PRAISE FOR

The Kindness of Strangers

"A moving novel about the ways in which healing can occur after a child's sexual abuse; Kittle's clear prose gives a luminous quality to her story of thriving against the odds."   —*People*

"Katrina Kittle's compulsively readable *The Kindness of Strangers* is a powerful public-service narrative about child abuse and its effects on a family." WITHDRAWN —*Chicago Tribune*

"[A] heartbreaking story [that] encompasses fear, fury and loyalty. . . . Thanks to the author's exceptionally fluent narrative skill, [this] novel . . . becomes utterly compelling. . . . Kittle unfurls her tale with absolute devotion."   —*Kirkus Reviews*

PRAISE FOR

Two Truths and a Lie

"A chilling, sensitive thriller . . . Readers will hold their breath as her tale comes to a suspenseful conclusion."

—*Publishers Weekly*

PRAISE FOR

Traveling Light

"[A] wonderfully moving book on love in all its variations. Kittle's novel is hard to put down, and harder still to forget."

—*Booklist* (starred review)

"An engaging debut."   —*Seattle Post-Intelligencer*

The

Blessings

of the

Animals

ALSO BY KATRINA KITTLE

The Kindness of Strangers

Two Truths and a Lie

Traveling Light

The

Blessings

of the

Animals

Katrina Kittle

HARPER PERENNIAL

NEW YORK • LONDON • TORONTO • SYDNEY • NEW DELHI • AUCKLAND

HARPER ● PERENNIAL

FIRST EDITION

Designed by Betty Lew

Library of Congress Cataloging-in-Publication Data

Kittle, Katrina.
    The blessings of the animals : a novel / Katrina Kittle.—1st ed.
      p. cm.
ISBN 978-0-06-190607-7
1. Women veterinarians—Fiction. 2. Mothers and daughters—Fiction. 3. Self-realization in women—Fiction. I. Title.
PS3561.I864M37 2010
813'.54—dc22   2009041740

---

10 11 12 13 14 OV/RRD 10 9 8 7 6 5 4 3 2 1

The

Blessings

of the

Animals

CHAPTER ONE

ON THE MORNING MY HUSBAND LEFT ME, HOURS BEFORE I knew he would, I looked at the bruised March sky and recognized tornado green.

I'd seen that peculiar algae shade before—anyone who grew up in Ohio had—but my intimate relationship with storms was a bit of family lore.

When I was eight, I tried to touch a tornado.

Trying to touch that tornado is my first complete memory-you-tell-as-a-story without details put in my head by somebody else. It is *mine*. The story makes it easy for my parents and brother to put any of my rash, reckless acts into perspective.

I recall standing at the breakfast nook window watching a tornado approach our horse farm—the last stubborn farm still standing amid new housing developments in our Dayton neighborhood—through the acres of pasture behind the house. My little brother, Davy, had followed Mom's instructions and huddled in the basement under the mattress she'd wrenched from the guest bed, but I stayed at the window, waiting for my father to return from the barn. I watched as hail—the first I'd ever seen—pinged against the house with off-note guitar plucks and chipped the glass under my hands. "Camden!" My mother grabbed my shoulders. "Get to the basement!" When I wrestled free, she chased me through the kitchen and living room, until I ran out the front door and into the yard.

I didn't want to go back and hide, not when *something was about to happen*.

I'd been waiting for this, whatever it was, ever since the sky had turned this sickly shade at the end of the school day. Friends had followed Davy and me home, as usual, our horses and hayloft a magnet, but my girlfriends wanted to "play wedding." I hated that game and was relieved that my brother didn't mind being the bride—he willingly donned that itchy lace prom dress Bonnie Lytle had stolen from her sister's closet. He put an old curtain on his head for a veil and even let the girls paint his nails and rouge his cheeks and lips. My best friend, Vijay Aperjeet, and I could usually be coaxed into playing the groom and the minister, which meant we could gallop around the barn lot in bare feet and dig in the dirt until it was time to stand there with my brother-bride and repeat the vows. I remember believing the word *holy* in "holy matrimony" was actually *hole-y*, as in "full of holes," and I swore I'd *never* marry for real.

On that third-grade day, though, I wouldn't even consent to be the groom. I just sat on the fence and looked at the sky— the sky so green and heavy with anticipation—even after my mother had told everyone to hurry home and called Davy and me inside.

Something was about to happen.

Pressure throbbed in my head and bones. The leaves turned their silver backs, flashing in the icy air. Candy wrappers, papers, and leaves floated in lazy circles at chest height. The horses sweated in the fields, their movements agitated. All I knew was that something was going to happen, that it might be dangerous, and that it filled me with a lovely, dreadful sensation.

I ran right out into the pelting hail.

The wind forced me to my knees. I stretched out on my belly and wrapped my fingers in grass. That screaming wind became the only sound. I knew it could destroy me.

I knew it *could*, but I also knew it *wouldn't*.

In my child's mind, this approaching tornado was a living, violent creature, just like my father's enormous, hotheaded stallion. Stormwatch was the horse that had carried my father to three of his four Olympic gold medals. My brother and I were told to stay away from that horse, even though we played around the legs and hooves of all the other horses on the farm. I believed that both the tornado and the stallion knew I was drawn to them.

Stormwatch would snort and rear, his hooves pounding the ground around the delicate bones of my bare feet . . . and never touch me. His teeth could've ripped the face from my skull, but he just gnashed and snapped, closing on air. I didn't cringe or cry. I was reverent. He liked it, that stallion. He looked at me, the way this tornado did, and something passed between us.

Stretched out in the mud, I let go of the grass with one hand and reached out toward the moving wall of air.

That tornado laid waste to our town. It crumpled homes to the left and right of ours, flipped one of our horse trailers upside down, tore off our roof, and kicked my canopy bed all the way to the grocery store parking lot a mile and a half away. That tornado ripped through our town for thirty-two miles. It killed thirty-three people, and injured one thousand one hundred and fifty others.

But it didn't injure me. All it did was take my outstretched hand and bowl me down the driveway. It never even lifted me from the ground, it only rolled me—the way I rolled myself down grassy hills—at high speed, over the lawn, through flower beds, across the blacktop road, until I smacked up against the Aperjeets' picket fence. The wind held me against the fence, right in the middle, without any of my limbs touching the ground. I was pressed there until the splintering of wood filled my ears, the smell of fresh cut lumber stung my nose, and that invisible hand pushed me down into the Aperjeets' muddy yard, on my back, where I watched the boards of their fence fly away into the whirling sky above me.

When the wind stopped screaming, running footsteps drowned out my breath. My mother dropped to her knees beside me and snatched me by the shoulders. "You, you," she said. "You." She ran her hands over my arms, my face, everywhere she could. She squeezed my shoulders again, hard, and shook me, my bloody nose showering bright red drops down both of our shirts. My mother was drenched, a small star-shaped gash on her forehead. I remember realizing with amazement that she had *followed* me into the storm. She grabbed my hair as if to yank out handfuls of it, then released the handfuls and smoothed the hair instead. "You," she kept repeating. She stood and vomited right there in the Aperjeets' yard.

My father ran down the driveway, carrying a wailing Davy and shouting, "Where *were* you?"

"You don't know when to stop," my mother said to me, quiet

discovery in her tone. It was the first of countless times she would say this. "You just don't know when to quit."

She was right. I knew I would do anything imaginable to repeat those last fifteen minutes.

When I grew too old to be doing such unladylike things as running out into storms or slipping onto that stallion's back and careening across pastures, I turned to more sophisticated means of re-creating that rush, some healthier than others. I asked for a hot-air balloon ride when I was ten. I convinced the family to go white-water rafting when I was twelve. By thirteen I fell in love, at first by accident, with the pure adrenaline that kicks in with starvation. The hyperfocus, the lovely sensation of floating, the reckless certainty that I'd become superhuman. Throughout my teens I'd flirt with starvation—as well as with rock climbing, flying lessons, hitchhiking and lots of solo travel, a variety of drugs, and boys with bad reputations.

Nothing could ever compare with that tornado, though—until I met Bobby Binardi, the man who affected me like an approaching storm. A man whose family was as volatile and loud as mine was reserved and decorous. A man with lashes longer than mine and tattoos I traced under my fingertips. A man who fed all the reasons I'd been starving myself. Fed me, quite literally, because he was a chef. So, the girl who said she'd never marry did.

In our wedding video, the thunder drowns out the vows. Eighteen years ago—*eighteen years? That couldn't be possible!*—a storm snatched the veil from my blond hair, toppled tables, and ripped the lily heads from my maid of honor's bouquet. Guests gasped, clutching one another as they turned their backs against the wind. It had always been a good story to tell, one that set our wedding apart. Our wedding day suited us.

At the reception, we found out that a tornado had actually touched down only ten miles away. My relatives laughed and told all the Binardis how fitting that was.

AS I LAY IN BED, MY LEGS STILL TOUCHING MY SAD, SLEEPING husband, I pulled one arm from under the flannel sheets to release some of his heat. The back of my neck was damp. Our dog, Max, paced the hallway, his toenails clicking on the hardwood floor. The bedroom door stood open since Gabriella was away on yet another overnight debate tournament—kicking butt, I had no doubt (I tried to be impartial and modest, but our daughter was brilliant). I tried not to move or make noise, knowing that once I did, Max would bound onto the bed demanding his breakfast. Already, Gingersnap, our latest failure of a barn cat, had crawled between me and Bobby, kneading her paws on my rib cage.

It was Saturday. I had worked every Saturday for the last fifteen years of veterinary practice, until I bought my own animal hospital six months ago. With my associate vet, Aurora Morales, I had worked my ass off, renovating an old, rundown clinic. Aurora and I had painted and grouted, had interviewed and hired, trained and instructed our staff of nine, named our practice Animal Kind, and opened three weeks ago. Starting today, I would only work two Saturdays a month. And today, Bobby had a rare Saturday off for us to savor together. His restaurant, Tanti Baci, was closed until Tuesday while a new bar was being installed. *Tanti Baci.* Many kisses. My wish for today.

This rare time alone with Bobby was a gift. I tucked my knees behind his, pressed my naked body to his back, and wished with all my might he'd find his way out of his restless depression.

Thunder rumbled like a warning growl from deep in a dog's throat.

Bobby had promised to make me breakfast this morning, something he hadn't done for months, and I hoped for his famous fluffy gingerbread waffles. We'd even joked that we might prepare *and* eat breakfast naked. We'd been silly and giggly, like we'd been when I was in college and his sister (my roommate) was gone, leaving us the entire apartment to ourselves.

I breathed in the musk of Bobby's neck. His happiness seemed so fragile these days that I put all my faith in that playful promise to eat naked. I felt this *need* to make the day monumental and sacred, as if one morning might save us.

For a moment, I even let myself fantasize about our fiftieth wedding anniversary, decades away. This was in my head because Davy—the former child bride, now happily out and with his partner, David ("the Davids," as they were referred to by family and friends)—had called last night to remind me, "You know this fall is Mom and Dad's fiftieth. We need to plan something. A party."

I pictured my parents, still on the same horse farm half an hour away. I didn't think my parents had a great marriage, but fifty years was impressive all the same. I created our own fiftieth in my head—I pictured us dancing somewhere in Italy, then calculated how much time that gave me to convince Bobby to learn to dance: thirty-two years.

In the meantime, I'd also use those years to convince him to sell the damn restaurant that visibly added burden to his shoulders, years to his face. I'd convince him he could find some other path.

So I lay there in that too-warm bed and felt flooded with the need to make this softly snoring man know how much I loved him and mourned for his unhappiness. How much I wanted him to emerge from his gloom.

The dog's tags jingled in the hallway. I considered sneaking out of bed, letting Max out before he barked, brushing my teeth, and slipping back under the covers. But I knew Max would bark the minute my feet hit the floor. Screw the toothpaste. It wasn't fair for one of us to have morning breath when the other didn't. Experience had taught me that Bobby's willingness never hinged on such minor details. Tanti baci. Tanti baci, baby.

I reached for Bobby under the covers, marveling at the heat he radiated. I slid my hands down his arm, over the gothic *SPQR—Senatus Populusque Romanus*, "the Senate and the People of Rome"—inked into his biceps, then let them wander to his hip and the small of his back. He stirred awake with an appreciative murmur and rolled toward me, pressing the length of his hot body against mine. "Hey," I whispered.

"Hey."

CHAPTER TWO

I SHOULD'VE KNOWN THIS WOULD BE EXACTLY THE MOMENT my cell phone would ring. Gingersnap leaped off the bed and Max barked the way he would if someone pulled into the driveway.

Bobby rolled over. "Max," he moaned, his voice more affectionate than irritated. "They can't hear you. They're on the phone."

I laughed and leaned across him for my cell.

"Is it Gabby?" he asked, rubbing his eyes.

My heart sank to recognize the number of Sheriff Stan Metz. *No, no, no, not today!* I volunteered as a court-appointed livestock agent for the Humane Society. "It's Stan Metz," I said, my voice part-warning, part-apology.

Bobby groaned and flung his arm over his eyes. I thought about ignoring the call. I didn't want to leave my warm bed, the anticipated waffles, my potentially laughing naked husband. But Bobby said, *"Of course* it's Stan Metz," with such petulant venom that I answered the phone.

"I know it's early, Dr. Anderson," the sheriff said, "but we need you. Immediate removal. We've got dead horses, dying horses, and an owner threatening to shoot us."

Dying horses? Not if I could help it. I swung my legs out of bed, pulse kicking up a notch. I tried not to look at Bobby as I pulled on jeans and a T-shirt while the sheriff gave me directions. "Helen's already here," he said of my best friend and fellow Humane volunteer. "She's calling potential foster homes. Bring your trailer. And a camera."

Bobby sat up. "You're *going*?" he asked. It sounded like an accusation.

"This sounds bad. But, I'll hurry. We'll have breakfast when I'm back, okay? I'm sorry." I leaned over to kiss him, but he pulled away. "Hey, this is my *job*," I said. Why was I apologizing? He certainly never apologized when he went to the restaurant at odd hours.

I ran my fingers through his thick black hair. "I'll be back as soon as I can."

He didn't say, "It's okay," or, "I understand." He didn't even tease me not to bring home another animal. I stood at the edge of the bed.

Although I'd never, ever say this aloud to him, he'd become worse than Gabriella ever was in her middle-school years. With Gabby it'd been easier. I'd simply leave the room when she used to say her seething, hateful words—a bit of healthy separation—because I knew it honestly had nothing to do with me. Bobby's sorrow, though, his moodiness, felt personal.

I stood there and wanted to ask him, "Are we okay?" but I'd asked him that yesterday, *finally*, after having carried the question like something burning in my chest for weeks. He'd assured me, "You're the one good thing I can count on in my life, Cam. You and Gabby." He'd held my face in his hands and said that his gloom, his drinking too much, his temper, had nothing to do with me but everything to do with his unhappiness with the restaurant (a thriving restaurant, mind you). Asking the question again didn't fit us. If he said we were okay, then I believed him.

I made myself kiss the top of his head, then went downstairs. I'd already told him he should sell the restaurant if he was that miserable. I assured him we would manage, I could work more weekends again. His happiness would be well worth it. I wanted the man I'd married back.

I stuffed several baby carrots into my back pockets, grabbed a video camera from my office, shoved my feet into green-and-pink striped Wellingtons (a birthday gift from Gabby, on an eternal quest, I believe, to make her mother more hip), and went outside.

The sky seemed a dark wool blanket slung just above the tree line. Of course my trailer wasn't hitched, and Bobby was already pissed and sulky so I couldn't ask him to help me. I looked up at our bedroom window. With a second person down here to guide me, this task would take three minutes, tops. Alone, it ended up taking nearly fifteen—backing and pulling forward repeatedly (under the watchful eye of my stone statue of St. Francis) until I got the trailer and truck lined up just right to lock and pin everything into place.

As I hit the road on the way to the emergency rescue, I vowed that I would *not* bring home another animal. That would be my sacrifice, my peace offering to Bobby, who'd recently dubbed our farm and its motley crew the "Island of Misfit Toys." Even though it irked me that a man who hated the holidays would use a Christmas special reference against me (that version of *Ru-dolph the Red-Nosed Reindeer* was Gabby's childhood favorite), I had to admit he had a point.

We had Max, a mutt with a permanent limp—Max had been hit by a car as a puppy after having been abandoned in the country.

We had Gingersnap, a cat with no ears. They'd been snipped off by two sadistic twelve-year-old boys who would no doubt grow up to be serial killers.

"Christ, Cam," Bobby said when I brought Gingersnap home.

"We have a barn," I said. "It has mice."

But poor Gingersnap was an uninspired mouser. I'd noticed a new stray cat—a big orange thing—hanging around though, which I hoped to convince to hunt in our small barn.

In that barn, which held four stalls, we had Gabriella's horse, Biscuit, a gentle Belgian with a spine defect that didn't allow him to pull or carry more than two hundred pounds (rather lim-iting for a draft horse). In another stall we fostered Zeppelin, a "wiener dog" version of a pony with legs too short for his long body, who was blind in one eye. We also had Muriel, a barren white goat abandoned after the county fair. Also a foster. Not permanent.

I had one empty stall as I headed to the rescue that morning. Well . . . perhaps two, since the goat—who escaped with exas-perating frequency—was rarely *in* her stall.

When I reached the rescue site, the sheriff es-corted me past a cluster of shouting people into a barn where skeletal horses stood in ankle-deep filth. Several Humane Society volunteers stood ready to take the animals away to foster homes.

A man and a woman I assumed were the owners argued with the police outside, their obscenities carrying in on gusts of increasingly colder air. A pit bull tied to a red Lexus with a plastic clothesline bayed nonstop. The sound of hammering and splitting wood came in bursts from beyond the barn's open back door. More thunder rumbled. This was not going to be an easy or quick removal. I thought of naked Bobby in the flannel sheets at home and felt a tangle release inside my chest. Our breakfast together was unlikely.

I stopped walking, shocked at myself. Was I honestly *relieved* that I'd be here instead?

I hadn't *really* thought that, had I?

Helen approached, face grim, pale-blond hair nearly glowing in the dim light. I pushed that horrible realization about Bobby away from me and focused on my terrier of a friend—short and petite but with no concept of her small size, never afraid, and fiercely loyal. She took my camera and began to film, while I set up a sort of triage. I had no time to think about my shameful relief to be away from Bobby as I examined each surviving horse, listening to their hearts, lungs, and guts and looking in their runny noses and eyes. As soon as I scribbled down instructions for a horse's feed and initial treatment, a volunteer loaded it onto a trailer and hauled it away.

In one stall, a chestnut horse lay dead. The face was already decomposed, its eye a black hole. A nauseating, sweet stench of decay choked me as rain began to tap the barn's tin roof.

"That was a lucky one." Helen nodded to the dead horse. She spoke quickly, in a monotone. "Here's what we know: wife catches husband having affair. Kicks him out."

Another round of hammering came from behind the barn. Wood cracked.

I moved to another stall and found a brown mare on her side who looked like a tossed-down bundle of thin firewood, her breath ragged and labored. I crouched to listen to the mare's struggling heart as Helen continued, "Wife gets a restraining order against husband. Fires the barn manager because he's the husband's brother. Runs the brother off the property, too. Then, the bitch leaves for Florida for five weeks with *her* new boyfriend and never hires anyone to *replace* the damn barn manager!"

Five weeks? I heard no gut sounds on the poor wheezing mare. The horse didn't stir or respond in any way when I touched her. Five weeks of starvation was a slow, tortured death.

Helen waited for the pounding out back to stop, then said, "A neighbor fed and watered every now and then . . . until the food ran out. He waited way too long to call the police."

I moved a hand above the mare's unresponsive eyes. I looked up at Helen; she knew what I had to do. I made too much noise, slamming my kit around as I prepared the injections, the first one to relax and anesthetize the mare—she was too far gone to register new pain, but I wouldn't allow even the possibility—and the second to end her sputtering heartbeat. I sat in the filth to cradle the mare's head and whispered, "It's okay. That's a brave girl. It's okay, it's okay," until first the drowning gasps stopped and then my stethoscope went silent.

"Get this on film." I pointed to the gnawed remains of the mare's feedbox.

Helen filmed and I narrated in a voice that sounded tight and swollen no matter how many times I cleared my throat. "The mare ate the wood. She was eating her own stall in an attempt to survive. Look." With gloved hands, I pulled back the mare's upper lip and opened her jaw. "Her tongue and gums are full of splinters, and her mouth is full of manure."

The shouting, hammering, and barking continued as we filmed empty feed bins, an empty hayloft, empty water buckets.

I euthanized a black gelding and shipped off four other raggedy survivors with the last of the volunteers. Helen got on her cell, trying to round up more foster homes.

When I opened the last stall in this barn, two fillies stared at me from dark, sweet eyes in deep hollows. Their hip bones pushed up so starkly that sores oozed where bone threatened to push through the skin, but their hearts and lungs sounded strong.

The sheriff returned and asked, "How we doing?" His tone left no doubt that we should hurry.

"Where will we take them?" Helen asked. "I'm getting nothing but dead ends." She looked at me and pressed her tongue against that tiny gap between her two front teeth.

I wouldn't, I *couldn't* take one home. I felt too guilty about preferring to be here rather than with Bobby. I couldn't stop thinking I was a horrible wife.

The hammering continued from the barn behind us. The pit bull barked and barked.

"—my girlfriend's horses!" reached me through the wind. "—can't just fucking *take* them!"

———

"These are the last two, right?" I asked. Maybe I could put them together in one stall, as they were now. Just to get them out of here. Just to get home and salvage the day.

Before Helen could answer, a huge crash came from the back barn.

"What is with that damn hammering?" I said. "Don't they have anything more *useful* to do?"

The look on Helen's face froze me. "*That*'s the last one," she said. "The last horse alive is in that back barn."

That god-awful racket was a *horse*?

Disbelieving, I walked into the gravel aisle between the barns in time to see a set of hooves strike out over a nearly demolished Dutch door. The hammering resumed as the horse pummeled the wall with his back hooves.

I peered into the kicker's stall. A dark bay reared. "Hey, hey, hey," I scolded. "You settle down." When he kicked again, I shouted, "*Hey!* Cut it out!"

The horse paused to regard me for a moment, snorted, then resumed kicking.

"Can you trank him?" the sheriff asked.

I frowned. "He's so underweight. Not a good idea." And even if it were, how was I supposed to inject him? With a dart gun?

Helen and I glanced at each other, considering our options.

"Sweet boots," Helen said, in her typical we're-not-in-the-middle-of-a-crisis way, nodding down at my striped Wellingtons.

I smiled. Helen had an identical pair from *her* daughter, Holly. Holly was four years older than Gabriella. Gabriella adored her.

Gabriella! Panic zipped through me. I *had* to get home in time for Bobby and me to have the house to ourselves. I had to make up for leaving him this morning. . . . But who was I kidding? There'd be no cozy, romantic morning. The truth was, I'd get home and Bobby would be moody and resentful all day because I'd left.

Just then, the horse kicked his door free of its hinges, slamming it into the gravel aisle. He barreled out of the stall and skidded to a halt two yards away from me. Close enough for me to smell him—a mildewy, sickly smell—and to feel the heat of his breath.

I held out my arms. "Where you gonna go now, handsome?" I asked. And he *was* handsome, even in that scraggy, dirty state. Hints of muscle remained on his frame. His leather halter, now far too big, hung crookedly across his nose, below the white crescent moon on his forehead.

He wheeled away from me, thankfully missing my head with the buck he threw in for good measure before he galloped away. I gasped from the adrenaline surge as I followed him.

He'd run into the gravel lot where my trailer was parked, so we closed the gates, confining him. As if on springs, the horse trotted across the gravel. Even in this feeble, eerie light, every rib stood out in stark relief. Blood trickled from one hock and from just above one hoof. He lowered his head to the small swath of grass at the fence line, stripping it in seconds.

"We can get him on the trailer with food," I said.

"And take him *where*?" Helen asked. "And what about the two fillies?"

I sighed—I had no choice. I ducked back inside the barn,

out of the wind, to dial my parents' number. I explained the situation.

"Well," my father said, in his slow, deliberate way. I'd rarely seen him do anything hurried or ungraceful my entire life. "How do they handle? Will they be low maintenance?"

I assured him they had lovely ground manners, which meant *I* was taking home the kicker. Great. Wouldn't Bobby just love that?

My father agreed. "Thank you, thank you," I breathed, giving a thumbs-up to Helen and the sheriff. "Helen's going to bring them right over, while I take one to my place."

"Try to beat this storm if you can."

When we left the barn, the woman screamed at us, "You can't just *steal* my horses!"

We ignored her, but I wanted to slap her hateful face. Someone needed to lock her in a cell where she had to sleep in her own shit and eat it if she wanted to live one more day.

Out in the rain, the kicker's wet coat made him look even gaunter than he had moments before. Keeping an eye on him, I opened the emergency escape door at the front of my trailer and piled an armful of clover hay from my truck into the waiting feed bag. I undid the pins holding the back door in place and lowered the door, turning it into a ramp for the horse to walk up. The kicker *whooshed* his nostrils at the ramp, which quickly grew slick in the ever-steadier rain.

As calmly as I could, I held a lead rope and reached for the horse's dangling halter. He shied away from me, then reared. I cursed. A horse should have his lead rope tied to a metal ring in the trailer wall. If he wasn't tied, he could send the trailer off balance, making it a rough and dangerous ride.

"Motherfuckers! This is against the *law*!" carried to me from the driveway.

Having the kicker loose in the trailer wouldn't be ideal, but it would get him the hell out of here. And it would get *me* out of here and back home to Bobby, where I should be. Where I should *want* to be.

Another rush of wind slammed several stall doors, along with the trailer's escape door, which clanged shut with a force that rocked the trailer and echoed in my ears.

I patted my pockets, wishing I hadn't given away all my carrots. Turns out it didn't matter, as the kicker saw the gesture and moved toward me.

"You guys be ready to shut this door," I called.

"Are you insane?" Helen yelled as she saw me step onto the ramp. But she and the sheriff already approached the trailer. The kicker barely glanced at them but followed me.

I slipped on the ramp and fell, bashing my shin on the frame. I felt the cold and wet before I felt the pain, but the pain was secondary to the exhilaration that rushed through me. *Get up. Get up!* The kicker's breath prickled my scalp as I scrambled forward.

I got to the front of the trailer and ducked under the measly protection of the hay bag.

The back ramp-door lifted up and closed with a thump. I prayed that Helen and the sheriff got the pins in before the horse gave the door the kick I knew he would.

His kick was a loud, echoing gunshot. I heard Helen's "Shit!" but the door held.

I yanked the escape door handle that had blown shut.

It wouldn't turn.

I wriggled it with my cold fingers, the metallic taste of fear filling my mouth.

The kicker turned his head to view me with one eye. I kept my right hand on the door handle. "The door is locked or jammed or something," I called. I heard quick footsteps in the gravel.

The horse snuffed the pile of hay before him then began to chew. He looked so serene that I believed for a moment I might be able to put a lead rope on him after all.

Then, he turned his head and bit me.

Startlingly swift, like a striking snake, he clamped his jaw on my right forearm.

The pain surged through my arm like heat. I pictured bones crunching in his powerful grip, his teeth meeting, my bones flattened between them.

Helen jerked open the door.

With my left hand, I smacked the horse on the front bone of his face, where it would hurt. When the smack didn't work, I punched him.

He released me.

Helen yanked me out of the tiny space.

I fell to the wet gravel in a ball. Helen and the sheriff crouched beside me. I curled up, trying to wrap myself around the pain. It pulsed through my arm in hot white waves that stung my nose and burned involuntary tears down my face. I clutched the arm to my sternum, my fist tight.

"Let me see," Helen insisted, but I was convinced it would hurt less if I held it to myself.

The kicker was now calm. Even through the rain, we heard his teeth grind the hay.

When Helen got me to release my arm, I was *amazed* to see no skin was broken. I expected to see spurting arteries. Instead, hard, bright red welts outlined a perfect set of tooth indentations. Purple swelling rushed into the indentations as we watched.

"You need ice," the sheriff said. "Your arm could be broken."

No. No. I had to get back to Bobby. I couldn't go to the ER.

I stood up, holding my arm to my chest as if it were in a sling. I wiggled all five of my fingers. "Not broken," I said. "What about that dog out there? Tied to the car? We taking him?"

The sheriff blinked and shook his head at me. "No. They brought him with them today."

I wondered if that meant the dog was more or less lucky than the other animals. "Okay, then, we're done. Let's go."

The sheriff looked skeptical. "You can *drive*?"

There was still time for breakfast. I still believed there was time.

AS I PULLED INTO OUR DRIVEWAY, I WAS GLAD HELEN HAD agreed to follow me, in case anything disastrous happened on the drive. The kicker (or was he now the biter?)—who had been an easy ride, content to eat his hay—turned himself around the moment the truck stopped and half-jumped, half-climbed out of the trailer. He raced at a gallop around the house.

I'm not sure if I looked up toward our bedroom window or just headed off with Helen as she leaped from her truck to grab a rake from our back porch. I snatched up a broom. Walking together and waving our utensils—me still clutching my injured arm to my chest—we herded the kicker toward the barn. I heard Max barking inside the house. That's when I remember wondering why the hell Bobby didn't come out to help us.

The horse put on an admirable rodeo show and tore up clumps of the yard. He wheeled and struck my St. Francis statue with his back hooves, sending the figure flying.

He ran straight for the barn and, once he found himself trapped inside, fled into the only open stall door. Helen shut the door behind him. Of course he immediately exited his stall's back door into his private paddock, but the paddock's gate was latched. I rushed to switch on the electric tape that ran along the top of the paddock fences—something I'd installed to prevent the goat from climbing out of her enclosure (it hadn't worked). Bobby and I had grown so used to her escape routine that a monotone, unruffled "goat's out" became a sort of joke between us.

Helen and I stood, panting, looking at the kicker. "He's gonna be a handful," she said, in that same no-crisis-here tone.

I burst into laughter. "More like a truckload."

At least the fillies in Helen's van still stood peacefully. The rain had lightened, but the sky remained that dark green of *something about to happen*. Helen still had to drive on to my parents' farm, about thirty minutes away. I felt I should go with her, but Helen shook her head. "I called Hank; he's going to meet me there. No worries. You go get ice on that arm."

I nodded, grateful, but the mention of Helen's husband, Hank—they were teased about sounding like a country-western duo—also caused me a flash of irritation. Was Bobby so pissed at my being called away, or at an additional animal being brought home, that he refused to help us? I hated how much I dreaded walking into the tension in the house.

"You kicked ass today," Helen said.

I waved good-bye to her and walked across the yard, flexing my fingers, wincing at the deep ache this action pulsed through my arm.

As the lightning flashed, I looked at that sickly sky and remembered running out into the hail. How could I have been so certain I wouldn't be hurt?

CHAPTER THREE

⁂

BOBBY

If only you'd given me a sign.

Any little thing I could have taken as a sign.

Bobby kept waiting for it, kept changing the deal in his head: "If she asks me to help hitch the damn trailer, I won't leave today." But, no, he watched her from the window stubbornly doing it herself like he didn't exist. She didn't think of him.

So he changed the deal again: "If she asks me to help catch this psychotic horse she's brought home, I won't leave." But she never even considered him.

He'd become invisible here.

He thought about making waffles when she left, but he'd learned these rescues sometimes ate an entire day. To be honest—although he realized he couldn't actually say the word *honest* with any fucking seriousness ever again—he didn't have it in him to perform this last gesture if the waffles were going to sit there cold on a plate. No way in hell could he picture himself staying to do the dishes after he told her, any more than he could picture leaving the dishes for *her* to clean up.

He sat in the spare bedroom he used as an office and waited. Sometimes when she came home he'd have this moment of panic—he didn't know what else to call it—wondering if she even remembered he was there. He knew it sounded nuts, like he was crazy, but it was this brief fear that he might've become invisible for real. More and more lately he had thoughts like that.

Cami called, "I'm home!" but he couldn't answer. He opened his mouth but it was like he honest to Christ couldn't remember how to speak. He couldn't do this! And just as fast a new level of fear layered on the first at the thought of continuing the way he had been.

When she plopped down on the guest bed beside him, he watched her face, this face he knew so well, as she went on about the horse, about Helen, about people screaming at them. He loved her face. He knew the next logical thought was, "Okay, whatever, if you love her, how could you do this?" but he *did* love her. Even now. He searched her face for signs of the woman he used to cherish. For hints of the woman who'd once cherished him.

She was drenched. Mud-splattered. She had goddamn gravel in her hair. It didn't seem fair to tell her his news while she looked so beat up, but he felt relieved, a little, at her appearance. He might actually find the courage to leave if she didn't look so strong, so fearless.

As she talked about the rescue, he kept thinking, *Do you not fucking see that I'm dying here? Can't you tell that something important is about to go down? Can't you sense it?* She used to know his thoughts before he even did, but she kept talking about these horses, and when she told a story about euthanizing a mare, the weirdest image flashed into his head. He felt nuts, but she always struck him as sexy with a syringe. He remembered the first rescue he went on, back when she used to invite him. He loved the way she pulled off an injection cap with her teeth. He'd seen her do it at least a hundred times. She'd have one hand holding the scruff of a neck—cat, dog, whatever—and she'd reach up to her mouth with her other hand and bite off the cap, exposing the needle, clenching the cap in her teeth while she injected the animal. The confidence in the move, the careless certainty—for some reason that picture of Cami defined her for him.

Why the hell did he want to think of her as strong and sexy at that moment? Was he truly going crazy? No, the point was she was strong enough that she'd be okay no matter what he did.

"I just don't understand people," she said, as she always did after a removal. It honest to Christ amazed him that she said it so sincerely every single damn time. He wasn't sure which was stronger: the way her perpetual horror annoyed him or the way it made her remarkable.

"These animals are living, feeling fellow beings," Cami said. "When you take one into your life you're making a *commitment*. How can you just throw them away like garbage?"

Bobby knew this should be his cue to take her face in his hands, to say, "My little crusader, Cami," but the word *commitment* made him mute.

Cami showed him her arm where that son-of-a-bitch horse had bitten her. He knew the blue and red welts should evoke something in him besides exasperation for her carelessness with her own body. He *hated* when she was hurt—it made him feel *sick*—and she hurt herself all the damn time. He knew he should get an ice pack or suggest they go get an X-ray—it really did look like her goddamn arm was broken. He almost took that as an out—a trip to the ER—but he knew she'd think the delay of this moment, once she knew what the moment held, was unforgivable.

"I need to tell you something important," Bobby managed to say. *There*. He could do it. He could speak. The words were out there in the room. There was no turning back now.

Her face was curious. She leaned forward and *grinned*. "Is it what I think it is?"

Not likely. Christ. He didn't want to humiliate her. He would cut off his damn arm not to have come to this point if he believed it would save them.

He opened his mouth and said the words he'd been dying to say for months: "I don't want to be married anymore."

This smile curled up her mouth like she wanted to *laugh*. Oh, shit. She didn't *believe him*. But he watched it dawn in her face as she studied his. She was blindsided. But why *wouldn't* she be blindsided after that pile of bullshit he'd told her yesterday? "Are we okay?" she'd asked him. He should've told her then. But he hadn't been ready. He'd still been trying to convince himself, still believing, even yesterday, that maybe he could change his mind and stay.

He clung to his scripted words. "You know I've been un-happy for a long time, Cam. I know I've been hard to live with lately."

She looked so . . . wounded. He'd never seen her look hurt. She *got* physically hurt all the time, but that didn't stop her. He'd never seen her look like she actually *felt* a wound, like she did now. She wore no makeup, which is how he loved her face the most. Her hair and clothes were stuck to her with rain, and she probably didn't know or care that blood was seeping through the left leg of her jeans. She'd smudged mud on the quilt Ma had made for them on their third anniversary.

"I think I should go away for a while," he said, "and then we should talk."

She shivered, fidgeting with a loose thread in the quilt.

He remembered them making love on this quilt when they first got it, this ugly quilt they'd relegated to the guest room. Ma had accidentally left a pin in the fabric that snagged a streak of red—like a cat scratch—on Cami's left hip. He'd run his tongue over that scratch. Her warm skin, her vanilla smell, rose up in him. *What am I doing? Why would I leave you?*

She kept pulling on the damn thread. "We should see a counselor."

For a second, he considered what she said—a reasonable request. But it took only a second to see what would happen: they'd cry, then they'd have sweet, careful sex and they'd tiptoe around each other and *nothing would change*. Bobby would still dream about drowning. "I don't want to see a counselor. I don't think there's anything to do. It's too late for us to—"

"Too late? But you just *told* me."

He stood and picked up his gym bag. "I'll call you in a few days."

She sat up straight on the bed. "Whoa. Wait. You're leaving *right now?*"

What the hell? Did she think he was going to sit here in this house after he'd told her this?

"Don't go, Bobby. We can figure this out. We can make things better."

This strangling sob came out of his throat. Then another. He hit the door frame with his fist; the pain felt good. "Shit. I'm sorry. Aw, fuck." He was lost, crying big, back-shaking sobs. He knelt beside where she sat, hugging her shivering legs, burying his face in her knees.

She put her hands in his hair and said, "It's okay, it's okay," as if she were talking to a crying Gabriella. Her comfort felt so familiar that he thought *I'm crazy. Just stay. You can get by on this*. But he knew it wasn't true.

How could he tell her that for more than a year he'd dreamed about drowning? Terrifying scenes that had him dreading bed and intentionally drinking himself too dull to dream. In sleep, a heavy anchor pulled him down in deep green water that he swallowed and choked on. He'd thrash his arms and kick, fighting for the surface, once even knocking the goddamn clock off the nightstand, another time socking her in the face with his elbow, giving her a shiner that cut him to the bone every time he looked at it.

That black eye made him feel like his father.

When he looked down through that green water, it was *Cami* holding him down. Cami holding his ankles, her jaw set, her nails digging into his skin.

One night, panting from the dream, he whispered in the dark when he was certain she was asleep, "You're drowning me." The damn dog whined at him, and Bobby'd had this irrational fear that Max would be able to *tell* Cami. She was closer to the animals than to him. She saw what they needed and gave it to them. He knew he was a small, coldhearted jackass for being jealous of a gimpy dog and a maimed cat, but there it was. That's what pulled him down.

———

He blundered on, desperate for her to know he did love her and didn't want to hurt her—all that lame-ass shit everyone says—even though he knew it was asinine to think that leaving wouldn't hurt her. "I couldn't tell you, Cam," he said into her knees. "I knew when I told you, I had to be prepared for us to be over. I had to be ready. It took me a long time to be emotionally ready for this."

The words she said next peeled back his skin. "So, *you* needed a long time, but you thought *I'*d be okay with, what? Ten minutes?"

Christ, how could he have said that to her? He should leave before he fucked it up worse.

But Cami wasn't done. She never knew when to quit. He should've known.

"Don't do this, Bobby. We're intelligent, creative people. Let's *fix* this."

In the flash of lightning that lit the room, he watched that funky raspberry-colored pattern crawl over her face like a rash. She flowered like this when she was pissed or embarrassed. And when she came. He knew under that damp, dirty T-shirt her breasts and belly would also be blotched. He knew she hated this trait in herself. He knew so much about her. He *knew* her.

Then she asked it. "Is there someone else?"

Tell the truth. Just tell the fucking truth. But he couldn't. "No. No. Don't think that."

It threw him when she yelled at him. "Don't fucking tell me what not to think. What am I *supposed* to think?" He thought she might hit him, and for a second, he wished she would.

"This isn't about anyone else." *That isn't a lie. Not really. We would be over regardless.* He remembered a line he'd rehearsed and grabbed for it. "I have to make peace with the fact that I may never be with anyone ever again. Not until I work out my own issues."

Something like hatred flashed across her face. "Where are you going?" she asked.

He couldn't tell her. Not yet. "Call my cell if you need me."

Then she asked, "Does Gabriella know?" Shit. He'd screwed this up so bad. Thinking about Gabriella, already missing Gabriella, almost drove him back to Cami's knees. This furious woman had given him Gabriella. They'd created her together. If Cami wanted counseling, he should go to counseling. If she wanted a trial separation, he should do that, too. He shouldn't leave until they both knew it was the right thing. He wanted, so badly it made him ache, to be able to stay and do this like a man.

But he took his bag and walked down the stairs and out the back door, where that goddamn goat jumped out of Cami's truck bed and came running toward him. Without even thinking, he turned to call up the stairs, "Um . . . goat's out." It hit him then, like a ball bat to the gut, the history he was leaving.

But when he stepped off the porch, he took a breath. He felt that breath go deep, all the way through his body, and expand in his lungs.

He'd done it.

He'd broken through the surface.

CHAPTER FOUR

IT WASN'T UNTIL AFTER BOBBY HAD LEFT THAT THE TOR-
nado sirens went off, jump-starting my pulse.

The howl rose and fell, mournful in the stillness.

Perfect. Some more destruction to top off this day.

I thought he was going to tell me he was selling the restaurant.

Before the sirens, I had no idea what to do. I watched the red
numbers of the digital clock across the guest room change for
seventeen minutes. I didn't cry. I didn't rage or break things.
Other than feeling chilled to my bones, I was numb.

When the sirens went off, there were things I needed to do.
And that was a relief.

MY LEG HAD GROWN STIFF FROM MY FALL IN THE TRAILER,
and my feet were so cold they ached. I limped down the hall to
our bedroom, Max limping beside me.

Rain released from the sky with a screech, as if someone had
turned on a faucet. I needed to get to the barn.

I opened the dresser drawer for the wool socks.

The drawer was empty.

My heart clutched.

I opened the drawer above it, which housed Bobby's underwear and T-shirts.

Empty.

I opened the third drawer down—his jeans and sweat pants. Empty.

I flung open and slammed shut drawers. Empty. Empty. Empty.

I opened his closet and stared at the bare rod.

He'd packed his car. He must have gotten up when I left and started packing. When I reached over to kiss him before I left this morning, he *knew* he was leaving me.

The erratic ping of hail began.

"*I KNOW I'VE BEEN HARD TO LIVE WITH LATELY.*" HE ALWAYS *had* been, with his operatic moods. He'd been *miserable* to live with lately, but I'd never once thought, "Oh, he's hard to live with, let's end our marriage." I'd only thought I should do all I could to get him through his crisis.

THE LAUNDRY. I BET THERE WAS A PAIR OF WOOL SOCKS IN the laundry. I opened the hamper. Four pairs of my own panties lay curled in one corner. *He'd even taken his dirty laundry.*

The hail sounded like someone pouring gravel on the roof.

INSIDE THE BARN, I DASHED INTO EACH STALL TO CLOSE the back doors and slide the thick Plexiglas panels into the windows, clenching my teeth against the pain in my arm. Of course the kicker refused to come inside, huddling instead in the corner of his paddock. He turned his butt to me when I called him. I didn't blame him since he'd been held prisoner in a stall for more than a month, but I felt horrible as I closed his door, shutting him outside.

I caught my breath until it hit me: *Bobby just left*. That really happened.

Was he caught on the road in the storm? Or had he reached wherever he was staying? Was he thinking of me, wondering if I was safe? Would he call Gabriella? Please, *please*, let Gabriella be safe, still far from here in Lexington and not on a bus yet. I dialed her cell, but my call went straight to voice mail. "Call me when you can, babe. We're getting a tornado here and I want you to stay safely put somewhere until it's over."

Something hit the barn door hard enough to knock down the pitchfork hanging on the wall. A hideous metallic screeching came from one corner of the barn, and I hoped the roof held.

Zeppelin, the pony, appeared to be sleeping, but his eyes were shut too tight and his tail swished. Perhaps it was denial or just his Zen way of waiting out the storm.

I opened Biscuit's stall. My daughter's horse was bombproof, never one to shy at invisible "goblins" on windy days. The storm didn't seem to faze him at all. Muriel, the goat, lay near Biscuit's hairy hooves, legs tucked under her. I didn't bother putting her back in her own stall.

A blur of motion caught my peripheral vision and I turned but saw nothing. I hoped it was that orange cat I'd been spotting on the property. A huge but scrawny feral creature abandoned when the neighbors to the north were arrested for the meth lab they operated deep in their wooded acres. It struck me I hadn't seen the cat for days. How many?

Bobby left.

That reality hit me behind the knees, sinking me to the floor. I leaned against Biscuit's stall, my knees to my chest, hugging my right arm. I ached all over.

Bobby made me a latte yesterday morning. He'd driven Gabby to school, with her suitcase for the tournament, and brought back my favorite orange-and-cranberry scones. He'd come into my office as I sat researching an iguana's skin condition. He'd kissed my neck before he left for the restaurant. He did all that when he knew he was leaving?

I huddled in the aisle and tried not to think about Bobby. Tried not to think of how he'd always made me feel *something was about to happen*.

Well. Something had happened. That's for sure.

Think about something else. Think about anything else.

But, of course, that never worked.

BOBBY AND I MET THROUGH HIS SISTER, ONE OF MY BEST friends. Olive Binardi—her name fit her Mediterranean skin, her round face, her ample curves—was one of those people whose car was littered with fast-food wrappers, who perpetually lost her keys, and who was late every single place she went. She was also, in my opinion, the best massage therapist on the planet. When I first met her she was a physical therapy major and my first roommate in the Ohio State University dorms. We rented an apartment above a pizza parlor after our sophomore year.

Olive's family lived in Columbus, and Olive received free tuition because her dad was a professor in the math department.

Olive's dad also drank a few bottles of Chianti a day, and sometimes Olive's mother, Mimi, would arrive at our apartment at three in the morning to sleep on our thrift-store couch.

Olive invited me to the Sunday dinners, where up to thirty other relatives would descend upon their house, all shouting, all smoking, all casually using profanities that made my jaw drop.

The combination of thick smoke and the need to yell to make myself heard left me hoarse each time I attended. No wonder that the first time I brought Olive home with me to Dayton for the weekend, she thought all of us Andersons were angry with one another. We were so quiet.

I'd seen photographs of Olive's brother, Bobby, long before I met him. He'd been banished by their father, for reasons neither Olive nor Mimi could make clear to me. That made him mysterious and bad, and therefore more appealing. Bobby lived in Brooklyn for a while and worked as a sous-chef in a relative's restaurant. He didn't go to college. When he came home to Columbus for Christmas, Easter, and Mother's Day, he stayed at the apartment I shared with Olive instead of at the Binardi house. I went home to Dayton for those holidays—an hour away from Columbus—so our paths crossed only briefly, but enough for us to flirt, for me to stammer and blush, and for Olive to warn me, "Don't go there, Cam. He's trouble."

With an endorsement like that, I was doomed.

Once, Bobby came back early for Mother's Day weekend. He and I ate ice cream. That ice cream became as much family lore as the tornado.

My mother might say I didn't know when to stop, but in my dabbling with starvation, I honestly didn't know *how* to stop.

I'd finally realized, as I arrived at my preveterinary program—existing on cigarettes, black coffee, and plain yogurt—that this had truly turned into an addiction. About the time Bobby and I sat down to ice cream, I'd grown afraid of my own behavior. When my brother arrived on a surprise visit to tell me he was worried about my health, I didn't confess that I lied about my weight to our parents on the phone, that Olive and I argued over the grocery shopping (when it was my turn I stocked the fridge with celery, Jell-O, and grapes), or that I had freakish white hair growing on my stomach. I told Davy I'd been on a "little diet." I sat on my hands so he couldn't see how they trembled, and said nothing, of course, about how I couldn't go from sitting to standing without white sparkles crowding my vision, about the bruises smudging my spine, or the scab on my tailbone. I said all the right things to him but told myself it was nothing dangerous, just enough to feel that lovely high.

And then Bobby walked into my life a day early and changed everything. I opened the door and there he stood with that curly black hair, that Roman nose, those ridiculous lashes.

I went for ice cream with Bobby. Yes, ice cream, which I hadn't eaten in three years. It felt too tense in the house, waiting for Olive—she wouldn't be home from work until midnight. I didn't want to leave him alone and return to my room to study, but I didn't know what to *do* sitting with him, so close to him and his clean leather smell. He'd already eaten but said he needed dessert. He opened our kitchen cupboards, then closed them. He opened our freezer, then closed it. He opened our fridge, chewed his lip while he considered a container of ricotta cheese (certainly not *my* purchase), then shut the fridge and suggested

Jeni's, an ice cream parlor down the block. I found it impossible to say no.

Inside Jeni's, I was stunned by the exotic flavors: Thai Chili, Mango Lassi, Lime Cardamom. Bobby ordered Riesling Poached Pear sorbet. He said, "These are together," to the girl behind the glass. I protested, but he took my hand, making me nearly swoon. "One scoop of ice cream. Just one," he said. My mind whirled—had Olive talked to him about me? Did he know?

"What flavor?" the server asked.

I opened my mouth, heart racing, but had no idea what to say.

Bobby's hand in the small of my back drew me toward the glass to look down at the tubs of ice cream. They were exquisite, but . . . my vision sparkled. I put out a hand to steady myself. I hadn't meant to pick, but Bobby said, "Okay, Gravel Road it is." The girl dipped the metal scoop in warm water and picked up a sugar cone, the scoop sliding into my not-choice.

I felt giddy. I'd handled a sedated tiger the previous week as part of my internship at the Columbus Zoo, but holding an ice cream cone felt more daring.

We sat outside on a bench. The dogwoods were bursting with pink and white bloom, reminding me, though I hated to admit it, of wedding cakes. The blossoms smelled like sex as the warm breeze scattered a confetti of petals upon us. Bobby had a white petal in his hair.

I kissed my ice cream cone. Sweet, cold caramel heaven on my lips. I touched it again with my tongue. Slivers of smoked almond. Grains of sea salt. Totally foreign. Forgotten.

I had only one thought: *I want this*. All of it. Sitting there with this man I'd been warned about who seemed to understand this bizarre, ugly thing about me and was patient and generous. I wanted his sudden smile, the way it lit up his face like a camera's flash, the way his hair curled at the back of his neck, the way my lungs seemed to expand in his presence.

Bobby held eye contact until I blushed and dropped my gaze. I say *blushed*, but my "blush" is to break out in itchy red mottles like I've thrust my face into stinging nettles. I've had strangers ask me if I'm okay. Bobby didn't seem to mind.

Back at the apartment, in my bedroom, when he undressed me, he looked away, and I knew it was because it hurt him to look. As he put his hands on my shoulders to guide me under the comforter, I mottled again, knowing exactly what my shoulders felt like under his fingers.

I covered myself, and Bobby crawled beside me, him on top of the covers, me beneath them. "You're too skinny," he whispered in a voice full of sorrow. Then he kissed me. Just one kiss, but it lasted. It didn't get hurried or rushed on to other things. I savored it, the kiss and his words, like I'd savored the surprise of sea salt in the caramel. A magic combination.

We slept, that puffy yellow comforter between us, until late in the night, when knocking startled us awake. "Cam?" Olive opened my door, light from the hall spilling in. "Was Bobby here? His suitcase is in the—"

She blinked at her shirtless brother. "Oh," she said. "Shit." She slammed the door.

"Ollie?" Bobby called. "Wait." He followed her.

Profanities flew, as they always did within his family. I put on a robe and joined them.

"Ice cream?" Olive raised her eyebrows at me. "Yeah, *right*." I was certain Olive didn't really believe me until she saw my changed appetite the next day. And I'm sure she didn't believe me, then or now, that "nothing but a kiss" had happened on that visit.

Bobby stayed for three days. I went home to Dayton only for Mother's Day instead of for the whole weekend, claiming I was swamped with homework. Bobby would begin each night on the couch while I lay awake until he crept to my room and curled up with me, warming my cold, no-body-fat self. He bought bag after bag of groceries, filling our pantry. He baked bread in our tiny kitchen. When the shiny, golden loaf came out of the oven, he pulled handfuls from it, like buttery cotton, which he fed to me, the act as charged as a kiss. He roasted a turkey and made a pot of soup with its stock and tender meat, adding ingredi-ents that amazed me: bacon, black beans, spinach—and *cocoa*. "Taste," he said. My mouth closed around his spoon. He pulled it slowly from my lips, both of us flushed.

The day he left our apartment, he told me he'd be back in a month.

I ate for his return.

As I waited out the storm, I tortured myself with memories of that ice cream, that warm bread, that turkey soup. When the hail stopped, the sudden release from the din startled me into the here and now. One ping, then three, then one. A churchlike quiet fell. Only a swish of horse tail. A snort. A soft storm-over rain on the roof.

When I opened the kicker's back door, there he stood, drenched but unharmed, thank God.

***

I called Gabriella again, but panic seized me as her phone rang. What was I doing? I shouldn't talk to her now. How could I not tell her? I couldn't lie to her; she'd know. I was about to hang up when she answered. "God, Mom. *What?*"

Her voice was sharp with impatience, which helped me find footing. She was safe. Good. *Fine, be a bitch.* That would make withholding the news easier. "Whoa," I said, in our usual banter. "Forgive me for caring about your safety."

"It's not even raining here, okay?"

I couldn't help but tease her. "Oh, and I'm fine, by the way. Your concern is so sweet."

She breathed something like laughter. "What's Dad doing?"

I opened my mouth, not sure what would come out. For a split second I thought I would tell her. "God only knows," I said, which wasn't exactly a lie. But immediately my nose burned.

Gabriella laughed. "Seriously, Mom, everything looks fine here. It's *sunny.* We're getting close to Cincinnati. The bus driver says the storm went north, so we'll be okay." She paused as if waiting for something, then said, "And we *won*, thanks for asking."

How could I forget to ask? So much for acting like all was normal. "Well, I figured you would," I said. She and her boyfriend, Tyler, always did. "Congratulations anyway."

Now Gabriella paused. "You okay? You sound . . . weird."

"Um, well, there was this tornado."

"You *worry*," she said, in the same tone someone might say, "You pick your nose." "I'll be home in an hour or so," she said. "Tyler will drop me off. Love you! Bye!"

I opened my mouth to say the same but before I could, she

clicked off. I stood there, phone to my ear, feeling tired, cold, and trampled.

Muriel butted her head against my banged-up shin. I hissed breath through my teeth, grateful for the distraction of external pain.

I WAS GLAD FOR MURIEL'S COMPANY AS I WALKED OUR property in the rain. I passed St. Francis, who lay facedown in the frothy, muddy mess of my lawn. I picked him up, but only his body rose in my hand. His head had been kicked clean off. Branches were down everywhere. The wind had stripped some aluminum gutter off the back of the barn, peeled some shingles from the house's roof, and collapsed the rickety shed with my tractor parked inside it.

Cradling my arm, I walked the fence line of our pasture, checking to see that fallen branches hadn't compromised any fencing that would later have me chasing goats and horses down the highway. Swirls of steam rose from each white gem of hail on the ground. In the northwest corner of the back pasture, I heard a noise that made the hairs on my arms stand up—I swore it was a child crying. I peered over the fence into the trees and scrubby brush on the other side. The new neighbors had told me they found the entire back property full of crude, makeshift booby traps—obviously to protect the hidden meth lab—and had to ask the local DEA to sweep those acres and declare them safe. "Are you okay?" I called. "Do you need help?"

The crying took on new force and volume, decidedly *not* human.

I climbed the fence and thumped down on the other side. A rustle of movement to my left, low to the ground, made me crouch and peer through the underbrush.

It was the orange cat.

Its front left leg was caught in a trap—a pair of metal jaws with ragged teeth. The trap held the cat up high on its leg, near its shoulder.

Ignoring the pain in my arm, I crawled under the brush to the dull-eyed bag of bones. How long had he been there? The stink of infection already hovered around him. The leg was nearly severed. I knew the minute the trap was removed bleeding would start.

I carried him, trap and all—once I'd wrenched the stake from the now-soggy ground—back to the house, Muriel trotting at my side. I braced myself for Bobby's reaction to yet another animal but then remembered, *Bobby left*. My phone rang in my pocket. Was it Bobby? Maybe he'd spent the entire storm worried about me, regretting his decision. Maybe he'd changed his mind and was coming back. With the cat in my arms, though, I couldn't answer.

The cat cried and hissed. "It's okay," I said, and flinched. I wanted to kick myself, and then kick Bobby. What he did was *not* okay. That *really happened*. My husband *left* me.

Because of the jostling of the walk, the cat's blood ran down my forearms by the time I got him on the kitchen counter. It's a good thing Bobby *was* gone at the moment because blood like this would keel him over every time. I grabbed a freshly laundered saddle pad and taped it around the cat's leg, the fingers of my injured arm puffy and numb.

I checked my phone, in case it was Bobby or Gabby who'd called, but the missed call was from my brother. I looked at the cat's pale gums and dull eyes. Davy would have to wait.

I called Aurora, my associate vet, to explain what had happened (my injuring my arm and finding the cat, *not* Bobby leaving). I drove with the cat swaddled in a towel to meet her at Animal Kind.

Aurora's eyes widened at my appearance. "You look run over," she greeted me. We considered euthanizing the cat, but I couldn't shake how he'd been my little shadow escort on barn chores, following me from twenty yards away—peeking around corners or down from the loft. I couldn't get close to him, but he'd begun to eat the food I put out for him when he thought I wasn't watching. No, I couldn't kill this cat. So we hooked him up to IV fluids, anesthetized him, and began surgery—or, rather, Aurora did, with her healthy, nimble fingers, while I assisted. There was no way to save the decomposing leg. We amputated below the shoulder.

While he was under, we neutered him for good measure, then we stood, watching him breathe as he was stretched unconscious on his side.

Only then did I pick up the faded green collar we'd cut off and examine the worn tag declaring him to be "Champagne Toast." A ludicrous name for such a tough guy. He had fur the color of pumpkin pie, not champagne, with white socks on his three remaining legs and white covering half his battered face. He was big, his head enormous, his nose broad like a wildcat's.

"Just what I need," I said. "But I'm a sucker for an orange boy-cat."

Aurora laughed, the tiny diamond she wore in her left nostril twinkling. The diamond looked classy and exotic on her, not absurd as it would on me, just like her close-cropped black hair. She was my age but looked ten years younger, something pixieish about her. "Every orange tom I've ever known has been pretty damn cool," she admitted. "I like how they get those huge boxing-glove paws in front."

We looked down at our patient. He still had his *one* huge boxing-glove paw.

"Are you okay?" She touched my shoulder. She'd been watching me watch the cat, and I felt naked, exposed, afraid she'd seen the truth of the day when I wasn't guarding it.

I still didn't tell her about Bobby, although I longed for the strength and comfort I knew she'd give me. I wasn't ready to share the news yet. What if he came back? We talked instead about the tornado that touched down five miles away. About Gabriella's win. About the biter. Aurora gave me a blue ice pack and sent me home, saying she would stick around until the cat came to.

I drove home past damaged buildings I hadn't registered on my way to the clinic. The hardware store had lost its entire roof, and several trees had been uprooted. Leaves, trash, and debris were everywhere, as if a giant tide had scraped away.

The last thing I expected to see as I pulled into my drive was the Davids' blue Jeep. They came out of my house the minute I parked, their faces serious, expectant. I realized in a flash: the storm, the unanswered phone call, and, *oh God*, the bloody kitchen counter.

I sat in my truck watching them approach, Max twirling

around their legs. I wasn't ready to tell them the real destruction of the day. I needed time, if only overnight, to absorb this. If they asked how I was, I'd tell them about the horse and the cat, then send them on their way.

But when my brother opened the truck door he said, "Gabby is freaking out."

"Gabby's here already?" Even as I said it, I saw Tyler's black Honda parked by the garage.

Davy offered his hand as I stepped from the truck and said, "She called us wigging out about Bobby. And, hey, your goat is loose. We tried to catch her, but we didn't know how."

My tongue felt pinned to the bottom of my mouth. Had Bobby talked to her already?

At that moment, Gabby stepped off the back porch yelling, "What did you *do* to him?"

CHAPTER FIVE

AT THAT POINT THE DAY WENT SURREAL.

Gabby's face was tear streaked, her eyes red. Tyler stood behind her on the porch, looking like he wanted to be here at this moment even less than I did. Gabby still wore the black suit that made her look thirty. The auburn ringlets of her hair that were not swept up in a sophisticated twist slowly began to wilt in the drizzle. "Did you *hurt* him?"

"No, Gabby, of course not—" I suddenly didn't believe I could remain standing.

Big, bald David Neumeister—built like a linebacker—seemed to sense this. He wrapped me in his arms, enveloping me with that yeasty aroma of fresh bread he carried with him. Big David owned the bakery, David's Hot Buns, that supplied Bobby's restaurant with all its bread. His hug infused me with strength even though it hurt my injured arm.

Davy kissed my cheek and said near my ear, so Gabby couldn't hear it across the yard, "Whatever he did, sis, we're gonna go hunt him down and kick his ass."

I adored my brother for the sentiment but had trouble picturing the Davids beating anyone up. Not that they *couldn't*— Davy was a sinewy, muscled marathon runner who only ever looked small next to Big David—but beating someone up was just so against their natures.

"But it looks like you already did," Big David whispered, as they led me inside.

"Please don't tell me you murdered him and dumped his body in the meth lab acres out back," Davy said. "We need you for a reference for our adoption, remember? It won't look good for us if you're in prison."

MY FIERCE, BALEFUL GABRIELLA SAT, ARMS CROSSED, AT the kitchen island. Tyler stood beside her, hand on her shoulder.

Tyler cleared his throat and said, "Dr. Anderson, I'm sorry, but . . ." he nodded toward the gory mess on the counter. "What happened?" He sounded almost scared.

I'd stopped bothering to tell him he could call me Cami. It was a sign of his good parenting that he'd always addressed Bobby and me as Mr. Binardi and Dr. Anderson. Tyler worked in my clinic (as did Gabby); he wanted to be a vet, and I thought he'd make a great one.

I quickly explained about the cat.

Gabriella's big brown eyes softened.

"Did he make it?" Tyler asked.

I nodded. I saw the interest in his eyes, knew he would've loved to see that surgery.

Then they saw *my* arm. Everyone stared at the now almost-black purple welts. Blood blisters shone from the top of each one. "Like I said, it's been a hell of a day." My words ran out of my mouth, gathering momentum. "I've been bitten by a rescue horse—who's in our barn right now if he hasn't dismantled it—left by my husband, and forced to amputate the leg of a cat."

A strange silence fell in the kitchen. Strange enough that it made me look up and into everyone's faces. I saw wheels turning, information being shifted behind their eyes.

"Whatever Dad did, you're going to let him come home, right?"

A slow dawning rose in me. "Babe . . . what did your dad tell you?"

"He didn't *tell* me anything. He . . . he left me a message."

"A *message?*" For a second I wished the blood on the counter *did* belong to Bobby.

"He said he wanted me to know before I got back that he couldn't be here and it looked like the two of you were splitting up."

Wow. That sounded so . . . reciprocal. I pressed my fingers to the angry bumps on my arm.

"What happened, Mom? What did he do? He'll be back, right?"

What did I say? Pretend it was just an argument? *Would* he come back?

I told the humiliating, scalding truth, then watched everyone reprocess this information.

Davy asked, as if sorting out complicated directions, "Wait. *He* left *you?*"

When my mother's car pulled into the drive (Gabby had called her), I put my forehead on the kitchen island. My parents were professional stoics, and at the moment, I was too depleted to do the work to put on a brave face. I clutched my hands to my muddy hair. I couldn't face my mother like this. My mother could stand in the dustbowl of a summer horse show, judging class after class of riders she'd allowed to remove their jackets in the savage heat—never removing her own jacket, of course—and look like she'd just stepped out of an air-conditioned room. Davy urged me upstairs to take a shower.

Bobby had taken his shaving mirror from the shower, but his razor stubble peppered the tub. This sight had greeted me nearly every morning of our life together.

Why hadn't I told the truth to my friends? Who had I been kidding? At our Girls' Nights Out (referred to by my friends as GNOs), Olive, Helen, and Aurora talked with equal passion of their love and irritation for their men. Nick wouldn't stand up to his mother. Hank always forgot to ask before he committed them to plans as a couple. One of Aurora's dates had never voted. Olive had turned to me: "So, your turn, Cami. Don't hold back just because he's my brother."

When I smiled and shrugged, they insisted, "Oh, come on. Don't make us hate you!"

Finally, I said, "He never rinses his damn stubble down the shower drain."

Silence. Then, joking, "You suck. That's all you've got?"

Now, with Bobby gone, I stepped into the shower—that stubble gritty under my feet—and wondered why I hadn't told them about the burden of his unhappiness. Or the fact that he'd never dance. That a gift certificate for salsa classes died a quiet death in his dresser drawer. That the holidays I used to love became tense with his gloomy moods.

He hadn't *really* left me, had he? He'd come back. He had to come back.

I washed my hair for a long time, partly because of my tender arm but also because I was stalling. I was too spent to talk to my mother. Oh, God. I didn't want to *be* my mother. Just thinking that made me crouch down under the shower's stream, my arms wrapped around my knees.

Suddenly I was eleven, scrunched down like that with Vijay, hiding in my parents' hayloft, overhearing my parents argue.

Vijay and I had been walking on the ceiling beams that went over the indoor riding arena, from one loft to the other inside the barn, pretending to be tightrope walkers. When we heard my parents' voices, we scampered off a beam and hid behind some bales of hay.

My parents *never* argued, but Dad's word *bitch* rose to me and punched my stomach.

Beneath us, my father saddled Stormwatch, while my mother followed his every step.

"I'd do anything, Cleve," Mom said.

Even at that age, my mother's desperation and pleading tone sickened me. Her repeated "please" stung me as much as Dad's rude insult.

"You ask a lot, Caroline," my father said.

But as far as I could see, my mother hadn't asked for *any-thing*. Ever. She toiled away behind the scenes. She wiped his boots. She wiped the horse's mouth. She walked the course. She timed. She carried. She fetched.

My father mounted Stormwatch, clucked his tongue, and cantered out the open door.

"Don't take it out on the horse!" Mom called.

When Dad rode away, Mom said, "That's not who you want to hurt." She stood, staring after him, hands on her head, frozen. When she finally left, Vijay and I climbed down and took off to report everything to Davy.

Terrified that our parents were going to split up, Davy and I spied on them both, recording observations and clues in black-and-white speckled notebooks. We witnessed more whispered arguments. Phone calls our father would end abruptly when we entered the room. I crept downstairs several nights to find Dad asleep on the couch, covered in our dogs and cats. Twice I found our parents' bedroom empty, Dad's truck gone, and Mom crying in the barn lot.

It didn't take much for Davy and me to figure out our father was having an affair.

Davy feared Dad would leave us, forcing Mom to sell us—just like what happened to Seabiscuit's jockey in a book we'd read. I, though, became scornful that my mother didn't leave herself. *I* would never put up with that bullshit. *I* would never beg *please*.

In the shower, I leaned my forehead against the tile.

My dad still got all the glory, even though he was retired from competition now. He won four Olympic golds before a brutal fall injured his brain and spine five years ago. While Mom walked him up and down the hospital hallways and oversaw every physical therapy exercise, it was my father who got his picture on the cover of magazines even then.

Now my parents were only months away from their fiftieth wedding anniversary. *Fifty years.*

❧

MY MOTHER'S GENTLENESS EMBARRASSED ME.

I sat on the edge of the tub, combing my hair, when Mom knocked. "Oh, sweetie," she said, the words full of heartbreak. She sat beside me on the tub's edge and put an arm around me. She smelled of wood smoke from their fireplace, with perfume faintly beneath it.

When she saw my arm, she stiffened. "What on earth happened? Did he *hurt* you?"

"No! No, no, one of the horses we removed this morning bit me."

The coiled snake of my mother's anger released a little. Mom knew Bobby's father had been a violent man when alive. When Bobby and I first dated, Mom had seen Mimi once with a bruise-smudged lip. I'm not sure she ever truly believed that Bobby had purpled my own eye by accident, thrashing around during one of his nightmares.

I wished in that shameful instant that Bobby *did* beat me. I wanted to announce that Bobby and I split up because he hit me. I wanted a *reason*. Something as clean and sharp as an elbow cracking into a cheekbone in the dark.

IN BOBBY'S IMMACULATE KITCHEN—SOMEONE HAD cleaned up the cat's blood—whatever Big David was baking filled the air with rosemary. Gabby had changed clothes, and polite Tyler had left for home. The evening blurred together with their comforts and conversations.

I turned to Gabriella. "Babe, you know this has nothing to do with *you*, right? This is between your father and—"

"If one more person says that to me I'm going to scream!" she said. "What am I? *Six?*"

I looked at the others, who shrugged sheepishly. Good. Good for them. I'd rather she heard it too often than not at all.

They asked me questions. I told the story. They talked. My mind drifted, hearing fragments.

I sat down at the tiled kitchen island with an ice-filled dish towel across my forearm. I traced the blue-and-yellow designs in the Portuguese tile we'd selected on one of our last trips together. It hit me—if he really was gone, that would have been our last vacation. The first of a series of lasts: the last Christmas, the last party, the last birthday dinner. Bobby's birthday was just a week away.

As angry and hurt as I was, I mostly felt fear—fear for Bobby. What was he *doing?*

Once Gabby left the room, Mom was brave enough to ask. "Is there someone else?"

Even though I'd asked Bobby the same question, my mother bringing it up rankled me. "He said there wasn't."

"Of course he's going to say that, right?" Davy said. "He's too big of a coward to admit it to your face. But who would leave *you* for no reason?"

I loved my brother fiercely at that moment even though I didn't want him to be right.

"That's the first thing my mom asked, too," Big David said. His sixty-seven-year-old mother, Ava, lived with them.

"You told your mom?" I was mortified.

Big David nodded. "While you were in the shower."

"Not that she'll remember it," Davy said. Ava had Alzheimer's.

Big David said, "She's with Carol"—his sister—"and when I told her, Mom asked me, 'Who did he leave her for? A man or a woman?'"

The floor seemed to tilt slightly. *What?* Bobby had talked often lately of "reinventing" himself. Well. *That* would certainly do the trick.

"Please," Davy said, seeing me consider this. "He left Gabby a *message*. A gay man would *never* have been that insensitive."

Even I laughed at that, grateful to Davy for breaking the grim mood.

"You should call Mimi," Mom said of Bobby's mother. "But otherwise, be discreet. He may realize he's made a mistake and want to come back. And when he does, you don't want to have dragged your dirty laundry through everyone else's backyard."

I wanted to say, *I'm not you, Mom!* But I didn't. I didn't like who I became in her presence—reduced to my eleven-year-old self. I did say, "Maybe *I* wouldn't take *him* back."

My mother's face flushed. She wiped nonexistent crumbs from the Portuguese tile.

I hated myself. Hadn't I just been thinking what she suggested—that he might return before anyone else had to know? Why was I so awful to her?

"You should eat," Big David said, always the peacemaker. "I'm baking you some rosemary bread. It'll be out in ten minutes. But we can rustle up a meal, too."

The rosemary bread was one of my favorites from David's bakery. We called it "funeral bread," because Ava always made it for friends when someone died. It seemed all too fitting.

A wave of memory crashed against me—the way Bobby held my face in his hands and bent his head to mine. How his fingers always carried a scent of citrus, or of basil.

"Don't tell anyone yet, okay?" I asked the Davids. That was as close to an apology to my mother as I could muster.

I HAD NO IDEA WHAT THEY HEATED UP FOR DINNER. WHATever it was tasted like sawdust, but I sat with them and forced myself to bring spoonfuls to my mouth to chew and swallow.

I was relieved when everyone went home and it was just me and Gabby. I showed her the new horse. We stood outside, since the kicker still refused to enter the barn. Gabby slid next to me, putting her arm around my waist, her head on my shoulder.

I was so sorry this was happening to her this way. A *message*? Really? I watched the horse scarf his new pile of hay. "You didn't really think I'd attacked your dad, did you?"

"Well," she said. "You can be pretty kick-ass, you know."

I kissed her forehead. I didn't feel very kick-ass at the moment, but the compliment warmed me. I loved this person with every rational thought (and plenty of irrational ones) that passed through my brain. Her opinion mattered more than almost anyone's to me.

I'd give my moody, morose husband time. I'd give him space. I'd get him back here and we'd make it better.

Because even though I'd never wanted to be married, there's no way in hell I wanted to be divorced.

CHAPTER SIX

⁂

MY PULSE'S DRUMBEAT THROBBED THROUGH MY BITE
marks. Max and Gingersnap both knew I was awake and were
staring at me. If I rolled away from them, they moved to face
me again.

"Stop it," I said. Max licked my face. I gave up and wandered
downstairs to my home office.

Hoping for something from Bobby, I checked my e-mail.
Nothing.

I e-mailed Vijay. My subject was "Emergency." I typed, "Are
you awake? I need to talk. Don't worry about what time it is."
As soon as I hit send, I wondered where he was—in New York
or still in Botswana? Although his "real" work was with HIV/
AIDS for Doctors Without Borders (sometimes in Zimbabwe
and Botswana for months at a time), he was most known for his
hour-long weekly show on the Discovery Channel. *Outbreak*
was, in spite of its melodramatic title and sometimes gruesome
coverage of infectious diseases around the globe, a well-respected
program with an almost cultlike following. Vijay's brother
Asheev jokingly called him Dr. Hollywood, but Vijay contended
that the show brought much-needed attention—and, more
important, funding—to the work of Doctors Without Borders.

Because of our last names—Anderson and Aperjeet—Vijay and I had been in homeroom together from first grade until we graduated. He'd helped me with my calculus; I'd helped him with his English papers. We'd represented China in the model UN trip to Chicago, and we'd been busted for having wine in my hotel room on the French club trip to Paris. If I hadn't missed so much school, traveling to my father's competitions (and landing in the hospital for starvation), we might have tied for valedictorian, but as it was he'd taken the honor alone. We'd shared sleepy rantings about medical and veterinary school and listened to praise and complaints about each other's various dates. I'd read a poem at his wedding. He'd been an usher at mine.

No e-mail popped up. My cell phone didn't ring.

I put my head down on my desk to wait.

Poor Vijay. Rita left him before Christmas, four months ago. I'd been sympathetic and supportive, but now I knew I hadn't done enough. I'd had no idea what this *felt like*.

WHEN THE DOORBELL WOKE ME IN THE MORNING, Gingersnap pushed off my lap with pinpricks of claws. Max scrambled from under my desk and tore for the door, barking ferociously. I sat up, stiff from all the abuse my body had taken yesterday. *Yesterday*. I'd done it. I'd survived that awful day. My arm throbbed. When my haggard face ambushed me in the hallway mirror, I tried to comb my tousled hair with my fingers.

"Maybe it's Dad!" Gabriella shrieked. She bolted down the stairs so fast I cringed, expecting her to fall. The hope in her voice bruised me. Why would Bobby ring the bell? Oh, God.

Don't let my poor daughter feel abandoned. If she was disappointed, though, she didn't let it show. She called out "Mr. Henrici!" Why would Nick, Olive's boyfriend, be here? Did he know our news?

As soon as Nick spoke, Max stopped barking and twirled in lopsided circles. Gabby laughed and said, "I did my Latin homework! I swear!"

Nick taught at the same school where Davy did. Davy, in fact, had introduced Nick to Olive. Gabriella had reported that Nick was the second most popular teacher at school—next to her Uncle Davy, of course. She got points for having an "in" with both of them.

"I need you guys to help me," Nick said.

He obviously hadn't heard our news: there was something too exuberant on his face. Gabby and I exchanged a look that was an unspoken agreement to let it slide for now.

"Look!" He held out an open ring box. The diamond on the delicate gold band glittered even in the dim entryway. "I'm proposing today, but you guys have to help me."

Gabby clapped her hands, but then shot me a worried glance.

Although I smiled, the back of my throat ached at the irony of the timing.

Nick laid out his creative, thoughtful plan. He'd told Olive they were going to a beer garden in Cincinnati with some of his friends. Really, he'd rented a room in a historic bed-and-breakfast. They'd go to dinner—alone—and he'd give her the ring.

He needed us to pack Olive's overnight bag. "She'll need a nice dress, makeup, shampoo, stuff like that. I'm picking her up around noon. I'll tell her I want to get a cup of coffee first. I want you guys"—he made a gesture up the stairs that I knew included the Bobby he believed was there—"to go into her apartment when you see us walk down to the corner."

So Bobby hadn't told Olive. I figured he hadn't, or Olive would've been here. Had he told *anyone?* If he came back, no one else would ever have to know about that horrific day.

"I'll try to convince her to sit and have our coffee at the café," Nick went on, "but she might not. I'll leave the car unlocked. Just pop the trunk and put the bag inside."

He never asked about Bobby, so we never volunteered.

DAVY, GABRIELLA, AND I PARKED DOWN THE BLOCK FROM Olive's apartment. Davy had shown up to check on us shortly after Nick had left, bearing a box of pastries from David's Hot Buns. He'd begged to be allowed to accompany us on our packing mission.

I was glad we had this project to keep our minds off Bobby. My heart pounded as if we were part of a covert operation. As we waited for Nick to arrive, Gabby asked, "How did Dad propose to you?" She hunched her shoulders, realizing how this question might pain me. "Sorry."

"Not like this," I said, hoping to make a joke of it. I patted her knee where she sat sandwiched between Davy and me in my truck cab.

I could practically *feel* all three of us scrambling for something to say after that.

"Any adoption news?" Gabby asked in too chipper a voice.

"Nope," Davy said.

I looked at my brother's freckled profile—he'd look youthful even when he was eighty, I bet. Helen—wonderful Helen, my fellow Humane volunteer—was an attorney for the county's Family Services, currently trying to help the Davids adopt.

Although they might have had better odds applying as single dads, they'd gone the honest route, and pregnant girl after pregnant woman had rejected them as the parents of her unwanted child. Helen assured us *all* couples could expect to be turned down a dozen or more times before they were chosen, but each time made me feel they'd been spat on.

"I wish you weren't doing an open adoption," Gabby said. "Are you *sure* you can't get a baby from a foreign country?"

"Gabby!" I said.

But Davy laughed. "We're sure. Besides, we really believe in open adoption, no matter what you say about it."

"But the kid's real parents could be at *our* Christmases?" Gabriella asked.

"*Biological* parents," Davy corrected her. "We'll be real parents. And, yes, they could be at our Christmases. And our Thanksgivings. And our birthday parties."

"Eww! What if they're freaky?"

I laughed out loud. So did Davy. "Freakier than our family already *is*?" he joked.

My daughter was so intelligent it often startled me, but she occasionally reminded me that she was only seventeen. She didn't—as she sometimes seemed to believe—know everything. *But please please please, Bobby, let her know she has two parents who love her.*

Gabriella turned Davy's silver band on his ring finger.

"Do you think he'll come home?" she asked, without looking up.

"I don't know, babe."

"It's too soon to tell, right?" Her tone dared us to disagree. When she was sufficiently certain that we wouldn't, she changed the subject again in a bright, cheerful voice. "I remember *your* wedding," she said to Davy. "I remember playing in the fountains at the park."

Gabby had been nine at their commitment ceremony. Bobby and my mother had been miffed I'd let Gabriella get in the fountains in her tights.

Gabriella kept turning Davy's wedding band. "I'm glad you wear rings even if . . ." she trailed off, not sure, I imagined, how to tactfully say *even if they don't count*.

"Even if," Davy said simply.

"If I ran the country . . ." Gabby started.

"Oh, brother, here we go again," Davy said.

" . . . I'd let you get married."

"Well, thank you," he said. "So under President Gabriella Binardi, let's see, we'd outlaw all plastic grocery sacks—"

"That's right."

"We'd outlaw all drive-throughs, and now we'd have gay marriage. Nice."

"Don't forget the birth control in the drinking water," I said.

"Whoa. Isn't that a little fascist?" Davy asked.

"No, no, no," Gabby said. "Anyone *can* have kids. They just have to *choose*. All they have to do is ask and I'd switch their water to normal."

Davy nodded. "I like it. I'd vote for you."

"And," Gabby said, "I'll pull that off in my first one hundred days. Just you wait. Law school first, though. Debate's gonna get me into Harvard."

She'd been saying that for four years now, ever since Holly, Helen and Hank's daughter, got accepted there. I feared I'd have to *make* Gabriella apply to other schools, too.

Nick's car appeared at the end of the block. The three of us fell into conspiratorial silence and my heart resumed its quickened pace. How *had* Bobby proposed to me?

Nick lifted his hand in a tentative wave when he spotted my truck. Gabby waved back.

Had there been a proposal? I remembered a conversation in my old apartment kitchen that would have to count. Bobby had made chicken korma, which had reminded me of Vijay and all the times he or his mother, Shivani, had cooked for me in high school.

Bobby's korma had filled my entire apartment with eye-watering garlic scent. He fed me naan bread dipped in the korma, his fingers lingering on my lips. "Our kitchen will be bigger than this," he'd said. "I'll cook for you every night."

"*Our* kitchen?" I asked.

"In our house," he said.

I licked a bit of korma from his lower lip. "We're getting a house?"

"Yep." He took my hand.

"Are we getting married?"

"Yes." He led me down the hall to my bedroom. This had often been our dessert.

A few halfhearted raindrops fell on my truck's windshield. "I think *I* proposed to him."

"What?" Davy and Gabriella turned their heads to me.

"I was trying to remember, since you asked me. I think I proposed to Bobby. I asked, 'Are we getting married?' and he said, 'Yes.' "

Gabby wrinkled her nose. "He didn't give you a ring?"

"Later. Not that night." His family had *made* him give me the heirloom ring I still wore. I self-consciously turned it with my thumb.

"He didn't get down on one knee?" Gabriella sounded heartbroken.

I shook my head. I'd always defended our low-key engagement and wedding to my mother, to my brother, to friends, and especially to Bobby's family. Bobby and I hadn't *needed* all those trappings, all those "societal conventions," as we called them.

"It should be romantic," Gabby declared. "Mr. Henrici is doing it right." No matter how many times Nick had told her she could call him by his first name outside of school, I'd never heard her do it yet. "That's how I want Tyler to propose to me, something creative like this."

"Not anytime soon, I hope," Davy said.

Gabriella laughed. "We're getting married as soon as we're eighteen!"

Davy made a choking sound. He knew as well as I did that she'd been saying that since middle school, back when she'd filled the covers of notebooks and the margins of schoolwork with hundreds of "Gabriella Reed"s (which struck me as odd since I'd kept my own name). Bobby always said, "Over my dead body," and Gabby would laugh and kiss his cheek.

Before I could speak, though, Davy said, "There they go!"

Olive and Nick strolled down the street holding hands. The little bit of rain didn't seem to bother them at all.

"Okay, let's go," I said. We crossed the street and approached the apartment. As soon as Nick and Olive rounded the corner, the three of us broke into a run, me cradling my arm.

It struck me, as I climbed the stairs to Olive's apartment, *I'm laughing. My husband left me and I'm laughing. Is this okay?* Something dreamlike hovered around the scene.

I unlocked Olive's apartment with trembling hands, the fingers of my injured arm numb, bumping her "Licensed Massage Therapist" sign so hard it nearly fell.

"You go out on the balcony," I told them, "and keep an eye on the street."

I ran into Olive's bedroom. She was still the slob she had been in college. Her bed was unmade, the crazy quilt Mimi had made her in a rumpled ball, the top sheet falling off one side. Her closet stood open, clothes heaped everywhere. I unzipped Olive's gym bag and tossed the sneakers, sports bra, and towel to the floor.

Okay. Pink dress. I'd decided on her pink dress. I saw it, still in a dry cleaner's bag. Perfect. I laid it on the bed. The dress was strapless. I dug through drawers and found a strapless bra and sexy panties. I selected a necklace and earrings that matched the dress.

"Hurry up!" Davy pleaded.

"Are they coming?"

"No, but it's taking you forever!" Gabriella said.

More adrenaline surge. I found a vintage, beaded cream cardigan and folded it into the bag in case she got cold. In the bathroom, I threw in everything—her shampoo, her lotion, her entire makeup kit. Her curling iron. Her hair spray. A million different hair clips and pins.

"Come *on*!" Gabriella called.

"Stop it! You're freaking me out." My fingers felt clumsy as I zipped the bulging bag.

When my cell phone rang, I yelped as if I'd been stung by a bee.

I checked to see who was calling, fearful it was Nick, hoping it was Bobby.

It was Vijay.

The phone rang again. I didn't know what to do. I'd said *emergency*.

I answered. "Hey you. Can I call you back in like, ten minutes?"

"What's going on?" His deep, velvet voice was a balm.

"I'm in the middle of something crazy. Everything's okay, but—"

"What's the emergency?"

"Oh. Well, I mean, *everything's* not okay, but there's something else going on . . ."

"Why are you out of breath? Are you all right?"

Davy stood in the doorway. "Who are you *talking* to?" he asked in his sternest teacher voice.

"I have to go, Vijay. I'm sorry. Thank you for calling. I *will* call you back in just a little bit."

"You're on the *phone*?" Gabriella appeared beside Davy.

A noise in the hallway startled all of us. "Someone's *here*," Davy whispered.

"*Shit*," I said. "Vijay, I gotta go. I'll explain everything in a minute." I clicked the phone shut and thrust the gym bag into Davy's arms, then picked up the dress.

But someone knocked on the door we'd left open. "Hello?" a female voice called.

It wasn't Olive. I recognized the voice but couldn't place it.

"Olive?" the voice called. Slightly frightened.

I carried the dress out to the living room, following Davy and Gabriella.

Zayna Arnett stood in Olive's doorway. Seeing her here, out of context, added to the surreal quality of this morning. I normally saw her assisting the vet techs in my clinic.

"Davy? What are you— Oh, hi, Dr. Anderson!" She looked, for a second, as surprised as I was, and I thought she might turn around and run away. Zayna was a spunky, fun, twenty-two-year-old theater major. She was completely footing her own bill through college because her parents disapproved of her "wasting her time" on an acting degree. I'd convinced Bobby to give Zayna a job waiting tables at Tanti Baci, too, even though he'd sighed and said, "You can't rescue everyone, Cam." Here in Olive's doorway, Zayna looked from Davy to Gabriella to me. "Where's Olive?"

Had Olive taken off and forgotten about an appointment? How did she stay in business?

Before I could explain, my phone rang again. I looked. Vijay.

"*Mom*," Gabriella pleaded.

"Here." I handed her the dress and bag. "Go put this in Nick's car."

As Gabriella ran down the stairs, Davy said to Zayna, "The best massage in town, right?"

Zayna smiled and nodded.

I answered my phone. "Vijay, please. I'll call you back. Give me a—"

"You don't sound right. What's going on?"

Zayna stood there, twisting a curl of her shiny red hair around one finger, watching me with wide eyes. Why was she so nervous? Oh, my God, did she think we were *stealing* from Olive?

"Look," I told Vijay and Zayna, "Nick is proposing to Olive today." Zayna opened her mouth in a little O. "It's a big, cool surprise, all is well, so *please* let me call you back—"

Gabriella clomped back up the stairs.

"But what's the emergency? Your voice sounds all wrong."

Gabriella stood in the doorway, contemplating Zayna. "Cool shoes," Gabby said.

I looked. Strappy sandals, with heels that made her legs look like a ballerina's.

"Let me finish this and then I'll—" *Shoes!* "Oh, my God. We need shoes!"

"You didn't pack *shoes?*" Davy grabbed his head in both hands.

"Mom!"

Still holding the phone I rushed back to Olive's closet.

"Cami?" Vijay asked.

Clutching the phone between my ear and shoulder, I dug

around on the closet floor and found the cream T-strap heels Olive always wore with the pink dress.

I stood up and turned around, barreling into Davy. "Here, Gabby, run these down."

"*Me?* I'm gonna get caught now!" but she snatched them and ran.

"Cami, talk to me." Vijay sounded panicked.

I took a deep breath. I had, after all, left a melodramatic message. "Bobby left."

There was a pause. "Left?"

"Yes. Left. As in emptied his closet, packed up his car, and left me."

Zayna put her hands over her mouth. I turned away from her.

"Oh, Cam. Cam." The tenderness in Vijay's voice prompted my eyes to sting.

"I should go——" Zayna said.

But Gabriella ran back into the apartment, blocking Zayna's exit. "They're coming!" she said.

"They'll just get in the car and leave now," I said. "We can hide up here until they go."

"*Hide?*" Vijay asked. "Why are you hiding? Who are you talking to?"

"I'm talking to Gabby. Don't worry. This is a *good* thing. It has nothing to do with Bobby——"

Suddenly Nick's voice boomed in the stairwell. Way too loud he announced, "Okay, just hit the bathroom and we'll be on our way."

I reached out to quietly close and lock the door.

"I *will* call you back," I whispered and clicked the phone shut again. *"Hide."* Davy and Zayna fled to the balcony, closing the door behind them.

I started to follow with Gabriella, but Olive's voice was right outside the door, her key rattling the lock, "Okay, Mr.-let's-go-get-a-coffee, don't be rushing *me* now."

Nick laughed, loud and forced. He was trying his best to warn us. I grabbed Gabby's hand, pulling her into the bedroom. She slid under the bed. I crouched down beside it, yanking the quilt over me. I still clutched my phone. I set it to vibrate.

"I just want to get on the road," Nick said as they opened the door.

"Quit *yelling*," Olive said. "What the hell is wrong with you?"

I heard Olive drop her purse and head for the bathroom. Oh, no—when Olive saw the mess I'd left, with cabinets and drawers open, she'd think she'd been robbed. But I heard only the sound of Olive peeing. Ah, thank God she was such a slob. I peeked out from under the quilt. Nick stood in the tiny hallway outside the bedroom and bathroom doors. I waved and gave him a thumbs-up. He beamed. When the toilet flushed, I curled into a ball and covered myself again.

The phone buzzed, wasplike, in my hand. I shoved it down the front of my pants and hugged my knees up to muffle the noise.

I stayed still until Nick and Olive's footsteps faded on the stairs. The balcony door opened and Davy burst into whooping laughter. Gabriella crawled out from under the bed. Zayna left quickly, and Davy and Gabby went into the kitchen and sat on the floor, laughing and eating a bag of Olive's Doritos, while I called Vijay and told him all about yesterday.

Talking to Vijay grounded me, as it always did. He grounded me before horse shows in high school, when I took my VCAT exam, when I got cold feet before my wedding.

I got cold feet before my wedding.

I'd forgotten, until now, how Vijay, looking dashing in his suit, had come into my little dressing tent, summoned by Olive. He'd taken both my hands in his—he had enormous hands with long, lovely fingers. "Having second thoughts?" he asked.

I nodded. His voice made me breathe. We whispered, since Olive kept watching us. "But not about Bobby. About me. Am I up for this? Worthy of it?"

Vijay's nostrils flared. "Worthy of *Bobby*?"

I'd been so quick to correct him, I'd never registered his reaction until this moment. "No, no, of *marriage*. What will happen to us? Will we do okay?"

He'd smiled, his teeth so white against his caramel skin. "Well . . . that would be reading the last page of the book, wouldn't it?"

Our favorite teacher in high school had fondly chastised Vijay, saying he needed to relax, he couldn't plan every aspect of his life, he couldn't—as I knew he *did*—make a list of goals, then move on-schedule through life checking them off. "If this were a book," Mrs. Norvell had teased him, "I'm afraid you'd read the last page!"

He'd looked at her, his expression revealing his opinion: *Of course! Who wouldn't?*

I wouldn't, I told him later. "Life is an *adventure*. Think how boring it would be if you knew right now how it all turns out. Where's the fun? The mystery? The discovery?"

Lying there on Olive's bed, years after those conversations, I said, "You know what? I want to see that last page."

He laughed, a rich, low sound that always made me think of dark desserts—chocolate mousse, sticky-toffee pudding, melt-in-your-mouth truffles. "I'll tell you what your book says: you end up happy and discover the life you're meant to live."

Hadn't *this* been the life I'd been meant to live?

"I meant Bobby's book," I said. "I'm really worried about him."

Vijay snorted. "I think he just changed his story pretty profoundly."

"And mine."

"He can *affect* your story," Vijay said. "He can change it somewhat, but he can't change *you*. You don't have to be reduced by those changes."

Maybe it was the doctor in him—that part of his nature he'd displayed since elementary school. He could diagnose and treat just with the sound of his creamy voice. He was in Botswana, leaving in ten days, and promised to fly to Dayton as soon as he was back on this continent.

I stayed on Olive's messy bed after we hung up. I listened to my daughter and brother rehashing the packing escapade and narrow escape. This project had occupied a couple hours and had kept me focused on something beside the fact that my life had been hurled upside down.

My arm hurt. I needed to tend to the biter. And check on the three-legged cat. Those would be the next projects to get me up off of Olive's bed.

CHAPTER SEVEN

ℛ

OLIVE

Olive sipped her mocha and wondered how she'd do it. How she'd break up with Nick. They were speeding along I-75 toward Cincinnati, and she dreaded another gathering of his friends with every muscle in her body. His goddamn married friends. There wasn't a single one of them not married.

Nick hummed and tapped his fingers on the steering wheel. Why was *he* so damn happy today?

Olive tried not to hear her mother's grating voice in her head: "Well, why shouldn't he be happy? He's sitting pretty, isn't he? Why should he buy the cow when he gets all his goddamn milk for free?"

Cow? Fuck you, Ma.

Olive had shut her up once with, "Why should I buy the whole pig when all I want is the sausage?"

Ma had scowled. Then she'd slapped Olive on the shoulder: "The sausage. That's good."

But it wasn't true. Olive had to pretend it was. Just like she'd have to pretend she was okay with not being engaged at yet *another* gathering of Nick's smug married friends. Did they pity her, showing up year after year, still with a bare left hand?

She looked at him, driving along, singing now—off key—and hated him. She didn't even *want* to marry him. If he asked her now, right this second, she'd say no.

"You're quiet today," he said. He put his right hand on her left knee and squeezed it.

Olive did the right thing. She put both her hands on his and smiled at him. "Just thinking," she said, making sure her tone was light, her voice pleasant.

"About?"

Should she just tell him the truth? Should she just say, *I was sitting here wondering if you're ever going to fucking marry me or if you think I'm the biggest goddamn patsy you ever met.* But she didn't. She made her voice all flirty and said, "You."

"Unpure?" Nick teased. "Your thoughts about me?"

"Always."

He laughed. She couldn't tell the truth because that went against the rules. Women had to be chosen. Men got to do the choosing, but women had to wait for someone to want them.

At a Girl's Night Out, Aurora had asked her once, "Why don't *you* propose to Nick?"

But the idea was preposterous. That wasn't how it was supposed to happen.

Sometimes Aurora and Helen got on her nerves. Like Helen had any room to talk, since she *was* married. Helen asked, "What difference does it make? You love Nick, right?"

"Of course I do," Olive had said.

"You're happy, you're having fun. How do you think marriage is going to change that?"

Olive hated questions like that, especially from *a married woman*, for Christ's sake. Marriage changed everything. It would say to the world that Olive was worthy, that she was partnered in a life that expected every grownup to be partnered. It said she was a success. Complete.

And yes, yes, yes, of course she could agree with Aurora, who'd said, "There are many paths to committed and satisfying relationships. Not just marriage." But deep in Olive's guts, there was something about the public, societal declaration of permanence she needed in order to consider a relationship "real." Not being married—or at least engaged—made her feel fundamentally unloved, unworthy, and unnecessary. No matter how great the sex was.

Really, did Nick think she would just keep on dating him indefinitely? She wanted to be married. She wanted to have children. If that's not what he wanted, it was time to move on. She'd tell him on the way home.

She leaned her forehead against the glass and watched the shopping malls zipping by. Christ, that would be awful. Starting again. Dating. There was nothing so demeaning as being a single woman over forty. She'd read desperation was a turnoff, but here she'd invested nearly three years acting as laid-back as she could—and for what?

Nick was *grinning*. Just pleased as fucking punch. Not a care in the world. Did she even *like* him? They had nothing in common. She didn't speak Latin. Or any foreign language, except a bit of Italian. He spoke Italian better than she did. He spoke five languages. He liked grammar and golfing and the goddamn opera. She liked sudoku and yoga and jazz clubs.

But she also liked having someone. She liked holding his hand when they went for coffee. She liked being in a pair.

Even if they weren't a match.

CHAPTER EIGHT

I CHECKED MY E-MAIL AND CELL PHONE OBSESSIVELY, BUT there was still no word from Bobby. Gabriella flew to the landline every time it rang. She carried her cell phone from room to room, leaving it beside her while we ate. Bobby's treatment of me was one thing, but his self-absorbed insensitivity to our daughter made me nauseous with anxiety.

I went out to do the morning feed a full hour earlier than I usually did—and ended up waking every single animal. I attempted to groom the biter, but he shied away from me and threatened to kick, so I leaned on his fence—the electric off— to contemplate my next move.

He faced me, his whole body hunched and defensive. I understood—abandonment *hurt*.

When he stepped toward me, I hid my surprise and stood still. He took another step, then another. I didn't breathe as he flared his nostrils to snuff my hair, my head, my shoulders.

Go ahead. Bite me. I longed for him to leave me looking as bleeding and wounded as I felt.

Raw, open sores peeped from where his too-big halter rubbed across the gaunt bones of his face. His forelock and mane dangled in dreadlocks of mud. But through this disguise of neglect and cruelty, anyone could see he was magnificent. "Hey, beautiful," I whispered.

He tossed his head up and down violently, the way a person might shake out a dusty rag. Then he wheeled around and let loose with one mighty kick before he tore across the small paddock. The little shit's hoof struck the fence just a foot away from my left shoulder.

When Gabby left for school—her red, swollen eyes belying her "fine"—I called Bobby's cell, not caring about the hour, and told his voice mail: "You need to talk to Gabriella. Call her, meet with her, something. She deserves more than a message left on her phone."

At the clinic, I didn't tell anyone what had happened. I was partly following my mother's advice, but mostly I still couldn't believe this really *had* happened.

The three-legged cat growled and hissed even when no one was near him. Aurora had told me he'd come out of anesthesia fighting, thrashing around and banging his head against the sides of his kennel. She'd had to hold him down until he was fully conscious. I ignored his ferocious sounds and rubbed his broad wildcat nose until I eventually earned a grudging purr.

"How's your arm?" Aurora asked when she came in. "Do we need to switch today?"

Mondays and Wednesdays were my surgery mornings, Tuesdays and Thursdays were hers. Whoever wasn't in surgery saw patients. I flexed my fingers. "I think I'm okay."

"*Are* you?" Aurora asked, and again I felt ashamed for withholding from her. "What's going on with you, Cam?"

I looked into her kind, concerned eyes and lied that I was fine.

My first procedure was a tracheal wash on a dog who'd been coughing and vomiting for a month. Since I hadn't scrubbed in yet, I checked my phone and computer again for word from Bobby while Bridget, my technician, and Zayna prepped the dog. Nothing.

After the procedure (we retrieved a sample for lab analysis), I checked again. Nothing.

Sweet Zayna took away the coughing dog and brought in my next surgery. She didn't let on to anyone else that she knew anything unusual about my weekend.

After a routine spay on a labradoodle, still no messages.

After a cat neuter, and another cat neuter, nothing.

I'd gotten all the routine surgeries out of the way and into recovery so I could concentrate on this last, likely to be complicated, case—a chow with a huge abdominal mass. I operated with a poor prognosis and ended up removing an enormous spleen full of tumors. The rest of the abdomen looked "clean"—no obvious tumors in the liver, lymph nodes, or intestinal tract. Probably still a poor prognosis, but we'd see what the pathologist said.

All through the afternoon appointments—in between a cat with an eye infection, two spay follow-ups, the Rottweiler with heartworm, and the expectant rabbit—I frequently stopped in the hall outside the exam rooms, braced my arms on the walls, and took deep breaths to stop my stampeding pulse.

Aurora caught me doing my brace-and-breathe routine. "I'm *fine*," I said, a rote answer. Aurora narrowed her eyes. Over her shoulder, I saw that Zayna had witnessed this act.

The only e-mail that came was from Olive: "I have big news to tell you! It must be in person! We need a GNO!" She obviously had no idea what Bobby had done or she wouldn't wait for a GNO. The fact that he hadn't told her made me hopeful that perhaps his leaving wasn't permanent, that perhaps he'd come home.

The only voice mail that came was from Gabriella: "Dad called me. I'm going to meet him for coffee after school. Tyler said he'd do my kennel work for me, okay?"

Her voice brimmed with giddy relief.

When we sent the surgeries home, that chow who'd lost his spleen walked out five pounds lighter. I watched his happy owners drive him away and figured I'd bought him some time.

Time.

Maybe I could buy some time with Bobby, too. Maybe I could get him back home before anyone else knew what had happened.

WHEN I LEFT ANIMAL KIND THAT EVENING, I AVOIDED MY own home and drove instead to my parents' to check on the foster horses.

I walked to the barn, wandering from immaculate stall to tidy paddock until I found the two rescue fillies. Their manes and tails were clean and tangle-free and their legs and jaws trimmed. I sheepishly pictured the biter's appearance at my own farm.

"Hello, Camden." My mother walked out of the barn, dressed in black field boots, suede tan breeches, and a green sweater I knew was cashmere. She stroked the fillies' foreheads. "If I'm not careful, your father will want to keep these two."

I grinned. "That wouldn't be so bad, would it?"

"You're no help," Mom said, but I knew it was only in jest. Just then Dad came around the corner in the slow shuffle he'd had since his accident five years ago. He carried a saddle.

"Camden." He rested his gloved hand on my arm. "How are you doing?"

I nodded, touched by his concern. I knew this was all I could expect him to say about Bobby leaving.

"Caroline, are you going to ride?"

"Yes, I'm going to school the Burgans' mare," she said.

"All right, then, I'll leave you the Passier," he said of the saddle they'd had for . . . it had to be nearly twenty-five years. He set the saddle on the fence beside her.

"How nice of you," I teased him, "to leave Mom the old, battered saddle."

My mother raised her eyebrows.

Dad chuckled. "This 'old, battered saddle' is the most comfortable, well-made one we own." He touched the pommel flap. "Looks like we may need another visit to Benny soon."

I couldn't count the times their saddler had tended to the Passier.

"Ever going to just give in and buy a new one?" I asked.

They exchanged a look full of meaning. "Nah," they said, smiling at something shared that excluded me, tilting me a bit off balance.

"I remember when Stormwatch bit that saddle," I said, hoping to bring them back.

Mom and Dad both reached out to touch the scar on the cantle. For no apparent reason, one day the stallion had chomped into the back of the saddle as it sat on his stall door.

I'd seen my parents rub countless hours of saddle soap and oil into the gash Benny had stitched together, each passing year making the mark less visible.

Dad ran his finger over the faint ridge. "These teeth marks?" he said. "These stitches? They add to the beauty of the saddle, to the value. They announce it was worth saving. I won't replace it until it falls off in two pieces from the horse's back."

Mom pursed her lips, as if to comment on his rare sentimentality.

Once I had examined the fillies, I drove home. I passed the decapitated St. Francis still lying facedown in the mud, the shingles scattered in the yard, the branches down everywhere. I walked straight to the barn, where Muriel wandered in the aisle and the biter wouldn't let me touch him.

What if you thought something was worth saving but you didn't know where to begin?

HELEN AND HANK SHOWED UP WITH THE DAVIDS TO TAKE us to dinner. Davy had told them the news at an adoption meeting. Helen put her arm around me. "I'm so sorry, Cami." She held me for a moment. "You pick the restaurant," she said. "We're not taking no for an answer."

My heart lifted at this command invitation, at being taken care of, but my skeleton felt like it weighed a ton. I didn't want to go anywhere but to bed.

Wonderful Hank—an attorney, like his wife—had brought a huge pot of homemade macaroni and cheese. "It has healing properties, I swear," he said. "It's good for the soul."

Hank had run Cincinnati's Flying Pig Marathon with Davy last spring. I envied these guys' ability to eat any damn thing they pleased and still stay so greyhound scrappy.

I lifted the lid on Hank's pot. Not your usual mac 'n' cheese— fusilli and thin strips of red bell pepper peeked through the layer of bubbly golden-brown.

Hunger awoke in my belly, but with it came the image of Bobby, a towel tossed over his shoulder, expertly whacking a clove of garlic with the side of his knife.

I pushed that image from my head and joked I'd be content to sit on the kitchen floor to eat from this pot, but they insisted we go out and I eat Hank's gift later.

I thought I could use Gabriella as an excuse to stay home and send everyone away, but when she returned, she seemed pleased to see everyone: "I'm starving. Are we going out?"

WE GOT A TABLE UPSTAIRS AT MY FAVORITE THAI RES-taurant.

My eagerness for scraps about Bobby embarrassed me, so I was relieved when Gabby dove right in. "I met him at his apartment," she said, "and we went to—"

"You met him *where?*" I asked.

I saw from Gabriella's eyes that she'd thought I'd known this. "He rented an apartment."

"Oh." When I pictured him looking at apartments, signing a lease, making arrangements to move, then coming home to the farm each night pretending all was fine, the image cut into me with the precision of a scalpel.

"Everything he said sounded rehearsed and stupid," Gabriella continued. "He said, 'How do you tell someone you still love them but just don't want to be married to them?' "

He *had* told me. He'd told me loud and clear last fall. My cheeks stung as I remembered.

A party at the farm. A crisp, first-sweatshirt-of-the-season night. A bonfire. Bobby grilled steaks. Gabby and Tyler searched the pasture edges to collect sticks for s'mores. The talk had turned to Ohio's proposition to ban gay marriage. Gabby, the Davids, and I had spent many weekends chanting at rallies and pounding yard signs into the dirt of willing properties.

"Why *shouldn't* gay people marry?" I'd asked. I'd stood on the patio overlooking our farm, surrounded by my tribe of family and friends. "No one's ever given me a worthy argument."

"Gay people?" Davy said in mock horror. "Gay people? Eww!"

"We don't know any gay people," Big David deadpanned. "There aren't any around *here*."

When the laughter had died down, Bobby asked into the silence, "Why do gays *want* to get married?"

Something about his tone slapped my cheeks.

"I mean," he went on, "nobody *needs* to be married. Not anymore. It's obsolete."

Olive smacked Bobby in the back of the head. "That's a nice thing to say to your *wife*, you stupid son of a bitch." But I'd pretended not to be offended. We were just talking politics, right? It hadn't been a judgment on our *own* marriage. I'd been quick to rush in to defend, to show I wasn't hurt, to make light of it.

Helen rubbed my shoulder, bringing me back to the crab rangoon they'd ordered that I couldn't swallow. What the hell had I been thinking, letting these people drag me out in public? I felt peeled back, everything inside me visible for anyone to sift and poke through.

Gabriella chased her half-eaten rangoon around her plate with a fork and told us more. "Dad said he's always hated that he doesn't know what his calling is in life—his purpose."

Whenever we'd had those conversations, I tried to be supportive and encouraging. I joked that "Your purpose is to love me." That always made him smile. It often had led us to the bedroom.

"He's a *chef*!" my brother said. "He owns a *restaurant*. What the hell is he talking about?"

"He really struggled with the restaurant." I hated my knee-jerk reaction to defend him. "He worked so hard to get it, but then it didn't make him happy the way he thought it would."

Gabriella pushed that same bite of rangoon around her plate. My breath snagged in my chest for the confusion I saw in her eyes.

She scooted her chair back and stood. Without looking at us, she said, "He looked horrible. He looked like he'd been crying."

Good. But I couldn't mean it. The thought made me feel empty and bleak.

After Gabriella excused herself for the restroom, Davy said, "I never liked Bobby anyway," his voice cold and dismissive.

"Yeah, me neither," Big David said.

"Here, here," Hank said, raising his glass and downing the last of his gin and tonic.

I couldn't breathe.

Then Davy put down his glass and sighed. A real sigh, swollen with sorrow. "No, I really did like him."

Helen rubbed the top of her wineglass and made it hum.

"Yeah," Big David agreed. "I wish we didn't."

We lingered over dinner (I managed a couple spoonfuls of my seafood stew). I made Davy promise not to tell Nick yet at school and convinced them all not to spread the news until I told them. I still needed time to talk to Bobby, to figure out what I was going to do. As we stood to go, the late hour—how much time we'd filled—felt like an accomplishment.

We walked downstairs, Davy and Gabby talking about some AP History exam at school.

Gabriella said, "Oh, my God," in such a chilling way I knew it wasn't in reaction to the test. I was pulling on my coat and sensed everyone freeze. A beat behind, I snapped to attention.

As I followed his gaze, Big David said, "Of all the restaurants in Dayton . . ."

Bobby sat at a small table near the door.

He was with someone.

He lifted that someone's hand to his mouth and kissed her knuckles.

He was smiling.

CHAPTER NINE

I'D NEVER BEFORE FELT THE BURNING IN MY BONES THAT I felt when I saw Bobby kissing another woman's hand. *Smiling* two days after he'd left me. The burning threatened to eat through my skin into blisters.

He turned and saw us.

The someone turned and saw us.

It was Zayna Arnett.

I stared, my arms still stuck in my coat sleeves. *Zayna Arnett?* That ungrateful little bitch! It had been *my idea* for Zayna to waitress at Tanti Baci. Oh, I was an idiot. I'd never questioned why Zayna had shown up at Olive's apartment Sunday morning. I just assumed she had a massage appointment. *She knew then. Was she coming to tell Olive? Why?* I flashed back to this morning at the clinic. *She was sleeping with my husband and she'd come to work at the clinic?* I imagined her telling Bobby, "She didn't tell anybody. She just ran around like crazy, doing this weird breathing thing." Had they *laughed* at me? My face blazed into its rash.

Bobby said something to Zayna, then he stood and came toward us.

I forgot how to walk. My coat was still half-on, half-off, cuffing my arms behind me.

He reached our frozen cluster. No one spoke until Gabby said, "I *hate* you," then walked out.

Davy said, "I'll follow her."

Helen followed Davy out the door, Big David and Hank two steps behind her, leaving me standing there alone with Bobby, hopelessly mired in my coat sleeves.

"Here," he said, reaching out to help me, sliding the coat up my arms. He turned me to face him, leaving his hands on my shoulders. I stepped back, almost recoiling, making him drop his hands. He held them awkwardly at his sides and I saw he wasn't wearing his wedding band. Two days and he'd already taken it off! I wanted to hurl my ring at his head. I wanted the diamond to embed itself in his eye and blind him.

"So," I said, "looks like you took care of those issues pretty quickly."

He frowned. "What?"

"Those issues you said were going to keep you from 'ever being with anyone ever again.' "

He stepped closer to me, lowering his voice. "It's not how it looks."

I barked a bitter, one-note sound. "Why didn't you just tell me the truth?"

He looked over his shoulder, and when I realized he didn't want other diners to overhear us, I felt a dangerous urge to cause a scene. "Why didn't you tell me that you rented an apartment?"

Zayna took two steps toward us but saw my expression and

stopped. *Don't you dare fucking talk to me. Don't you say one word.*

I looked from her to Bobby, then turned for the door. "I need to see to our *daughter.*"

I thought he might follow me, if not to talk to me then at least to comfort Gabriella.

But he didn't.

IN MY BEDROOM, I LOOKED AT OUR WEDDING PHOTO ON THE bed stand. In it, Bobby held my left hand in both of his, and I reached up with my right to keep my veil from flying away in the wind. I kicked the table. The frame fell flat. The lamp wobbled but righted itself.

Max, who'd been asleep on the bed, sat up.

Well. That was not at all satisfying.

I kicked the stand again, harder, and tipped the whole table. The lamp wrenched its cord from the socket and fell to the floor. The frame fell but didn't break. *God damn it!* I flung the picture against the wall. The glass finally shattered and sprinkled the hardwood floor. *There.* I kicked the wall. Pain shot through my toes and up my leg. Max whined.

I clutched my aching foot, cursing, but in a weird way, the pain felt *good.*

I thought of the biter sulking down in his paddock. *Ah, my friend,* I thought. *I'm on to you.*

THE NEXT DAYS BLURRED TOGETHER IN THE TOO-BRIGHT, headache-y cocktail of heartbreak, sleep deprivation, and hunger.

I buried my ring in my lingerie drawer. My thumb continually sought the ring, to spin it, startling me each time it touched only pale flesh, causing a zip of *I lost it* . . . then I'd remember.

Zayna quit at the clinic, "for personal reasons," which forced me to finally gather my nine employees and tell them the news.

Aurora was outraged. "Is she even legal?" Her nose diamond flashed as she shook her head. "Classic midlife crisis. Idiot man makes ass of himself. Cami, I'm *so* sorry this is happening to you." She asked if I needed some time off. But even if the clinic could afford that, what would I *do* with myself if I stayed home? I *needed* this place of emergencies and decisions. I needed the constant focus, assessment, and reaction the job required.

I caught myself doing things more characteristic of Big David's mother, Ava: I left my keys in the car, I put my stethoscope in the refrigerator at work, and I was confused to pull a half-sandwich from my pocket when I needed to hear a puppy's heartbeat. I found a bowl of Hank's macaroni and cheese in the microwave a whole day after I'd put it there.

I had no appetite. *Stay busy, stay busy,* a frosty voice whispered in my head. I would show everyone just how strong and together I was. I'd put on a brave face for my desolate daughter.

I let the three-legged cat—who could *not* be called Champagne Toast—loose in our office during our lunch break, so he could try out his new moves. It never ceased to amaze me how quickly cat skin healed—after all these years I still marveled that no sutures were needed on a cat neuter. Bobby had flinched as I'd explained once, "You just anesthetize, shave, scrub, cut the scrotum, remove one testicle, tie the vas deferens on itself, then repeat with the second testicle. Done. No sutures. No fuss, no muss. Healing quickly within twenty-four hours."

I pondered what I'd like to do with a scalpel and a certain scrotum right now.

Bobby didn't call or e-mail. I checked at every opportunity.

I ignored another message from Olive. I could tell she *still* didn't know. I loved that Davy could keep a secret sacred, just as he could be counted on to do when we were kids, but I hated Bobby for leaving the telling up to me. Was he just going to *disappear*?

Mimi left a message, too, in her too-loud, bossy voice, "My wayward son isn't answering my messages, so I'm asking you: how many people are coming to this boy's birthday? I need to start my shopping." *Oh, my God, Bobby's birthday.* "Maybe he doesn't deserve a birthday dinner, if the son of a bitch is too busy to talk to his own mother. You tell him I said that, all right, doll?"

He hadn't told his mother. Or his sister. The big coward. Couldn't he *at least* leave them messages like he had for our daughter? At first the fact that he hadn't told anyone had made me hope that he might still return. But now that Zayna factored into the equation, I fumed when I imagined he was simply too . . . *busy* to think of informing his family. Picturing Bobby and Zayna in bed together made me break slides at the clinic. Made me look at an X-ray and forget if I was looking at canine or feline bones. Made me miss an exit on the way home.

We'd been planning a birthday dinner at the farm. His mother was going to make her "gravy" and all his childhood favorites. I

knew the relatives had already been given their assignments—
Aunt Frannie would bring the roasted peppers, Aunt Louisa
would bring the baked ziti, Uncle Tony would make his stuffed
mushrooms, cousin Michael would make veal marsala, and on and
on. My side of the family was never given food assignments—
we brought the wine—except for Big David, who made the cake.
Bobby would not be allowed to prepare a thing.

I let Mimi leave her voice mail as I watched the orange cat
move about the office, trying out his new rabbitlike gait.

"FUCK THAT BASTARD'S BIRTHDAY," OLIVE DECLARED
when I found her sitting between Max and the goat on my porch.

Olive had been informed of the news by Cecile, a Tanti
Baci hostess. Since Bobby hadn't returned Olive's calls, she'd
stopped by the restaurant, to show Bobby her ring and pick
up some take-out lasagna. As she was sitting at the bar waiting
for the order—and for Bobby to emerge from the kitchen—
Cecile had given her the scoop. Olive abandoned the lasagna
and rushed to the farm.

She hugged me while Muriel nibbled my calf. "That bastard.
I'll kill the son of a bitch. And that little whore! What is she,
twelve?"

"Twenty-two," I said. As I unlocked the front door, Muriel
pushed past my legs and tried to barge inside. I grabbed her
leather collar, instructing Olive, "Go. Get inside. Quick."

We headed into Bobby's kitchen, where I felt like an in-
truder. I pulled a Chianti I knew Olive liked from our rack. She
opened a cupboard for the wineglasses. Gabby was at a movie

with Tyler, so I was relieved not to be home alone. Distraction kept me sane.

I apologized for not having told her myself, then, at her request, recited the story yet again. I told her how Zayna had dropped by her apartment. "I just assumed she had a massage, but I think . . . I think she may have been coming over to tell you, or ask advice or something."

"Advice? My advice would be to keep her slutty self away from my very married brother."

The thing was, I'd never thought of Zayna as slutty. I'd thought of her as funny and bold, vibrant and striking enough to actually make it as an actress with her penny-red hair and sharp, feline features. Mostly I'd thought of her as far too smart to ever fall for this man-in-crisis bullshit. Oh, I was an idiot. But forget about Zayna for the moment. "So Bobby never told you anything about this? He never hinted to you that he was unhappy with . . . with the marriage?" That felt easier than saying, "with me."

"Are you fucking nuts? I wouldn't keep something like that from you." Olive cocked her head and did this thing she did with her lips, like she was blowing a smoke ring, even though she'd quit smoking years ago. The smoke ring was her unspoken way of saying, *I think that what you just said was full of shit*. "He may be my brother, but you're my best friend, Cami. You were my sister long before you married him." She set down her wineglass with a clink. "That jackass is going to make *me* tell our mother, the damn baby. For Christ's sake, is he just going to let everyone show up here for the party? Shit. He doesn't deserve a damn party."

I agreed wholeheartedly.

Olive paced the kitchen. Her ring caught the light and sent sparkles across one wall.

"Your ring. Let me see it."

She hid her left hand with her right. "I feel bad . . . under the circumstances . . ."

"Don't be silly. You have something monumental to celebrate. Your happiness doesn't mean you care about me any less. Now let me see the damn ring."

She showed me. "It was so perfect. He actually got down on one knee at Fountain Square."

"And I take it you said yes?"

She beamed. "When we got back to the room at the bed-and-breakfast, there was champagne and roses. He thought of *everything*. He made it wonderful."

She slid down on the floor, her back to the cupboards. She patted the floor beside her, but Max moved into the place first, so I sat on the other side, my head on her shoulder. We looked up at the glasses we'd left on the counter. Neither of us had the energy to retrieve them.

We sat that way for several minutes before she said, "I would do *anything* for you, Cami. What do you need most right now?"

"I need to sleep. I can't sleep. I'm a zombie."

"I can remedy that." Olive stood, then held out her hand and hauled me up. She directed me into a hot shower. When I emerged, she had lotion ready and warm. I crawled into bed and lay on my stomach. Olive massaged my neck and shoulders with her miraculous hands. She expressed dismay over my wounded arm and put her hands on it in a magical way, soothing it better than any painkiller or ice.

Olive kneaded the bruised tenderness in my muscles, working them loose and fluid again. Before long I drooled. And blinked. Unable to hold my eyes open, I drifted off into blissful sleep.

I WOKE UP LATER TO ANXIOUS SORROW AND A RACING heart. I was buried under quilts and blankets, Gingersnap sprawled on my chest, snoring her slightly fishy breath into my face.

It was nearly 1 a.m. My massage had to have been around 7:30 or so. This was the longest I'd slept since Bobby walked out. I got up and dressed. Gingersnap stayed in bed, but Max followed me as I stood in Gabriella's doorway listening to her deep, sleeping breaths. I felt guilty for missing her return, missing the chance to wish her good-night.

I thought about going to the barn but was stopped by a childhood memory of standing in the shadows, watching my mother, in her nightgown, weeping in the barn lot.

You're not like her. You're strong. You don't need him.

I hadn't eaten and was ravenous, but most of the containers in the fridge were full of food Bobby had made. Knowing it was melodramatic, I emptied every last one of them into the sink and forced the mess down the disposal with a wooden spoon. Pesto. Seafood risotto. His fried polenta I craved like a junkie every time I had my period. Some old rigatoni. I wouldn't eat his food. I didn't need anything from him.

That bastard *left me*. For a *girl*. The same age as Helen's daughter, Holly, for God's sake! I'd put up with his bitchy moodiness! I'd walked on eggshells around him! I'd offered to support him, and all the while he was fucking a waitress? Okay, she was only a waitress *at my suggestion*, but that thought made me shove the food down the drain until the disposal's motor groaned.

When I turned off the disposal I almost shrieked as someone rapped on the front door.

Max barked once, then stopped. He whirled his greeting dance.

It's Bobby. Max wouldn't bark at Bobby. Relief flooded through me. He *had* come back.

But when I stepped into the foyer, I saw Mimi. I wanted to run back down the hall, but she saw me. "Oh, Cami, doll, thank God. Open up."

How long did I think I could avoid her? I was ashamed at how quickly my anger at Bobby fled when I thought he was on the porch. How pathetic.

Mimi hugged me. *She knew*. Bless Olive. She hadn't taken long. Mimi smelled as she always did, of cigarettes and garlic, but it was not unpleasant. She stood on tiptoe to kiss my cheeks. "Oh, doll. I had to see you. I need you to tell me where my son of a bitch of a son is staying. The restaurant was already closed. If he won't answer my calls, I'm going to hunt him down."

God, I loved this crazy woman.

"Cam, doll, what did he do that was so awful? You're a strong woman, but the longer he's gone, the bigger the risk you take. You can't work on things if he's not here. Men are weak—"

I started as if I'd touched the electric tape (which I'd done more than once by accident).

"Mimi, Bobby left *me*. It was *his* decision to leave, not mine. He's rented an apartment."

Mimi's eyes blazed. "Where is this apartment?" She looked like she might kill him.

"He wouldn't tell me."

"*I* know the address." Gabriella stepped into the room, making us both jump. Mimi hugged her. They swayed together, looking for a moment like they were dancing.

When they broke away, Gabriella picked up a piece of junk mail off our foyer table and scribbled down the address. When I saw it, goose bumps shivered across my back. Only *blocks* from Animal Kind. I'd pass Bobby's apartment every day.

"Thank you, *bella*. Now go back to sleep. I'm sorry I woke you." Mimi looked at the address. "I'll go right now." I could picture Mimi pounding on Bobby's door, ripping into him. Maybe Mimi would interrupt Bobby with Zayna. I felt more gleeful than I had in days. Mimi turned to me. "I'll knock some sense into that head of his. Whatever problems you have, they belong here, in your home, not all over town."

The glee fell away. "Mimi, he's—he has someone else—"

She clucked. "That's what men *do*, doll. You don't have to forgive him. But he needs to be here. We can't very well have the birthday party without the guest of honor."

I didn't know which was worse, my daughter hearing that her grandmother believed that all men were unfaithful, or that Mimi still thought I was hosting Bobby's party. "Mimi. No. I am not hosting a party for a man who left me."

Mimi puffed herself out like a rooster. My heart thumped. I'd seen this woman rant and scream, but she'd always been sweet as can be to me, saving me extra pignoli cookies, not letting me do any little chore when I was pregnant, always patting my cheek and saying, "You're so good to my boy." If I was about to go face to face with Mimi Binardi, then bring it on.

But Mimi only looked flustered and, suddenly, very old. She folded up the piece of paper in her hand. "You kids. Nothing but extremes! I'll talk to him. Your husband will come home."

I didn't believe her. But I didn't correct her.

When Mimi was gone, Gabriella said, "I told you you were kick-ass."

"You're the one who gave her the address."

She grinned. "Was that evil?"

I considered this and admitted, "Yes."

"He deserved it," she said, the sudden venom in her voice surprising me. I wasn't sure what to say. I agreed—hell, *yes*, he deserved it!—but felt I shouldn't in front of her.

I realized I still held the wooden spoon I'd used to shove Bobby's food down the disposal. I pointed it at her. "Not *all* men cheat."

"I know."

"Not all women take it."

"I know. Why are you holding a spoon?"

I looked down at it. "Because I am kick-ass." I broke the wooden spoon across my knee.

Gabriella shook her head. "No. Now you're just weird."

In spite of the good start, I got no more sleep that night.

CHAPTER TEN

I BROUGHT THE THREE-LEGGED CAT HOME, PRAYING HE wouldn't destroy my house before he completed his antibiotics and could go outside again. He fumed, resenting his plastic Elizabethan collar—but he required it since he kept tearing out his stitches (an amputation required a longer incision than a neuter, after all).

Gingersnap responded by sulking out of the house to pout in the barn. Max's nose-in-the-butt greeting earned him a swipe across the nose, but he didn't seem offended.

Gabriella and I agreed that Champagne Toast was too stuffy a name for such a raggedy guy. *Champ* sounded silly. *Pagne* sounded like "pain." Toast? Hmm. "Hey, Toast," Gabriella said.

The cat snarled at Max, ears flat, the name making no apparent impression.

WHEN DAVY TOLD ME BOBBY'S BIRTHDAY PARTY HAD BEEN moved to Tanti Baci, the news leveled me. I'm not sure what I'd pictured—that the party would be canceled altogether, or that Mimi would have a family-only gathering in Columbus? But imagining people gathered to celebrate the man who'd just been an utter shit to me and my daughter made me feel kicked to the curb.

Davy had tried to convince Big David not to make the cake after all, but Big David felt he had to—he'd committed to it months ago, and it was his business after all.

On the phone with Davy, I couldn't disguise the hurt in my voice. I sniffed, amplified in his ear, and in just the right way, apparently, because an hour later, he and Big David were at the farm, Ava in tow, bearing ice cream—a pint for each of us.

Gabriella groaned and said, "I need to study!" as if they were torturing her, but she sat on the kitchen island to eat straight out of her pint.

"By the way, your goat is out," Davy said. "She's standing on your mailbox."

I let them pamper us. I opened my ice cream, now perfectly soft. Davy remembered my favorite flavor—caramel with almonds. I tried not to think about eating ice cream with Bobby on our first date. *Who were we? Who were those people?*

Ava, immaculately made up and dressed, as always—she never *looked* like someone slowly losing her mind—ensconced herself on the couch. To my amazement, Champagne Toast loped in and curled up next to her. "Gerald!" Ava cried. "What's this absurd contraption?"

We all looked at one another, curious. Ava didn't comment on the fact that the cat was missing a leg and had a line of stitches marching like blue ants across his shaved shoulder.

Ava spooned the cat ice cream from her pint. She scolded him for bringing a mole into her bed. "Oh! My skin just shivers thinking of it, you naughty thing!"

Big David shrugged and said, "We never had a cat named Gerald. The memory must be from when she was a kid."

The cat fished his way into Ava's purse, pulling tissues and a compact from it, proving to be quite dexterous with his one front leg. I returned the items, then put the purse on the mantel.

"Well, the cat does need a name," Gabriella said.

I told the story of his tag. "I was thinking of Toast."

"Toast?" Davy asked. "Don't you already have a cat named Gingersnap? And a horse named Biscuit? What is this? The all-carb barn?"

"All right, fine, he can be Gerald," I said, laughing. "Well, Mr. Gerald, what do you think?"

The cat blinked his celery eyes.

"It's decided, then," I said.

If only the rest of my long list of decisions could be so easy.

I STARTED SMALL, WITH THOSE DECISIONS. I OPENED NEW accounts of my own. I called Helen and asked for referrals for a divorce lawyer. I made an appointment with one for next week.

After school, Gabriella and Tyler showed up for work. I'd worried about hiring them both, since I didn't want to deal with any romance drama, but they were great.

Davy, and Olive, and even my mother—in a rare break from Anderson decorum—had wondered if Gabriella and Tyler had sex (or, as my mother had primly asked, "Do you think they're . . . active?"). I hoped not but hated the look on everyone's face when I admitted that they probably did. "Come on," I said. "We were all having sex in high school! And we were 'good kids.' " I'd asked Gabriella, of course, and her eyes flashed with disdain, "God, Mom. No," but I'd told the same lie to my own mother. Working with animals had made it easy to talk with Gabriella about sex and reproduction from the time she was a toddler.

I made sure she knew I didn't *want* her to have sex yet. (But I certainly didn't tell her that I'd had sex in high school!) I'd tried to be honest about how sex changed things, how there was no going back once you had it, how you gave a little of yourself away. Maybe I was wrong; I didn't know *for sure*. I'd be disappointed, but I wouldn't be at all surprised if they were, indeed, "active."

Bobby had refused to talk to me about Gabriella having sex. He'd actually said, "I can't go there. I don't want to even think about it."

I wanted to ask Gabby if she'd heard from her dad and see how she was doing, so when I had a break, I entered the kennel, braced for the inevitable bedlam of barking. The noise crescendoed, then quelled when the dogs saw who it was. What I liked about Gabriella and Tyler both was their ability to calm the animals with their presence. A quiet kennel is a lovely thing.

So is a clean kennel. These kids were thorough. I paid them well, but it went beyond that. Good help, real work ethic, was hard to find.

Zayna had had it, damn it. Now I was scrambling to hire a replacement. I couldn't help wondering about Zayna's family's reaction. If her parents were so rigidly disapproving of her acting major, what the hell would they think of her sleeping with an older, *married* man?

THE BLESSINGS OF THE ANIMALS

Not my problem, I reminded myself. She *deserved* whatever hardships they threw at her now.

I was surprised to see dog poop in the three runs nearest the door. The kids should've gotten to this by now. Where were they? I saw them outside through the window. Oh, God, were they lost in one of their endless political debates again? It never ceased to amaze me that they actually discussed public policy. They made my high-school self seem so shallow.

Gabby had a beagle on a leash. Tyler had a springer spaniel. The poor dogs, though, were just standing there, bored, looking longingly into the distance.

I went to tap on the window, just to wave, say hi, perhaps jolt them into action, but I stopped with my knuckles a breath from the glass when I registered Gabby's tearstreaked face.

Oh. Oh, poor Gabby. What a mess we'd made for her.

Comfort her, I willed Tyler. Why was he standing so far from her? *Hug her, Tyler.*

Gabby moved as if to walk away and Tyler reached out to stop her, which gave me a view of *his* face—he looked like Gabby had just told him his entire family had died.

Gabby led the beagle away. Tyler watched her go but didn't follow. Devastation was loud and clear in his hunched shoulders, his frozen spine. The spaniel looked up at him and wagged her tail uncertainly.

What had just happened?

What had I just witnessed?

Long minutes crept by. He didn't move.

I heard someone ask, "Where'd Dr. Anderson go?"

When Tyler finally walked back into the kennel, I busied

myself with an Irish setter, treating her to a cursory exam she didn't need. I looked in her ears and eyes, not seeing them at all, only seeing Tyler's wounded expression.

This was about something more than the divorce.

I tried not to worry, but my next appointment was an expectant collie. As I palpated her abdomen, telling her beaming owner I felt four, possibly five puppies, I scolded myself. Don't immediately jump to the worst-case scenario.

My anxiety ratcheted up several notches when Gabby waited outside my office for a ride home instead of going with Tyler, like she usually did.

When I asked about it, she shrugged and pointed to a red brick building we drove past. "There's Dad's apartment," she said. Closer than I even thought. Depending on what floor he lived on, he might actually be able to *see* the clinic, an unsettling thought.

We drove home in silence, except for my desperate questions. "You okay?"

"Nope."

"You wanna talk?"

"Nope."

I squeezed her knee. She put a hand on mine and left it there while I drove.

After a moment I asked, "Did you hear from your dad today?"

"Nope." She turned her head, looking out her window, so I couldn't see her expression.

DURING THE NIGHT I CONVINCED MYSELF I WAS OVERREacting. They'd simply argued. People argued, right?

Then I heard her vomiting in the bathroom.

When I asked her about it, she denied it. "God, Mom, what are you doing? Spying on me?"

She and Tyler barely made eye contact with each other at the clinic.

I focused on breathing in and breathing out.

I finally broke down and called Bobby. I was furious he'd ignored Gabriella for as long as he'd ignored me. I needed to talk to him about Gabby. If Gabby were in trouble, she'd need him. He'd be there for her . . . wouldn't he?

"Sure, we can get together," he said, as if I'd called to invite him for drinks. "I wanted to come get a few more of my things, anyway."

I bit my lip so hard I tasted the rusty tang of blood.

After work, while Gabby was at debate practice, I found myself in the bizarre position of figuring out how to dress for my soon-to-be ex-husband. I didn't want to "doll up" for him, but I felt compelled to look somewhat good. I put my hair up in a loose twist and settled for jeans and a fitted T-shirt. V-neck. I stood before the mirror and remembered Vijay telling me—when we took high-school anatomy together—that I had beautiful clavicles. I traced those bones with my fingers, remembering how stark they'd been when Bobby first met me.

I counted in my head. There were still three days left before Vijay left Africa.

Bobby knocked on the door, like a guest.

I froze, relieved he was here and full of dread that this moment had arrived.

We ended up in the kitchen, which bothered me because it

seemed like Bobby's turf. Before I could bring up my concern about Gabby, he started in on a list of things we needed to do: separate cell phone accounts, close joint accounts at the bank, discuss the farm. He'd made a budget of the utilities and mortgage to show me I couldn't keep the farm. Oh, that's not what he *said*. He said sweet things like, "I know you love this place, but this will be a *lot* for one person. How will you take care of it on your own?"

Smoldering began under my skin. "I'm not moving, Bobby."

"Cam, I'm not trying to be an asshole, but have you even called anyone to look at the roof? Or that corner of the barn? It's been almost a week."

"Well, you know, this week was, um . . . exceptional. I've been a bit overwhelmed. See, my husband left me and is sleeping with a twenty-two-year-old."

He didn't deny it this time. He pushed the budget across the kitchen island. "Just look at this, okay? We have to be practical about the finances, with Gabby going to college next year."

At least he still remembered he *had* a daughter! I glanced at the budget and my nostrils flared. My ribs rose and fell in short breaths I imagined as puffs of smoke.

There was a print date in the corner of the paper. "You made this budget before you left."

He closed his eyes a fraction too long, signaling his impatience.

"This is dated *two weeks* before you left. You knew you were going to walk out and what did you do? You sat at your damn desk and made a *budget*? You couldn't give me even a *hint*?"

I wadded the budget into a ball in my fist.

He spoke to the Portuguese tile. "Cami, please know I just wanted to take care of you both."

I flung the paper ball at him. It bounced off his chest onto the island between us.

"That isn't taking care of us! You were taking care of details, of logistics, not of *us*."

He picked up the crumpled budget and smoothed it flat.

"You don't even see the difference, do you?"

My hands trembled so violently I clutched the pepper grinder to still them.

"I'm so sorry," he said. "I did this so badly. I . . . I'm sorry."

When I put my hands flat on the tile, he grabbed for one as if it were a lifeline. I gasped at the pain in my bite wounds, but he didn't notice. He grasped my hand in both of his own, then pressed my palm to his cheek. "Oh, Cam, I'm sorry. I'm so sorry."

The familiarity of that unshaven jawline felt right. I concentrated on his hands, hands that had caressed me, massaged my feet when I was pregnant, rubbed oil into my monstrous belly. He'd croon Frank Sinatra tunes to my navel. His raspy chin tickled in my memory, his voice buzzing through my taut, tight skin. These hands had held Gabriella before I even had. That image, of this man holding his naked newborn daughter, rocked into me and stole my breath.

I know you, I wanted to say. For a second the energy in the kitchen changed. I thought we might laugh and look at each other and say, "Shit! What did we just almost *do?* That was close!"

But, still holding my hand, he said, "If I could go back and do it differently I would."

I pulled my hand away. He may want to leave me differently, but he still wanted to leave me. "I can't imagine you not in my life," he said. "You've been my best friend. You *are* my best friend. I hope you know that."

I stared at him. *What the hell?*

His hand went to the gold cross he wore around his neck—a gift from his grandmother. He moved it back and forth on its chain, then brought it up over his chin and held it before his lips. The movements were so boyish.

"I don't know if that's how your little fantasy runs in your brain, that I'm going to be your *buddy* while you fuck around and make an ass of yourself and your family, but it's not going to play out like that." The poison that welled up in me astonished me—an urge to *hurt* him. "I wouldn't be friends with *anyone* who's behaved in the cowardly, self-absorbed, narcissistic"—my brain scrambled for adjectives that would cut him—"despicable, dishonorable way you have."

The injured look in his eyes was what I was after, but it enraged me further. How could he be hurt by what I said? How could he not already know it was true?

I took a deep breath, to get a grip, before I started throwing things. "We're not going to be 'friends,' but we are Gabriella's parents. We *have* to be good parents to her, no matter how we feel about each other."

He nodded. "Absolutely."

I wanted to scream, *Then why haven't you called her?* but I fought to keep level and sound sane. "I'm really worried about her. That's why I called you."

I saw him snap into focus, bringing that cross to his lips.

"I . . . I'm scared she might be pregnant."

He stared at me for a second, as if translating what I'd said. Then he let the cross fall back to his chest and made a face, exasperated. "Cami," he said disapprovingly.

I told him the scene I'd witnessed at the kennel, how they both walked around dazed.

Bobby crossed his arms and set his jaw.

"She threw up this morning," I said. "Then she lied about it."

He closed his eyes too long again. "Cami, I know you're upset, but this isn't fair."

What did he just say? A year seemed to pass as we stared each other down. I finally formed words, "You think I'm making this up?"

He sighed. "I think you're very upset and not thinking clearly—which is my fault, I admit—but Cami . . . I'm not coming home."

Gravity seemed to triple, rooting me to my spot. I wanted to stab him with his own expensive, snooty knives—they were within arm's reach. The image was too satisfying and frightening. I stood up and turned my back on him. "We're done. You should go."

He stood quickly, probably relieved to be dismissed. He paused, then asked, "Do you know if Gabriella is coming to the party tomorrow?"

"I don't know if she's going to your party because I don't know if she even knows she's invited!" I yelled. "Why don't you *talk to her* and ask her yourself? You're breaking her heart, you asshole!"

He at least had the decency to look sorrowful. But then he

asked, "If people ask, Uncle Tony or whoever, what do you want me to tell them? About, you know, why you're not there?"

I opened my arms. "How about the *truth*? I know that's apparently not your first instinct, but seriously, are you just going to avoid talking about it to people in hopes they don't notice? Like you did with your mom?"

"That was low, giving her my address. You know *I* can handle her, but—"

"But what? *Zayna* was a little thrown by the wrath of Mimi?"

I've never seen someone look so ashamed. "You shouldn't have given her the address."

As sweetly as I could, I said, "*I* didn't *know* your address. You wouldn't tell me, remember?"

"You woke Gabriella up just to get back—"

"No, I believe your *mother* woke Gabriella up knocking on our door at two in the morning! Which she wouldn't have had to do if you hadn't been too big of a chickenshit to return her calls! What did you *think* she would do?" Bobby's face told me he'd never considered this. Had I always been married to the village idiot and never noticed? I repeated, "You should go."

The cross came back to his lips. He nodded. "I want to take a few more things with me."

I stayed in the kitchen while he went upstairs. It was torture waiting for him to leave. I found Mr. Gerald, who'd scattered my purse's contents across the living room, happily shredding a tampon on the couch. I cleaned up the mess, then put my purse in the microwave for safekeeping. I gave Gerald his antibiotic (accompanied by *Exorcist*-worthy yowls). I made an appointment with Enterprise Roofing. Finally, I could stand it no longer and walked up the stairs.

I stood in the doorway just as Bobby finished up. "Hey, Cam," he said, his voice revealing a sense of hey-how-perfect-you're-here. "You wanna give me a hand with this?" He picked up his computer monitor and gestured to a box that contained the keyboard, speakers, and assorted cables. "If you help me, we could do it in one trip. It's starting to rain."

I exhaled sharply, not really a laugh, not really a gasp. I walked down the stairs empty-handed.

Muriel pranced in and out of the open garage as I listened to Bobby take the two trips to the car. He didn't say good-bye.

He didn't tell me the goat was out.

I WAS AWARE OF BOBBY'S BIRTHDAY FROM THE MOMENT I woke at 3 a.m. on Saturday.

He always woke me on my own birthday with a dozen roses. He never seemed to remember, no matter how many times I'd drop it into conversation, that my favorite flowers were gladiolas.

Stop it, you're being pathetic.

After doing the morning chores too early, I took the newspaper and went back to bed. Max snuggled up alongside me. Mr. Gerald even sat on one corner of the bed—having finally graduated from his Elizabethan collar—looking pissed, but I wasn't fooled. He could just as easily be pissed downstairs by himself. Gingersnap had taken up camp in Gabriella's room in protest, snuggling in my daughter's armpit. The two cats couldn't pass each other without hissing.

Just as the crossword was beginning to make me feel like a moron, Gabby came into my room and crawled into bed with me. My heart pounded. Was she about to tell me? If she didn't, how long before I asked? Please, *please*, let me be wrong. Gingersnap followed and sat on the opposite bed corner from Gerald, both of them facing away, like gargoyles. We just lay there looking out the skylight above the bed, until I thought she'd fallen back to sleep.

"Dad wants me to come to his party," she said. "Will it hurt your feelings if I go?"

"No! No, Gabby, no. You mustn't think that, okay?" I rolled on my side, to brush her auburn hair off her forehead and touch the blue shadows under her eyes. "I don't want you to feel you're taking sides here. You should go."

"I'm going to his apartment first," she said, "then we'll go to the party together. But I don't want to act like everything is normal! I can't pretend it's just a birthday party. I mean, I haven't seen him since Monday!"

"Did you tell him that?"

"No." She made a face.

She looked up at the skylight again.

"Are you okay?" I asked.

She sighed, this one irritated, not sad. "You can't keep asking me that!"

"Sorry. What's going on? Did you and Tyler fight?"

She shot me a look, wary. "Nothing is going on. Why are you always so dramatic?"

"You just don't seem like yourself these days."

"Well, my life isn't like it used to be these days."

The truth of her words cut like an incision. "I'm sorry. I'm truly sorry about that."

We lay there in silence.

"I guess I better go feed the crew," she said.

"I already did."

Instead of thanking me, she snapped, "God, are you ever going to let me do my job again?"

I picked up the newspaper. "You're welcome."

"Whatever." She sounded as if I'd insulted her. She didn't huff out, though. She sat on the edge of the bed, her back to me.

No one tells you when they place that fragile, blood-tinged baby in your arms just how much shit you will take from this person. No one warns you that you will take it and take it and take it. Because you have to. You will have no choice. Because you will love them beyond all reason.

"Do you think," she asked shyly, "that Zayna will be there?"

"I have no idea, babe." Surely he wouldn't be idiotic enough to invite her. Not if his daughter would be there. But . . . everything I *thought* I knew about Bobby had blown away in the storm.

Even though I told Gabriella I didn't want anyone to take sides, that was a big, fat lie. Reduced to eleven-year-old vulnerability, I wanted everyone to take *my* side.

After Gabriella left and party time approached, I called Helen.

"I'm coming over," Helen said. "We're gonna have a slumber party."

CHAPTER ELEVEN

HELEN

HELEN WENT INTO EMERGENCY MODE AT THE SOUND OF CA-mi's voice. Her friend was about to crash, and she wanted to do all in her power to soften the landing.

Helen knew Cami would be better off for crashing. Knowing Cami the way she did, though, she expected Cami to fight it. That was just delaying the inevitable, but she knew better than to say that to Cami. Words like that may as well be a triple dog dare.

As she drove to the farm—after hitting the grocery for comfort food—she wished there was a way to make Cami believe how much better life would get. Because it would, Helen knew. She'd been in Cami's shoes.

She should've told Cami that before now, but it wouldn't have been valuable until this moment. Just like Cami waiting for the moment Helen needed to know about her former life of starvation. A few years ago, one of Holly's best friends was battling an eating disorder and Helen told Cami, "I don't get it. I want to smack this girl and say, 'Just *eat*. How hard can it be?' "

Cami said, "Actually, it can be really hard."

That was a turning point in their friendship. Helen remembered Cami saying, "Okay, when I tell people this I see the 'oh, she's crazy' light go on in their eyes. Believe me, I *know* it's crazy." Helen thought Cami was so brave that day, advising her on how to help Holly's friend, taking her chances that Helen wouldn't think she was a freak. She'd given Helen a gift that day, dusting off a skeleton from her past—a fragile skeleton at that—and entrusting Helen with its care.

Helen had always wanted to give Cami something back. To-night might be the night she could.

Of course Cami wasn't in the house. Helen unloaded the groceries, then wandered down to the barn just in time to see the devil horse lurch toward the hay Cami'd just given him. Helen gasped at the obvious stagger. "Damn," she said. "Lucifer is lame."

Cami didn't even turn around when she said, "You can't call him that."

Cami's forearms dangled over the fence, so Helen checked out the wound from Saturday—the purple-and-green bruises, the actual teeth marks now nearly black.

Cami turned to her and Helen saw betrayal glittering in her friend's eyes. "I felt *sorry* for Bobby," Cami said. "I would've done *anything* for him. I feel like such an idiot."

"Oh, sweetie. You're no idiot." Helen hugged her. She wanted to encourage Cami to keep talking, to keep letting it out, but before she could, Cami switched topics, as if afraid.

Cami gestured to the devil horse. "If one of us held his halter, the other could lift that leg."

Helen saw that she was serious, then shook her head. "You're insane. You never change," she said, but didn't try to argue. She just opened the gate when Cami handed her a lead rope. Helen would prefer not to be the one near the horse's mouth, but knew Cami was the one with the skills necessary to diagnose that foot.

The horse ground his teeth as they approached, a hideous, skin-contracting sound. "It sounds like he's sharpening them," Helen joked.

"Tie his mouth shut," Cami said. She was probably trying to joke, too, but Helen wasn't sure if Cami was brave or crazy to risk another bite so soon. Helen wrapped the chain of the lead rope over the horse's nose and pulled it tight, ready to apply painful pressure if needed.

Cami tried to pick up the hoof in question, but the devil horse resisted. Helen held his nose still while Cami leaned into his shoulder to sway him off balance. He finally gave in and lifted the hoof. Helen immediately felt the weight as he then leaned into the lead rope.

"I can feel the heat through the dirt packed in his hoof," Cami said. "Shit. I can't believe I didn't bring a hoof pick!"

Helen felt like she held up the horse's entire body weight as she watched Cami scrape out what dirt she could with her fingernails. "He might have an abscess," Cami said. "Yep, I think right at the base of his frog." Helen wondered, as she always did, why on earth that V-shaped mark on the bottom of a horse's hoof was called a *frog*. She might've asked, but she didn't want to do anything to prolong the torture of her arms straining to hold up the horse's many pounds.

He groaned a low note that ended in a whimper.

When Cami released his leg and stepped away, Helen let go and shook out her arms.

Cami brushed the dirt off her hands. "Tomorrow we should do this again, ready with a hoof pick. We could soak him. While he's like this, I might be able to clean him up."

She reached in her jeans pocket and produced a sugar cube.

"Do you *always* have sugar in your pants?" Helen asked.

"Sugar, dog treats. You don't want to know."

Helen studied her friend's drawn face while Cami stared at the horse before them. "When you're ready," Helen said, touching her shoulder. "I'll tell you about some of the truths I found."

Cami looked at her with bloodshot, hollow eyes. "Truths?" She frowned. "About what?"

"About divorce."

Cami blinked. *Oh, sweetie, your eyes. You need sleep.*

"You were divorced?" Cami asked.

Helen nodded. A million emotions flashed over Cami's face. Pissed she didn't know this, disbelieving, skeptical, then . . . *baffled*, Helen thought.

"Hank's not your first husband?"

Helen laughed. "Nope. And he's not my second husband either."

"Whoa, wait. You were divorced *twice*?"

That wasn't really fair of her, but she laughed again. "No, no, no. Married once, divorced once. Hank and I aren't married."

Cami's mouth hung open. "H-how did I not know this?" she finally mustered.

"*Please* don't take it personally that I never told you." Helen loved this woman. They'd vacationed together, with Hank, Bobby, and the girls. Cami had every right to feel confused and a little miffed. "It's not the sort of thing that just comes up, you know? When I first met you, I wasn't going to say, 'Hi, I'm Helen, and I had a husband before Hank,' any more than you were going to say, 'Hi. I'm Cami. I used to be anorexic, but I've been fine now for decades.' "

When Helen took Cami by the shoulders, everything under Cami's skin jangled. Maybe it was too early to tell her anything. "I've been where you are," Helen said, as gently as she could. "My husband left me in a way very similar to what Bobby did. Don't go holding your breath that Bobby is going to figure it out and be able to explain his insanity to you. Because you know what? Skip hasn't really gotten his act together yet, and that was, like, almost twenty years ago."

Helen saw the flicker of disbelief and curiosity at *Skip*. But Cami didn't ask.

"Do you still see him? Skip?" Cami said it as if to try out the name.

"I kinda have to on occasion. He's the father of my only child."

"*He*'s Holly's father?" Her voice was so shrill, the devil horse snorted.

Helen tried hard not to laugh, but, really, Cami acted like Helen had just told her she had a hidden third arm or could fly. "Hank's acted more like her father. Holly adores him, but she was four when I met Hank."

Cami kept staring at her, which was getting a little creepy. She said, "You know, I heard you sometimes refer to 'Holly's dad,' but I'd always assumed it was just a silly semantic trick you played when you were pissed at Holly or Hank."

"Look, I'm telling you now because I think it's important for you to know that I've been where you are. And it gets better."

Cami shook her head. "I thought you were one who got it right." She sounded so sad.

"I *did* get it right . . . eventually." Did she ever. She'd struck gold with Hank. "Don't get all swept up in that 'we failed' bullshit. I swear, one day I'm going to write a book about my *good* divorce. My divorce made four lives happier, maybe five if you wanna count Skip's new wife."

Cami looked at her as if every word she'd said was bullshit, but when she spoke she didn't contradict anything; she just asked, "Why aren't you guys married?"

Helen hated that question. "You know, no one ever asks, 'Why *are* you married?' of married couples, so why am I always expected to have some brilliant answer? Most married people have no damn clue why they're married." Helen shrugged and admitted, "I'm afraid of the marriage jinx." Before Cami could ask, she explained, "Skippy and I were great until we got married and then it turned into a disaster. I see it happen day in and day out in my line of work. I want Hank to be with me because he *chooses* to be, not because he *has* to." She pulled her ponytail out of its band and redid it. Hank chose to be with her, and every single day she counted that as a monumental, joyous blessing. "That may sound stupid, but it's the honest-to-God truth."

"It doesn't sound stupid," Cami said. "The only thing that sounds stupid is—"

She didn't finish. Helen *knew* she wanted to say, *The only thing that sounds stupid is your ex-husband's name*. But she didn't.

She would, Helen knew. A whinny interrupted them. The devil horse shook a mouthful of hay, doing this crazy head toss that rattled his teeth.

"He needs a name," Cami said, and it took Helen a moment to realize Cami had jumped topics again, back to the horse.

"He *has* a name," Helen reminded her. "I just haven't had any luck getting his papers. His owners are real assholes. They're fighting to get him back. Him and all the others we took."

Cami shot Helen a look. "Please. They're not getting him back." She leaned on the fence again. "I need to call him something. Something to do with that crescent moon on his face."

"Well, getting him handleable is a moonshot, that's for sure."

"Moonshot?"

"It means getting to the moon, you know, a snowball's chance in hell. So, see? There's still the devil connection."

"Moonshot. I like it. That's what we'll call you, beautiful."

He ground his teeth, the horrendous noise as if he chewed on rocks.

"I guess that's his opinion of *that*," Helen said, laughing. She stopped laughing, though, looking at her friend's haggard face. "You need to *slow down*. That's today's piece of advice, okay?" She put a hand on Cami's back. "You *must* sleep. You look like a madwoman, my friend. Get your cute doctor friend to write you a prescription for something."

"I want to sleep," she said, and Helen heard the gravel deep in her throat. "But my heart races. My brain races. My arm hurts. I—" She stopped, then said with a bit of brightness, "Cute doctor friend is coming to town next week. I'll see what he says."

"I lied," Helen said. "I have another piece of advice for to-day. Are you listening? Post-breakup sex may seem like a good idea at the time, but it really just confuses a lot of the issues."

"*What?* You think I'm going to sleep with Vijay?"

"Hello? Who *wouldn't* want to sleep with Vijay? Plus, I've seen you two together."

"The last time you saw us together we were both married!"

"Mmm hmm. And now you're both *not.*"

Cami stared at Moonshot but then turned with a genuine smile and said, teasing, "Hmm. That thought gives me an appetite. I feel hungry."

Helen laughed. "Good. Indulge whatever craving you have. What are you hungry for?"

Cami said, as suggestively as she could, "Curry."

Helen pushed her. "Seriously. What do you want?" *Let's see if I know you like I think I do.*

Cami slumped her shoulders. "What I really want is the grilled calamari at Tanti Baci."

"Crap. Okay, what *other* cravings do you have?"

She thought a moment. "Pizza," she said. "Or ice cream."

"Or both," Helen encouraged. "I brought both."

And, good for Cami, she did eat both, along with copious amounts of wine, while they were stretched out in front of the fireplace. Max and Gingersnap curled up with them, but that new three-legged cat sulked on the back of the couch.

Cami told her about the budget conversation with Bobby. Helen listened, thinking how much Bobby had in common with Skippy. He'd left while Helen was frying pork chops, so to this day, that sizzling could bring her back to that hideous moment.

Holly had had the chicken pox, and they'd just put down their blind, arthritic fourteen-year-old Labrador that very day. *That*'s when Skippy decided to skip. His timing was golden. The pork chops burned in the skillet, the smoke alarm went off, and the house stank for days.

Helen leaned back on the pillows and said, "They break your heart, don't they? They're so pathetic. Skippy was the same way."

Cami sat up and said, "Tell me his name wasn't really *Skippy*!"

Helen laughed. "Finally! Of course it wasn't. His name was Stephen. But when we were splitting up, he was being such a baby, just a total ass. Doing things like taking the ice cube trays out of the house because they were his before we were married and hiding the remote to the TV. I was so tired of being angry, you know? It was taking up all my energy and time, being pissed at him. And I decided one day, after I'd come home to find that he'd taken the shower curtain away because he was the one who picked it out so therefore it was 'his,' that he was behaving like a child, so I should give him a child's name. When he did crappy things like send my mail back—because I'd stopped using his name, so he'd mark it 'unknown'—I could just shake my head and say, 'Oh, that Skippy.' It's hard to be mad at a Skippy, you know? *Stephen* I could be mad at. Murderous raging take-a-hatchet-to-his-car mad. Skippy was absurd and easier to take."

"You are a genius. That's brilliant. So, what's a baby name for Bobby? Butthead?"

Helen laughed but shook her head. "You wouldn't call a *child* butthead."

"Boo-boo?"

"That's better. Not it, but better."

"*Binky*."

"Perfect."

"Binky." Cami tested it. "Did I tell you that big, stupid, clueless Binky asked me to help him carry his computer out of our house?"

Helen choked on her wine. "Tell me that you didn't."

"Hell, no. I should've though. I should've picked it up and heaved it down the stairs."

"Attagirl." *Good, good for you*. The anger was good. The anger would help.

"Fucking Binky."

Helen burst out laughing. "He *asked* you to help him carry his computer? *Really?* Like, oh, by the way, I don't want to be married to you anymore, but, hey, could ya help me carry my stuff out of the home we shared?" Helen laughed so hard, the wine burned in her nose and she had to wipe tears from under her eyes. Cami laughed, too. "That is *such* a Binky thing to do!" Helen said.

For a split second, Helen saw the laughter leave Cami. She watched her friend remember. Watched the sorrow and exhaustion tug down her face. *Go ahead and feel it, my friend*, Helen wanted to plead. *Let it take you. Get it out now*.

But then damn Mimi had to call and postpone the crash further.

CHAPTER TWELVE

I DON'T KNOW IF IT WAS THE WINE OR THE FACT THAT I WAS an even bigger naïve idiot than I'd thought myself to be, but when I saw Mimi's name on my cell, my stupid heart lifted, believing she might be calling to say she missed me or to see how I was doing.

Her first words, however, were, "I don't care what's going on between you and Bobby, but you have no right to interfere in his relationship with his daughter."

I let out breath as if she'd punched me. The possessive pronoun rankled in particular.

"Gabriella should've been at her father's party! You had no right to keep her away."

I recovered enough to speak. "Gabby *did* go to the birthday party. I thought—"

"Don't you tell a goddamn lie to my face. When I called her to find out where she was, Gabriella *told* me you wouldn't let her come."

The room seemed to slant. Helen watched me, eyes wide, ready to spring into action. "B-but she would never say that," I said. "Nothing could be further from the truth. I . . . I wonder—"

"Well, of course she didn't say it outright. But I could read between the lines. You made her feel guilty for wanting to go. Your marriage problems have nothing to do with them."

"That's exactly what *I* told her. She left the house hours ago and I thought, until you called, that she was at the party with you. Oh, God. Where is she?"

When Mimi was silent, I thought she might be worrying like me, wondering if Gabriella had been in an accident or was with her boyfriend doing God knew what, but then she said, "That's pretty low, calling your daughter the liar when it's plain as day you're just trying to punish Bobby. You need to get off your high horse about whatever it is you think he's done—"

I hung up on her.

How *dare* she speak to me that way! I fought to catch my breath.

Forget Mimi. I didn't care about Mimi. Gabby. Gabby. Gabby. Where was she? I'd never known her to lie to me so blatantly. My hands shook as I filled in Helen. "Shit," I said, shaking my wine-fuzzy head. "Shit. I hope she's okay." I opened the phone I was still holding and called her. When the call went to voice mail, I hung up. Damn it. Damn it. "I don't know whether to be pissed or terrified." I took a deep breath. "I'm calling Tyler."

Helen snorted. "Don't expect him to pick up if Gabby didn't."

But, to my surprise, he *did*.

His "Hello?" was cautious.

"I need to speak to Gabby."

"Oh—I thought . . . I . . . she . . . she's not here, Dr. Anderson."

"Tyler, this is an emergency. Put her on." My hard, icy voice surprised me.

"She's not here. For real. I'm sorry."

My head whirled. "Where is she?"

"I . . . I don't know, Dr. Ander—"

"Tyler. I'm not kidding. This is urgent."

"Honest to God. *I* don't know. She won't even talk to me."

I froze, but inside my brain I scrambled for a toehold.

"She broke up with me."

The room slanted again. I shut my eyes. Nope—that was worse. I opened them and took a deep breath. "I didn't know that," I said, willing my voice to soften. "I'm sorry. *Why?*"

He didn't hesitate. My question opened the floodgates. The poor kid was dying to tell. "She wouldn't even give me a *reason.* She just kept saying she had to. She said she was breaking up with me because she loved me, but if you really love someone, then how—"

"Is she pregnant?"

Oh, God. Oh, God. Oh, God. *Had I said that out loud?* Why? Why?

Helen stood, her face horrified.

"Uh," Tyler said, making the word last several seconds. "I, uh. I . . . uh, no. I don't think . . ."

Tyler was smart, but I'd thrown him too much to say the simple no. His answer told me what I'd long suspected, but at least I knew now that what I'd witnessed at the clinic was not her telling him she was pregnant. Now I knew I'd probably witnessed the actual breakup.

Max leaped up and scratched at the door as car lights flashed across the room.

Helen went to the window. "She's back," she said.

———

Thank God, thank God. "Tyler, I'm sorry," I said. "You know it's been stressful here. I didn't mean to make you uncomfortable. I need to go now. I'm sorry I called so—"

"Is she okay? Do you want me to help look for her?" His voice was so hopeful, so worried.

"Actually, she just pulled up the drive. So, I should go, but I'll—"

"Do you want me to quit?" he asked. "At the clinic?"

"What? No! God, no!" I couldn't lose him *and* Zayna. I wanted to beg, *Please don't quit,* but then I thought how awful it might be for them to work alongside each other every day.

Poor kid. I wanted to hug him. "I'm *so* sorry, Tyler. Breakups are . . . breakups suck. I don't want you to quit, but I'd understand if you needed to."

I heard the car door. Max began to spin his greeting circle.

"I love my job," Tyler said.

"Then it's yours as long as you want it."

I wish I knew the right words to comfort him. His voice about broke my heart. I managed a good-bye and hung up the phone just as Gabby walked in.

Helen busied herself with cleaning up our food mess.

I wasn't sure how I'd play this. I *wanted* to corner her and force a confession out of her, but getting this right was too important. I needed to gather my thoughts. I didn't want to scream at her. I didn't want her on the defensive, like I'd been with Mimi. The issue was too fragile. If she hadn't been at the party and she hadn't been with Tyler, then where *had* she been?

I hugged her. "How was it?" I asked, feeling like a bitch for trapping her.

She shrugged, her eyes glittering. "Awful."

Helen squeezed Gabriella's shoulder, then passed us to enter the kitchen and give us privacy.

"You wanna talk about it?"

She shook her head and went upstairs. She didn't slam her door, but when she closed it, the sound echoed through the quiet house.

Helen appeared in the kitchen doorway. "I'm gonna go," she said. So much for our slumber party, but she knew what I needed to do. "But I'll be back in the morning to soak Satan."

"Thank you."

She stepped close and whispered, "You don't *really* think she's pregnant, do you?"

I shook my head. "I misinterpreted something, I think."

Helen exhaled. "Thank *God*." She hugged me and said, "Good luck."

I was going to need it.

MAX LED ME TO GABRIELLA'S ROOM. I KNOCKED. WHEN she didn't answer, I opened her door. She was lying on her back in bed, surrounded by books and papers. She had her iPod on, so I flicked the lights to get her attention. She pulled the buds out of her ears.

"Hey, babe, I need you to talk to me."

She sat up, stretching, and said, "Sure. I was just thinking I could use something to eat."

I could be devious and ask, *Didn't you have enough at the party?* Binardi gatherings were feasts. But I couldn't stand the deception between us for one more second.

"First, talk." I moved a pile of the papers off the bed and sat down beside her.

She narrowed her eyes.

"Why didn't you tell me you broke up with Tyler?"

She sighed, then rolled her eyes. "When did he tell you?"

"I called him earlier to find out where you were."

She stopped breathing a moment, wheels turning behind her eyes.

"I need you to tell me why you lied to me, babe."

She didn't protest. She didn't say, "I don't know what you're talking about." She knew.

"I've always counted on our honesty." I didn't sound angry, and I made sure not to have that horrible I'm-so-disappointed-in-you tone. "So, I'm really thrown by this. Mimi called and accused me of not letting you go to your dad's party."

Her head snapped up. "I never said that!"

"I didn't figure you did. But the bottom line is that you didn't go to the party. What's worse is that when you came back and I asked you about it directly, you lied to me."

"I'm sorry." Her words were swollen with heartfelt regret.

"I'm sorry, too. I'm sorry all this crap is going on and causing all this upheaval in your life, but, babe—we *have* to be honest with each other or we'll never survive this. Where've you been all this time?"

"I just drove around. I was pretty upset. I ended up walking along the river downtown."

Oh my God, not exactly the safest choice, but I let that go for now.

Gingersnap jumped on the bed and curled up in Gabby's lap. Gabby idly stroked her.

"Did you go to your dad's apartment?"

She nodded. I saw the corner of her mouth twitch.

"Did you two fight or something?"

"No . . ." More twitches in her face as she struggled not to cry. "Zayna *lives with him*, Mom. I went to his apartment and he acted like everything was fine. Like he'd always lived there and it was no big deal that I had to stop by to see him. I went to the bathroom and there was girl stuff everywhere. Makeup, shampoo, a pink razor in the shower, *birth control pills*. She *lives* there! It's a one-bedroom apartment!"

Gabby's reaction surprised me. She'd been there at the Thai restaurant, after all. Tears hung on her lower eyelashes. Her voice climbed high. "I tried to talk to him, but while we were sitting there, *she* came in. She has a *key*. She just let herself in, she didn't knock or anything. And she said, 'Hey, sweetie,' before she saw me! He left us for Zayna!"

My poor daughter. That she had to see this, that it had to unfold in just this way. The tears spilled over and she gave in to them. "C'mere." I put an arm around her and pulled her close. She cried into my shoulder. It hurt my arm, but I wasn't about to suggest we change positions.

"Oh!" she said, jerking away from me, as if she'd just remembered something, "Oh! He had the nerve—before Zayna came back—he had the nerve to ask me *if I was pregnant*!"

She actually got off the bed, leaving Gingersnap looking miffed, and paced the length of her room. "Can you *believe* that? Where did *that* come from?"

My cheeks warmed. So he couldn't give me any credit to my face, but he'd listened to me.

Gabby's face was murderous. "I told him *I* wasn't the one running around like a whore!"

I choked. "You did not!"

I *almost* got a smile. "No," she admitted. "But I thought it. And it's true. I did say it took a lot of nerve to ask me that right then, and that I thought he was changing the subject. It seemed like awfully weird timing to suddenly want to have the sex talk with me!"

When she was furious like this, she seemed like herself, but as I watched, the energy of the anger left her and she shrank before my eyes. She looked so . . . defeated. She sat back down on the bed and spoke to her own knees. "They have a *dog*, Mom. They bought a dog together!"

That was a stab to the belly. I actually flinched.

"They bought a puppy! A boxer puppy. It's *their* dog, not hers. That's how Zayna introduced it—'*our* puppy,' she said."

A puppy. That was a commitment. That was a shared undertaking. It *hurt*. It . . . it hurt almost worse than knowing Bobby was sleeping with Zayna.

"I looked at Dad, and he shrugged. He *shrugged*. Zayna looked all embarrassed and took the puppy into the bedroom, and Dad leaned across and took my hands"—her voice was a snarl now—"and he said, 'If I hadn't done this, Gabby, I'd be dead.' "

I gasped, the pain as sharp as Moonshot's teeth clamping on my arm.

"Dead?!" Gabby shrieked. Gingersnap fled from the room.

"Living with us was killing him? What the fuck does that mean?" The profanity washed over me, inconsequential at this moment. "'If I hadn't done this, I'd be dead,'" she repeated. "I got up and walked out. I just left."

I hugged her tighter. I whispered into her hair, "I'm so sorry."

I held her while she sobbed, back heaving. I wanted to muster some fury, but I felt flattened.

Soon she was able to speak again. "But, Mom, he didn't do *anything*. He didn't follow me, he didn't try to explain. He just *let me* walk out and he stayed in there with *Zayna*." She spat Zayna's name as if it tasted bad. "I had to wait, like, five minutes for the damn elevator, and he never even opened the apartment door to look down the hall! And he went to his birthday party! I sat in the parking lot and followed him to Tanti Baci. I mean, does he even *care* about me?"

After a few staccato breaths, she said, "I . . . I'm sorry I lied. I just . . . I didn't want you to know . . . you know, about Zayna."

"But, sweetie, I saw him with her at the restaurant. She quit at the clinic. I already knew."

"I know, but . . ." She burst into tears again.

"What, baby?" I had to hold her a good long while. My injured arm grew numb, my fingers cold, but I would have stayed this way all night.

She sniffed, her anger making her words hard. "It was one thing to think he was having some stupid, disgusting *affair*. But he left us. He left *us* to live with *her* in some tiny little apartment. He left Max and Biscuit and Gingersnap to buy a new puppy. From a *pet store*," she added, saying it the way someone might say *pedophile*. "He chose *that* over us."

"Not us," I whispered. "Not you. This is just between me and him."

"He's not *here*, is he?" she yelled.

I absorbed that. I ran my fingers through her hair and she let me. I idly braided and unbraided her hair. "I'm so sorry you're stuck in this mess your parents made."

She jerked away from me. "God, Mom! How did *you* make this mess? He *left*. He left us for a girl practically my age. Listen to yourself!" Disdain glittered, feverlike, in her eyes.

Gerald wandered into the room, exploring the perimeter in his jerky, marionette-like gait.

"You don't really want to break up with Tyler, do you?" I asked, as gently as I could.

"That's none of your business, Mom," she said, but it was halfhearted.

"Your happiness is always my business."

I tried to stroke her hair again, but she pulled away.

She got off the bed and shuffled some papers from one stack to another. I watched her, amazed when Gerald jumped up on the bed and butted his head under my hand for me to pet him. I cautiously scratched his ears.

"I'm never going to be where you are," she said, her back to me. "No man is ever going to wreck me. I won't let him."

She may as well have swung the lamp at my head—I was about as prepared for that action as I was for those cutting words. She thought I was *wrecked*?

I stuttered, trying to form a coherent response. Before I could find any traction, though, she swiveled to face me. "You know I blew my debate yesterday."

I blinked. "You think I'm wrecked?"

"I *sucked*," she said, ignoring me. "I blew it."

Was she going to pretend she hadn't just said that?

"I *blew* it," she said. "We were using gay marriage again for our affirmative rounds, should've been a shoo-in. I went totally off topic, ranting about how marriage is a worthless, archaic institution that obviously doesn't work, and how instead of granting gays the right to marry we ought to institute a complete marriage ban not allowing anyone to do anything so damaging."

For years I'd gritted my teeth as she prattled on about marrying Tyler. And now . . . I wanted nearly the opposite. If she didn't want to get married I wanted it to be her choice, not an escape tactic, not a knee-jerk reaction to the cruelty she perceived.

I wanted to go back to that "I'm never going to be where you are" but was suddenly mortified. My daughter thought I was wrecked? "That's not hard, working with Tyler now?" I asked.

She said, "No," but her eyes told a different story. It hurt, I could see it. "We have another one tomorrow, you know. He's picking me up, so we can review some of the argument on the way to Cincinnati." She surprised me by laughing and covering her face. "Oh, my God. A marriage ban. I actually said that. You should have seen their faces!"

It seemed like I was supposed to offer her something here. Something of hope, something of reassurance. But I had no idea what it was. I found myself defenseless, idly scratching Gerald's ears until he reached up and snagged the skin of my wrist with the claws of his one front paw.

CHAPTER THIRTEEN

AFTER GABBY WENT TO BED, I E-MAILED BOBBY, SAYING, "Gabriella is very upset about what happened today. Please talk to her."

I tried to sleep, but I worried over that "No man is going to wreck me" like a terrier with a bone. Is that how Gabby saw me? And when I wasn't mulling that, I was picturing Zayna and Bobby with their puppy. The image made me feel like someone sat on my chest.

I woke up in the wee hours, with a slight hangover headache, to Gerald and Gingersnap growling at each other at the foot of the bed—deep, demonic rumbles, punctuated by spitting and hissing. "Shut up," I warned, but they were in full throttle. Max stood with his two front feet on the bed, whining, trying to be the peacemaker.

I finally kicked the two cats out of the room and managed to get back to fitful sleep for an hour or so before the whole routine started again. This time, there was no Max trying to moderate. It was barely light outside.

I padded past Gabby's room, but her door was already open, her bed made. Max must be with her, down in the barn. Poor Gabby. I lay briefly on her bed, breathing her pillow.

Downstairs in my office I cursed to discover Gerald had emptied my purse and shredded my checkbook, a pad of sticky notes from the Advantage drug rep, and what appeared to have fortunately been only a one-dollar bill. "You little paper-loving shit," I muttered. I cleaned up, then checked my e-mail. There was one from Vijay, saying he was heading to the airport to fly back to the States. While I sat there, an e-mail popped in from Bobby. Just one line: "Please tell Gabriella to talk to *me*." You bastard. Why did *she* have to do the work? Why would you put the burden on the child? Okay, a seventeen-year-old intelligent young woman, but still a child. I rolled my eyes at the way we both said "please."

While I was waiting for the coffee to brew, I jumped when Gabby's cell phone went off in her backpack on the floor. The ring tone was the *Sopranos* theme song. I dug out the phone, even though I knew who it was—and sure enough it said "Dad."

We'd teased Tyler the first few times he'd encountered Bobby's crazy family. "So, what do you think of the Binardis?" I asked him after one Sunday family dinner.

He smiled, wide-eyed, and said, "It's kinda like *The Sopranos* without all the guns."

I couldn't help myself. I said, feigning surprise, "You haven't seen the guns?"

I had him for a minute.

Here in the kitchen, Gabby's phone beeped. New voice mail.

I was not a snoop. But I *was* Gabriella's mom, and occasionally I scrolled through her call history to make sure I recognized who she talked to. I didn't listen to her messages—I just liked to be sure there wasn't some name I couldn't identify. So, I flipped open her phone.

"Dad." "Dad." "Dad." I scrolled down. Since seven o'clock last night, Bobby had called her fifteen times, and she'd never answered. There was not one call dialed from Gabby to her father.

Here I'd been e-mailing Bobby to call her. But, damn it, where *was* he? Why wasn't he showing up? Tracking her down? Why wasn't he trying *harder*?

The coffeemaker finished dripping, and I carried a steaming cup outside, where Muriel met me on the porch and escorted me down to the barn, her little tail twitching.

Biscuit's stall was empty. I looked at the rosy sunrise and figured Gabby was out on a trail. A bike path and bridle trails ran between the end of our back fence line and the highway.

I gathered the buckets, hoof pick, and Epsom salts I'd use once Helen arrived, then sat on an upside-down bucket in the barn lot. I watched the sun rise, cradling my coffee cup in my lap. Muriel knelt beside me, only her front legs folded, her rear high in the air.

My daughter's soft laughter—one of my favorite sounds in the world—made me turn to see her approaching bareback on Biscuit. "You two look like you're praying," she said.

I smiled. "Maybe we are."

Gabby walked Biscuit close to me. "Yep," she said, lying down along his neck and hugging him, her dark hair intermixing with his golden mane. "This is my church."

I scratched the coarse hair along Muriel's back. "Mine, too."

Gabriella wore a helmet but it wasn't snapped, and she had only a cotton lead rope looped through Biscuit's halter, no bit.

Biscuit nickered amiably to Moonshot, who bared his teeth. Biscuit flicked his ears, nonplussed, then bent his nose to Muriel. They exchanged breath. "I read somewhere," Gabby said, watching them, "that if you blow into a baby bison's nostrils, he'll follow you anywhere."

"Hmm. Too bad I don't know any baby bison to test this." I'd personally always thought that animals smell our breath because they're able to smell our intent. I'd lately become envious of this ability. "I wish you would talk to your dad."

She sat up and entwined her fingers in Biscuit's mane. "Did he call you?"

I didn't answer one way or the other. "We're all trying to figure out how to make this work, but he's your father, Gabriella. I don't want you to lose your relationship with him."

"He's *your* husband, and he threw your relationship down the toilet."

I swallowed. Her anger seemed to radiate from her in waves. "I just want you to know," I said, choosing my words carefully, "that what happened between your father and me has nothing to do with you, and it did *not* 'wreck' me. It's a whole separate—"

"And what *did* happen between you?" Her face was flushed, her lip curled back. Even sweet Biscuit raised his head, agitated. "Nothing, right? He just up and left. He's an asshole."

"Gabriella. It's more complicated than that. He's been very unhappy for a—"

"God, listen to yourself, Mom. Why are you defending him? Have some self-respect."

Thank God, she swung herself down from Biscuit and led him into the barn before I could speak. If a horse hadn't been between us, I might have yanked her by that auburn hair and slapped her face. I felt like *she*'d slapped *me*. But what smacked the hardest against my cheekbones was the realization that I'd said those same things to *my* mother.

I sat seething until Tyler walked into the barn lot. He carried a box from David's Hot Buns. He could barely meet my eyes, and two red spots appeared high in his cheeks.

Oh, God. I remembered what I'd asked him. He was smart enough to know what his bungled answer had revealed.

"Hey," I said lightly. "I've got a veterinary situation you might be interested in."

When Gabby walked out of the barn, I saw the flash of pain that crossed her face before she hid it behind a mask of cool indifference. "You're early," she said.

"I know." Tyler held up the box. "I thought we could have breakfast. I got your favorite."

"I still have to shower," she said, walking away, not even thanking him.

I itched to follow her up the path and shake her shoulders. She was a better person than this! Why was she being so cold-hearted? She was acting just like *Bobby*.

Tyler looked crushed. "She and I just had an argument," I said to him. "I think you got blasted with the aftereffects."

He looked grateful but said, "That's more than she's spoken to me all week, unless we're talking about debate."

Fortunately, Helen arrived, distracting us.

Helen held Moonshot's halter as she had last night while I leaned into him to pick up his foot. Again he seemed in worse pain when the foot was held off the ground, which didn't make sense to me. I tried to work quickly with the hoof pick, prying loose the embedded layers of dirt, gravel, and manure. I got down to his frog and felt the hard, hot lump. "Yep. He's going to abscess. Feel that?" I let Tyler feel the hoof. The way his face changed heartened me. The interest, the curiosity—the heartache with Gabriella temporarily forgotten. I strained to keep Moonshot's leg up while Tyler pulled the bucket of hot water and Epsom salts into position.

Moonshot was so eager to put his leg down that half the bucket's contents splashed out on my jeans. He snorted in surprise, then groaned a sound that was unmistakably relief.

I bent over, hands on knees, peering at his back feet. "Look at that." I pointed to his left rear hoof, near the coronet band. "He's abscessing in *two* feet. This poor guy."

Sure enough, the head of the abscess was visible—angry, hot, and ready to open.

I tried to clean that back hoof, but Moonshot was too inclined to kick with it. I managed to pry some layers of muck from the bottom before my aching back insisted I give up. Three tries got that back hoof finally planted in another bucket of hot water.

While Moonshot stood in buckets, I took off his too-big halter. Ideally, I'd leave his face naked to let those raw rub marks across his nose heal, but he was still too tough to handle. I rustled up another halter that fit him properly, with lambskin pads across the noseband.

Tyler helped watch Moonshot's head while I took scissors to the worst of the dreadlocks in his mane and clipped the clumps of matted hair hanging from his belly and legs.

"Can't you just give him antibiotics?" Tyler asked. "Wouldn't that be faster than all this soaking and dealing with . . . pus?"

I rested a hand on the horse's withers. He let me, although he ground his teeth, the munching-gravel sound making my skin shudder. "Some people do. But you know what I've found? It makes the infection *appear* to get better. Everything clears up for three or four weeks, and then, just when you think you're out of the woods, it comes back. There aren't any shortcuts. You're better off going slow and letting the ugly stuff come through."

Helen looked at me from across Moonshot's back. "You gonna take your own advice?"

I looked away.

AFTER THE KIDS AND HELEN HAD LEFT, I CALLED A FAR-rier to check Moonshot's hooves and a large-animal vet I liked to take a look at the abscesses. With their help, I discovered that the back hoof's abscess was caused by a nail—probably from the stall he'd been in the process of dismantling when I'd met him—but the front hoof was still a mystery. I was to soak him three times a day.

I welcomed the time this ritual was going to take. I wanted every moment filled up. I was *not* wrecked. I would show Gabriella I was fine.

I hauled branches to the county refuse yard, chatted with the roofer who came out to fix the missing shingles, and managed to reattach the gutter to the barn myself, injured arm and all.

I propped St. Francis upright, balanced his head in place, and stuck my chewing gum in the space between as a temporary fix. Unless you looked closely, you didn't notice the split.

❦

My "stay busy" routine didn't prevent me from see-ing my daughter's heartbreak. She returned around four that afternoon. My "How'd it go?" was met with a shrug as she opened the fridge.

That *Sopranos* ring tone sounded again from her backpack, but she ignored it.

"You think we're ever going to have real food in the house again?" she asked.

I winced but didn't answer. "Are you ever going to talk to him?"

"Maybe." She took a pear, a Diet Coke, and a yogurt from the fridge. "Maybe not."

She carried her food up the stairs to her room and shut the door.

I sighed, glad to know the ring tone she'd picked for me was *Wonder Woman*. That is, unless she'd changed it.

My own cell phone rang while I was in the shower. I didn't have special ring tones for different callers, never having both-ered to program such things. When I checked the display and saw it was Helen, I shut off the water and answered, standing in the tub naked and dripping.

"Feel like tackling a crazy cat lady? Got a report on one downtown."

"Aren't we supposed to handle *large* animals?" I complained, already knowing I would do it. It would fill more time. It would show Gabby that I was just fine, thank you very much.

Gabby's door was still closed, so I stood in the hallway and called her cell. I listened. Yep, sure enough it was still *Wonder Woman*.

"You're such a freak," she said into her phone. "Why are you *calling* me?"

"I'm going on a rescue with Helen."

She opened her bedroom door and we stood there, yards away from each other, phones to our ears. Still speaking into her phone she said, "Okay. Good luck. I'm sorry I was a bitch."

"Apology accepted. Call your father."

She made a face at me and snapped her phone shut. "Sorry! We got disconnected!"

"You *are* a bitch."

"But you love me anyway, right?"

I thought about saying something like "maybe" or "don't push it," but some things you don't mess with. This was my daughter. There was only one right answer. "Of course I love you."

She stood in her doorway. "I love you, too."

"Call him."

She slammed the door.

CHAPTER FOURTEEN

By the time Helen and I were in my truck, that raw, insistent rain of Ohio springtime had begun. "What is it about us?" I asked. "The day began beautifully. I watched the *sun* rise."

From the initial drive-by, the house looked normal. We saw two cats on the porch. A cat in the window. The house, painted several different shades of green with purple Victorian ginger-breading, looked well cared for. "Doesn't look too bad," I said as I parked.

"The guy next door made the call." Helen looked at the paper in her hand and said, "Stuart Duberstein. He said it was like something out of a Stephen King book."

Stuart Duberstein. Hmm. The name conjured a crotchety old opinionated guy, the sort who wrote letters to the editor that began with, "How dare you?" Maybe he just didn't like cats?

Two more cats appeared in the windows. Nothing abnormal yet.

But the unmistakable odor reached us as I began heading up the front walk. "Uh-oh," I said.

I still hoped this was a case where we could humanely capture a few cats, take them to the spay and neuter program, and offer some education to a little old lady with good intentions.

As I put my striped Wellingtons on the bottom step of the porch, I had my first inkling that this was not to be. Cats poured forth as if someone had turned on a cat hose.

The front curtain moved and I glimpsed a human hand. "Someone's home," I said. The windows filled with more cats. I tried to count. Thirty? More?

"Oh, my God," Helen said. "There's just as many *inside*."

I slid my feet without lifting them, dragging my legs through the river of cats to ring the old-fashioned turn bell. The sound seemed to summon even more cats to the windows and from under the porch. I suddenly had a new opinion of curmudgeonly Mr. Stuart Duberstein.

I rang four times and pounded on the glass.

"This is freaking me out," Helen said. "Get *off*!" She edged her way to the steps, using her folded-closed umbrella as a deterrent. She reentered the pelting rain, her white-blond hair immediately plastered to her head. "If it's not Stephen King, it's Alfred Hitchcock for sure."

I fled to the rain, too, where only ten or eleven cats followed. The rest stayed on the porch, crying and mewling at us.

"Oh. My. God," Helen said. She opened her umbrella and shielded me while I took photographs of the porch and the crowded windows. We walked around the house, a few cats hop-trotting along, flicking their paws at the rain.

I waded through the cat sea again to knock on the back door. Since it had no curtains, I cupped my hands around my eyes and peered into the kitchen. The floor was solid with cats—

they crawled on the counter, in the sink, on top of the stove. What struck me the most were the signs of normal life: a bowl of apples, funny magnets on the fridge, a nice espresso maker.

A gray tiger kitten succeeded in hooking itself to my jean-clad right thigh. While I tried to peel it off, another cat climbed up my back. I plucked the tiger kitten off me by the scruff of the neck and dropped it into the pillow of cat bodies below. The cat on my back had almost reached my shoulder. I dropped my umbrella and plunged back into the downpour. "Get it off me!" I shouted to Helen. She grabbed the cat, but it clung to my coat. I heard fabric rip.

Once she flung it to the ground, it turned and sprang on *her*, while more cats cascaded down the steps at us. I yanked the cat from her coat, dropped it, then grabbed her arm to run.

As we fled, the back door of the neighboring house opened and a man shouted, "In here!"

It wasn't as if we were being chased by rabid wolves or movie zombies, but we ran for that door as if our lives depended on it. A tall, blond man let us into a warm kitchen, where we dripped on his black-and-white tiled floor. A handsome Australian cattle dog sat smiling at us.

"We're from the Humane Society," I said, catching my breath. "Thanks for the refuge."

"Thank *you* for finally coming. I'm the one who called. I'm Doobie."

I shook his hand, even though the image in my mind was now turning three hundred and sixty degrees. *Doobie?* So much for my grumpy old man. Now we had a hippie pothead.

As if he read my thoughts, the man said, "Not Doobie, like,

you know"——he mimed taking a toke. "It's *D-U-B-E-Y*. You know, from Duberstein? Stuck since childhood. No one calls me Stuart." He dug around in a plastic tub and handed us each a towel. I dried my face, then looked around the kitchen. Several cardboard boxes stood in stacks, with more visible in the hall.

"Are you moving in or out?" I asked. I'd move out if I lived next door to that nightmare.

"In. Unfortunately. Let me take your coats." He gestured us to a red Formica table. I sat, still mopping my hair with the towel.

"What a great dog," I said.

Dubey grinned. "Booker, would you like to meet the ladies?"

"I love Australian cattle dogs," I said as Booker sniffed my hands and let me rub his large, fruit-bat ears. He was freckled white and tan, with an intelligent face and a stump of a tail.

"You know that breed? Lots of people don't."

"Cami's a vet," Helen said. We did introductions.

Dubey had been in the house for only a week. His coffee-maker was unpacked, so he started a fresh pot. While it dripped, he unpacked some mugs. "Cream or sugar?" he asked. He was tall, fit, with hair dark blond like antique gold; like the honey sold at a farmers' market——real, fresh honey with the comb still in the jar——deep golden with a hint of red.

"Cami?" Helen asked.

I shook myself. "Oh! Cream, please."

Helen grinned, raising one eyebrow. I rolled my eyes at her when Dubey's back was turned.

Dubey handed us our mugs——Helen's had a picture of Beethoven on it, mine had Mozart.

"Classical-music fan?" Helen asked.

He joined us at the table. "I teach piano and music theory at the University of Dayton."

I took a sip. This was *good* coffee. I could be a bit of a coffee snob—no doubt influenced by Bobby—and I had been expecting only warmth, not quality.

"Well, welcome to Dayton," Helen said.

"No, no—I've taught at UD seven years. I just moved—I'm only renting this, I don't know how long—" He stumbled over this sentence three or four times before stating, "I'm getting divorced. My wife is in our old house. This is temporary, until I figure out what I'm doing."

"I've been there," Helen said. "Cami's getting divorced, too." I kicked her under the table.

Dubey nodded at me. "Sucks, doesn't it?"

"Big-time." I wondered whether he was the leaver or the one who was left. I gestured to the house next door. "My husband once told me that without him *I*'d become the crazy cat lady."

"Oh, please," Helen said. "Not a chance. Well . . . at least not *that* bad."

Dubey shook his head. "My wife never said anything remotely that kind to me."

We talked easily, Dubey refilling our coffee. We learned that Dubey's wife, Susan, an opera singer, had cheated on him after having become convinced that he was cheating on her—which, he told us, he hadn't been—and had taken a hatchet to his piano. Although she'd never wanted a dog in the first place, now she wanted possession of Booker in the divorce settlement.

Even my bone marrow chilled. "She's fighting for custody of the *dog?*"

"I think it's just because she knows he's something I value," he said. "When we started dividing stuff, I told her I didn't care about anything but my piano and the dog, and, of course, those are the two top things on her list. She doesn't even *play* piano."

He filled us in on the house next door. "The woman's name is Charisse Beaumont-Clay. She looks normal—leaves her house in a suit, has a job somewhere. You'd never know from looking at her that she's . . . God, I don't even know what you'd call it."

I nodded. "It's like a mental disorder. We mostly see it in women. It's like they *collect* animals. Sometimes it's all different kinds of animals, sometimes it's just one kind, but most commonly it's cats. It *begins* with good intentions, but then it crosses a line."

"Booker killed a couple of her cats," Dubey admitted, looking sheepish. "That's how I discovered how bad it was over there."

Booker looked up at me, fanning his enormous ears.

Dubey continued. "I let him out and saw him dash for something. He caught a cat, shook it, and that was that. The cat was dirty and didn't have a collar, so I just assumed it was feral, but the next day he killed *another* one. And then, one evening, I saw Charisse back by the garages. She was calling the names Spike and Maxine over and over. I went out to talk to her, and she said she was missing two of her cats. She described them perfectly, and I felt horrible."

"Wait a second," Helen said. "She can't possibly—"

"Right!" Dubey said, nodding. "But at the time, I had *no idea*. I was heading into her yard, gearing up to confess, when all these cats started coming from everywhere and following her. She has names for each and every one of them."

"This is weirder than we thought," Helen whispered.

"I told her we ought to call Animal Control about all the strays, and she said they were hers. And I said, 'Isn't there a limit? Some kind of city ordinance about how many you can keep?' and she changed in an *instant*. She got nasty about Booker and said she bet he'd harmed her cats, but at that point I was too freaked out to tell her the truth. By then I pictured her being crazy enough that I'd come home someday and find Book's head in a boiling pot."

"This is too big for us," I said. "We have to call the police and Animal Control."

We made the appropriate calls. Our description was horrifying enough, and the day quiet enough on the crime front, that within an hour we were in business. The police ordered Charisse Beaumont-Clay to open her door or they'd force entry. I'll be damned if Dubey wasn't right—she looked furious, yet totally normal. She wore stylish jeans, a pretty sweater, makeup. She was my age, perhaps younger, which tipped me off balance. How did someone end up this way? There was nothing to indicate why she shouldn't have friends in her life who would intervene.

Once inside her house, I blinked against the ammonia sting of tomcat urine. Each room was full of cat beds, climbing platforms, and scratching posts. In the basement were five plastic kiddy wading pools acting as litter boxes, and I had to hand it to her—they were relatively clean. But there was no masking the accumulative stink, especially with so many unneutered toms.

Charisse was in tears, but not hysterics, as Helen and I tried to explain the health issues—similar to a refugee camp's—in keeping so many animals together.

"There are pretty rampant fleas," I said—they visibly peppered the coats of the white cats and speckled my boots. "With fleas come other health problems."

Only when Animal Control began to remove cats did Charisse reveal signs of disorder. "My babies," she cried. "Who do I keep? How can I choose? You can't ask a mother to choose!" She picked up a beautiful calico and cried, "Gina? How could you forgive me?" but as she did, her sleeves fell down to mid-forearm, revealing an almost scabies pattern of flea bites.

We helped Animal Control put plastic collars on each cat and label them with permanent marker, and sure enough, just as Dubey had indicated, Charisse told us the names of *each one* of her cats.

"How will I know what happens to them?" she asked. "Will they kill them?"

I couldn't make promises. "Not if they don't have to. They'll only euthanize them if there are health problems, like feline leukemia."

Her eyes went wild. "That's so unfair! They live a *long time* with leukemia before they get sick! The vets always want to kill them right away. Monsters!"

I murmured what kind words I could, then Helen and I went outside, where I told the Animal Control guys, "Don't let the shelters put any of these cats in their general population. They need to be quarantined. There's a whole slew with leukemia."

They nodded, their eyes sad and pained. We hated this, all of us.

Animal Control loaded cats into carriers and humane traps

and carted them away, a process that was still going on as we left and that would fill five county and two private animal shelters.

Dubey was leaving his house with Booker as we got in the truck. "You ladies need anything? More coffee? More towels?"

"You're very kind," I said, "but I think we need to burn our clothes."

He grimaced. "That bad?"

I nodded. I looked down at Booker. "I hope you get to keep him."

Helen leaned across me to hand him my clinic card. "If you do, Cami's the best vet in town."

He smiled and put the card in his shirt pocket. "Well, then, I want the best for Booker."

By the time we made it out of Dubey's neighborhood, the sun was shining, the fallen rain shimmering on the spring grass. A rainbow even flirted in the sky. "It *is* us," I said. "The two of us on a rescue wreaks havoc with the weather."

Helen didn't answer, so I glanced at her. She grinned. As I wound my way back to the highway, she said, "He was sweet on you. And I'd venture to say you're a little sweet on him. Here"—she handed me the note with his original message on it—"keep his number."

My stomach tossed. I couldn't *call* him. I didn't know the rules anymore. It'd been too long. I'd make an ass of myself.

Helen put a hand on my upper arm. "You know what? You will *never* be a crazy cat lady, Cami. *Bobby*'s the one as sad and crazy as Ms. Beaumont-Clay, if you ask me."

Did sad and crazy equal *wrecked*? I was *not* wrecked. I'd save Gabby from her marriage ban.

CHAPTER FIFTEEN

OVER THE NEXT WEEKS I MOVED IN A FRENZY THAT KEPT me from feeling much of anything except heartbreak for Gabriella. How did I offer her hope when I felt none myself? "Why marry?" she asked. "Why risk it?" Because, I wanted to tell her, when you got it right, it was the most liberating, inspiring state of being on the planet—a true partner in your corner, a mate who witnessed every aspect of your life. But the flip side was so stabbingly evident: when you got it wrong, it was at best anesthetizing, at worst a splintering kick to the teeth.

Vijay e-mailed. He was back in the States but unable to come to Dayton. He was working on a three-part pandemic flu story for his TV show. "*Haraka haraka haina baraka*," Vijay wrote at the end of one of his e-mails. He didn't translate it, which was unlike him. I didn't ask. I assumed it was in his parents' native language.

I dismantled my shed to free my tractor. I had three potential adopters out to meet Zeppelin the pony. I did the Humane Society paperwork on the removed horses and cats, logging long hours into the night, downloading photos, preparing evidence. Aurora marveled at the casework, "You did all this yesterday? Are you sleeping *ever*? Are you taking cocaine?"

Olive came over often. Her expansive nature and dramatic stories fed us. I liked letting her feed us literally as well, cooking us spaghetti and meatballs and leaving Bobby's kitchen a train wreck. Her spaghetti was not nearly as good as Mimi's or Bobby's, but it passed for "real food" in Gabby's eyes, letting me off the hook for just a bit longer.

When Gabby went down to the barn one day, I found out Zayna *hadn't* been at the party, but my relief was short-lived when Olive said, "But Nick and I had dinner with them last night."

"Them?"

"Bobby and Zayna."

Olive made a face, but the words clawed open my chest. I knew Bobby was her brother. I knew Olive loved me, but it ripped my heart out to picture them all being nice to one another.

If someone had hurt Olive the way Bobby had hurt us, that someone would be dead to me.

And Nick! Sweet Nick—how hard would it have been for him to tell Olive, "I'm not okay with this. I don't really want to pretend to like Bobby right now."

Was I being a baby? Was there no loyalty? Did it not *matter* to them what Bobby had done?

Olive might call Bobby a bastard and Zayna a slut, but the bottom line was she'd sit and laugh with them in a restaurant. I wanted to choke on the spaghetti I'd pushed around my plate.

I headed for the barn after Olive left. I leaned on Moonshot's fence—I'd given up on the electric tape and never bothered to turn it on anymore. Muriel stood beside me, butting her head against my leg.

I thought of what Gabby had said: *You look like you're praying.*

So I practiced the form of prayer I'd practiced all my life, being in the presence of animals. I soaked Moonshot's feet again. As I got his hooves settled in the buckets, I watched in awe as Muriel scaled the paddock fence as nimbly as a child. She and Moonshot snuffed each other's breath, then she pulled mouthfuls from his hay pile, nibbling her sideways chews.

I brushed Moonshot's matted coat. I'd put off trying to comb his tail, wary of those back legs, but now I eyed that gnarled mess—it looked like three or four bird nests knotted together. I pulled the tail to the side, out of range of those hooves, and began loosening the tangles, pulling out straw, clumps of dirt, and manure. To my surprise, Moonshot didn't just tolerate this attention but seemed to enjoy it. He stopped eating, eyes half closed, ears drooped to the sides.

I massaged his tail's dock—the portion with the bone and muscle—and his lower lip relaxed. He began to snap his front teeth together while bobbing his head, the equivalent of a dog involuntarily thumping his leg when you get just the right spot.

I tried to be in the moment, just as Moonshot was. I emptied my mind of Gabby's bleakness, Zayna's betrayal, Bobby's cowardice. I just combed this horse's tail.

The water in the buckets cooled. When I stopped finger-combing Moonshot's tail, he moved his hind end abruptly toward me, knocking over both buckets, startling all three of us—Muriel springing to her cloven hooves and climbing out of the paddock.

After a rush of adrenaline, I recognized he was saying, "Don't stop." So I moved the buckets and combed his tail for twenty more minutes, soothing us both. He tried to get me to continue again, but I patted his rump and said, "That's all for now, handsome."

I exited his paddock, feeling calmer and centered. Feeling fine.

I SAW MY FIRST ATTORNEY AND HATED THE ENTIRE EXPERI-ence. I sat in the lobby, repeating, *People do this every day*, to calm myself, but I felt I should have had a giant red *D* emblazoned on my forehead. The attorney herself was too slick for my taste, whippet thin, with a face taut from plastic surgery. She wanted to take Bobby for all he was worth, the restaurant, all of it, even though I told her I only wanted to protect Gabriella and keep the farm. When the attorney tapped some figures into a calculator and told me the monstrous spousal support Bobby could owe me "for five years or more, and that's before we even *talk* about child support," I glazed over, wrote a few notes, and knew I would never return.

EACH TIME I SOAKED MOONSHOT, I WAS ABLE TO HANDLE him a little more. Whenever he grew agitated with my other ministrations, I returned to his tail. Over the course of two weeks, with nearly a bottle and a half of ShowSheen, a wide-toothed plastic comb, and my fingernails, I could run my fingers through the elastic black hairs with no knots or tangles stopping me.

❧

BOBBY AND I WENT THROUGH A BRIEF SPATE OF E-MAILS AS he continued to call Gabriella seven to ten times a day (I checked; she never answered or responded, to his or to Tyler's messages).

When I called Bobby on the "If I hadn't done this, I'd be dead" statement, he wrote that "Keeping this secret was killing me. A good day was a day when I didn't think about killing myself." I'd suspected he'd been depressed, but the idea that he'd been *suicidal* and never shared it with *me*, his wife, supposedly his closest friend, brought me to my knees. Literally.

DAVY FOUND ME SITTING ON THE FLOOR OF MY OFFICE AFTER I read that e-mail. He'd come over to accompany me to Gabriella's choir concert that evening. I'd heard him knock but couldn't pull myself together. He came in, cursing as Muriel tried to squeeze past him. When he found me, I saw sympathy in his eyes, but only for a second before he turned tough. "Get off the floor."

He pulled me, roughly, when I didn't stand on my own. "Get the fuck up off the floor."

Once I was on my feet, he said, "No man puts my sister on the floor. You hear me? You wanna cry, you can cry in a chair. On the couch. In your bed. But not on the floor."

The thing was, I *wasn't* crying. I'd been too stunned, too leveled to cry. When I nodded, he kissed my forehead, then held me at arm's length. "Let's get you dolled up. You look like shit."

As he supervised my makeup and hair and selected clothes from my closet, he asked, "Bobby's gonna be there, right?"

I shrugged. "I told him about it—but who knows."

"He better not bring that little slut with him."

Slut made me wince. I thought Zayna had proven herself terribly misguided and much more shallow than I'd originally thought her, but I didn't blame her the way I blamed Bobby. I could see her line of reasoning and understood it: this seductive, sad man—*of course* she wanted to try to save him, to lift him up, to be the reason for his smile. It was an instinct old as time—*I* will be the one. *I* will love him the way he needs to be loved.

Turns out Bobby did attend the concert, but with his mother, not the slut. My parents attended, too. Fortunately, Davy and I were late. The auditorium was crowded enough that we all ended up far away from one another, and no one had to worry about logistics.

Two soft, hymnlike songs in a row made me close my eyes. When I did, I pictured the farm. Pictured Moonshot. Could feel that clean, luxurious tail under my fingers.

Afterward, I expected to feel gleeful when Gabby came to me first with a big hug, but instead I felt wretched to realize: this is her life, forever dividing her affections, doling out her love. We'd failed her.

ONE AFTERNOON—AFTER ZEPPELIN HAD BEEN HAULED away by a family with an eleven-year-old girl who would *worship* him—I filled groundhog holes way out in the back pasture (which is a chore that does indeed need to be done, but perhaps not with such daily diligence as I'd been doing it lately). After I'd emptied the wheelbarrow of gravel, I returned to the barn to find a horse—a fetching gray mare I recognized as one of my dad's old event horses, Caroline's Cantata—dozing in the goat's stall. One of my parents was here.

Their trailer stood by the scrunched-necked St. Francis. An aroma startled me as I went into the house—lemon roast chicken. One of Bobby's recipes. The aroma ambushed me with the image of Bobby rubbing butter over the chicken's skin and putting half a lemon into the chicken's cavity while we talked over the day in the kitchen.

I walked into that buttery-lemon smell and found my mother in Bobby's kitchen.

"Hello!" She smiled too brightly, not making eye contact, and spoke quickly. "I was in the mood to cook and thought I'd bring you girls a nice meal. I hope you don't mind. I brought Cantata and hoped you and Biscuit would join us for a trail ride in this lovely weather."

Was it lovely? I hadn't noticed as I shoveled gravel from the wheelbarrow. I tried to think of an excuse. Why didn't I want to? "I need to go back to the clinic this evening. I'm sorry."

My mother's frown bruised me, a frown of sorrow, not of judgment.

To divert her, I asked, "Is this the chicken Bobby always made?"

Mom nodded. "He told me how to do it once, when I asked." She said it absently, looking inside one of the stacked ovens. Then she turned, took a deep breath, and said in a rush, "I'm afraid you kids are going to wreck this. Things are being set into motion that can't be undone."

Oh. That's why she came. "It's already wrecked, Mom. No 'going to' about it."

"Have you tried talking to him? I mean sitting down and really talking?"

My sleep deprivation and hunger made me vicious. "To say *what?* Look, not everybody forgives a cheating spouse, okay? Some people have more self-respect than that!" *Oh, shut up. Shut up. Why couldn't I stop myself? I knew what this felt like!*

Mom flinched but didn't look as offended as I thought she deserved to be. "It takes great self-respect to forgive," she said.

"You forgave too much. I'm not you, Mom. I can't do it."

She watched my lips move as if she were deaf and trying to lip-read. She spoke slowly, as if figuring out a puzzle. "You think *I* forgave too much?"

I nodded, feeling sick. *Shut up. Just shut up.* I wasn't mad at *her*. I needed to eat.

"What are you talking about?"

I fought the urge to run from the room. "Well, you know. That year . . . that year, Davy and I figured it out. We knew."

Mom watched me for a moment. "What exactly did you and Davy think you figured out?"

Why had I opened my poisonous, hateful mouth? Here was my mother sweetly cooking for me, and how did I repay her? "You know, that Dad was . . ." It seemed callous to say he was "cheating on you" or "sleeping around." I scrambled for the words. Mom waited, her face open, as if she honestly didn't know what I was struggling to say. "That he was . . . unfaithful."

"Oh, no." A horrible sound came from her mouth, and her face drained of color. "No, no, no. You thought that? All these years?"

She put a hand out for the tiled island as if she needed support. Her face was anguished. "No, Camden. It was *me*."

What the hell was that supposed to mean?

"*I* was the one who was unfaithful," she said. "*I*'m the one who had the affair."

The lemon smell intensified. A whirring sound filled my head as events, snippets of conversations, and snapshots realigned themselves in my head.

Oh.

"*I* didn't forgive *anything*. He forgave it all, Camden. All. Oh, I hate that you thought badly of him. Davy, too? This is really what you thought? All this time?"

I wanted to ask so many things, but our family had never been much for divulging. We stood several minutes, facing each other.

I knew my mother was never more comfortable than when on a horse.

"Do you still want to ride?" I asked.

CHAPTER SIXTEEN

CANTATA AND BISCUIT STROLLED IN THE SUNSHINE. THE periwinkle sky, the pear tree petals sprinkling down on us, and the pastel blossoms made me feel as if we moved inside a Monet canvas.

I waited for my mother to speak first. While she collected herself, the horses clopped along, Biscuit's rocking walk massaging my lower back.

The memory of the contempt in Gabriella's eyes nipped at me.

When we came to the creek, we let out the reins so the horses could drink. I'd been judging my mother for putting up with Dad's cheating. Surprise and shame filled me as I realized I didn't have the same disdain for my father, now that I knew the true story. Talk about a double standard.

Something Bobby had once said returned to me. Knowing nothing about my parents' true history, he'd asked, "How come when a woman abandons a marriage, everyone says, 'Oh, good for her,' and it's seen as this liberating act of independence, but when a man leaves a marriage, he's nothing but a cad?" He'd repeated this question more than once, whenever we watched a movie or a play in which either spouse left a marriage. Had he been thinking of *himself*? Already wanting to leave?

My mother let Cantata walk out into the creek. Caroline's Cantata. Dad's last Olympic ride. It was hard for me to look at that horse and not flash back to Dad's accident. I remembered sitting in the mud cradling the mare's head—those panicked eyes, the foam from her nose. I shook myself. A little puffiness in her left front leg was the only remnant of her own injury.

Caroline's Cantata. My father had named that horse *after* the infidelity.

Cantata put her nose under the water, then tossed her head, sending small splashes dancing across the stream's surface. Biscuit and I stood on the shore, watching.

Mom combed through Cantata's mane at her withers and finally spoke. "Your father and I had changed as people. We'd grown up, we'd evolved, really, as people do, as people *should*. We had problems, but instead of dealing with them, I took the easy route and became convinced that the marriage itself was bad." She squinted through the sunlight. "I was wrong."

Biscuit ambled down the slope to stand in the water, too, as if he wanted to be closer to hear Mom's soft voice over the lapping of the water.

"We needed a change. I fell in love with another person because I needed a catalyst." She made a face at some expected disdain from me, but what she'd said made sense. "I can explain it now, but at the time, of course, I had no idea what I was doing. But now I know that when someone's in need of *big* change, the most common thing to do is convince yourself you're in love. Not real love, either, but ridiculous besotted infatuation. The kind that's so predictable it's become a cliché—the midlife crisis, the trophy wife. My therapist said you typically fall in love with something missing in *yourself*, not in your spouse."

I couldn't help but wonder what Bobby was missing that he saw in Zayna. What was he missing that he couldn't find in me?

"I was missing a sense of purpose," Mom said. "I didn't like who I'd become at competitions. I didn't like who your father had become. I didn't like our coach. I didn't like how we treated our horses. I didn't like the stress, the anxiety, the—"

"You *are* Dad's coach."

"I am, now."

"But." I tried to take all this in. I remembered other coaches, vaguely. Way back when Davy and I played or napped in a giant dog crate while Mom and Dad competed at shows.

She looked up at the sky, then returned her gaze to mine. "I convinced myself I was in love with someone else. It swept me away, consumed me—don't worry, I won't go into detail—but I wasn't in love with that man. Not like I love your father. I was in love with what he *did*."

We watched the water in that hypnotic way one might stare at a fire. I thought of the many male coaches her age who could have been her lover, but I already knew—in spite of all she'd revealed today—that my demure, private mother would never tell me his name.

Eventually, Cantata crossed the creek and climbed the opposite bank. She chose a path wandering up a rolling hill and we let her, Biscuit and I following behind. We moseyed along in single file for about fifteen minutes. When the path widened, I squeezed my calves against Biscuit's sides. He picked up a lazy jog and we caught up to Mom, our boots nearly touching.

I listened to the creak of the saddles, the occasional clink of a horseshoe on a stone, the whisk of the horses' tails. I wanted to tell her I was sorry, but I didn't know words that would include my regret for *all* of it. All the misunderstandings, all the lost opportunity, all the pain and distance. How I'd judged her. What a bitch I'd been.

I reached out to her. Mom saw the gesture and reached to meet my hand with her own. We held hands between horses until Cantata stepped sideways to avoid a puddle, tugging us apart.

LATER, BACK IN THE BARN, WE UNTACKED THE HORSES AND hosed them off. Sweaty foam had gathered between their legs and along their necks. Finally spring.

"How did you mend it?" I asked. "The marriage?" I ran the hose over Cantata's back, watching her coat change from white to gunmetal gray.

Mom stopped scrubbing the mare's neck. "We just *decided* to. We said if we were going to end it, we had to *earn* our way out. We had to pick up every single stone and look beneath it for a solution. We vowed we weren't walking away until we'd exhausted every possible option."

I hosed the mare's tail. "How do you even begin, though? What did you *do*?"

"Talked. Fought. Cried. It was *hard*, Camden. The hardest thing I've ever done."

The hardest thing she's ever done? My mother didn't say those words lightly.

I thought again of the accident.

I thought of my father's face, freckled with mud. I saw the

burgundy blood bubbling in one nostril. I heard my mother saying, "Just move. Just open your eyes. Show me you're all right."

I thought of how it took a crawling century of a week for my mother to get that wish.

That day was among my favorite being-married memories—that is, up until the clipped, British announcement that Cleveland Anderson was "unseated at the Broken Bridge." Our whole family was present at the Kentucky Horse Park for the Rolex Kentucky Three Day Event. Crisp but sunny weather. My husband holding my hand. My funny daughter teasing us. Eating funnel cake and onion blossoms. Walking the miles of the cross-country course, Bobby animated, asking me questions about the sport and its confusing rules.

Bobby, Gabby, and I had waited for more than an hour to stake out perfect bleacher seats at the series of water jumps. The Davids were farther behind on the course, at the Broken Bridge. The water complex and the Bridge promised to be the most spectacular jumps of the day. Mom would be zipping to strategic places on the course in a golf cart, and all of us would be at the finish.

The rider before Dad had fallen here at the water. She and the horse were unhurt but disqualified. Now, five minutes later, Dad could be approaching any moment.

When I heard Dad was "unseated" I wasn't worried. He'd get back on. It would cost some points, some time, and perhaps his wide first-place lead after the dressage, but he'd be fine.

I expected the announcer to declare him "away," but instead we heard, "Both horse and rider are still down at the Broken Bridge."

I stood up. "Let's go."

Gabriella took my hand to stop me. "Are you sure?" We'd *earned* these perfect seats.

"'Horse down' means they're done. They can't finish the course."

I was still thinking more of Cantata than of Dad as we picked our way down the bleachers.

It wasn't until the announcer told us that the rider on course after Dad had been stopped, and that no other riders would be sent out until the accident was "cleared," that my limbs went to ice.

I remember whispering, "This is bad," to Bobby.

I remember him nodding and taking Gabby's hand.

I remember running. It was more than a mile from the water to the Broken Bridge. An ambulance passed me, both of us cutting across the open pastures. For a while I almost kept pace.

I remember the splintered top rail, the demolished stone wall, my father and Cantata down inside the gap in the bridge. Cantata's panicked breathing filled my ears as I took in Davy holding my mom out of the way of the EMTs.

An EMT unsnapped Dad's helmet and it fell in two halves, like a coconut.

I see that helmet in my dreams.

Big David ran his hands over his bald head, saying, "It was that dog. This damn dog ran out from the crowd." He pointed as if the dog was still there. "They tripped on the dog!"

My mother grabbed my wrist—so hard she left a bruise—before she got on the helicopter and pleaded, "Please. Cantata. If she . . . if she has to—" and I knew she was saying, *I want it to be you who does it if it has to be done.*

Cantata stopped thrashing when I crawled into the narrow ditch and stroked her head. With the official event veterinarians, I ran my hands over the bones of her legs and felt almost sickening relief to find nothing obviously broken. She was trapped, unable to extend her legs to get out of the ditch. They had to dismantle the entire bridge to free her.

It was only after Cantata stood and lurched to a waiting veterinary trailer on trembling, caving legs—the anxious crowd cheered—that I followed the others to the hospital.

Davy met me first. "They think he's paralyzed."

You could call that day *hard*, I'd say.

Or the week that followed while Dad lay in a coma.

You could call the next half year *hard* as Mom refused to accept that he'd never walk again. Dad's physical pain, his emotional despair—she took it all with a consistent, giving-up-is-not-an-option commitment.

She taught him how to eat with silverware again.

She taught him words with flash cards.

In the first days after the coma, she'd had to remind him of her name.

"IT WAS THE HARDEST THING I'VE EVER DONE," MOM REpeated, bringing me back to the soapy Cantata. "And the best."

Mom had taken that scarred Passier and set it on the gate. I replayed my parents' exchange over the saddle. Dad was right. The repair proved the saddle's worth.

The mare put her head down to sneak a mouthful of grass while the cool water ran over her. "I feel *sorry* for Bobby," Mom said. "I managed to salvage my mistake in time. If he doesn't, it will be a tragedy."

Mom and I skimmed sweat scrapers over the mare, sweeping the water from her coat. "You have the hardest work," Mom said. "Forgiving is the hardest. Regret isn't hard, but you carry it forever. Once you forgive, though, then you're free. You just have to be clear about what you want."

The mare whisked her tail at a fly and wet horse tail smacked me in the face. I shut my eyes against the sting.

CHAPTER SEVENTEEN

YOU JUST HAVE TO BE CLEAR ABOUT WHAT YOU WANT. MY TER-
rier mind gnawed on the bone of my mother's words.

What if . . . what if Bobby and I tried to mend our marriage?
What would Gabby think of that?

I saddled Moonshot. And sat on his back. That's all, I just
sat. He was still a little gimpy but certainly mobile, and I wasn't
going to *ride* him for real. I slipped onto the saddle for fifteen
seconds, then slid off.

Head tossing. Teeth gnashing. But he stood still.

I did it three more times before I made Gabriella stop studying and went to bed.

My mother's words kept me awake.

The cats had been quiet that night, and 2 a.m. was long before their usual witching hour. It was even too early for Max to
follow me to the barn. Without lifting his head, he tapped the
end of his tail twice before he shut his eyes again.

I wasn't on my guard. My mind was full of the Passier, those
bite marks, our trail ride conversation. I opened the door and
out rushed the three-legged cat.

"Gerald!" I called. I stepped into the dark. "Gerald, c'mere!
Come back."

I grabbed the flashlight from the back porch, but Gerald was long gone. I called and called and shone the light into bushes, the pile of wood that was once my shed, and the flower bed of the slouching St. Francis. In the barn, Biscuit grunted in mild protest at the disturbance, and Moonshot paced fretfully outside. I walked through the back pasture, rustling up nothing but three deer who rose and galloped away with my pulse.

Maybe . . . maybe the riskiest thing in the world would be to try to fix things. Part of me felt heavy at that thought, as if my bones had taken on more weight. What would it feel like for everyone to know all that crap that had passed between Bobby and me—the "dirty laundry," as Mom had called it—and to try to forge ahead, all exposed like that?

Wouldn't it be worth it to present Gabriella with a model like that?

What if the greatest adventure in the world was to do this right? To do it well? In this day and age—this time period in which I found myself alive on this planet—maybe we would be the boldest, bravest explorers if we tried to repair a marriage instead of throwing one away?

IN THE MORNING, I SADDLED MOONSHOT AGAIN AND SAT ON him before searching the pasture for Gerald. The tuna I'd set out for him was gone, but the footprints around it looked like raccoon, not cat. I scanned the horizon. I'd grown fond of that raggedy cat, with his broad, lionlike nose. How would he fare out there with only three legs?

After work, I searched for him again. Gingersnap, in the

meantime, lorded over the house, positively swaggering every-where she went.

I was about to get on Moonshot again that evening, when I saw Bobby's car come up our drive. I grudgingly gave him credit for finally showing up.

I couldn't help but gasp at the punch in my stomach of the puppy tumbling out of the car after Bobby. A floppy Boxer clambered on too-big paws beside my husband as they walked down to meet me at the barn. I wanted the puppy to steel my fickle heart against Bobby's betrayal, but when the puppy toppled into a somersault at the slightest nudge from Max, then looked up with its tongue poking from the side of its underbite, I didn't have a chance.

I knelt to pet the ungainly baby, who climbed onto my thighs and covered my neck with slobbery kisses.

When I looked up, Bobby was smiling. *God, he's beautiful.* At his smile, my heart stuttered, then gunned with adrenaline. That was a fear rush. Why was I afraid? Because I couldn't stop thinking of my mom's words, of that stitched-up saddle. Could we be repaired?

"This is Zuzu." Bobby's eyes were bright, his expression sheepish.

Zuzu? I hid my face, ducking away from her bubblegum tongue. That name was *ours,* that was *our* private joke. Watching *It's a Wonderful Life* was one of the few Christmas traditions Bobby didn't just tolerate but actually enjoyed. We could quote dialogue from the entire film. When good news happened, we were as likely to exclaim, "Zuzu's petals!" as "Congratulations."

You can't call her that! I wanted to snap as I let the puppy lick my face. *That name belongs to our marriage, it doesn't belong to Zayna.* I felt like some kind of store open for Zayna to stroll through and select what she wanted. *I'll take this, and this, and this* . . . until my shelves were bare.

When I was able, I looked up at Bobby.

He shrugged. "I know. I—" He opened his hands, as if helpless.

He'd never shown the slightest interest in any of our animals, but his dopey grin made it clear—he was smitten. Well, well, well. Binky had a heart after all.

The puppy spilled from my kneeling thighs, then splayed on her back, exposing her round belly for Max's inspection.

I stood, brushing my knees, shaking away the bit of dizziness as I rose upright.

Bobby frowned at me as I unfolded before him. *What did I look like?*

"I'm here to talk to Gabriella. Or to try to anyway."

"I'm glad." My own voice startled me with its warmth, its welcome.

He looked into my face, wary at first. Then gratitude softened his eyes.

Gabriella came out the back door. "Dad?"

She ran down the path to him. As they embraced—Max and the puppy stumbling around their feet—my own arms ached to touch Bobby. See? You forgave—you *decided* to, as my mother had said—just as Gabby did right before my eyes.

I watched them and thought, *Maybe, just maybe . . . we could do this.*

But not right now. This moment was not about me.

When the two of them left for dinner, I sat on Moonshot again. I touched my heels to his ribs and he stepped away from the mounting block. I let him walk across the barn lot, then closed my hands on the reins. He halted, and I slipped my feet free of the stirrups and slid off his back.

EARLY IN THE MORNING, AN E-MAIL FROM BOBBY SAT waiting.

> It was so good for me to see Gabriella. She says you never sleep or eat. I thought you looked way too thin. You've been on my mind and if there's anything I can do for you, please call me. I mean that. Love, Bobby.

My face broke out in a hot, scratchy flush. I read the e-mail again.

I'd been on his mind? *Please call me? Love?*

I walked down to the barn at dawn.

This time, I put on a helmet and rode Moonshot around the perimeter of the barn lot. His walk was classic thoroughbred, forward and gliding, his stride long and low.

If there's anything I can do for you.

Love.

You've been on my mind.

Back in the house, Gabriella scrambled eggs. "If you did my morning feed again," she said, "then the least I can do is feed you."

"Oh, babe, that's sweet." I sat down to eat the eggs. *See? See me eat? I'm fine, just fine. Why did you tell your father that?*

But a small, shameful slice of me wondered, *If I were thin enough, would he rescue me again?*

Gabriella had a stack of printed-out Internet research beside her. Her suitcase stood by the door.

I turned over a few forkfuls of eggs. "Is this tournament one night? Or two?"

It shocked me to hear my mother and myself echoed in her sigh. "One," she said. "We'll be back tomorrow night. I wrote it down because you don't remember anything anymore."

I made a face at her. What if . . . what if when she returned, I could offer her some hope?

Don't be stupid. Don't call him. He walked away. You already know his answer.

When she left, I waved good-bye, then dumped my eggs in the disposal.

I WAS NEVER SO RELIEVED AS WHEN MY CELL RANG LATER at the clinic and I saw Vijay's name appear. "If I were at the Dayton Airport at seven p.m., could you pick me up?" he asked.

"Yes!" I didn't check a clock. I didn't need to.

"Good, because I'm at La Guardia, on a plane, and finally about to take off."

I wanted to fall to my knees and kiss the floor. He'd closed two e-mails lately with that line: *"Haraka haraka haina baraka."* I needed to ask him what that meant.

I tried to dress with care, but my clothes all felt too big and slovenly. I chose a black V-neck sweater (those clavicles) and jeans I had to belt.

I stood in the Dayton airport, waiting for a lifeboat to be tossed to me.

Vijay strolled around the corner and out toward the baggage claim. I took in his lankiness, the sureness of the sweet, bow-legged gait I used to tease him for in high school. When he saw me, the flash of his white smile against his cinnamon skin made something dissolve within me.

He engulfed me in a hug and kissed my cheek, as he always did.

Once he'd collected his suitcase and we were in my truck, he said, "You're too thin, Cam."

He said it simply, a scientific observation. He was the only person who could say this without raising my hackles. "I'm try-ing to eat. I just . . . can't."

"I remember that feeling. I lost about fifteen pounds when Rita left."

"And you don't have fifteen pounds to spare."

"Like you have any room to talk, Miss Skeletore."

I laughed. He used to call me that, even when I was hospital-ized. It made the nurses gasp.

"You understand you have a disorder, right?" Vijay asked. "Even though you've managed it for years, you're susceptible in times of trauma or stress, kind of like an addict."

"You must be a good influence on me," I said, "because I'm starving. Where are we going?"

He chuckled as we approached downtown. "You know what really sounds good? The grilled calamari at Tanti Baci."

"I was craving that just the other day!"

"Great minds, you know. Wanna go? I could pretend to be your boyfriend. I'll make out with you in front of Bobby."

I laughed. "Oh, my God. You're so wonderful. I love you."

"I love you, too, Cam. I'm so sorry you're going through this." He reached across and put a hand on my knee. "So, what do you think? The Pine Club? Jay's? El Meson?"

I thought a moment. "I'd go to Tanti Baci. I really want that calamari." Bobby made it the old-world way, not thick strips of tentacle but tiny squids fried whole that you ate like popcorn.

"Really? I was kidding."

"What, am I not allowed to go there? Am I supposed to hide?" What was I doing? This was a stupid idea and I knew it in my bones. But, maybe, if I saw Bobby again, it would be natural and easy like yesterday. It had felt so . . . *good* to see him.

"You're just being Reckless Diva again," Vijay said.

I laughed. "No, honest. It's just I'm *craving* some of that food. Nothing else sounds good."

He didn't say anything.

"And you don't have to make out with me."

"Oh." He feigned disappointment. "Well, if you change your mind, I'm willing."

My belly fluttered. Was he just trying to make me feel good?

I drove us to Tanti Baci, but Vijay said, "I'm not eating here. I don't know what you're trying to prove, but if you want to have dinner with *me*, we're eating somewhere else."

I was half-relieved, half-disappointed to be saved from my own childish willfulness.

We ended up—at Vijay's request—at another Italian place,

one I'd always liked, but which after Tanti Baci had opened felt disloyal for me to patronize.

The hostess led us to a romantic corner table by a window. Vijay held out a chair for me, and we ordered a bottle of Chianti and grilled calamari.

And, as I had done all my life, I told Vijay everything. Zayna. The puppy. The trail ride with my mother. The scarred Passier saddle. Gabriella's marriage ban.

My new plan to salvage my marriage and make it better, like my parents had.

Vijay unfolded his napkin with his huge hands. He'd grown into his hands, but they used to look all out of proportion to the rest of him. He spread the napkin on his lap, then said, "Cami. Are you sure you want to offer him this? Think about what he did. He did a shitty, *hurtful* thing to you. I mean, marriages end. Relationships end. The reason this one ended is one thing that only you and Bobby will ever know or understand. But *how* it ended? That's another thing altogether. The how it ended puts Bobby on my shit list until the end of time."

I thought about how it had felt the day Bobby left. Opening that sock drawer.

If there's anything I can do for you.

Love.

The waitress brought our wine. After the opening and pouring ritual, Vijay raised his glass. I raised mine, too, even though my hand trembled. "To surviving life."

"Life," I repeated. This was really happening, messy and surreal. Vijay's "Are you sure?" left me unsteady. I set my glass down and tucked my shaking fingers under my thighs. "This sure wasn't what I thought would happen," I said. "I've been dumped by my husband like a shelter dog. My life is falling apart."

Vijay frowned his disagreement.

I wanted to drink my wine, but I didn't want Vijay to see the telltale tremors in my hands. "I feel like such a failure," I admitted.

"You can't fail a test you weren't allowed to take," Vijay said.

I shivered, and hoped he didn't notice. Why was it so cold in here?

"Your husband left you for a child waitress and you're feeling that *you* failed?"

I let that sink in. I thought about Bobby's e-mail, but it suddenly seemed so obviously hopeless. I couldn't think of the reasons I'd gathered for why I should try to fix the marriage. My brain felt fuzzy even though I'd had only one sip of my wine.

"You're confused and hurt, Cami. Don't rush into this. I don't think Bobby deserves it."

Simply smelling the calamari when it came brought my appetite to life. The meat melted on my tongue. Vijay took a bite, too, and for a moment we simply savored. A ravenous urge overcame me to consume a plateful of this stuff, plus the entire bread basket.

"What about *you*, Cami?" Vijay asked. "Were you happy? Really?"

The question turned my one bite of calamari to cat litter in my mouth. "I knew we had problems," I said. "I knew we had flaws. But . . . until that morning he left, I would've told anyone who asked that we had a happy marriage."

Vijay tilted his head. "But did you hear what you just said? *You would have told anyone who asked* that you were happy, but that's not answering the question: Were you happy?"

How did he *do* that?

"Do you know how many years I've listened to you defend him and make excuses for him?"

My neck and cheeks itched.

"You were a master at rationalizing any insensitive thing he did."

I longed to scratch the blossoms I knew were crawling across my face.

"Why did you spend so much energy apologizing for him? You'd always have some sweet explanation of why he was the way he was, why it was okay with you. It made me sick."

The calamari steamed like a punishment before me. I knew I couldn't touch it. "Why didn't you ever say anything before?" I asked. "You sound like you hated him!"

"I never hated him . . . although I might *now* for the cowardly way he did this. I could never say anything to you because you loved him, Cami. I couldn't risk losing my friendship with you, so I kept my mouth shut."

Dizziness sparkled in my head.

"So, let me take that back," Vijay said. "About hating Bobby now. I think I may like him better now than I ever have before. I think he just did you the biggest favor of your life."

"*Favor?* Vijay, I— Remember, he saved me once. He—"

"No," Vijay said. "I think *you* rescued *him*, just like you try to rescue everybody. *He* was *your* shelter dog." He took my hand.

My face felt as though I stood before the pizza oven at Tanti Baci.

"Cami, don't you see? Your life isn't falling apart. It's about to fall *together*."

CHAPTER EIGHTEEN

IT TERRIFIED ME, THIS NEW DESPERATION, THIS NEW HUN-
ger. I had to know if Bobby and I could—or should—save our
marriage.

Did I *want* to?

I had already struggled with this question. Did I truly miss
Bobby? Or did I miss the *idea* of Bobby?

I thought of my fierce, wounded daughter.

I thought of that tattered saddle and had to know.

I dropped Vijay off at his parents' house; I didn't go inside.
He usually alternated every other night with our house when he
was in town, a tradition we'd kept even when we'd both been
married, but I was glad to be alone this night. At my own house,
I didn't even bother to go through the motions of getting in bed.
I wandered the pasture calling for Gerald. I scratched Moonshot's tail. As the sun rose, I tried to talk myself out of it.

Vijay was right. Bobby doesn't deserve this. Don't call.

But I did.

I flipped open my cell phone and dialed his number. He answered on the third ring, his voice grumbly with sleep. I looked
at the microwave clock. Oops. It was three minutes before
seven.

After an excruciating, babbling start, I said, "I need to ask you something. Can we meet in person?"

"Uh . . . okay. When?"

"Now?"

He paused. He coughed. He agreed to meet me at the Second Street Market downtown.

WE SAT OUTSIDE AT A PICNIC TABLE, WHERE BOBBY GREETED me with "Gabby's right, Cam. You're too thin."

But thin *enough*? I sensed his impatience, his irritation— what was this burning question I had?—but I didn't know how to begin. I was desperate for a sign of some kind.

As I took a deep breath, I felt real fear, this sense of *do NOT do this*. Bobby watched me, expectant. I asked, "Do you want to work on our marriage?"

I swear I could hear a woman breathing a hundred yards away. Bobby's panic hung in the air, a palpable thing.

Each second of silence burned in my chest, scalded my face. Which answer would be worse?

"I . . . I wouldn't even know how to begin," he finally said, fidgeting with the cross at his neck.

"That's not what I asked you." My voice was harsh in my attempt to cover my shakiness. "I asked if you *wanted* to try to work on it."

He opened his hands. "I . . . I just . . . I don't think that would be fair to you, Cam."

"I didn't ask you that." My own voice frightened me. "I asked if you wanted to work on it before we say we're done."

He rubbed his face with his hands. In that gesture I saw the answer: *no*. No, he didn't want to work on this. I saw the weariness.

He didn't want to try.

I was an idiot.

"Your answer is no," I stated.

He nodded.

"All right," I whispered, suddenly feeling I might crumble into ash. I looked into those espresso eyes and girlish lashes and wondered how I hadn't seen what was so obviously there. How I couldn't see he didn't love me.

Dizziness careened through me as I stood. Bobby reached out, as if he feared I'd fall. "Cam?"

I cleared my throat. "What did you do to fix it?"

He crinkled his brow.

"What did you try? I know you didn't talk to me, you didn't share what you were feeling, but were there things I didn't see that you attempted?"

He shoved his hands into his pockets, the SPQR tattoo sliding into view under his T-shirt sleeve.

"Please tell me you tried *something*. Anything. That you didn't just quit."

The signs were all around me, but I had to let him reject me *again* to know for sure?

"I had to know. Thanks for coming." I walked back to my truck, lightheaded and wobbly.

To exit, I had to drive past the picnic tables and when I did, Bobby was still there.

Zayna sat beside him.

Zayna wearing a soccer jersey I'd bought for Bobby when we'd last been in Rome.

He'd brought her *with* him? Had she been watching our conversation?

Zayna ran a hand over Bobby's back and leaned her head on his shoulder.

Bobby turned, lifted her chin with his hand and kissed her on the mouth.

And when they parted from the kiss, of course, *of course*, Bobby saw me. The goddamn red truck was so conspicuous. Our eyes met. I turned my head and drove away.

By the time I was on the highway, my cell phone buzzed. *Bobby.* I opened it, then shut it, cutting him off. In seconds, he called back. He called three times on my way home. Each time, I hung up on him. At home, I left my phone on the kitchen counter. It kept buzzing like an angry hornet.

I stormed my way through my late morning feed. Unforgivable that I'd left the animals hungry for *that*. I slammed doors, hurled grain into boxes, and tossed the empty cans, relishing the racket. Why had I called? Why had I allowed myself to be hurt *again*?

Were they laughing at me? Was Zayna asking, *She called you for* what?

I saddled Moonshot again. I put on my helmet and led him to the outdoor arena.

The gliding motion of his walk soothed me. With each fluid stride, my pulse slowed to normal.

He lifted his ears and looked at something to our left. When

I turned my head to see, a wave of dizziness prickled through my skull. A glimpse of orange in the weeds. Was it Gerald? I blinked against the faint white sparkles and they retreated to my peripheral vision. Before I could focus, Moonshot picked up a trot. We probably shouldn't do that yet . . . but it felt so flowing, so forward. I indulged in it for a moment, then closed my hands in half-halts to ask him back down. He slowed but didn't walk. Another wave of dizziness. The white sparkles crowded my vision. Okay. Time to be serious. More aggressive half-halts on the inside rein. He turned sharply. The arena slanted. I dropped the reins and grabbed his mane to keep myself seated. I looked down but could barely see my hands through the narrowing tunnel of my vision.

Another sharp turn. I was sliding. Shit. I kicked my feet free of the stirrups and tried to dismount, but the ground didn't meet my feet like I thought it would.

Spinning. An image of outer space. Which way was up?

My left shoulder found the ground first. Surprise as well as pain jolted me awake as I bounced.

The second landing was on my side.

I heard the crack. Felt the pop, like an internal flashbulb going off.

CHAPTER NINETEEN

I FELT PAIN LIKE I'D NEVER KNOWN BEFORE, NOT EVEN GIV-
ing birth.

Moonshot snuffled the length of my body, then brought his
muzzle to my face.

It hurts. My shoulder throbbed. Bone ground deep within me.
My helmet's strap chafed my neck. Thirst cottoned my mouth.

Okay. Think. My phone. On the kitchen counter. Shit. Shit.
There was a landline in the barn.

I tried to visualize myself getting up, walking the distance to
the gate, crawling through. I managed to move only my right
arm, though, before I gave up. *It hurts it hurts it hurts.*

After more time had passed (ten minutes? two hours?) I tried
to sit up. The alternative was to stay here until Gabriella returned this evening. It couldn't have been much past 9 a.m. now.

There was water in the barn. And the phone. Phone and water. Phone and water. My mantra. Eventually, I used my right
arm to push against the ground to raise myself to sitting.

Unbearable. I looked at the barn. Might as well be on Mount
Everest. I slid back to the ground.

Max trotted into the arena, whined, sniffed me all over, and
curled up against my back.

When I heard knocking on wood, joy surged through me: *Someone is here!* Vijay? But it was Muriel, climbing the fence. She crossed the arena to me, her tiny hooves *scritch-scritch-scritch*-ing in the sand. She looked me over, then paced like a little old lady wringing her hands.

How could I have been so stupid? When had I eaten last? Eaten for real?

Vijay would spend the night here tonight. When would he arrive? Lunch? Late afternoon?

Your life isn't falling apart. It's about to fall together.

Falling. That seemed to be the key word. *It hurts it hurts it hurts.*

Moonshot lowered his head to mine, and his reins slid down his neck, catching on one ear.

Scritch-scritch-scritch. Back and forth, back and forth, Muriel paced.

What would stupid baby Binky do if he knew I was lying here? I tried to shove that image away; I didn't want his help. Bullshit. I'd take *anyone*'s help right now. Hell, even Zayna's.

AFTER WHAT FELT LIKE AN HOUR, THIRST PROMPTED ME TO attempt sitting again. I shut my eyes, psyching myself up for the effort. When I opened them—step one—Gerald perched before me, his one front paw curled under. He mewed as if he'd been waiting for me to wake up. He touched his nose to my eyelids, forehead, and lips as if trying to taste what had befallen here.

This time I made it to my knees, thinking I might crawl, but when I tried to put weight on my hands, waves of pain ripped through my torso. A low, deep grinding sensation made my vision darken. I slumped to the ground again, this time on my right side, facing away from the sun.

From this new view, I saw that the far side of the arena held a broad strip of lush grass. Moonshot was opting to stand near me rather than graze.

Don't panic. If nothing else, Gabriella would come home. 6 p.m. Maybe earlier.

Max sat up and barked, then bounded off. *That's right, boy. Be like Lassie. Go get help.*

Think of something else. I imagined myself boarding a plane. Going to visit Vijay in New York. I pictured the choreographed way the flight attendants mimed pulling those yellow oxygen masks over their heads. The way they'd say, in an almost admonishing tone, that you must secure your own mask first before attempting to help anyone else.

An image of Bobby holding out a spoon appeared to me.

Oh. Those oxygen masks. You had to put your *own* on first. You couldn't rescue anyone until you'd rescued yourself.

An image of my heartbroken daughter appeared to me.

Oh.

Max returned, still barking. I hoped. I waited. But no one materialized.

It's okay. I wasn't going to die. My daughter wouldn't return to find my body in the arena. The panic was near, though, circling like sharks. *Scritch-scritch-scritch.*

I craved water enough to try to shuffle on my knees. Nausea rolled over me, so I slid back to the sand and concentrated on Lamaze breathing. *I can't throw up.* Who knew how many hours

I had before I'd be discovered? If I got dehydrated and went into shock, I really could die.

Stop thinking like that. You're not going to die. You've obviously broken something.

What about you, Cam? Were you happy?

Stuck there, shivering, then sweating, I was desert-mouthed and riding waves of bone-grinding pain. Hunger growled in my belly. I'd known better. It had been willful, self-destructive. I'd known that grief and anxiety would push my metabolism soaring *even if* I ate properly, which I *hadn't*.

Had I really believed if I got thin enough, Bobby would return to feed me?

MOONSHOT WOKE ME, MUZZLING ALL ALONG MY BODY, HIS long whiskers tickling. The reins fell forward off his head, dragging on the ground. *Please, don't get a hoof stuck in that loop.*

The sharks bumped against me. My breath was shallow, my pulse too fast. I shivered.

Gerald resettled himself inches from my face, peering at me with his pale-green eyes. He'd spent *days* in a trap and he'd survived, I reminded myself. He began to purr. I knew cats purred not only in pleasure but also in times of stress and pain. Cats will purr in labor. He stared into my eyes and purred with ridiculous volume. I began to breathe in rhythm with the purrs. I entered into the purring, imagining it spreading warmth through me, radiating comfort through my torso. The sharks became peripheral and then faded as I concentrated on purring, like meditation.

Like prayer.

I don't know how long we purred together, Gerald and I. I lost myself in it until Max barked and ran away again. Muriel climbed the fence crying her bizarre shout. Gerald kept looking at me as if we were playing a game of Concentration. His purring never faltered. I tried to focus on him, not wanting to get my hopes up, but I was distracted.

When Max returned alone again, I closed my eyes and moaned. Gerald touched my cheek with his one giant boxing-glove paw, claws concealed, *Hey, pay attention*.

Max sat behind me, barking, the sound stabbing me. Moonshot whinnied. Biscuit answered. I tried to shush them, the sand gritty against my teeth. My head throbbed with Max's barking. Moonshot whinnied again. *Shut up, everyone*. How much time had passed?

Gerald dashed away, out of sight. Oh, God. Oh, no. What would I do without him? Max kept barking. "Shut up," I begged in a cracked old-lady voice.

"You talking to me?"

Gabby knelt before me in her suit, her face pale but resolute. "I called nine-one-one, Mom. When I first saw you. I looked up here when I heard Max barking."

Lassie. "Fell off. Broke something. Hurts to move."

"Oh, Mom. Mommy. What can I do? You're shivering. I'll go get a blanket."

"Yes, blanket. And water. But, first, could you put Moonshot back in his paddock?"

She'd kicked off her shoes and was barefoot in hose. She reached for his dragging reins. He lowered his head, standing still as she ran the stirrups up the leathers, but he balked when she tried to lead him away. "I . . . I don't think he wants to leave you."

My lips cracked as I smiled. "Okay. Just untack him."

She did, then returned with Biscuit's purple horse blanket. She draped me in dusty warmth and gave me sips from a water bottle. Heaven. "Could you take my helmet off, babe?"

She unsnapped my helmet and slid it off my head without moving me. Ah, blessed relief.

I heard the sirens in the distance. The worst was over.

But when Max barked and took off running, Gabby shouted, "We're up here, Dad!"

CHAPTER TWENTY

IF MY LIFE HAD BEEN A MOVIE, THIS WAS THE MOMENT Bobby would have dropped to his knees and said, "I made a horrible mistake. I want you back."

This was no movie. There was no going back, but our history counted for something.

Muriel put her front hooves on his shoulder and nibbled his hair. He shook his head, face pale and grim. Poor man always went to pieces when someone was hurt, so it surprised me when he was able to joke, "Goat's out."

The worst pain came with the paramedics.

Damn, but it hurt when they moved me. Bobby hovered, murmuring, "Oh, Cam." When I moaned, he held my hand. I clung to it and had a strange, vulnerable flash of giving birth.

He squeezed my hand.

In front of my daughter and soon-to-be ex-husband, I told the medics from the backboard, "I haven't eaten anything but one bite of calamari in probably three days, and not much for a couple weeks before that. I passed out from the back of that horse. Something popped when I hit the ground."

They began to scold me for not wearing a helmet, but Gabby set them straight.

They carried me the jolting, excruciating way to the driveway but then had to leave me there for about five minutes while they chased Muriel out of the ambulance.

They started IV fluids. I'd performed that procedure thousands of times myself and was grateful at how quickly I felt their effect. I listened to Bobby answer questions about insurance, my allergies, and history. I hated to picture Gabriella trying to navigate all of this alone.

At least there was no blood, so he could be helpful. Once, when Gabby was eight, she'd shut her fingers in the car door. Bobby had dropped to his knees, muttering what sounded like prayers in Italian while I wrapped her hand with ice and towels. "It's a long way from your heart," I told the brave, gasping Gabby, examining her fingers once the bleeding stopped. "You'll live." Gabby, who'd never gone into full-fledged tears over the injury, giggled and sniffed, but Bobby'd been pale and shaken all day.

One EMT reminded me that I'd need ID at the hospital.

"Bobby?" I asked, "could you go get my purse?"

"Sure. Where is it?"

"In the microwave."

"Uh . . . okay." I heard him ask Gabby as he stepped out of the ambulance, "Did she hit her head? Are you positive she had on that helmet?"

Gabby laughed. "I know that sounds alarming, but her purse actually is in the microwave."

"Why?"

"Long story." Then Gabby's voice hardened, "Maybe if you still lived here, you'd know it."

I closed my eyes. This was not my problem. The paramedic started some painkiller in my IV, so I quite willingly floated away.

TURNS OUT I HAD TWO BROKEN RIBS.

Not cracked, mind you, but *broken*, and slightly overlapping at the broken places.

I wished I'd had Gerald there to purr with me when they did the traction necessary to make the ends meet up again. I called on every colorful combination of the worst profanity I'd ever heard Bobby's family deliver.

Mimi showed up with Olive, followed shortly by my parents and the Davids. Helen and Hank, too. Then Aurora. My heart lifted when Tyler came with different clothes for Gabby to change into. She was still in her suit, her filthy hose in tatters.

Mimi patted my hand, humming. She kept saying, "It will all turn out fine."

Vijay strode into the room, looking only at me. "Oh, Cam." He took my hand, pushed back my dusty hair, and kissed my forehead.

Bobby stood. Vijay nodded to him but kept hold of my hand. He let go only when Gabby crossed to hug him and when my father came to shake his hand.

Fortunately, a couple of nurses and a PA recognized Vijay from his TV show and made a fuss, deflecting the tension. "Are you here for a story?" a nurse asked, looking gleeful.

"No, I'm here for a friend." He looked at Bobby. "But there *is* quite a story here, isn't there?"

Before anyone could speak, my own doctor returned.

"Okay," I said, wanting to simply get out of here. "What do you do for broken ribs?"

"Nothing," my doctor said. "You rest. You take it easy. You heal."

I looked up at my assembled posse. Vijay nodded. Gabby snorted. Helen arched an eyebrow. Davy put his hands on his hips. My mother pursed her lips.

"Don't say it," I begged.

Aurora shook her head. "Damn, but you like to do things the hard way."

EVERY TIME VIJAY LEFT THE ROOM—TO ANSWER A CALL, to talk to a doctor, to get me ice cream from the cafeteria—Bobby would take my hand. Were these guys going to plant flags next?

At one point, while we waited for "care and feeding" instructions—Vijay had gone to try to use his influence to speed things up—I found myself in the exam room with just Mimi, Bobby, Gabriella, and Tyler.

"Where'd you get that three-legged cat?" Bobby asked.

Gabriella's face lit up. "He came back?"

I smiled at Gabby. "He kept me company today."

Mimi snorted. "That's what you need like a goddamn hole in the head, a three-legged cat."

Bobby leaned close, intimate, in my space. "Cam. You can't collect every stray in need."

Is that what I did? Or what *he* did?

Mimi rubbed his arm. "You should move back in, Bobby. It's the right thing to do."

No, no, no. I *couldn't* collect every stray in need. I saw his need now. It was a need that I'd never fill, that Zayna couldn't fill. That a million puppies wouldn't fill.

Bobby didn't know how to love me unless I needed him.

"I could do that," Bobby said, looking back down at me. "For a while. To help."

Mimi beamed. I knew she believed "for a while" would become forever.

I closed my eyes. Why couldn't these painkillers knock me out?

"Could you all give us a minute?" Bobby asked.

Mimi and Tyler left quickly, but Gabriella stared at us for a moment before walking out.

"You're going to need help," Bobby said. His voice was kind.

I kept my voice kind as well. "You don't get to help me, sweetie. Not anymore." I returned to that prayerful calm of Gerald's purring. "I can't go from you packing your car and leaving to allowing you to care for me while I'm injured. The leap from A to B is too big. It asks me to act like A never happened. I can't make that leap. I . . . I'm really surprised that you can."

Bobby nodded, and when Vijay returned with the discharge nurse, Bobby quietly left.

ONCE HOME, THE INJURY GAVE ME THE PERMISSION I hadn't given myself to just unravel. I slept, usually at ten- to twelve-hour stretches at a time. I'd wake up with Gerald cuddled up to me. When I was awake, he'd work himself under my hands; the "self-petting cat," I came to call him.

I ran my hands over his shoulder, where the new coat growth

pleased my fingertips like velvet. We'd done a good job on that surgery.

Gerald hadn't stressed himself out pretending he still had all four legs, acting maniacally like his amputation had never happened. He'd acknowledged that he'd lost something and then set about learning how to move on without it.

Vijay stayed at the farm for three days before he had to return to New York. When he presented *saag* from his mother, I ate every last bite.

"Did you ask Bobby?" Vijay asked. "About working to fix things?"

I nodded.

"What did he say?"

I shook my head.

Instead of saying, "I told you so," or railing at Bobby, Vijay just said, "I'm sorry." He knew what I needed, he knew how much it hurt. Even if it was the right thing, he knew how horrifically it hurt.

My mother did laundry, helped me wash, and kept the pantry stocked.

The Davids came over daily, Davy on his way to school each morning. Big David stopped by on his way home from the bakery, bringing scones and watering plants.

Olive and Nick brought dinner and movies.

Hank made more mac 'n' cheese and called from work each day to entertain me.

Aurora handled Animal Kind on her own without complaint, and even though I knew the schedule had to slam her, she still found time to visit me almost daily.

Gabriella and Helen took care of the feeding and stalls.

Gabriella came in one evening odd and aloof. I was desperate for conversation, but she was monosyllabic in her responses. She sat on the couch, distractedly petting Max. "The crew okay?" I asked. I missed Moonshot.

She nodded.

I waited, and when she offered nothing else, I said, "You wanna eat with me?"

"I ate already." She looked only at Max. "Dad brought me some veal marsala."

Before I could think of a response, she said, with a defensive edge, "I invited him."

"You two could have eaten in the house, you know. He's allowed inside." It didn't trouble me so much that she'd invited him but that she hadn't told me, that neither of them had included me.

"Is he?" she said, her voice icy.

Keep breathing. "Gabriella, anytime you want to see your father, he's welcome here."

Her face contorted as she fought not to cry. "Why did you say no?" she wailed.

When I looked confused, she said, "At the hospital! He was going to move back in!"

Oh.

"You said no! We could've all gone back to normal."

I breathed as deeply as my ribs allowed. "Gabby, when your dad said he'd stay here, he meant temporarily, to help out while I recover."

"How do you *know?* If he were here, who knows what would happen?"

How much should I tell her? Would it help her? Hurt her? I felt like I walked a tightrope. "Did your dad tell you that he and I met for a talk the morning I fell?"

She shook her head.

I told her about our conversation. I tried to speak neutrally, just reporting the facts. I didn't tell her Zayna had been there.

My daughter studied my face. "Really? You would've let him come back and tried to fix it?"

I nodded. "I think we *could* have, but to be fair to your dad, I'm not sure that would've been right, for any of us. When you said we could go back to 'normal' . . . well, now that I've had some time to look at it, I don't think our normal was very healthy."

We were quiet a long time. I stroked Gerald, and Gabby stroked Max.

"I wasn't trying to be mean," I said. "I just don't think it's good for me to accept help from him. Remember how you told me to have some self-respect?"

She groaned and pulled her hair over her face. "I'm sorry!"

"No, no, no, you were right. I wouldn't feel good about myself letting him stay here. Okay?"

He would come here and do barn chores, sure. That was *easy*. He wasn't capable of or willing to do the harder work, the work that mattered.

After a long silence, Gabby asked, "Is it even *possible*? Marriage?"

I laughed, then winced at the pain.

"No, Mom, I'm serious. In Philosophy we just read this ridiculous Plato myth about how for every person there's a missing other half and you're never a complete person until you find it. That's just . . . bullshit. No *one* person is going to fulfill every single one of your needs. When did everyone start *believing* this crap? They stand there and say those vows that they'll cherish each other *until they die*. And nobody does. Nobody can."

"Some people can," I said. "Some people do."

"Like who?"

"Well, like your uncle Davids."

"They're not dead, Mom," she said, as if I were a moron.

Oh, so by Gabby's standards, Mimi and Frank had had a successful marriage just because one of them was now buried?

"I'm never getting married," Gabby said.

I smiled. I used to say that.

"I'm glad you're not like women who think they're not complete until they get married," I said. "That's why I used to hate it when you talked about your wedding all the time. But why say never? Don't you think that's a lonely way to live?"

Gabby gently pulled on Max's ears. "You think Aurora's lonely?" she challenged.

She'd caught me. Gabby had once wondered aloud to me if Aurora was lonely and I'd used the "teachable moment" to talk about how Aurora—one of the busiest, most accomplished and interesting women I knew—was content, complete, and unwilling to settle for a man who didn't enrich her life.

I laughed, then gasped at the pain the laughter produced in my ribs. "No. No, but remember Aurora has never claimed she wants to be single forever. She dates. She's just not willing to be with any ol' guy just to be with someone."

Gabriella shrugged. "Maybe I'll be like Aurora."

"Maybe you will. Or maybe someday you'll find a strong, competent partner—maybe Tyler, maybe someone you haven't met yet—and you're going to want to spend your life with him."

She kept her eyes on Max's ears. "Maybe."

"It was good to see Tyler at the hospital with you," I said. "Are you guys going out again?"

She shot me a look. "We're friends, okay?"

"Just friends?"

She didn't answer.

She kept looking at Max, holding his muzzle in her hands, stroking his face with her thumbs. "I miss Dad. I miss *us*. All of us together, the way we used to be." Then she said quickly, "I know, I know, you said the way we used to be wasn't all that hot, but it was . . . it was *easier*."

Those words set off a new pulsing ache in my broken ribs.

CHAPTER TWENTY-ONE

GABRIELLA WAS RIGHT. IT *HAD* BEEN EASIER TO LIVE WITH blinders on.

Easier . . . but not better.

I found there was more space and light in my thoughts. More room and energy in my head.

I felt as if I'd taken off a blindfold. I didn't know when, I wasn't sure why, but it was a blindfold I'd quite deliberately tied into place myself.

Vijay was right: Bobby had done me a favor.

After Vijay had to return to New York, I was touched by visits from his mother. Shivani would bring fresh flowers and massage lotion on my legs, because it hurt to bend.

"You and Vijay are both single now," she said. "I do not understand this way, this ending."

"I don't understand it, either," I said. "Not really."

Shivani rubbed lemon-scented lotion into my calves, an act that seemed strangely intimate and made me shy. "We must fatten you up, my girl. I will bring you your favorite."

"Oh," I said. "I *love* your halva." I longed for it with the fervor of a junkie.

Shivani nodded, businesslike, taking the order. "It should

not be," she said. "The two of you alone." She tilted her head at me as if trying to read something. I remembered that when Vijay and I were in school, Shivani had always called me their "other daughter."

Mimi swept the porch and took the "pails" (as she called the garbage cans) down to the road. She also vacuumed, mopped the kitchen floor, cleaned the bathrooms, and lectured me on how men "strayed" but it was our job as women to forgive them and guide them back.

Olive came over and helped me shower, gasping more at my ribcage than the shockingly deep bruise. "Oh, Cam, you're so thin again it's scary."

"I know," I said, to her surprise. "I'm fixing it."

Everyone brought food. Big David always brought a box from David's Hot Buns—my favorite scones, cinnamon rolls, marbled rye bread with orange molasses, cream horns.

I ate it. I ate it all.

This time I ate it for me.

THREE WEEKS AFTER THE ACCIDENT, VIJAY FLEW TO OHIO again, the second time in two months—a record for him.

The minute Gabriella left for school, I called Helen. "Can you come over before you go to work?" Helen helped me shower and blew dry my hair (it still hurt too much for me to hold my arms up). She even put earrings on me that Vijay had given me last Christmas. She helped me put on some mascara and lipstick. "God, you look better," Helen said, "now that you finally *slept*." She parted with "Remember what I said about post-breakup sex."

"Are you kidding me?" I said. "It hurts to *breathe*."

❧

VIJAY ARRIVED WITH A BUNDLE OF PURPLE GLADIOLAS, a box of Klondike ice cream bars, and a bag of books and movies—none of which I'd already read or seen. Ah, a man who remembered *details*.

He sat on the edge of my recliner. We ate two Klondike bars each, and he helped me fish a piece of the chocolate coating from my neck. His fingers there, along my collarbone, made me flush. When he found the piece, he held it out to me.

I opened my lips to say something—I wasn't sure what—and he placed the chocolate there. My lips closed, ever so briefly, on his fingers. I let the chocolate melt in my mouth.

Vijay stood, gathered the silver Klondike wrappers, and took them into the kitchen. My heart rapped against my aching ribs, but the pain was almost delicious. Was I crazy? Was Helen right?

When he came back, the mood had shifted, and I wasn't sure whether to be relieved or disappointed. He asked about my pain very professionally, what meds I was still taking, when I'd have a follow-up.

"Can I see?" he asked.

I hesitated, mottling. "I don't have— It hurt too much to put on a bra."

He laughed, his gorgeous white teeth flashing. "Please. I'm a doctor."

I liked that he waited, though, until I said, "Okay," before unbuttoning my denim shirt.

He left the top two buttons alone, and when he opened the shirt he left my breasts covered. He sucked in breath as if something had stung him.

"Hey, doctors aren't supposed to do that," I said. "It freaks your patients out."

When he touched the undamaged side of my ribcage with his fingertips, my skin shivered.

"This bruising," he murmured. I'd seen it in the mirror. Deep blue-black, a sickening red-purple underneath. It didn't look natural. It looked as if I'd dipped half my torso in ink.

He lifted the left side of my shirt, his eyes following the bruise up my ribcage. He leaned over to peer at the site, and the proximity of his mouth to my breast made my nipples contract.

Surely he could see my heart pounding through my chest. He lifted the rest of the shirt up to my neck, exposing both breasts, and then, to my held-breath surprise and delight, cupped my white, undamaged breast in his nutmeg-colored hand.

There was nothing diagnostic about his touch.

I thought I might melt into the couch.

"Is . . . is this ethical, Dr. Aperjeet?"

"I'm not *your* doctor."

He kissed me, his lips and tongue stealing back the taste of chocolate he'd salvaged for me. Only our lips touched, my injury looming fragile beneath us, and there was something luscious in knowing this was all we could do. The care the moment called for made it reverent.

"Hey," I asked Vijay the next day, after the delicate, careful kissing had moved on to other unbruised areas of my body, "What did that mean? That phrase you kept sending me?"

He narrowed his eyes, thinking.

"It starts '*harina harina*' or something like that."

His brown eyes lit with recognition. "Oh, that. It's Swahili. It means, 'Hurry, hurry brings no blessing.' "

Then he continued blessing me in the slow, unhurried way my current condition required.

I'D MISSED A SCHEDULED APPOINTMENT WITH ANOTHER attorney because of the accident. I'd called to explain, had apologized, and then had been amazed to discover I was talking to the lawyer herself, not a secretary. The woman answered her own phone. That seemed promising.

Sue Ellen Lippincott looked like she could be my grandmother. Her office was a cozy house, not at all like the slick attorneys' office I'd visited downtown.

Davy took half a personal day and drove me there. I spotted three different cats—one who sprawled on the lawyer's desk, belly up. Yes, this was the attorney for me.

Sue Ellen made me a cup of tea, then asked me about what had happened with Bobby. I realized I was tired of talking about it. Finally. That felt good.

"I want this divorce to be as clean as possible. I don't want to screw him over; I just want to protect my daughter and keep my farm."

She instructed me to make a list of our belongings and draw up a list of how I'd like to divide them. "You have to list everything. Anything of real value we'll need to discuss."

It felt wrong to move through the house, in my stiff, careful gait, filling a notebook with our possessions. Is this what a marriage came down to? Accumulated stuff?

The kitchen stopped me. All the pots and pans, the gadgets, the cookware, the spatulas and spoons should be Bobby's, right? But . . . without him in the house, I would have to cook.

I realized I *wanted* to. I'd wanted to all along.

Once, Bobby had come into the kitchen as I was pouring pasta into a colander, but instead of saying thanks he'd snapped that the pasta was ruined. The colander had no legs, so, temporarily, the pasta sat in its own water until it drained. What the hell was the big deal? It had been sitting in its own water seconds before on top of the stove, but Bobby threw it out.

He'd often taken knives from me in a condescending manner, as if I were a child. He'd added more salt or spices to anything I'd put on the stove. It'd always been good natured—"Oh, Cami can't boil water," that sort of thing . . . and it *was* true that twice I'd put broccoli in a steamer with no water beneath it, filling the house with the smell of char and ruining two good copper pans. We'd laughed about it, but now I felt insulted. I realized I'd been insulted at the time but had stuffed it down, because, as Gabby had pointed out, that had been easier.

Those memories made me list quite a few items from the kitchen I'd like to keep.

In the bedroom, I came across my wedding band and slid it on. How much would it be worth? The ring, with its four tiny sapphires and diamond, had belonged to his great-grandparents. They'd been named Roberto and Carmella, so inside the ring, our own initials, R & C, were already engraved, along with the words *Amore per sempre*.

When I tried to take it off, it stuck, and I had a moment of panic before I managed, with some flaming in my ribs from the effort, to pull it off.

❧

I TOOK TO MAKING MY TURTLELIKE WAY DOWN TO THE BARN in the mornings to sit in the barn lot. I'd bring a cup of coffee to watch the sun rise and the horses wake. Gerald always followed me, then sat on my feet. I noticed spiderwebs bejeweled with dew, deer rising from sleep in the far reaches of the pasture, and a mockingbird who surveyed the start of each day from our weathervane. One morning, six fat rabbits grazed on the hillside while Max lay at my side. "Some dog," I scolded.

I tried to be present with an open heart as the bones in my torso knitted and healed.

I prayed for the ability to forgive.

I began to find it. When I played with a twig and watched Gerald leap and twist to catch it—marveling at his agility in spite of his missing leg—I felt sorry for Bobby. He wasn't happy. Even with his little adoring waitress lover and their perfect puppy.

Most mornings I did wake up happy. This was enough—this goat trotting to greet me, tickling my legs with her beard.

This was enough—this gorgeous, wounded horse who'd protected me.

This was enough—my sleepy daughter sweeping the barn aisle. This amazing person in the world—Bobby and I had failed in many ways, but not in this. That made it impossible to hate him.

I also recognized I hadn't seen these things when I was with Bobby. I'd been too busy tending to *his* happiness, checking in on his moods, walking on eggshells around his gloominess.

I'd totally lost sight of what *I* wanted. I'd become the woman I'd never wanted to be; I'd become the woman I'd disdained my mother for being, but that she hadn't been at all.

———

I ached when I thought of Gabriella's statement: *I miss us. All of us together, the way we used to be.* I missed the idea of having a partner, someone in my corner, a soul mate. But Bobby had never really been those things. I'd spent lots of time and energy, oh so much energy, creating the myth that he was.

Which meant I now had a lot of free time and energy on my hands.

What was I going to do with it?

CHAPTER TWENTY-TWO

SHIVANI

SHIVANI APERJEET STOOD IN A HOT KITCHEN GRATING CAR-
rots to make *gajar ka halva* for her oldest son's birthday. Vijay,
who would be forty-three—forty-three!—had not asked her to
make halva, but she remembered how he always put his fingers
in it, plucking out the cashews and all the golden raisins.

Shivani wiped her forehead with the loose end of her fuchsia sari. The young ones, the grandchildren—although none
of them were Vijay's kids, which was not right, he was *forty-
three*!—would turn up their noses and complain that this was not
"real" pudding. Whoever told them halva was pudding? Shivani
kept on grating, the juicy, orange mound growing before her.
She remembered who. Rita. Vijay's wife.

Shivani snagged her knuckles on the grater. Not his wife.
Not now. She couldn't get used to saying "ex-wife." Forty-
three! He was forty-three and left a marriage just like that, the
way a person might toss out rattan furniture that wasps had
burrowed into.

She sucked the coin taste of her bloody knuckles and pictured
Vijay scolding her for using the metal grater. "Mom," he would
say, "why don't you use the food processor we bought you?"

Shivani picked up the last carrot and grated it down to a quarter-thin nub. She didn't *want* to use a machine. She didn't *want* it to be easy.

She scooped up the slick, orange gratings and plopped them into the gallon of whole milk waiting in the stockpot. She turned on the flame, lowered it to a hint of blue, then put her hands on top of the empty gallon jug. A marriage did not come with an expiration date like this gallon of milk. The idea was as foreign to her as the gas flame she could turn on twenty-four hours a day when she first came here.

The milk had already turned pale orange as Shivani wiped her forehead and under her eyes again. Now she must stir the halva for an hour or more, until the carrots drank up nearly all the milk. She remembered Rita's wide eyes. "An *hour?* No wonder this is never on the menu at Indian restaurants," she said. "It's too labor intensive." As if that were a bad thing. A reason not to make it. "If we turned up the heat, we could speed it up, right?"

Wrong. If you turned up the heat, you would scorch the milk on the bottom. Even if you peeled off the black strips, that ashy charred taste would remain. No. You must be patient. You must tend to the stockpot while the milk simmered and the carrots swelled over the low flame.

Shivani sighed. She'd been married by the time she was twenty. She knew her children were embarrassed to talk about their parents' arranged marriage. Shivani had known that would not be the path for her sons or even her daughter. She'd been happy for them, with their choices.

But their freedom had not done them any good. For all their

choices, for all their "practice"—Vijay and Rita had shared a home before the wedding—it had not protected or prepared them. Only Asheev was married now. Kinnari was thirty-five! She claimed there were no good men but was outraged when Shivani had offered to arrange some meetings with sons of their friends.

Shivani dropped eight cardamom pods into the orange milk. "I will marry for love," all of her children had declared. Did they think she hadn't? She and Lalit had love. But they loved the marriage as something far greater than just either one of them. She had not known what to say when Vijay told her of Rita, "This just isn't working. We don't make each other happy."

"Well, you must begin to," Shivani had told him, bewildered. Her son was an intelligent man!

Shivani would take more of this halva to Camden. It was she who would eat it, even cold from the refrigerator. It was she who had eaten it always, even during that nonsense in high school when she'd whittled herself down to the bones of a beggar child.

Camden Anderson without a husband. Shivani stirred and knew the wish in her heart.

Shivani and Caroline had wished for it back in the college days. Even Lalit didn't mind the idea of their pale dark-haired children. They suited each other. And they were *friends*, which is what mattered beyond all else. "I will marry for love," they'd all declared.

She snorted. Couldn't they see the deep love, the enduring love, the real love that was already there? Ah, these movies that gave them such ridiculous notions of romance!

She stirred the thickening milk, now a rich, reddish color. Her back ached from standing, but there was still much time to go before she could melt the ghee in a skillet and brown the cashews.

Lalit came into the kitchen. She took in his white temples, the hair that grew so abundantly from his ears, the owlish look to his eyes behind such thick glasses. "Ahh, halva," he said. He stood beside her and kneaded the small of her back, that open patch between the bottom of her shirt and the top of her petticoat, just where she ached. Shivani leaned into his touch.

"This will be good," Lalit said, with certainty.

"It *is* good," Shivani said. She turned her sweaty face up to his and kissed him.

CHAPTER TWENTY-THREE

VIJAY CAME BACK AS OFTEN AS HE COULD DURING THAT long summer of my recovery, sometimes for little over twenty-four hours before flying back to New York (or on to Accra or Gaborone or Harare). There was safety in the fact that we couldn't actually be lovers yet.

"Maybe we shouldn't be each other's rebounds," I said. "That's always a disaster."

He played with the inside of my wrist. "I don't think anything about us getting into bed together would be a disaster."

"You've been my friend for so long," I said to him. "What if we mess it up?"

"You worry too much," Vijay said. "Why would we mess it up?"

"Promise, then. No matter what happens to us as a couple, we'll stay best friends."

"I promise."

My ribs felt better much sooner than my doctor or the emergency team had predicted. I swore by the healing properties of fabulous kissing, the presence of horses, and the halva Shivani brought over (and that Vijay fed to me with his fingers).

GABRIELLA HAD ALWAYS LIKED VIJAY. HE'D OFTEN BEEN A guest in our home, so having him around wasn't an unusual occurrence for her. We were discreet, and he slept in the guest room. When she saw us together, we were as comfortable as we'd always been. She milked his medical knowledge for all he was worth, drilling him on stem cell research, partial birth abortion, and AIDS policies.

"You like Vijay, don't you?" she asked one morning as we both ate breakfast.

"Of course I like him. He's been my best friend since I was six!"

"No, you know what I mean. You *like* him—like him, don't you?"

No matter what I said, that splotchy blush spoke for me. "I think I do. Yes."

I held my breath, but she grinned. "It's obvious he likes you."

"*Likes* me—likes me?"

"Hello? He worships you!"

I felt I was blushing even inside, so delectable was this thought. "Are you okay with that?"

"Of course!" she said. "You should be happy."

I looked at her. "What about you? Tyler worships you. Shouldn't *you* be happy?"

"You know what, Mom?" She stood up from the kitchen island and put her dishes in the dishwasher. "You think I broke up with Ty because of you and Dad. But maybe I broke up with him because we've been going out since sixth grade and I thought it was time to date someone else."

Oh, I hated when she threw my own arguments back at me.

I *liked* Tyler. I had not one single thing against Tyler except for the fact that for years my daughter's love for him had given her tunnel vision about her options.

I should be rejoicing. I should feel relieved.

But I didn't believe her.

DAVY BEGAN TO PICK ME UP IN THE MORNING AND DRIVE ME to work. I could at least do paperwork and diagnostics and let the vet techs and assistants do most of the manual labor. I wanted to relieve Aurora as much as possible, plus help the clinic bring in more money.

I especially liked letting Tyler assist me. He was excellent at knowing exactly how I could move and how I couldn't.

As I listened to a puppy's heart—a wriggling puppy Tyler held still for me—I looked at the blue shadows smudging Tyler's eyes.

In between appointments, I asked him how he was doing.

"I just . . . I wish I knew what I'd done wrong. If she'd just tell me, then I could fix it."

Since hugging him was physically impossible, I closed the exam room door and turned to him. "Tyler, you didn't do *anything* wrong."

"But I—"

"Did she say that?"

"No, no, she said it wasn't me, it was her, but—"

"You know what I've learned? And don't forget, I'm in your exact shoes."

His cheeks pinked a bit.

"If someone says it's not you, *believe them*."

❦

HELEN CALLED ME AT THE CLINIC. "YOUR MOONSHOT HAS a name. I have his papers in my hand. And guess what? I was right—there's a Satan connection. His registered name is Devil May Care."

I blinked. "Devil May Care? Is he— Sounds like he's sired by Devil Made Me Do It."

Devil Made Me Do It was a Kentucky Derby winner, currently the highest-paid stud in the country.

"He is," Helen said. "This horse is *valuable*."

I bristled. "I already knew that."

"This is going to court. And it doesn't look good."

I started to protest, but Helen interrupted me. "There's another sister who wants them. Ginger Avalon. She wasn't involved in the—"

"*What* is her name?"

"I know, I know, it's ridiculous. She sounds like a porn star. It's like that game, where you use the name of your first pet and the name of the first street you lived on to find your porn name."

"Please," I said. "I can't let a porn star take this horse."

But Helen didn't laugh. "The porn star wasn't involved in the abuse. Cami, I'm on your side. You know I am. I'm just saying, friend, don't get too attached."

Too late.

Way too late.

THE IDEA OF MORE POTENTIAL LOSS MADE ME GET PITBULL-ish about the farm when Bobby's attorney pushed. I was not letting go.

The wedding ring finally came up. That ring was worth *much* more money than I'd known all those eighteen years I'd worn it. I'd had it appraised, nearly choking when the jeweler told me the high five-figure sum.

I already knew from Sue Ellen that legally I had to return the ring—it was a family heirloom. I assumed Bobby's attorney had told him this, too, which is why one night at the farm visiting Gabriella, Bobby tentatively brought it up.

"That ring is worth a lot of money," I said, "which is exactly what you're asking me for right now, expecting me to give up my home."

He never mentioned it again. I bought Bobby out of the farm, giving him half the equity in the place already. When I wrote the check and presented it to him, I knew he thought it was the ring's money I was handing him. I let him believe that.

The day we divorced, the ring was still safely tucked away under piles of my underwear.

DO YOU KNOW HOW EASY IT IS TO GET DIVORCED? I HAD NO idea. Depressingly easy.

Everyone called while I was getting dressed (a process that still took twice as long as before my injury)—Vijay, Olive, Helen, my brother, my parents, Aurora—offering me support, volunteering to go with me to the courthouse.

I declined their offers but was filled with gratitude. As I headed into the court building, I turned off my phone. I'd do this alone, but I felt loved and surrounded walking in.

The hallway was packed with other couples ending their marriages. I couldn't stop watching an older couple—they looked my parents' age—who both read novels while they sat in the hall, as if they were in a doctor's waiting room.

Before I knew it, we were "up." A bailiff ordered everyone into lines and used such terms as "in the hole" and "on deck," which made me think of horse shows and waiting your turn to jump. "Here we go," my father always cheerfully said as he trotted from the "on deck" warm-up ring into the stadium. I thought it myself as we were ushered into the courtroom. *Here we go.*

It was such an assembly line, though, that we stood in the courtroom and watched two other couples divorce before we were moved—all of it carefully choreographed—to stand in front of the grandmotherly judge ourselves.

"Do you agree to the terms set forth here?" The judge peered over her turquoise bifocals.

"I do," I said.

"I do," Bobby said.

Our wedding vows in reverse.

We signed our names.

And that was that.

Our attorneys whisked us back into the hallway and told us to wait while they made copies of our divorce decree. When they returned, we all shook hands, and then we left, walking out the front door together, into a summer morning with a chicory-blue sky.

Bobby and I paused at the crosswalk, where we turned to each other. Bobby shoved his hands into his pockets and kicked at the sidewalk with his toe. *He looks like a little boy*, I thought. *Binky.*

The moment turned into another.

"Have a nice life." I said it as kindly as I could, then I started walking. When I looked at my watch I was shocked to see the entire procedure had taken less than twenty minutes!

Once in the car, I began calling everyone, as I'd promised. Davy answered with "I can drive right over. I took a personal day, just in case."

"Aw." This touched me. "But it's over. The whole thing was frighteningly efficient. Could've been a drive-through."

Olive had wanted to meet me for breakfast. I had to call her and ask to move it a full forty minutes earlier. When I got to the café, it felt good to sit down; my ribs were throbbing.

I was sick of talking about the divorce. Rather than feeling bitter or sad, I wanted to look forward, so when Olive plopped into the chair across from me, I asked about her and Nick's wedding plans and said, "Let me know if I can do anything for the big day, okay?"

Olive made that smoke-ring mouth. "Are you kidding me? You're my maid of honor! I was yours and you're gonna be mine. We've talked about that for years."

I swallowed my latte too fast, burning my mouth. "B-but, I mean, now that Bobby and I—"

"This is not about my stupid-ass brother. This is about me. This is my day. This is how I always pictured it, and I'm not changing my mind just because my brother went insane."

"I'll actually get to be the *maid* of honor," I joked.

Olive laughed. "That's right! See, how perfect? No frumpy ol' *matron* for you!"

I looked at her round cheeks, those long outrageous lashes,

like her brother's. What she was attempting was so *hard*. I wanted her to be happy. I wanted Olive and Nick to get it right. On the morning of my divorce, I wanted to be a part of this couple attempting to take it on. I swore I could almost hear sappy music in the background, or a scene from some grown-up version of *Peter Pan*—I *do* believe in marriage! I *do* believe in marriage! And the dying institution rallying to life like poor Tinker Bell's light growing brighter and brighter.

Almost.

But I couldn't shake that doubt that Gabriella might be right.

CHAPTER TWENTY-FOUR

OLIVE MADE AN APPOINTMENT FOR OUR FIRST FORAY INTO wedding dress shopping.

I'd been taken aback to learn she was going for the white dress, the giant wedding party, the whole nine yards. "Just because I'm over forty doesn't mean I can't have the wedding I want," she said. "I've dreamed about this my entire life."

Just like Gabby used to draw designs of her wedding dress and buy *Brides* magazine.

Maybe it was time girls had something different to dream about?

My torso ached from being back at the clinic, but I went anyway, determined to be a good sport. Olive seemed much more wedding savvy than I'd been. Salespeople had been disbelieving at my lack of an answer whenever they asked me, "What had you pictured your wedding day to be like, as a little girl?"

I *hadn't* pictured it, and the question only conjured images of those ridiculous play weddings in the barn, wearing that prom dress—yellow under the arms and gray at the hem.

All the wedding gowns I'd tried—even the one I ended up with (which Davy had found for me in a vintage boutique)— felt like costumes for a play I'd underrehearsed.

The saleswoman cooed and fluttered over Olive's ring. "He must love you very much."

I expected Olive to bristle, as much as I did, but she beamed. What did this woman know about Nick's love for Olive? The ring was a just a *purchase*, no way to tell if he loved her or not.

I remembered my own exasperation with my ring, that ring now hidden in my lingerie drawer. The way total strangers had felt free to comment on its beauty, its worth—and therefore my worth to Bobby—was when I'd become aware of how *public* marriage is, what a huge community ritual it represents.

As I shopped with Olive, my bare left hand bugged me like a pebble in my shoe. Whenever the conversation forced me to reveal I was divorced, I sensed the slightest bit of recoil, as if I were tainted, or worse—contagious. I caught myself intention-ally talking about Vijay in front of the saleswomen. I even called him "my boyfriend" and found myself saying, "my boyfriend—he's a doctor," inwardly rolling my eyes at myself. But I'd gotten swept up in what I'd forgotten—that just showing up and shop-ping for gowns puts you in a sorority, a sisterhood, a *tribe*, and that all these women rooted for you, *approved* of you, and took care of you. *Welcome to the club.* Being there, clearly not a mem-ber in good standing, made me feel like an outcast. Then pathetic for falling for it. Then angry for the fact I felt pathetic.

The intellectual part of me could rationalize it, see it for what it was. But the emotional part of me thought of my childhood pony, Roscoe. Roscoe had needed a winter blanket when he was old and no longer grew a healthy winter coat. The other horses had turned against him in that blanket. They'd tormented him, yanking on the blanket with their teeth, even chasing him.

In spite of their bullying, Roscoe had been miserable alone in a paddock, even one adjoining the others. I knew he would've rather been blanketless and wretchedly cold than alone. Belonging to that herd was everything.

ON THE MORNING THAT THE BINARDI CLAN ARRIVED TO help move Bobby's things, I left the farm. I stayed away until Gabby called to say they were done and she was going to lunch with them.

When I returned, I steeled myself before entering the house. Spaces on the walls where paintings used to be. Furniture gone. In the kitchen, Bobby had taken his share of things, but it did seem that his presence was still there. It still felt like a room I entered as a guest.

Standing there, though, I looked outside and saw Muriel moving through the front yard in what could only be described as a dance, skipping, leaping, and striking out with her front cloven hooves. Whimsical and joyous. I had a revelation: I could do whatever I wanted. And what I wanted was to make this kitchen mine.

It took me ten minutes to form a plan, then I drove off to Lowe's to buy paint.

I enlisted the help of Gabby, the Davids, Helen and Hank, and Aurora (who jokingly complained, "Didn't we just paint the clinic?"), and it took two days to complete the job, but I— or rather, they, with their healthy ribs—created the kitchen I wanted. We covered the staid cream, painting each wall a different color to match the Fiestaware I loved (which had been relegated to a bottom cupboard because Bobby said food presented best on plain white plates): a juicy tomato red, a turquoise, a bright sunflower gold, a lime green. The Portuguese tile was stunning in this setting.

The kitchen was now as whimsical and joyous as my dear little white goat.

ONE WEEKEND WHEN VIJAY WAS IN TOWN FOR FORTY-eight hours and his parents had a party, we cooked at their house. I watched Vijay make *saag* without a recipe, chopping fresh spinach on a wooden block. I admired his angular cheek-bones, the slope of his nose, his graceful hands working the knife. "You are so incredibly sexy," I whispered.

He turned off the flame and walked toward me. It seemed as if he were going to pass me and walk out into the party, but he took my hand and pulled me—gently—into the pantry, where he pressed me against the shelves lined with bags of rice, spices, and *dahl*. He kissed me. We groped and fondled each other as best we could. I didn't care that my own parents, much less Vijay's, plus a ton of other people, were just a room away from us. But when Vijay reached around me, the slightest pressure on my ribs stole my breath with a yelp.

"I'm sorry. I'm sorry. Are you okay?" he whispered.

I nodded but couldn't stop the tears in my eyes. Damn. It *hurt*. I pressed a hand to my ribs. "God, when will these be healed? I can't stand it!"

"Vijay?" We heard Shivani's voice and froze like high-school kids.

"Yeah, Mom," he said. He reached behind me, picked up a bag of rice, and walked out as if he'd come into the pantry for that alone. I followed, after adjusting my shirt and running fingers through my hair.

Shivani spoke to Vijay about the *saag* and asked him to get more wine from the basement when he had a chance. She didn't seem to have noticed a thing, but on her way out of the kitchen, she nodded toward the pantry, lifted a lush eyebrow, and said sweetly, "Your ribs are better, yes? I am glad."

CHAPTER TWENTY-FIVE

※

My ribs slowly mended as summer came to a close. I found myself the mother of a high-school senior. How the hell did that happen? A high-school senior applying to Harvard who wanted to be an attorney before she became president.

The start of the school year coincided with Helen's birthday. Hank planned a "rib fest" birthday party for Helen at their house, joking that "rib fest" had a double meaning that year.

Vijay had to change his flight twice, but he finally made it and we arrived at the party late but in time for the decadent food. Squeezed in shoulder to shoulder we slurped down tender ribs, corn on the cob, and watermelon doused in vodka.

Hank stuck candles in the peach cobbler (compliments of Big David), we sang, and Helen blew out the candles, everyone urging her, "Make a wish! Make a wish!"

She looked at Hank and smiled a little kid smile. "One of my wishes has already come true."

Hank kissed her cheek.

After we'd moaned over the warm cobbler and homemade vanilla ice cream, Big David pushed back his plate and put both hands on the table as if about to make an announcement. "Okay," he said. "We have some good news. We—"

"Oh, my God! You got picked!" Gabriella said.

"Aagh! *I* wanted to say it!" Big David said. "But yes—we got selected by a mother!"

I couldn't speak. Something pressed against my ribcage, the pain exquisite. Vijay squeezed my hand. "I'm so happy for you," I choked out. "This is wonderful! Yay, Helen," I said. "Thank you, thank you."

Helen lifted her shoulders, looking shy. "Actually," she said to the cobbler crumbs on her plate. "This had nothing to do with me."

"Helen is great for understanding," Davy said. "We found another attorney, not through the agency. We were only trying to increase our chances. He just made it happen sooner."

"Tell us everything!" Gabriella said.

It didn't take much prompting before Davy was reciting, as well as anyone can speak clearly with a gigantic smile on his face, "The mother's name is Kim. She's nineteen, not married, already has two kids and doesn't think she can handle a third. She works at Kroger, but she's been going to school at Sinclair to be an X-ray technician, so she can provide better for the kids she already has. An infant, obviously, is going to keep her from going to class. She worries it will interfere with all the progress she's made."

I winced at the word *interfere*. How many times had I been asked to euthanize a healthy cat simply because it peed outside the litter box? At least this woman, this Kim, bless her, was not going that route. She was opting to let my baby brother be the dad I knew he was born to be.

Davy still beamed. "And she chose us!"

"When we met with her and her mom," Big David said, "being gay never even came up. They asked us about income, about our house, about our family traditions—"

"About holidays," Davy said, "and who would be with her during the day and how we'd—"

"Her?" I asked.

They both nodded, eyes shining.

"I'm going to have a cousin!" Gabby said. "A little girl cousin! What are you going to name her?"

"Brooke," Davy said at the exact same moment Big David said, "Nicole."

Everyone laughed.

"We don't have that much time to decide," Davy said. "Kim is almost eight months along."

"So," Gabriella said, "are her two other kids my cousins, too?"

The Davids looked at each other, as if for an answer. Davy shrugged. "I honestly don't know. We'll have to sort all that out."

"It just seems like it will be so confusing," Gabriella persisted.

Neither of the Davids looked at all angry, fortunately, but I was mortified.

"A toast," Vijay said, coming to the rescue. He raised his glass. "To this new family."

I touched his knee, grateful.

After the toast, Gabriella asked, "Whose last name will she have?"

"Mine," my brother said. "I'll be the adoptive father first, since I have better benefits. Then David will have to adopt her, too, but we can't do it together, as a couple."

KATRINA KITTLE

That knowledge put a momentary chink in the happiness but wasn't enough to drown the fact that they were *going to be fathers*. They may have to jump through extra hoops, but they were *doing it*.

A BABY. I DREAMED ABOUT HAVING ANOTHER BABY THAT night. In my dream, it was little, like a kitten, and slippery. It kept sliding out of my grip like a bar of wet soap.

I woke up and padded down the hall to the guest room where Vijay slept. The door was open a hand's width (we had to leave doors open because Gerald, for whatever reason, hated a closed door and yowled and pounded with his one front paw until it was open). I stood in the doorway, my face in the opening, and listened to the sound of Vijay's deep sleeping breaths.

The Davids would have the baby they'd dreamed of. A *baby*. Did *I* want another? Or was that only part of the Vijay fantasy? I tried to picture my life again with interrupted sleep, interrupted meals, interrupted conversation.

A vivid memory flashed into my head. In my first year of marriage, I'd already had doubts. I wore an orange wool sweater and had been riding on an early spring morning, steam rising from the leftover piles of gray snow. At that moment, with the snow mist and the itchy wool, I'd felt flawed in some way, incapable of loving anyone forever. That belief made me desolate to learn I was pregnant. Each pound I gained felt like an anchor, trapping me in my mistake.

But then . . . how do I describe it? The overwhelming, buoying love I felt for my daughter *immediately*. She proved that I did have it in me to love someone as long as they lived, or even after. I loved Bobby more than I ever had for making it possible for me to know this about myself.

The Davids were going to experience this love that ripped you wide open and defenseless.

This man, sleeping here in the very room where my husband had told me he was leaving—did we have it in us to love like that?

"Whatcha doing?" Vijay whispered from the darkness.

"Breathing you," I whispered back. *Breathing your intent.*

"Come breathe me closer."

So I did.

THE THIRD WEEK OF THE NEW SCHOOL YEAR, WHILE GA-briella and her friend Amy worked on their college application essays in my kitchen, my daughter presented me with an invitation to a baby shower for the Davids.

"What do you think?" she asked. "Our AP History class came up with the idea."

"No," Amy said, looking pointedly at Gabriella. "*Tyler* came up with the idea. It just happened to be in History."

Gabriella looked momentarily sunburned but shrugged.

I looked down at the pink card in my hand. "You are invited to a baby shower for the impending adoption of one lucky girl by Mr. Anderson and Mr. Neumeister."

I took a deep breath, something my ribs were allowing more and more. "How can I help?"

"We've got it covered," Gabriella said. I saw this belonged to her.

"Actually, we could use some help with the food," Amy said.

"I'll help with food," I said.

"You don't cook," Gabriella said.

I prickled but tried not to show it. "I *can* cook." *Of all the jobs, it had to be food?*

"I've never seen you make anything. That's Dad's thing."

Was that a dare? "I'll do the food. I'd like to. What do you need?"

Gabriella looked skeptical, but Amy jumped in. "Mostly finger foods. You know, appetizers."

"I can do that. How many people?"

"A hundred were invited," Gabriella said, still fixing me in her steely gaze.

"But only sixty have RSVP'd yes so far," Amy said.

Sixty? What had I just committed myself to? "Sixty people at a baby shower?"

"Everybody loves Mr. Anderson," Amy said.

When Amy bent over her essay again, Gabriella said, "You can just cater it, you know."

Well, I'd be damned if I catered it. I could do this. I could do appetizers, for God's sake.

So what appetizers did I know how to make?

There was a recipe I loved from my childhood called "Hanky-Pankies"—a savory cheese-and-sausage mix baked on squares of toast. Mom used to make them at my parents' postshow and posthunt cocktail parties, along with little wienies and other such things that made Bobby sneer.

I used to eat myself sick on those Hanky-Pankies as a child. Davy and I would lie upstairs and peer down the heating vent, looking at the tops of the guests' heads. Whenever possible, one of us would sneak down and bring back plates full of goodies.

So that brought my list to: Hanky-Pankies.

I was in trouble. But admit it? Not my style.

I had a brilliant idea, if I may say so myself—Big David's mother, Ava, was the Appetizer Queen.

AVA'S HUSBAND, MYRON, HAD DIED BEFORE I KNEW BIG David. When I first met Ava, she lived in a tiny two-bedroom apartment on a fixed income but managed to throw legendary dinner parties for miniscule amounts of money. Those parties in Ava's apartment, before she moved in with the Davids (when she started leaving the burners on or her door wide open), were sweaty, too-crowded affairs filled with laughter. And the food? Divine. Even Bobby had admired her food, although he called it "kitschy."

When you arrived, Ava would fix you a cocktail (she loved her Bombay Sapphire gin, and the way to her heart was to arrive bearing a new bottle), then usher you into the second bedroom, which was always the Appetizer Room.

She made bourbon wienies bubbling in a warmer, meatballs to rival Mimi's (although I never said this to Bobby), a spicy dip called Jezebel—cream cheese with a hot, peppery sauce over it—and my favorite, "egg on egg," a fabulous molded egg salad adorned with black caviar.

I'm sure her main courses were excellent, but I ate myself to oblivion on her appetizers.

THE DAVIDS WERE THRILLED WHEN I ASKED TO COME OVER and look at recipes with Ava. "Could you stay with her an hour or two?" Davy asked. "We need to do some baby shopping."

Baby shopping. The hair stood on my arms and my heart fluttered.

"The only thing better than being at a party is planning one," Ava said when I told her why I wanted her recipes. Then she frowned. "Oh, dear. I don't have things for a baby theme. Hmm." She put one finger across her lips, then clapped her hands. "We'll use my Valentine's Day things. Come on." Ava led me down the basement steps to three tubs full of pink tablecloths, pink napkins, pink serving dishes, and heart-shaped trays. I could hardly believe the coup.

Ava wanted to look through other boxes, too, so I let her while I went upstairs and thumbed through a faded red gingham binder containing the goldmine of her appetizer recipes.

When I returned to the basement, Ava sat, cross-legged, on the floor, surrounded by papers and photos. "Come look," she said.

I sat on the floor beside her. Wedding photos. "Oh, Ava. Look at you."

"So young and skinny," she said wistfully.

In the photo, she wore a tea-length dress and held the hand of a tall, bearlike man. The two descended the church steps, rice raining all around them. Ava looked at the crowd, laughing, while Myron looked at her, his pride and joy unmistakable.

"Are you glad you got married, Ava?" I asked.

Ava laughed a little trill. "What a question! Of course I am. Gladder about that than anything else in my life."

———

I was surprised. "What about having children?"

Ava frowned. "Oh. I'm supposed to say that was better, aren't I? You won't tell, will you?" Before I could answer, she asked, "Now, did I have two or three?"

"Children?"

She nodded.

"Two. David and Carol."

"No . . . seems to me there's three."

Was she remembering a child who'd died? "I've only met two."

"Oh, well." She waved her hand cavalierly as if she were talking about pets or teachers. "That was hard. Having those children. I don't think I was a very good mother."

I corrected her, even though I knew she spoke the truth. "You were a very good mother."

"Really?" Her voice went high and girlish. "How do you know?"

"David and Carol say so."

"What about the other one?"

"I've never met her."

"Him. It's a him. I wish I could remember his name." She picked up another photo.

David and Carol had said nothing of the kind. Ava had been high strung and distant. She'd melted down at David's coming out, calling the Davids in the middle of the night crying, "What did I do wrong? Why are you doing this to me?"

"He made bread, you know," Ava said.

"David does," I agreed.

"No, no. Myron. Myron made bread every evening, for the family. He could whip up a loaf quick as a cat could wink its eye. Every day. That's how we decided love would be. You have to make it fresh every day. Oh, dear. That sounded naughty! I don't mean *make love* every day, although he would've been very happy to do that, too. Goodness. No, I mean, you had to decide to love every single day. If you did, you could do quite well, no matter who you married."

Really. Was it that simple?

"All those weddings we went to. I could tell right away who had a shot at lasting. So many weddings. I'd take the cake."

Yes, you do, I thought. *You take the cake.*

"Yes, ma'am," Ava said. "The worst was when you'd know they *would* last but shouldn't."

"What do you mean?"

"Not every marriage that lasts should be celebrated." Before I could even react, Ava set down the photos and put her hand on my knee. "And not every marriage that ends is a failure."

My scalp lifted in goose bumps. Footsteps sounded above us. "We're down here!" I called.

Both the Davids came tromping down the stairs.

"Cool," Davy said, sitting on the floor with us. "I've never seen these." He sifted through photos, chuckling. He looked up at me. "We used to *play* wedding, remember?"

"You did. I tried to avoid it." I told Big David and Ava, "Davy was usually the bride."

"You *were?*" Big David asked. Even Ava giggled.

Davy picked up the wedding photo. "Lucky you, Ava. Myron sure was a good-looking man."

Ava's smile faded. She stammered a moment, then asked shyly, "Myron?"

With exquisite tenderness, Davy said, "Your husband."

"I . . . I don't know who— I'm not married." In a matter of seconds, she had changed from her classy, witty self to an old lady with Alzheimer's. "I don't know who you're talking about."

"It's okay, Mom," Big David said. "We know you're not married anymore."

"Is . . . is he here? Myron?" She looked around the basement and up the stairs.

"Nobody's here but us—you, me, Davy, and Cami."

"I don't feel well." Ava stood, photos and letters falling off her lap. "I want to lie down."

The Davids exchanged a brief glance. I'm not sure what passed between them, but it was my brother who stood and said, "Let me help you, Ava." He followed her up the stairs.

I reached across the pile of photos and took Big David's hand. "I don't want that to happen to me," he whispered. "I don't want to be alive for one single minute and not know I'm with Davy."

CHAPTER TWENTY-SIX

$\mathscr{R}$

DAVY

WHEN DAVY FOLLOWED THOSE PINK HELIUM BALLOONS UP to his classroom, he stood gaping. "Wow. My room," he said. "Wow."

The desks were pushed together to make banquet tables, covered in pink tablecloths. More pink cloth was draped from the ceiling in canopy-like loops, the way Bobby hung fabric at Tanti Baci. Baby mobiles hung from the intersections of every loop.

Gabby ran to greet them both with huge hugs. "Mrs. Bair brought in the crib. Isn't it cool?"

Very cool. Tanya Bair taught science in the room next to his (and he bet it was her oven that was being used by whoever catered the food he'd smelled all the way downstairs). The crib she'd brought was an old, white, sleigh-style one now piled high with wrapped gifts.

His room had been transformed. He looked at David and realized that this shower also transformed the two of *them* into something else.

The shower was everything their "wedding" hadn't been. Everyone who'd come to their wedding had known it wasn't real. They had a nice ceremony, threw a killer party, but it hadn't meant anything in any legal or societal way. There was no officiant, no license, no announcement in the paper. All during the planning, he'd felt a little like the kid he'd been playing dress-up wedding in the barn lot, just with a grander budget.

But the shower, now, *that* was real. They'd registered at major no-joke stores. Suddenly, his colleagues—those who'd always been good to them and even those who'd *never* been good to them (Tanya Bair had displayed a "Protect Ohio Families" sign in her yard, supporting the ban on same-sex marriage, and don't think he'd ever forget that)—treated them differently. Davy had to admit he loved every minute of the belated acceptance.

Gabby shushed everyone for a toast. She lined up Tyler and Amy, reminding Davy of Cami as a kid—always bossing everyone around, "directing" them. Gabby nodded at Tyler, who said, "This day is to honor you and the important journey you're about to embark upon—oops, sorry, Mrs. Wilcox: the journey upon which you are about to embark." Everyone laughed.

Amy spoke next. It touched Davy that they'd *rehearsed* this. "We know how much Mr. Anderson has affected our lives just in the fifty minutes he sees us each day," Amy said. "So, we know how the two of you will affect the life of this little girl."

Davy took David's hand. *We're going to have a little girl.*

Gabby finished the toast: "This little girl not yet in the world—but being awaited by so many people—is one of the luckiest little girls I know. Here's to her two daddies."

"Cheers!" "Here, here!" and "To the Davids!" rang out.

"And when is this baby supposed to arrive?" Tanya called out.

In unison, he and David answered, "Friday." More laughter.

"Not that we're counting," Davy said.

But they were. They had been counting for years. *Friday.* Six days, counting today. Six days and their lives would completely change.

Davy'd known he wanted to be a father since he was a kid—he'd cared for all of his sister's abandoned stuffed toys, taking them in like foster children. Ever since he'd met David, he'd known David was the one he wanted to have a family with.

Gabby directed everyone to begin eating. The food smelled incredible, and Davy was starving after his eight-mile run that morning. Cami slipped an arm around his waist just as he recognized the Hanky-Pankies. "Look what Mom made! Oh, my God, I love these!"

"Mom didn't make them," Cami said as Aurora, Hank, and Helen encircled them. "I did."

Davy closed his eyes, savoring one. "Remember how Bobby said these look like vomit?"

Everyone laughed.

"Who catered the rest?" Davy asked.

"I did," Cami said.

His jaw dropped. He held up a Hanky-Panky. "You mean, you made more than these?"

Cami's chin lifted a little, and he saw the little kid still in her.

"Everything but the cake," Hank said.

"I had help," Cami said. "Thank God. What was I thinking? These guys saved me this morning."

"Nah," Aurora said. "You had it. You just needed some sous-chefs."

"Whatever," Helen said. "We saved you and you owe us."

Davy thought his sister looked downright giddy. She *glowed*.

He leaned close to her. "Sis, you have something on your fore-head." Some orange smear edged her hairline.

Helen peered at Cami's face and laughed. "Oh, my God! It's bourbon wienie sauce!"

Cami almost cried with laughter. She put her arm around Davy again. "It was a little crazy getting this food here," she said. "My kitchen is a train wreck." She nodded to the Hanky-Pankies. "So, *enjoy* it."

"I am," Davy said. "I am." This food, from his sister, was such a gift, it truly touched him in a way not even the pile of pink-wrapped gifts in that crib did. He gazed at her for a mo-ment, thinking what a strong, kick-ass fighter she was.

Before he could figure out how to say this to her without sounding like a sap, Mimi and Olive interrupted them.

"Congratulations," Olive said, kissing Davy on the cheeks. "My God, it smells *favoloso*."

Davy watched Mimi squinting at the tables of food. Davy knew full well that Bobby would've made all the food if he and Cam were still married. "Who catered?" Mimi asked.

"Cami did," Davy said. "Everything but the cake."

Mimi nodded, in a grudging show of approval.

Davy didn't give a shit if it was petty, he hoped Mimi would give a full report to Bobby. He made eye contact with his sister and tried not to grin as Mimi ate a Hanky-Panky, then put four more of them on her plate.

"These are delicious!" Mimi said.

"These are one of our mom's old party standbys," Davy said. "They're called *Hanky-Pankies*." He said the name clearly, hoping Mimi would relay this to Bobby.

Cami looked down at her plate, biting her lip. He could tell she was trying not to laugh.

"Where's Vijay?" Olive asked, scanning the room.

Cami sighed. "He had to work. Couldn't come after all."

"He *always* has to work," Aurora said.

Cami looked at Davy and shrugged.

Gabby announced the start of the games. Oh, God, *games*. They warranted games. Long-standing traditional shower games were being played in their honor.

Gabby supervised a diaper change race and then a series of candy bars crushed into diapers that had to be identified. Davy's students loved that one and took photos with their phones as people sniffed and even tasted the diapers. Helen won this game in no time flat. "Please. I know my chocolate," she said. *Thank God for Helen. The best kind of straight ally you could hope for.*

Davy watched Tyler laughing with Amy across the room. *Good.* For once, he wasn't mooning after Gabby. Damn, that poor kid had fallen *hard*. It had been six months and Davy still caught him staring sadly at Gabby in class.

Recently at cross-country practice—Tyler had quit debate this fall and joined cross-country instead—he and Tyler had found themselves running side by side, the rest of the team spread far ahead or behind them on the loop at Sugar Creek Reserve.

"It's the worst thing that's ever happened to me," Tyler said of the breakup.

Davy let their footfalls fill the silence. Tyler should count his blessings that that was the worst thing, but Davy knew it wouldn't help at all to say so.

With each *slap-slap-slap* of his feet on the dirt trails, Davy's own tragedies flashed like video clips: His sister starving herself almost literally to death in high school. His father pitching head first into a stone wall and coming to not knowing their names. Being despised for who he loved.

All in all, though, Davy knew he was lucky. Besides, this was *his* life, not Tyler's. There was nothing more individual than grief.

Except maybe love.

"Nobody gets the good stuff *all* the time," Davy said to him as they ran. "Remember that."

He wished he knew something more comforting to offer. He wished with the fervor that haunted his entire teaching career that he could spare them, his students; that he could pass them the cheat sheet for their future lives.

He looked around his classroom at them, trying to picture *his* own high-school class throwing a party for a couple of old fags. These kids were *such* good people.

Davy started across the room to talk to Tyler and Amy when Gabby called out, "Okay! It's time to pit the Davids against each other in the 'Stressed-out Parent' game. You guys are going to each try to hang as many of these clothes as you can in two minutes"—she pointed to a basket and a clothesline she'd hung up. "You have to hold this crying baby the entire time. I'll be calling out real-life distractions that you also have to deal with. You can't put the baby down."

"I'll go first," Davy said. "Gimme that baby."

The game was ridiculous, set up to be impossible, with the doorbell ringing, a pot boiling over on the stove, and a cat puking on the carpet.

"We don't *have* a cat!" Davy protested.

"Mom's gonna give you one as a shower gift."

He found Cami in the crowd and pointed to her. "I'll kill you."

When Gabby called out more distractions and reminded him, "The baby's still crying," Davy cradled the doll in the nook of his arm and pulled out his cell phone. While the crowd hummed the *Jeopardy!* song, he dialed David's number.

Big David jumped when his phone vibrated in his pocket. "Hey, can you come home and give me a hand?" Davy asked. "We're a little stressed."

"Sure thing." David stepped into the scene and rocked the baby, while Davy quickly hung up everything in the basket. Everyone cheered.

David pulled out his phone again and said, "Hello?"

Davy wanted to see what game he concocted next, eager to play along, to go wherever he led.

"Okay. Wow. How long?" Davy realized David was talking to somebody *for real*. "We'll be right there." David clicked his phone shut. "Kim went to Miami Valley Hospital about three hours ago. She's in labor."

THEY TOOK HER HOME THAT DAY. A TINY, WAILING CREA-ture they named Grace. Davy swore he felt his chest crack open to make room for this new love. He had *thought* he was prepared, but he marveled like a goon at her miniscule toenails, her deep-lake eyes, her chubby thighs, her dimpled knees. *Our daughter.*

The effect on Ava was amazing. Grace made her happy, lucid. "I'm so glad I lived to see this," Ava whispered, holding their sleeping Grace.

"I'm glad, too," Davy said. He was glad she got to see David have a family, have such love.

And then, two days later, it was over.

CHAPTER TWENTY-SEVEN

AFTER WORK, I DROVE OVER TO SEE GRACE. I OPENED THE Davids' front door and listened for crying or happy babble. The house seemed to hold its breath. "Hello?" I called.

The nursery was empty, but when I peeked in the bedroom, there they were, the Davids, curled like spoons. "What's going on? Where's Grace?" I tried to soften the panic in my voice.

After what felt like a million years, Big David managed to croak out words. His voice was hoarse, shredded. "Kim changed her mind," he said.

I slid down the door frame and sat on the floor.

The Davids had paid for everything, not that there was a price tag for this, and she'd *changed her mind?* How could this happen? I wanted to find Kim, scream at her, shake her. *What the hell are you thinking?* This couldn't be true.

VIJAY'S GIFT ARRIVED, A BEAUTIFUL, MONOGRAMMED PINK fleece blanket. When Gerald puked up a paper-filled hairball in the kitchen I used the blanket to wipe it up without thinking. Later I rinsed it out and took it down to the barn. Standing with Moonshot as he snuffled comfort across my face, I felt a shift inside me. It was time to reach out, to be there for someone else.

Friends told the Davids, "You can start the process again," and "You'll be selected for another baby," but with my own loss still fresh, I knew that such offerings were insulting, that no matter how well intentioned, such platitudes trivialized the real pain. I said many times a day, "I am so sorry this happened to you." And truly, I was sorry it happened to *Grace*.

Their goodness, even in the face of such grief, leveled me. After a discussion with Helen—their new lawyer had proven to be worthless—they decided not to contest Kim's decision. They also decided not to ask for the money back—the money spent on her prenatal care, the groceries, the vitamins, the hospital delivery—even though by law and the adoption contract, they were completely entitled to do so.

"What would it accomplish?" Big David asked. "Kim's got no money. What money she has, we want her to spend on Grace."

They even gathered many of their shower gifts—the diapers, baby wipes, and blankets—and took them to Kim. Kim accepted the gifts but wouldn't allow the Davids to see Grace.

I contemplated kidnapping.

I asked Helen, "Tell me the truth. Would this have happened if they'd stuck with you?"

When she exhaled, she seemed to deflate. She shook her head. "You can't lose the baby to second thoughts if the birth parents' legal rights are properly upheld. This bonehead tried to shortcut the procedure. He screwed the Davids—and probably Grace—in the process."

This heartache had an added dimension in that it sent Ava on a downward spiral. She became prone to panic, constantly opening the closed nursery door and crying out, "Where's the baby?"

The fourth time I witnessed this, it pained me to see Davy walk away from Ava.

"Why isn't she here, the mother?" Ava demanded. Then, whispering, "Now, which one was married to her again?"

She'd sometimes confide to one or the other of the Davids, "If that other *man* wasn't here all the time, she might come back. It isn't natural, you know."

I thought back to my unraveled days and realized that when people said, "If I can do anything to help, please let me know," I hadn't been *capable* of asking for anything.

So, I brought the Davids flowers, cheerful movies, made sure they had good food, and, whenever possible, I'd take Ava away for a while, giving the Davids some time alone.

Ava was happy to accompany me on my evening barn chores. Mr. Gerald would hop over to her and allow Ava to carry him like a baby, on his back, in her arms. She'd sing to him, in a surprisingly lovely voice, songs like "You Are My Sunshine," "Swingin' on a Star," and "Embraceable You." He'd reach up and rest his one front paw on her cheek while she sang.

ANOTHER MONTH PASSED. NO COURT DATE WAS SET YET for Moonshot, but other Humane Society volunteers had come to document his progress. I was told rules I already knew—for instance, that I had to allow Ginger Avalon to visit him. When the volunteers asked for receipts for Moonshot's bedding, feed, and the vet visit so they could reimburse me, I told them to consider it a donation.

My ribs felt stronger with each passing day. Every morning, I crossed to the window and looked down on the farm in the first hint of light. I loved the paths in the diamond dew that deer had made, the ripe promise in the air, the last of the honeysuckle fading on the fence.

Although my heart held room to mourn for the Davids and to dread the loss of Moonshot, in another, new way I recognized I was *happy*. Happy to watch Biscuit roll in the dust to scratch his tabletop back, happy to notice the barn swallows dive-bombing Gerald (who caught and killed a surprising many of them, even with his missing leg), happy to notice Max and Muriel playing a game of head-butt tag. I saw so many things I hadn't seen before.

It was with this new vision and with my eyes wide open that I accepted Vijay's invitation for a weekend in New York.

"Someone should be having fun," Davy said.

VIJAY WAS WORKING LATE WHEN I ARRIVED AT LA GUARdia. An apologetic voice mail waited for me when I landed. I took a cab to the *Outbreak* studio to collect the keys, and Vijay kissed me in front of his coworkers—a kiss that made my head swirl. I almost walked into a wall as he ushered me back to the street. A second kiss, longer, followed when he tucked me into another cab.

When I unlocked Vijay's brownstone—yes, the whole brownstone—on the Upper West Side, I couldn't help but think, "This could be my house." Right inside—beside a giant slanting pile of mail, as if he hadn't been home in days—I slipped off my shoes and lined them next to his.

As I wandered from room to room, I learned that Vijay had a prescription for Ambien and that his fridge was empty, save for an old take-out container. I learned that he sent his clothing out to be laundered and that he slept on only one side of his bed, the other side piled high with clothes.

I looked at that bed and knew Vijay had been too busy to prepare for my visit. He'd had a tough week, apparently. Well, I could certainly understand long hours.

He called around 7:50. "A couple more hours," he promised.

I decided to walk through the neighborhood. I noted a good Italian grocery store Bobby would've liked. My nose and growling stomach took me to a small Middle Eastern place, where I dined alone on lamb so succulent I hardly had to chew.

Back at Vijay's house, it felt odd to be in a home with no other beings—not even plants, I realized. I watched TV until 11 p.m., then chose to sleep on the sofa rather than move his mountain of clothes from the bed.

Lips brushed my cheek. Vijay knelt beside the couch. "I'm so sorry," he whispered. His eyes were bloodshot. "This just came up. A huge MRSA outbreak. We're trying to finish a new episode to squeeze it in out of order. I'm sorry. After we planned for you to come—"

I pressed my fingers to his lips. He kissed them. My entire body yearned for this man kneeling beside me. Sleep had relaxed me; I felt open, fluid. But Vijay's skin seemed gray, every line on his face etched deeper. "Oh, Vij. Go. Sleep. We have tomorrow."

His forehead crinkled. "I have to go in tomorrow."

Disappointment pushed me deeper into the couch, but I remembered Bobby's poutiness when I'd left on rescues or other work emergencies. I convinced Vijay to go down to his bedroom and sleep. I loved this city. I'd go exploring. When he came home the next day, then we'd play.

It was 2:07 a.m., but I heard the musical chord of his computer coming on in his office below me and the quick clicks of keystrokes. I padded downstairs and stood in the doorway. Pictures of methicillin-resistant *Staphylococcus aureus* showed up on his computer screen, and he furiously typed notes. I tiptoed away and went back to sleep on the couch.

I WOKE UP TO THE SHOWER RUNNING. SEVEN-THIRTY. UGH. How did he function?

"I'm sorry, Cam," Vijay said, coming into the kitchen, where I'd made him coffee. "I didn't even get the house cleaned. You slept on the couch! I feel like a total shit."

"Please. Stuff happens."

My heart soared as he kissed me with careful, undivided attention. I kissed back, with fervor, and just as I was hoping I might be able to delay his departure for the office, he pulled away. "I have to go," he said, in a strangled voice. "God. I don't want to, but I have to."

He swayed, his eyes vague, as if drugged. "I'll be home around four. Maybe earlier." He made a move as if to kiss me good-bye, then stepped back, realizing the danger.

When he left, I wanted to claw my own skin off. I crawled into his bed and smoothed my hands over some of those silky black hairs left on his sheets, as if a sleek panther had slept there.

❦

I WANTED TO MAKE A FABULOUS, SEXY MEAL FOR VIJAY.

I decided on carbonara. When Bobby and I traveled in Italy, I'd ordered it at every opportunity. Bobby disliked it and didn't put it on the menu at Tanti Baci. I'd once, years ago, asked Mimi to show me how to make it. I'd paid attention. I didn't think I needed a recipe.

"Buongiorno, bella," the man behind the counter said when I returned to that Italian market.

"Buongiorno," I answered. *"Come sta?"*

"Bene, bene, grazie. Parla italiano?"

I laughed. *"Lo parlo poco."* Then I admitted, "You caught me. That's the limit of my Italian."

"No, no," the man insisted, his cigarette-stained grin wide, "your pronunciation is good. Good. You had me fooled."

In spite of the grocer's prominent Adam's apple and slightly marred teeth, there was something so welcoming about his laughing eyes and dimples that I felt charmed. His name was Antonio (of course), and he carried the basket for me as I roamed the aisles. When I told him I was making carbonara, he feigned a swoon, clutching at his heart. "For a lover?" he asked.

My blush told him the answer and he laughed. "Lucky man, *bella*. I hope he knows this."

Nearing 4 p.m., I started the meal in Vijay's kitchen. I sloshed wine over sautéing pancetta cubes, relishing the furious bubbling this produced. I beat eggs and cream, stirring in Parmesan. I was carried along on the cooking, enjoying it, and didn't even look at the clock. I boiled the spaghetti (I was going to go with penne, but Antonio suggested spaghetti for its more sensory, chin-slurping qualities), then tossed it with the egg-and-cheese mixture and the syrupy mess of the pancetta. Only after having added the chopped parsley did I look at the clock. 6:10.

Hmm. Well. I poured myself a glass of wine and cleaned up the kitchen. I set the table.

At 7:15, I called Vijay again but hung up when I got his voice mail.

By eight o'clock I was so famished, I made myself a plate of the carbonara, lit some candles, and sat down to try my creation. I held my irritation at bay, which was easy in light of this decadent meal. Even alone I moaned with pleasure. I wished Antonio the grocer were here to share this.

My heart leaped when my phone rang. But it was Davy. Poor Davy. Why had I left them?

"Are you guys doing it *right now*?" I loved that his voice was its normal, naughty silly self.

"Not right now," I teased back, "or I wouldn't have answered. That would be the epitome of bad manners, don't you think?"

"Hell, yes. But . . . you have, right? Just calling for the report."

"Actually," my throat tightened, "we haven't." I explained.

"Damn," Davy said. "Here I was thinking that one of us was having a good time."

"How are you guys? Have *you* done it, at least?"

He sighed. "Not yet. Not since . . ."

"You need to remedy that. Don't let it go too long." We talked for nearly an hour, and then I fell asleep on the couch again.

"Hey, Cami." I dreamed that Moonshot spoke to me in English. But then I opened my eyes to Vijay, again kneeling beside the couch, apologizing. Outside, rain poured and thunder rumbled. Vijay's hair was damp, the front of his blue shirt spotted with raindrops.

We sat on the kitchen floor, the pan of carbonara between us, instead of using plates. We twirled up spaghetti, our conversation teasing and seductive. When Vijay leaned over to kiss the creamy sauce from my lips, we were lost.

I melted from the inside. Oh, this was good. This was very, very good . . . until we reached *the* moment and realized neither of us was prepared. We were ready in every possible way, except the most crucial. "I'm not . . . I don't . . . I don't have anything," I said.

Vijay's face fell. His shoulders slumped. "Oh, my God. I don't either."

For a second it seemed the world had come to an end. Or that we might decide to blame each other. But knowing someone since you'd gone trick-or-treating together counted for something.

"You're a *doctor*," I teased him. "An infectious-diseases doctor. You specialize in HIV! How can you not have a condom?"

He thumped his forehead on the kitchen tile.

I started laughing.

We considered going out to a drugstore for a purchase, but the driving rain made us lazy. We lay naked on the kitchen floor, glistening with sweat, and ate more carbonara.

WE SHARED HIS BED THAT NIGHT, AND IT SURPRISED ME how right it felt to have a body beside me. Vijay slept, exhausted from his day, but I stayed awake longer, content to listen to the rain and breathe the scent of his neck. I pictured being this man's wife, living here in this house. I imagined Gerald and Max here on the bed. I wondered where I'd board my horse.

My horse. Moonshot could not be taken from me.

WHEN I FINALLY DRIFTED OFF, I SLEPT AS IF DEAD, NOT hearing anything, not remembering any dreams. I rolled toward the bacon-y post-carbonara scent of Vijay, pushing my arms through the sheets. My hands met pillow. I was in the bed alone. The clock shone 8:30. "Vijay?" I called.

Outside cabs honked, a distant police siren yelped twice, and two people carried on a conversation in Spanish. Inside the house, I heard nothing. No. Way. No goddamn way.

Next to the coffeemaker was a note. "New MRSA case— interview with patient this morning. Hated to wake you. I promise to do some 'shopping' before I come home."

I wadded up the note, then threw it at the fridge. I called Vijay's cell, got his voice mail, and left a message, "Call me, okay? When will you be back? I need to talk to you. Soon."

I showered. I dressed. I drank coffee. I missed my beautiful daughter.

Church bells tolled, and an unbearable longing to be near animals rushed into me.

CHAPTER TWENTY-EIGHT

ALMOST IMMEDIATELY UPON REACHING CENTRAL PARK, the faint perfume of horse manure comforted me. I watched a dappled gray Belgian pulling a carriage, the hollow clop of hooves on the pavement releasing my shoulders and clenched fists.

I stood on the sidewalk, reveling in the hints of autumn colors to come, when my attention was caught by a magnificent harlequin Great Dane leading its owners on a walk.

Across the street, a girl with her parents walked a Maine Coone cat in a harness. It looked so jaunty trotting stiff-legged down the sidewalk that I laughed aloud.

Although I'd planned to head into the park, I decided I'd follow this rakish cat for a bit. As I waited to cross the street, a young girl beside me held what I first thought was an old-fashioned muff but then recognized was a live rabbit.

We crossed with the light, following the marching cat and the Great Dane, along with a couple walking two standard poodles.

At the next intersection, all of us going in the same direction, I saw a girl with a Persian cat in a carrier. A woman in a fur coat carried a Chihuahua. A white rat rode on an old man's shoulder. Was this a dream?

Across the street, as this procession of animals headed up Amsterdam, I saw people unloading a llama from a van. Several of the dogs bristled at the llama, who imperiously surveyed the street from its tall neck. "What is going on?" I asked aloud.

A woman walking a corgi laughed and said, "It's the Blessing of the Animals." I fell into step beside her, and she continued, "Just up ahead at the Cathedral of St. John the Divine."

Friday had been the Feast Day of St. Francis, the patron saint of animals. How lucky that I stumbled onto this!

But when I reached the neo-Gothic cathedral and saw a table of good-postured St. Francis statues for sale, the saint's kind face seemed to tease me, "Now, you don't really think that was just *luck*, do you?"

Hundreds of people lined the sidewalks with their pets. Hundreds more were already inside, where a service was underway. Someone explained to me that a procession of "special" animals to the altar would take place—large animals mostly brought in from outside the city—then the entire congregation was invited to the side lawn, where several priests would bless all the animals in attendance. Dogs of every breed, including several good-natured and curious mutts, snuffled one another. Children carried hamsters, gerbils, and even fishbowls. One little girl in a green-checked coat carried a tortoise as big as a hatbox.

A hideous noise jolted me—a noise like a rusty engine trying to start. An exasperated man in a white robe pulled two donkeys with lead ropes. One donkey brayed.

The crowd hushed. A few dogs trembled. One near me growled, his tail between his legs.

The man acknowledged, "I know. A god-awful sound, isn't it?" Everyone laughed.

The donkeys stopped, causing the man to hold up the procession. A white-robed woman led a camel past him into the church. The man sighed, leaning on one donkey, wet stains under his arms. "I have to do this," he said under his breath. "I have to." He looked at me and said, "I hauled them all the way from Connecticut. I promised my wife. We'd been invited for years but never made it. Now she's in the— She's in hospice." He swallowed, scratching the black stripe that ran down the donkey's spine. "I promised. We're supposed to be after the camel."

"Can I help you?" I asked him. He looked far too young for his wife to be in hospice.

He looked hopeful. "You know donkeys?"

"Not at all," I admitted, "but I know horses."

He shook his head. "Not the same thing at all. These guys are a piece of work, I tell ya."

"Well, that camel is getting a huge head start."

"Worth a try." He handed me the lead rope for the male donkey. "If Jack goes, Jenny will usually follow him."

I reached into my coat pocket. Sure enough—I should've been embarrassed but instead was grateful—I found a rubbery carrot and a piece of apple going leathery. I rubbed the mummified apple on Jack's bristly muzzle. He stepped forward, eager to follow.

At first Jenny brayed again, which made a beagle in the crowd begin to howl, setting off a chain reaction of mournful wails. But Jack followed me, clomping right up the steps of the cathedral as if he did it every day. Once we were about to disappear into the church, Jenny shut up. Over my shoulder, I saw her marching forward, ears laid back, eyes glaring as if she couldn't believe Jack had the audacity to leave her.

Inside, barking and howling punctuated the sermon in progress, but the sheer magnitude of the sanctuary caused a certain awe.

A ripple of panic zipped through me as I approached the priest. Everyone in the procession wore white but me. Was there something I was supposed to know? To do? I looked back at the man, but he was keeping a wary eye on Jenny—who seemed dead set on catching up to Jack, and if looks could kill, I'd be dragging a dead donkey.

The priest read words of St. Francis; they managed to penetrate my brain while I kept the donkey moving forward. "Creatures minister to our needs every day," he said. "Without them we could not live, and through them the human race greatly offends the Creator every time we fail to appreciate so great a blessing."

With those words, Jenny caught up to Jack and bit him on the butt. He squealed and kicked her, then bucked three times for good measure, causing people on the ends of the rows to crowd outward. I was mortified, but a collective chuckle rose up and echoed in the chamber.

Swack. I flinched as water dashed across my face. Jack snorted in surprise as it hit him, too. We were being blessed. I laughed, which may not have been appropriate, but the priest laughed, too. Before I knew it we were outside again and I wiped holy water from my face.

The man thanked me. "Why I ever agreed to bring these hooligans into a church . . ."

Why? Because he loved his wife, that's why.

It'd all happened so fast. A boy stood on the lawn holding a goat. The goat looked up at me with yellow curry—colored eyes that seemed to laugh.

When Vijay hadn't called me back by noon, I got online and ate the fee to change my flight. I packed my suitcase, left a note by the coffeemaker, and flew home a day early.

CHAPTER TWENTY-NINE

I'D LANDED, DRIVEN HOME, UNPACKED, AND WAS IN THE barn by the time Vijay called.

He apologized earnestly, but I was glad I'd made this choice; he clearly had not returned home until nearly 8 p.m. again.

No one was home, but I was happy to let the animals minister to me. I imagined my crew parading through the cathedral. "You would've been the most beautiful ones there," I told them.

I wanted to ride. I hadn't been on a horse since the broken ribs, and sitting in that saddle felt like coming home. This time I was well fed and clear-headed. It was near dusk, I was alone, and I'd forgotten a helmet—all reasons to walk once around the arena and get off, but it felt so healing. Moonshot's free, swinging walk made me think of dancing.

Dancing. I wanted to dance.

I'd always wanted to dance.

ONCE NICK AND OLIVE HAD DROPPED GABRIELLA OFF AND I explained why I was home early, Gabriella said, "Men suck."

I slid off Moonshot's back and led him to his paddock. "Vijay doesn't suck. He just didn't have time for me, and I had more interesting things to do than wait around for him."

Gabby leaned on the fence while I untacked Moonshot and brushed him. "Aunt Olive and Mr. Henrici just asked me to write something to read at their wedding."

"Baby, that's lovely. What an honor." I scratched Moonshot's tail. Ah, I'd missed this.

"What am I supposed to *say*?" Gabby asked the ground, putting her forehead on the fence. "That I give them less than a year? That I think the whole thing is ridiculous and meaningless?"

I stopped scratching. "You didn't *say* that, did you?"

She lifted her head to roll her eyes at me. "I *should* have. We were at the restaurant. With Dad and Grandma Mimi. And *Zayna*." She spat Zayna's name. "I don't even want to *go* to the wedding."

I stopped scratching again, but Moonshot moved his rump at me so quickly, he almost knocked me down.

"That woman came here while you were gone," Gabby said. "Moonshot's owner?"

My heart stopped.

"Ginger something."

"Ginger Avalon," I said flatly. *The porn star.*

"Yeah, that's it. Is that a cool name or what? She came out here Saturday. I was down in the barn already. She seemed nice enough, but Moonshot wouldn't let her touch him."

I breathed again. *Good for you, old boy. Good for you.* I scratched his tail with new vigor.

"Could she really get him back?" Gabby asked.

I nodded. I couldn't find my voice to say, *She really could.*

❧

I RETURNED TO ANIMAL KIND MONDAY MORNING, EVEN though I wasn't scheduled—I wasn't supposed to even be in town yet until that evening.

"I'm glad you're here," Aurora said. "I need your help with a diagnosis."

She led me to the kennels and brought out a dog I recognized. "Booker!" I said. His fruit-bat ears stood up, and he wagged his whole rump.

"You *know* this dog?"

"Absolutely. Australian cattle dog. Belongs to Stuart Duberstein, right?"

Aurora's face was blank.

"Dubey?"

She shot me a *what the hell?* look and led the dog to an exam room. She handed me the file. "Verdi," the chart read.

"Verdi?" I asked the dog. He licked his right foot. His owner's name was Susan Weiss. Mrs. Weiss had brought this dog here on Saturday. She said the dog had begun to have seizures and behave aggressively. She wanted to have him euthanized.

I lifted my head in disbelief. "Aggressive? This dog?"

Aurora nodded, arms crossed. We both knew this was a crock of shit.

"His name isn't Verdi." I made sure to speak in a neutral voice, not specifically addressing the dog. "His name is Booker."

At his name, he looked up sharply, wagging his hind end.

I crouched down to pet him as I explained the story to Aurora—about the crazy cat lady and the cute man next door.

Aurora thought a moment. "I sensed she didn't want a diagnosis. She'd already made up her mind. I convinced her to at least let me keep him until today for observation."

"And what did you observe?"

"I took him home. He's well mannered, socialized. He played with my two dogs. He likes to chase cats and is pretty damn quick. He presented no illness or aggressive behavior whatsoever. I did blood work, even though she didn't want me to. All normal." Aurora moaned. "If we refuse, she'll find someone else to do it."

I nodded, thinking.

The vet tech poked her head in the exam room. "Dr. Morales, your first appointment is here."

"Thanks, Bridget." Aurora turned to me. "This is her. Help me think of a plan!"

I chewed my lip. "There's no way in hell I'm letting her euthanize him," I said. "I'll come with you." I shrugged my arms into a white lab coat and followed Aurora into Exam Two without Booker. I wanted to tell this woman I knew what an evil, vindictive monster she was. Instead, I shook her hand and introduced myself. "Frankly, Mrs. Weiss, your dog presents with absolutely no health issues."

Her spine stiffened. "Look. He has these seizures. They're very frightening."

Aurora reported what she'd observed . . . and what she hadn't.

"He *has* them," Susan Weiss said, her voice icy. "And they're awful. He's attacked me."

I wanted to attack her. "We can't euthanize a healthy dog,

Mrs. Weiss." It was the closest I could professionally come to calling her a liar.

She stood. "Would you please bring me my dog then? I'll have to get a second opinion."

"Let me keep him," I said.

"No. I don't want to do any tests or more observations. I just—"

"No, no. I mean, let me keep him permanently. Then he's off your hands." I worked to make my voice sincere, not condescending. "I'd like to have him, if you'll agree."

She squinted at me, considering. "You wouldn't take him anywhere? Like, out in public?"

When I frowned, confused, she had the decency to blush—a faint ladylike tint high in her cheeks. "I'd hate for him to be in public, at music festivals or what not. What if he had a seizure and attacked someone? I'd feel responsible even though the dog wasn't mine anymore."

"Music festivals?" I was astonished she'd be so brazen.

"You know, like they have at Riverscape. Outdoor concerts, that sort of thing. The fireworks downtown when the Philharmonic plays."

All the places where Dubey was likely to be. Places where he'd recognize his dog.

"No, I'd never take him to anything like that." *But your ex-husband might, you bitch.*

She looked at her watch. "Well. All right. Do I sign anything?"

After Mrs. Weiss had signed a release and clicked out the door on her high heels, Aurora said brightly, "Well, he should fit right in with your crew."

———

"No, no, no," I said. "I'm not keeping him. I'm taking him to his real home right this second."

When I got to Dubey's house, though, a *For Rent* sign stood in the yard and no one answered the door. Booker whined.

We walked around to the back, just in case. I glanced at the cat lady's house but was relieved to see only two cats on her porch.

I peered in the back-door window of Dubey's house. The kitchen was empty.

Back in the truck, I dug in the glove compartment, past a syringe of horse wormer and some dog treats, to find Dubey's original report. I called the phone number listed there, but it'd been disconnected. I called the Humane Society, but they had no other information.

Booker wagged his rump at me when I clicked shut my phone.

Great. Now I had an Australian cattle dog "with seizures."

THE NEXT DAY, WE WERE SLAMMED AT THE CLINIC—TWO hit-by-cars coming in within an hour of each other—so we were performing surgeries long into what was normally our lunch hour. I had to bring Booker to the clinic, since I couldn't leave him at home (he chased cats and I already knew that unlike Max, Booker would kill them).

It turned into the kind of day where I was scarfing down cold bites of sandwich between afternoon appointments. Even so, at every spare moment I made unsuccessful phone calls to the three Dubersteins in the phone book.

After I sent the last surgery patient home (an hour and forty-five minutes after usual closing time), I Googled Stuart Duberstein. I found several old notices about him performing at various places around town. Nothing to indicate an address or contact information.

I drove to visit the Davids with Booker panting in my backseat. I left the dog on the Davids' screened-in porch, collected their mail and papers, and went inside.

Big David was cooking dinner. Davy stood with a Scotch, staring into the fireplace. "Where's Ava?" I asked Davy.

"With Carol."

"What number is that?" I cocked my head toward his Scotch.

"Who cares?" Davy asked.

I took his Scotch from him and set it on the coffee table, then hugged him. He put his cheek against my hair. I saw Big David in the doorway, watching. I gestured to him to come over. To my relief he did. I opened my arms to include him, too. I twisted myself so that the two men embraced and I was on the outside hugging them both.

"I'm so sorry," Davy said to Big David. "I pretended not to see you cry this morning."

"I know. It's okay. I pretended to be sleeping so you wouldn't know I was crying last night."

"I . . . I wish I knew what to say to help you," Davy said.

"I don't know, either."

The smoke alarm went off in the kitchen. "Shit," Big David said.

"I got it!" I ran into the kitchen, snatched the smoking skillet from the burner, then waved a dishtowel at the alarm until it stopped. The chicken thighs were black on the bottom but, once extricated from the skillet, not really burned.

Eventually the Davids came into the kitchen and apologized.

"Don't," I said. "Think of all you saw me through."

They invited me to stay, and, sensing they wanted a buffer, I agreed. We talked of my trip, I defended Vijay to Davy, they talked about Kim, and by the time Big David brought out the dessert—a perfect cherry pie from David's Hot Buns—we'd even laughed a little.

As we lingered over coffee, Big David sorted the pile of mail I'd brought in.

"Wow, look at this," he said. He'd opened a thick, creamy envelope. Was this Olive and Nick's wedding invitation already? He handed us a card that read, "Join Cleveland and Caroline Anderson as they celebrate fifty years of marriage."

Well, damn. We'd forgotten all about it.

"Dinner and dancing at the Hunt Club."

Dancing.

How long had I been wanting to dance?

WHEN VIJAY CALLED THAT NIGHT, FROM HEATHROW AIRport, I said, "I'm finally doing it. I'm taking a ballroom dance class." I'd spent the last half hour searching for classes rather than for Dubey. "Wanna be my partner?"

I'd been joking, sort of, and was surprised when he said, "Absolutely."

"Right. Whatever. In all your free time."

"I'm serious. When is it?"

"Mondays at seven."

I heard clicking and tapping—he was checking his crackberry. "I could do that."

"Vijay, be serious."

"I can do it. I want to. I want to make it up to you for our botched weekend. I feel terrible."

He said he'd come in for the weekends, or at least Saturday night, and fly out late Monday after the class. "We'll learn to dance," he said, "and then we'll dance at your parents' anniversary party. I got an invitation yesterday."

"You did?" Hmm. My conniving mother.

Booker clacked into the office. Gerald growled.

"Will you be my date for the party?" I asked Vijay.

"I'll be your date for *every* party. Maybe we'll hit fifty years ourselves."

My heart fluttered. *What did he just say?*

Just then, though, Booker dashed for Gerald, so I had to hang up. Gerald was fast, thank God, even on three legs, but when I got Booker by the collar and called Vijay back, he'd already boarded his flight and I only reached his voice mail.

VIJAY CALLED SATURDAY TO POSTPONE HIS TRIP. "I'LL BE in Sunday evening," he said. "I promise."

Sunday turned into Monday morning, and on Monday afternoon, I called Davy. "I need you to come dancing with me." I explained and added, "This way, we'll know what we're doing at Mom and Dad's party. All their friends at the Hunt Club know how to dance for real."

"I can't. I've got stuff to do."

"What stuff? Drinking? Sitting around feeling sorry for yourself? You can do that later. I'll pick you up at six-thirty." I remembered the Davids showing up and taking me to dinner after Bobby had left. "I'm not taking no for an answer."

❀

DAVY WAS READY, IN SPITE OF MUCH COMPLAINING. HE'D even shaved and didn't appear to have been drinking. He got in the car and said, "Remember going to those dances as kids?"

My parents had belonged to a genuine hunt club with hounds, horns, and all that hoopla—galloping through fields and leaping over fences. Sometimes we stayed home with a babysitter for the parties afterward, but occasionally we were dragged along with the warning to be "seen and not heard." I thought my mother looked like Grace Kelly, with that upswept blond hair and long neck, in her floor-length gowns. My father looked right out of a Fred Astaire movie, in his tux. And they could *dance*.

I'd been picturing that scenario when I'd imagined a dance class.

I was a wee bit disappointed.

We met in a big gymnasium at a recreation center. We signed in, Cami and David Anderson. The instructors, Opal and Vick, didn't look glamorous at all—they looked . . . dowdy, really. Opal's hair had that chicklike fineness that frizzed out of her bun. She wore *pants*, not a gown. Pants that looked like gabardine, along with very sensible black shoes. Vick was handsome but had a paunch that marred the picture.

Once this couple began to move, though, all my doubts were dispelled. They started the class—as if they sensed my skepticism—with a demonstration. They moved together fluidly, pot belly and frizzy hair forgotten. While they danced, they gazed at each other so lovingly it made my throat ache.

When they weren't dancing, though, Opal was mean. She

ordered Vick around, and her corrections to us were curt and impatient. Vick's corrections were gentler but not as specific.

There was one couple around my age who looked like they were having fun and an older couple who already knew what they were doing. Most of the other couples, though, looked strained and uptight—the men, especially. Throughout the evening, as we made our way along the line of dance in fox-trot and waltz, I overheard hissed exchanges.

"God, you owe me. You know that, don't you?" one man said to his partner.

One woman tried to coach her man, "Your left foot, honey, start with your left foot," only to have him drop her hands and say, "You're such an expert, why aren't you teaching the class?"

Davy and I spent most of the night laughing—so much that Opal shot us scolding looks.

I predicted that probably half of this class wouldn't return the following week.

I WAS RIGHT. THE NEXT MONDAY, THE CLASS HAD MORE room and we received more instruction. Vijay had actually made it in for the weekend, arriving Saturday at noon. On Sunday, he spent many hours on his laptop and BlackBerry, then came to me with that look in his eyes.

"You're leaving."

"I'm sorry. They need me back in Botswana."

Davy called that evening. "What time is dance tomorrow? Wanna have dinner before we go?" He never even knew he'd almost been "bumped" from the class.

When Helen walked into my barn lot one brisk, sweatshirt evening, I knew what she was there to tell me. "We have a court date."

My legs went weak. I sat on a bucket. Maybe I could hide Moonshot, move him somewhere and not tell anyone. That had happened to us on a few occasions when we'd gone to remove an animal after a court decision.

As if she read my mind, Helen said, "You gotta do the right thing, Cami. You've brought him a long way. You brought him back, really. C'mon, you've fostered a million times, and every time you've made their lives better."

But *he*'d made *my* life better.

Davy and I took to practicing dance a couple of times a week. It kept me sane, and on dance nights I actually slept rather than stewing about Moonshot. Davy would teach the dances to Big David. Ava already knew them and would join in.

"Thank you so much for this," Big David said, walking me out to my truck one evening.

"Are you kidding? Davy saved the class for me when Vijay had to bail."

"I think the class saved Davy for me." His face in the streetlight showed he wasn't kidding. "We weren't doing so hot, you know. You brought him out of his sorrow."

I hugged him and he held me so tight, it hurt my old injured ribs. I kissed his cheek.

"You're keeping that damn freckled dog, aren't you?"

I punched his shoulder and got in my truck. "He's *temporary*."

If only Moonshot's owner had been so hard to find.

CHAPTER THIRTY

I NEEDED TO GET SERIOUS ABOUT HUNTING DOWN DUBEY. I couldn't keep another large dog, especially one that threatened my cats. I dug around on the University of Dayton's Web site and found an e-mail address for Stuart Duberstein. Woo-hoo! I happily left a message:

> Remember me? From the Humane Society—we took away all those cats from your neighbor? Well, I happen to have Booker safe and sound with me. Long crazy story. Call or e-mail and I'll get you reunited.

I expected an immediate response and was astounded when two entire days went by.

I tried again. This time I attached a digital photo.

Still nothing. I felt a bit of panic. Damn. I'd really wanted to do a good deed. I called the music department and got put through to his voice mail. I did this four times.

BOBBY WAS AT THE FARM ONE NIGHT TO TAKE GABRIELLA to dinner, and we ended up in the kitchen together, waiting for her to return home from debate practice. Bobby looked at

Booker lying in the corner next to Max, both of them gnawing chew toys. "Christ, Cam, another dog?"

"A good deed backfired. He's not staying."

Bobby smirked. "I've heard that before."

Asshole. As soon as he left with Gabby, I called UD again. I played around on the phone menu, calling *anyone* in the music department, until I got an actual person. Hallelujah! The man's name was David Perrella. "Dubey's on sabbatical," he said.

I put my forehead on the Portuguese tile. On sabbatical in a *monastery* somewhere? "I've sent a couple e-mails. Isn't he at least checking e-mail?"

David Perrella chuckled. "Dubey's real bad about that. None of us ever e-mail him."

Well. Wasn't that just my luck? "Do you happen to have a cell phone number?"

"Sorry, we can't give out personal information."

"Please. It's important. I have Dubey's dog."

"Uh . . ." Now the man sounded skeptical. "Booker's dead."

"No, no, no, he's not." I told him the story.

"But . . . it can't be the same dog. I mean, Dubey has an urn of the ashes and everything."

"Oh, my God. That's hideous. But this *is* Booker. I swear." I fired off the digital photo.

"Holy shit," he said. "That sure looks like him. Susan told Dubey he got hit by a car."

"That's an outright lie. He's alive and well and terrorizing my cats."

"Okay, here's his cell number."

❧

I WAS THROWN, THOUGH, WHEN A *CHILD* ANSWERED. I guessed she was four, maybe?

"Hi. May I speak to Stuart Duberstein, please?"

"Who?"

Was this *his* child? "Dubey?" I tried. "Is Dubey there?"

"Uncle Dubey plays piano."

Oh. *Uncle.* "Yes, he does. Is he there?"

"I play piano, too."

I could not get the child to round up any adult for me no matter how I begged. She did write down my phone number, though, and I hoped she knew her numbers. "This is an *emergency*," I said in my sternest voice. "It's very, very important. It's about his dog, Booker."

"Booker is in heaven."

"No. He's *not*. I have Booker, sitting right here on my kitchen floor."

The line went dead. That precocious brat hung up on me. I called back but got a message saying the voice-mail box was full.

I looked at Booker. "I'm trying, dude. We're jinxed."

I FORGOT ABOUT DUBEY AS I HEADED TO COURT WITH Helen the next morning.

We didn't have a prayer—I knew that as soon as I laid eyes on Ginger Avalon. She would never make it as a porn star. She was petite and flat chested, with the weathered skin of a horsewoman. She wore a beautiful burgundy suit and was articulate and warm.

She said all the right things. The farm had been their father's farm, and there'd been terrible confusion over possession of the property when he'd died last winter. She didn't associate with her other sister much. Ginger had been in Florida, at their winter training barn, when "the atrocity," as she called it, took place. The other sister would *not* be handling any of these animals.

She thanked us—most genuinely it seemed—for the care we'd taken of the animals. She praised my care of all of them, Devil May Care especially.

My photos, my testimony, were moot points, and I knew it. There was no case.

The judge ruled in Ginger Avalon's favor.

From this date forward she would pay all the various "foster homes" a competitive board rate, until she'd collected the animals. I felt numb.

Ginger approached me. "Thank you, Dr. Anderson." She shook my hand. "Because of some travel on the show circuit, I can't bring him home for another month. May I continue to board him with you or should I—"

"Yes," I said too quickly. "He can stay with me forever if you ever change your mind."

She laughed but said only, "He's special, isn't he?"

An ache flared in my forearm and, without thinking, I moved my hand to where he'd bitten me. It helped to press on it, as if the wound had just happened.

When I got home from court, an e-mail had come in from Vijay. Not only was he not going to be able to make dance class yet again, but he was going to miss my parents' anniversary party tomorrow. Well. Icing on the cake of this stellar day.

I WENT TO THE ANNIVERSARY PARTY, DATELESS AND MO-
rose, but at least Gabby told me I looked like a movie star in my
new black backless gown.

Gabby looked stunning herself, in a purple dress, Empire
style. She'd even invited a date—Steven Choo from her debate
team. Choo, as she called him, turned heads in his tux.

"Look at all these good-looking men," I said to the debonair
Davids, kissing them both.

Mom and Dad, looking as classy as they had in their Olympic heyday, greeted guests, beaming. They *couldn't* have been
married fifty years. They couldn't be that *old*.

Shivani and Lalit greeted me with hugs, and we went through
the "Where is Vijay?" routine again. I basked in their attention,
especially since I realized halfway through the filet dinner that
I appeared to be the only person there without a date, except for
Nancy Hartigay, the eighty-year-old horse show judge, whose
husband had died two years ago.

When the dancing began, I consoled myself with the thought
that even if Vijay had been able to come, he wouldn't know any
of the dances. Davy and I had a blast.

I danced with my dad, who knew how to lead like a master
even with his postaccident shuffle. "Congratulations, Dad," I
said as we moved like royalty around the ballroom.

He spun me out in a complicated turn and pulled me back.
He gazed across the room at Mom dancing with Davy and said,
"How lucky am I? That's my gold medal right there."

My mother's wedding dress was on display. Beautiful in its
classic simplicity—white satin, modest crew-neck collar, tiny
seed-pearl highlights, full skirt—she could most likely still

wear it. I stood staring at it, remembering our play weddings in the barn: one of the only times I'd been the bride was when I'd snuck this gown from its cedar chest.

"Mom? Hey, Mom." Gabby handed me my black beaded bag. "Your purse is buzzing."

"Thanks, sweetie." I unzipped the purse and pulled out my phone. Not Vijay . . . but a number vaguely familiar. I answered, praying it was not some emergency from the clinic.

"This is Stuart Duberstein. I understand you left a message about my dog?"

CHAPTER THIRTY-ONE

DUBEY BEAT ME TO THE FARM. HE WAS ALREADY IN THE barn, where I'd told him to find Booker (shut in Muriel's stall, since she never used it).

Dubey squinted into the light when I said hello. "Hey." He stood up from where he sat with Booker. "Wow. You look different from when I last saw you."

I swear, I felt the damn mottles in my *legs*.

"Wow," he said again, looking me up and down. "What's the occasion?"

"My parents' fiftieth anniversary party."

"You look . . . amazing."

"Well, thank you." The blotchy rash went into overdrive.

"Thank *you*. For Booker." He hugged me. I wasn't prepared for his fingers on my bare back.

The poor man probably hadn't expected to touch skin, either. He looked away, flustered, then bent to ruffle Booker's ears.

Moonshot nickered, peering in the back door of his stall, and my heart fell to my shins. He had yet to stay in the stall; I don't think I'd ever once changed his bedding since he'd been here.

"I need to visit my friend," I said to Dubey. "I can't come down here and not speak to him. It would be rude." I took a box of sugar cubes from the shelf, shaking three out into my palm.

I hiked the skirt of my gown and slipped through the fence. "You're a tough man to find," I said to Dubey as I fed Moonshot his treats.

"I apologize. I kind of wanted to disappear for a while. I've been staying with my sister."

Moonshot rested his muzzle on my bare shoulder, his whiskers tickling my skin. I was not prepared to lose this horse. "I was pretty unraveled, too, for a while," I said. *And this horse helped to bring me back.* "I can relate." I'd simply chosen a different way to disappear.

As I scratched Moonshot's tail, I told Dubey the story of his ex at my clinic. When I finished, he shook his head, horrified.

I patted Moonshot's rump. "Would you like a drink?" I asked Dubey.

"That would be great."

I led the way to the house, hyperaware of my bare back, feeling naked but bold.

Dubey admired the kitchen. "These colors. I would never be brave enough to try this. They're great."

He opened a bottle of wine while I took out cheese and crackers from the fridge. I'd bought romantic food, thinking Vijay would be here. Blue-cheese-stuffed olives, Brie, smoked almonds.

He raised his glass. "To your parents," he said. "Fifty years. That's longer than we've been *alive*. How come some people pull that off and some people end up with nothing but a maimed piano? No, that's not true. I have my dog." He bent to rub Booker's face.

"You know, when you told me she took a hatchet to the piano, I wasn't sure if you were serious, but now that she tried to kill your dog, I believe you."

"I'll show you when you come over."

I'll show you when you come over? Of course, I would be coming over.

"She was a plate thrower. A photo ripper. She came to UD once and drove her car into mine. All that melodrama is perfect for the opera but unbearable in real life."

"My ex threw kitchen appliances," I said. "He once threw the waffle iron out the back door."

Dubey laughed and popped an olive into his mouth. "It's not really fair. You've met Susan, so you have a visual. I wish I'd met your ex, so I could picture him."

"You ever eat at Tanti Baci?"

He tipped his head. "I used to play there all the time. With a jazz trio. For a while we were there every Friday night."

I'd most likely seen Dubey before. "Then you probably know my ex. Bobby Binardi."

"The *owner*? You were married to him?"

I nodded, watching his eyes roam around the kitchen as if seeing it anew. "Huh. I always thought he—" He shrugged.

"What?"

"Nothing."

"Come on. What were you going to say?"

"Well, since you insist, I always thought he was with this other woman."

My spine stiffened. "A *young* woman? With red hair?"

He nodded.

"Well, apparently he was with her. Is still."

"I'm sorry."

I shrugged and whispered, "What does it matter now?"

"It matters." He whispered, too. Both dogs lifted their heads from where they'd been slumbering as if they noticed the change in the room. "It'll always matter. Betrayal hurts."

He leaned across the island toward me. I leaned toward him.

The back door opened and we both jumped. Gabriella walked in, followed by the Davids. I pressed a hand to my chest. "You scared me! The dogs didn't bark."

Gabriella squinted her eyes at Dubey, then at me. "They only bark at strangers."

I felt the mottles. *Damn it.* We weren't doing anything wrong. We were just talking.

I was about to introduce Dubey when Muriel clicked into the kitchen on her little hooves.

"Who didn't close the door?" Gabriella yelled.

Muriel bolted for the stairs.

Oh, my God. The goat was in the house. This was my life.

I hiked up my skirt to follow her. She clattered through the bathroom, through Gabby's room, over my bed—where I finally tackled her, but she squirmed away—then back down the stairs.

Gabby held the back door open and Dubey herded the goat out onto the porch. "Well done!" Davy said as Gabby shut the door.

"This is Stuart Duberstein," I said, when I'd caught my breath. "He's Booker's owner."

Everyone made introductions. Gabby looked at the clock. *Yes, he called two hours ago.*

Davy grabbed a wineglass and went to pour some for himself. "Oh," he said. The bottle was empty. Gabby raised her brows. She looked like my mother.

"I should get going," Dubey said. "Thank you. Truly. I can never thank you enough. I'll see you tomorrow." He slipped quickly out the door with his dog.

When I turned back to the room, Gabriella had her hands on her hips.

"*What?*"

"What are you doing with him tomorrow?" Gabriella asked.

I blinked. "I have no idea."

"Do you *know* it's after midnight?" Gabriella scolded.

Big David said, "He's cute."

"He is," Davy agreed. He poked his niece in the shoulder. "Come on, admit it, he's cute."

She smiled, sort of, but said, "Did Vijay ever call?" The Davids hooted and laughed.

"Actually, no, he did not. Why are you acting like this?" I asked her.

"You *blushed*," she said, pointing at me.

"Okay, listen, this is weird," I said. "He came to get his dog, we started talking and—"

"—and drinking wine," Davy pointed out.

"—and the time just flew. He's a nice guy. We have a lot in common."

"And you look like a million bucks," Big David added.

"Thank you." I curtsied.

Gabriella started laughing. "Except for all that goat hair."

I looked down at my gorgeous new gown, covered now in coarse white curly hairs.

THE NEXT DAY, DUBEY ARRIVED WITH BOOKER AND A GI-
ant picnic. "I want to show you the piano and where I live right
now. Would your daughter like to come?"

His invitation expanded through my chest as if I'd swallowed warm cider. I went into the house to ask her.

"Really?" Gabriella looked suspicious but pleased. She came
outside to chat for a while. She ended up saying that she needed
to stay home to study, but she seemed charmed.

Dubey drove me to his sister's farm about half an hour
away—past beautiful sage-green fall pastures filled with puffs
of sheep. He pulled into the drive, approaching an old stone
house, then parked near a magical little guest cottage about two
hundred yards from the main house. I loved its hardwood floors
and expanse of light-streaming windows. The front room was
mostly taken up by a majestic grand piano that, sure enough,
had big ugly gashes cut into its top and legs.

"She did that the day I told her I was leaving."

So he was the leaver. I was curious, as if he might have clues
for me.

We walked up a rise behind the cottage, where some twisted
apple trees still clutched a few of their vibrant leaves. Bees
floated among the fermenting apples on the ground on this
unseasonably warm November day. Dubey spread a quilt out
on the ground and unpacked a picnic basket of grapes, cheese,
wine, good bread, and tart apples. A breeze carried the sheep's
murmurs up to us. Booker napped beside us.

"Why'd you leave her?" I asked Dubey. "What was it that
made you finally do it?"

He took his time, his expression as if he listened to music in a distant room. "I caught myself staring out the window all the time," he said.

I stopped the apple on the way to my mouth.

"That's exactly what Susan's father did. Susan's mother is just like Susan herself, and when we first started dating, I felt sorry for him. I'd watch him stare out their patio doors, like a man in jail. I caught *myself* doing that and it scared me. I thought I'm way too young to have settled for this misery. I wanted joy and a partner to celebrate with. A few days after I recognized her father in me, I worked up the courage to tell her."

I looked up at the clouds—whiter versions of the sheep below them—and thought about Bobby. Had he felt that way? That he'd settled for misery?

"I was dying," Dubey said.

Bobby had thought about suicide.

I wanted joy and a partner to celebrate with.

We sat, our arms wrapped around our own knees, bees buzzing around us. I breathed the hint of beer in the fallen apples, the spice of dried grass, the warm musk of the sheep.

I lifted my wineglass. "To beautiful days."

He clinked his glass to mine. "To beautiful days."

"I CAN'T BE YOUR PARTNER FOR THE LAST DANCE CLASS TO-morrow," Davy said on the phone.

I felt my happiness deflate. I no longer even pretended Vijay would show up. "Why?" I asked, hating the childish whine in my voice.

"Because . . . David and I have an interview with another prospective mom."

To beautiful days. "That's wonderful!" I said, actually doing a little hop.

"We'll see," Davy said. "I'm trying not to get my hopes up."

But I heard the hope already in his voice. "Are you working with Helen again?"

"Hell, *yes*." His vehemence leaped through the phone line. "Listen, I know it's short notice for class. Any chance Vijay could come?"

"Please. Vijay who? The workaholic?"

"I can't believe he didn't come to Mom and Dad's party."

"I know. I'm getting used to it."

"No. Don't get used to it. 'The biggest human temptation is to settle for too little.' "

"Who said that?"

"I don't know. It was in my tea bag this morning."

We laughed.

I dialed Dubey's number. "Do you like to dance?" I asked him.

THE DAY AT THE CLINIC WENT LATE WITH AN EMERGENCY (A German shepherd had swallowed an entire bathrobe sash), so I rushed to get ready for dance class. As I stood at the mirror, curling a strand of hair I'd left hanging down from my French twist, my phone buzzed. *Vijay.*

I *wanted* to hear that chocolate pudding voice. But . . . I looked at the clock. No time. I let it go. As much as I hated "keeping score," let *him* have a message unanswered for a while.

Gabriella came to my bedroom door and narrowed her eyes at me. "You look really hot."

"Thanks. I think. Why are you glaring at me?"

"You never dress like that for Uncle Davy."

"I'm taking Dubey tonight."

"You can't be dating a man named Dubey!"

I laughed. "It's a nickname. It comes from Duberstein. And we're not *dating*."

She played with the doorjamb with one pink fingernail and wouldn't make eye contact. "I thought Vijay was supposed to dance with you."

"So did I." While I applied lipstick and mascara, my phone buzzed again. Vijay. I slipped it in my purse.

"Who was it?"

"Helen. I'll call her later." This time I was the one not making eye contact.

TURNS OUT DUBEY COULD DANCE. VERY WELL. I THINK THE musician in him gave him a natural rhythm and ease. At the last class of the course, he was far better than any of the other guys who'd been there for the entire six weeks.

"Where is your husband?" Opal asked, looking down her nose at Dubey.

I laughed (we'd signed in with the same last name, after all) and said, "Davy's my *brother*. He couldn't make it tonight, so I brought a substitute."

My purse buzzed as I set it down. I checked, out of habit, but it was Vijay *again*. Sometimes he didn't call me back for days; was he going to call me every hour now?

Dubey and I took to the dance floor, standing expectantly before each other as Opal gave instructions. So far we'd done formal dances like the waltz and the fox-trot, with a little swing. For the final class, we were spicing it up with salsa and merengue.

Dubey's face changed when he listened to music. You could see him absorb it with his whole body. We fit together well, and he led with confidence. I hated each time they shut off the music. When Opal announced the last dance of the night, I turned to check the clock. Dubey laughed at the disbelief on my face. " . . . when you're having fun," he said.

We pulled out all the stops on the final salsa number. "More hip, Cami!" Opal encouraged and I delivered. Dubey looked at *me* when we danced, not at his feet, like my brother did. I wasn't sure what to do with his gaze—it held a dare, a bit of boyish "Look at us!" and an invitation all at once. By the end, I was sweating, and more strands had fallen from my twist.

As we walked out to the car, I felt like I floated. Why hadn't I been doing this my whole life?

"I'm sorry this was the last one," Dubey said, holding the car door open for me. "We'll have to find more classes somewhere else."

"I'd love that."

We pulled into the farm drive, which he remembered without being reminded. Another car sat by the garage, with Muriel standing atop it. "That goat is something else," he said.

"Yes, she is," I said, peering through the dark at the car. Whose car was it? Was Choo here? Bobby? It couldn't be Ginger Avalon. She wouldn't be here so late.

The kitchen lights were on. Muriel hopped off the car and

came trotting to Dubey's. She butted me in the knees and then stood on her back legs in a hopping dance.

"Want to come in?" I asked. "Have a glass of wine?"

Dubey hesitated. "I'd love to, but it's late. Thank you for a lovely night." He took me in dancer stance and did a series of underarm turns, spinning me down the walk to my back porch, Muriel following us, bucking and rearing. At the end, I thought, *Here it is, here's the natural place to kiss if he's going to try it*. He thought about it—I saw him, but he pulled away. "We'll dance again," he said as he walked to his car.

I stared after him a moment, then turned to go inside.

I jumped as if I'd touched the electric tape to see Vijay standing at my back door.

CHAPTER THIRTY-TWO

I LET MURIEL RUSH RIGHT INTO THE HOUSE. I'M HONESTLY not sure if I didn't do it on purpose. "Vijay! What are you— Oh, shit, the goat!"

"Hey, Cami, I've been trying to call you all day."

I kissed him. What the hell was wrong with me? Had I really wanted Dubey to kiss me? What if poor Vijay had *seen* that? "I'm so glad to see you. What a surprise."

Muriel's hooves clattered on the stairs, like someone in high heels. Max followed her, barking.

"Let me get this goat out of my house," I said, wanting a moment to clear my head.

"*I*'ll get the goat," said Gabriella, rising from the kitchen island. Two bowls and an ice cream scoop sat on the counter. How long had Vijay been there?

I stood in the kitchen, unbalanced, confused.

"You went to dance class without me," he said, looking like a little boy.

"I've gone to dance class without you every single time."

"I know. But I was *here*. I really wanted to go."

The hooves sounded like an avalanche above us, accompanied by Max's barking and Gabby's muffled profanities. "I didn't know that. It would have been fun to finally go with you."

"That's why I busted my ass to make it here today. I tried calling."

"Vijay, the first time you called, it was, like, ten minutes before I had to *leave* for class."

"But I was already here, at my parents. I wanted to surprise you."

He'd *been* here? "That's sweet, but . . ." The racket of hammering and barking was deafening, and it seemed absurd that we were talking calmly as if nothing were going on. "A little warning would be nice. I can't always drop everything because you've decided to show up."

His expression might have been the same if I'd intentionally stomped on his toe.

"Oh, Vijay. That sounded so much harsher than I meant it." I touched his chest. "Truly." The hooves now sounded like someone dropping a bag of pool balls in the hall. "Let me get the goat."

He looked so sad that before I went upstairs, I kissed him again. "I'm glad you're here *now*."

The flash of his smile warmed me. He held my hands and kissed them before releasing me.

I ran up the stairs, pushed past Max barking in my bedroom door to where Gabriella had a squirming Muriel cornered and was trying to get a grip on her writhing head. Vijay's things were laid out in my room—his suitcase, his laptop—all on my bed.

I used my sternest, meanest voice to say, "Muriel! *Enough!*"

Muriel stopped struggling. She wheezed a little sigh, minced down the stairs, clicked through the kitchen, and waited by the back door like a house-trained pet. When I opened it, she looked up at me with those odd yellow eyes. I dug in my jacket pocket and unearthed a sugar cube. She crunched it daintily. I crouched down to scratch between her horns. She only wanted to *be* with us, after all. I thought I might cry, but when she'd finished her sugar, she lifted her stout little body onto her back legs, kicking out all her limbs like a spastic ballerina.

ONCE GABRIELLA HAD GONE TO BED, VIJAY AND I MADE out against the fridge like teenagers. I nibbled his lips and ran my fingers through his hair. "What you said in the kitchen earlier—" he asked: "Do you really think that? That I expect you to drop everything at my whim?"

He had his hands under my shirt. His earlobe was between my teeth. "Well . . . a little. But I don't think you do it on purpose."

"Who was that guy?" I heard the overly casual tone, the way he'd slipped it in among other questions, his nose buried in my hair. "The one who danced you to your door?"

"He was my dance partner tonight because Davy couldn't go." Why did I feel like I was lying? I had to actually remind myself that I *wasn't*. "His name is Stuart. I treat his dog."

I was still against the fridge. Vijay leaned on one arm beside me and with the other played with my hair. Looking at the strand I'd curled he said, "I don't expect you to drop everything."

"Okay," I said. "I didn't say it to hurt you. It just gets frustrating."

His eyes widened. "Work interfered! Things came up."

I laughed. "And did I ever, a single time, give you a hard time about that?"

He shook his head.

"Right. And I've been stood up by you how many times? Six? Seven?"

"Wait, not that many, that's not—"

"It's not important. The point is I never gave you any crap about it, and here you are, stood up one time. *One time!* Stood up for something I didn't even know I was standing you up for!"

"I never said I wasn't coming."

"You never said you *were*."

"I said I was coming to *all* of them, and I always told you if I wasn't going to make it."

"I was supposed to assume you'd show up if I didn't hear otherwise? You're not being fair."

"But we could've—"

"*Stop.*" I pushed off from the fridge and moved away from him. "Was I supposed to wait, without a partner, to the *last second*? Was I truly supposed to believe that you were going to swoop in for the final class? Can we please drop this and concentrate on being here now?"

He opened his mouth, then closed it. "Yes. We can."

I smiled. "Good. Let's start over, shall we? But we'll skip the part where the goat ran in."

We kissed. He whispered, "So, listen, I know I've been frustrating, with my—"

I wanted to kick his shin. "We're starting over."

"No, this is about something different. I wanted to apologize and make things better, even before we . . . even before I messed up this evening." At least he said "I."

I started a fire, then we sat on the couch, legs entwined. He played with that loose strand of my hair again. "What do you wish for . . . for us?"

"I wish you were more available. I wish I could see you more often."

This seemed to please him. "What if I wanted that, too, and we took this to the next level?"

I turned my head, unsure what he meant.

"What if," he said, an almost teasing tone to his rich voice, "you moved to New York and we saw each other every day?"

My breath stopped. His face glowed butterscotch in the firelight. "What if we got to wake up next to each other each morning? What if I came home to you every day?"

I was afraid to breathe. The slightest movement might tip the balance.

He swiveled his long legs from under mine and knelt. He took both of my hands in his and looked up at me with that face I'd known, counted on, and adored for so many decades. "Camden Anderson, would you marry me?"

I squeezed his hands. "Vijay. Vijay." *I cannot screw this up. I cannot hurt this wonderful man I've loved for so long.* I had an immediate sense of the momentous consequence of whatever I said next. There was so much at stake. I pulled him back up on the couch. Where did I begin? Hadn't I wanted this? Hadn't I wished for this? "Thank you," I said. I had to do this just right. *Was* there any way to do this right?

He laughed. "So?" he asked.

"So," I breathed. *How did I do this? Don't make me do this!*
I'd paused too long. "Cam?"

I shook my head. "I can't answer you right now."

His lips parted, his eyes immediately wounded. I felt his natural recoil, the pulling away from me, but I grasped his hands and said, "I'm not saying *no*. I'm saying *not yet*. I'm saying there are too many issues that need to be resolved first, before I can . . . before we can know if this is right."

His eyes glittered orange in the firelight. "It *is* right. I've never been more sure of anything."

"I'm sure that I love you, Vijay. But . . . you're . . . you're not really available."

"What do you mean?"

"Your job. Or, I guess, your *jobs*. They consume you—they're important, and you're fabulous at them. And I would never, ever be the woman who asks you to give any of that up. It makes you who you are and I understand that. But it also makes you not available."

"It would be different if we were in the same city. It's the distance that makes it—"

"Half the time, *you're* not in your city."

"But when I am, we'd be together, which would—"

"Vijay, sweetie, I was *in* your city, remember? I spent the entire time alone."

"It's not always like that, Cami. That was a rare thing."

I nodded, kindly, but said, "The baby shower? The fiftieth anniversary? The six dance classes? Vijay, I love you. I truly do, but I think if I lived with you, I'd be alone all the time."

"Those are— No, seriously, Cami. It won't be like that."

I stroked his high cheekbone with my thumb. "Then we'd need to keep dating a while, until I saw that. Until I believed that. That's what I mean by 'not yet.' I love being with you. But for me to leave everything, my practice, my farm, I'd have to know I was getting something to make all that loss worth it. *You* would be worth it—well, well worth it—but not if I never saw you."

He stared off into the fire. "I . . . I don't know what to say. I'm—" He looked at me, more humbled than I'd ever seen him.

"Vijay, I love you. But I'm not sure we'd have a partnership. If I'm going to do this again, I want it to be *better*. Don't you?"

He didn't answer.

"We . . . you and I feel very unbalanced." I scooted sideways, so that my entire body faced him. "I'm not saying any of this to hurt you." I took his hands. "Everything we do, every time we get together, every single time we communicate, is your choice. You control it all. And I know it's because of your work. But I want you to imagine what that *feels* like."

He mulled this. "But you have your *own* work. You're devoted to *your* work, too."

I nodded. "And what about that? I own my own practice here, Vijay."

"Veterinarians can work anywhere."

"*Doctors* can work anywhere."

He frowned.

"See? There are some things we need to work on. Work on *together* to find solutions that satisfy us both. Let's not have some half-assed, un-thought-out marriage that fails, like we've both already had. Let's have a kick-ass marriage. Let's figure out a way to be remarkable."

Gerald hopped to the back of the couch and butted my shoulder, then rubbed his face against my cheek. He lay on the top of the couch, as if to watch the proceedings.

Vijay's expression about killed me. I felt like something had been irretrievably lost. We sat, leaning together, my head on his shoulder, his head on mine, staring at the fire, holding hands, Gerald's tail gently tapping our heads on occasion.

"I'm going to go," he whispered.

I didn't question it. "Will I see you tomorrow?"

He nodded. I followed him upstairs while he gathered his things. Gabriella's door was closed, the light out under the door frame.

After I kissed him at the back door, he paused. "Did you say no because of—" He looked out the door. "That guy? The one you danced with?"

I shook my head. "No," I said. The very fact he'd asked it made me certain Vijay didn't get it, that he hadn't understood my hesitation, that he'd only heard rejection.

CHAPTER THIRTY-THREE

⚘

BY THE FOLLOWING SATURDAY I WAS IN FULL FREAK-OUT mode.

From the moment Vijay had left Monday night I'd known something was lost.

On Tuesday, he didn't answer my calls, texts, or e-mails. By the time I'd left the clinic (checking my damn phone between every spay, neuter, and dental), I drove to Shivani's house only to be told he'd flown back to New York.

The way Shivani said, "Work, work, work. What will we do with that boy?" I could tell she didn't know what had happened.

Was I insane? Had I just made the mistake of a lifetime?

Olive seemed to think so. I'd called for an emergency GNO on Thursday. After clinic closing time, we took a corner table on the heated, covered patio at El Meson. With the fountain trickling, we could pretend it was summertime or some other country, not Ohio on a raw, gray, almost-Thanksgiving day.

"You said *no*?" Olive asked. "What's wrong with you? You're over forty. He's a doctor!"

Helen—thank God for Helen—laughed. "Over forty? You say that like she better grab the last man she's ever going to get!"

Olive opened her hands. "He's loaded. You'd live in the best city in the world. You told me his place is fabulous—"

"And I'd be alone all the time."

I saw from her face that she wouldn't mind that one bit. That she might, in fact, prefer it. For the first time I saw clear as a compound fracture in an X-ray the fundamental split between us: I wanted a *partner*. Olive only wanted to be married. To anyone.

Aurora stirred our pitcher of sangria when it arrived and filled our glasses.

My phone rang and I snatched it from my purse, hoping it was Vijay. At first my shoulders slumped when I saw that it wasn't, but then I recognized the number—a new number I hadn't yet added to my contacts. I couldn't stop the itchy mottles from blooming. I dropped the phone back in my purse. I'd listen to the message later.

"Who called you?" Olive demanded.

When I mumbled my confession, Helen sat up straight. "Dubey? Well, well, well."

"No, no. It's not like that. Truly. There's been nothing—"

"Who the hell is Dubey?" Olive looked outraged.

I brought her and Aurora up to speed.

"You turned down *Vijay* for a musician named *Dubey*?" Olive asked.

"No, listen, I turned down Vijay for reasons having *nothing* to do with Dubey." I scratched at the rash on my neck and admitted, "But, it is true that . . . Dubey is . . . he's really present and spontaneous, and . . . when he says he's going to be there, he actually shows up."

"And Vijay sure didn't," Aurora said.

"But what he *does* is important!" Olive said.

"Sure it's important," I said. "But if it's *more* important than our relationship, then the marriage is destined to tank. For it to work we both have to want it more than anything else."

The entire patio hit a lull in conversation at the same time, the only sound the trickle of the fountain.

Olive made her smoke-ring mouth again. "But, Cami, it's not right. You're beautiful and you have so much to give to somebody. You shouldn't be alone."

I spewed sangria, I laughed so hard. *Alone?* I pictured my crowded house. I wiped up the mess I'd made and asked, "What about the so much somebody has to give to *me?* When does it get to be *my* turn?"

Helen and Aurora grinned and raised their glasses.

HERE IN MY CLINIC, I SIGHED, THE SWEETNESS OF THAT sangria long gone.

It had been my Saturday to work. All had gone well, no surprises, but interesting enough to be distracting. When noon rolled around, I was sorry. I lingered in my office long after the staff had left. What did I want to do with the day? Fly to New York? Arrive on Vijay's doorstep?

Gabriella was at another debate tournament. Aurora was hiking in Red River Gorge with an interesting new man she'd met in her To-Shin Do class. Helen and Hank were in Chicago. I didn't have the energy for Olive and her wedding mania right now. Davy was swamped with end-of-fall-term papers and had asked not to be bothered (I'd called to ask about their meeting with the prospective new mom; they were optimistic but hadn't heard her decision yet).

The clinic phone rang, and I mouthed the answering-machine message along with my receptionist's recorded voice. For once I wished we *were* open all day on Saturday.

Should I call Dubey? I'd texted him after his sweet El Meson message (thanking me for the dance class), telling him this week was crazy busy but I'd call soon. I wrinkled my nose. No, no, no—not until I figured out what was going on with Vijay. God, I wish I'd known how to tell the truth without hurting him.

As I started a search for flights from Dayton to New York, my phone rang. *Bobby.* Ugh.

I let it go to voice mail and kept scrolling through flight options, waiting for the trill that told me I had a message.

What would I *do* if I went to New York? What could I say or do differently to make Vijay understand?

After a moment, I realized that the musical chord indicating a new voice mail had never come. Was Bobby talking *that* long? I checked my phone. Nope, he hadn't left a message.

As I stared at the phone, he called again.

I sighed. Whatever. He still didn't leave a message.

I could be in New York around 5 p.m. if I left right now. What did I need to take? Anything? Why not do it? That would show Vijay how serious I was, right?

I clicked "Book Flight" and began to fill in my information when my phone rang *again*.

This time it was Gabby.

"Hey, baby," I said. "Guess what I'm—"

"Where *are* you?" Her clipped, panicked tone made me go still and alert.

"At the clinic."

"Thank God. Hang on."

What the hell? After about twenty seconds of waiting (I watched the clock on the wall, trying to steel myself for the crisis behind her voice), she clicked back on.

"Okay. Dad's bringing Zuzu to you. He's already driving, actually, about—"

"No, no, no. I'm *closed*."

"It's an emergency, Mom!"

"Then he should go to the emergency clinic. You know that num—"

"You're closer."

"Gabby! This isn't fair. I don't have a staff here!"

A car peeled gravel in the employee parking lot. I looked out my office window. Bobby. With Zayna in the backseat. "They're here. Damn it, I can't—"

"Mom!"

When I got to the employee entrance, I saw through the window that Bobby held the back car door open for Zayna, but she didn't get out. I couldn't hear exactly what they said to each other, but the body language and raised voices were clear: they were arguing.

Great. Just great. How was this *my* problem?

When Zayna finally got out of the car, I took in the details— Bobby and Zayna, both with blood on their shirts, arms, and hands. Zayna carried the puppy wrapped in towels. Towels with bright-red spots. Blood *dripped* off Zayna's elbow as they walked toward me.

"I gotta go," I said to Gabby, unlocking the door.

"You *can't* send them to the emergency clinic!"

As I opened the door, I saw the way Zayna had her hand clamped on Zuzu's distal left foreleg, saw the blood that welled around her grip. Saw the puppy's shocky eyes and pale gums. There wasn't *time* to send them to the emergency clinic.

"Take her to a treatment room," I said, holding the door open, then asked, "What happened?"

"She fell out of our apartment window," Bobby said, his bloody hands in his hair. "The screen popped out and she fell."

"How long ago?" I yanked a light over the stainless steel table where Zayna laid the too-still Zuzu on her side, wounded leg up. Zayna kept pressure on the wound, knuckles white.

"Ten minutes?" Bobby guessed.

Zayna shook her head. "Less."

Okay. She might have a chance. I opened cabinets for pressure bandages and clamps, wishing I had a vet tech to get IV fluids ready. "Why would you waste time coming here?" I asked, snapping on exam gloves. "You should've gone straight to the emergency clinic."

I turned around in time to see Zayna shoot Bobby a furious look. She hissed an "I *told* you!"

"Let's see what we're dealing with," I said.

Bobby hovered near the table, his face gray, grim. "Is she okay? Can you make her okay?"

I peeled open the towel and, through the bubbling stream of deep, thick blood, saw bone.

Bobby wheeled around and bent over a linen basket, as if to puke.

"No!" I yelled, startling him enough to make him freeze. "Those are sterile surgery packs! We'll need those." I pointed him to the metal trash can.

He nodded, breathing deeply, and moved away.

I dabbed a four-by-four gauze sponge on the wound, then lifted it, over and over, each time able to see the damage for a few seconds before it filled back up with blood. *God, what I would give for a technician!*

Another dab of gauze and I managed to get a clamp on the severed bleeder. Three more dabs and I clamped the other end. The bleeding stopped.

"Is she going to be okay?" Bobby asked, looking at the floor.

I wiped away all the blood, checking the puppy's entire body. Other than a fairly deep abrasion on her pink-and-black freckled nose and several minor abrasions, the leg was the only external wound. "This looks like she was sliced with a scalpel," I said. "How'd a fall do this?"

"She slid down a canopy over the entrance," Zayna said. "I think she got cut on the canopy frame."

Bobby moaned and paced the room.

"I'm going to tie off this bleeder before we do anything else," I said.

I opened a sterile pack for my suture materials. Zayna brought me a cassette of catgut and pulled out the thread for me. I cut it under where she'd held it—so that only my gloved hands and suture scissors touched it. I threaded a tapered needle and began to work. "This'll be quick," I said. "I just don't want these clamps flopping around while we X-ray."

I tied off both ends of the bleeder, suturing them closed. Then I released the clamps one at a time to make sure I'd been successful. I had been. *Bleeding stopped. Next, treat the shock.*

I grabbed an IV bag of sodium chloride, hung it on a pole, and bent over the puppy's uninjured foreleg to place the IV catheter. "Zayna? Remember how I showed you how to hold the vein off for me?" Like I did with Tyler, I often had Zayna assist me, since she was so good with the animals and such a quick study. *Please, please let her remember how to do this.*

Zayna nodded but just looked at me expectantly.

"Well, could you do it?" My voice was harsher than I'd meant.

She still stood there.

"Now?" I prodded her.

She stepped forward and took Zuzu's uninjured foreleg in her hands. She rolled the leg correctly—even though I knew I'd only showed her once—so the vein was straight and popped up for me. Puppy veins were tough. Puppy-in-shock veins were tougher. I felt the vein with my thumb and slid the catheter in. *Got it. First try.* "Perfect," I said to Zayna.

I attached the IV and fluids to the catheter, then turned the knob to start the flow. "We're gonna run this wide open for a while," I said.

"What is that?" Bobby asked.

"Shock makes her blood pressure low," Zayna said. "The fluids will bring it up."

I nodded and taped the catheter to Zuzu's leg. I checked her pupils. They responded to light. While I listened to her chest, Bobby asked again, "Is she going to be okay? Can you fix her?"

"Her heart and lungs sound normal," I said, beginning to feel her belly. "How many stories did she fall?"

"Three," they said in unison.

I cringed. I needed to rule out internal injuries. Diaphragmatic hernia. Ruptured urinary bladder. Ruptured spleen. Broken back. Broken ribs. My own ribs ached at the thought.

"She fell two stories," Zayna said, "but then she hit the canopy. She slid off the canopy and into some big bushes."

That helped. The canopy and bushes probably saved her life. "We need to do some chest and abdominal X-rays. You carry the bag," I said to Zayna, pointing. Just as I worked my hands under Zuzu's body to lift her, she peed. I leaned over, scrutinizing the urine. Clear. Normal. Good. We could probably rule out a ruptured bladder. I scooped her up and carried her to the X-ray table.

"Will she be okay?" Bobby asked.

"I'm trying to find out!" *Would you stop asking me that?*

Once I'd measured the width and depth of Zuzu's chest and abdomen so I'd know how to set the X-ray machine, I put on my leaded gown. I looked at Bobby and Zayna. I'd need help for the ventral-dorsal view. Zayna knew how to do this, but . . .

"Any chance you might be pregnant?" I asked Zayna.

I thought *I* blushed badly? Zayna's face flushed red like a poisonous reaction.

"I . . . I don't think . . . I—" She looked at Bobby.

"Bobby, put this on," I said, handing him a lead gown.

Zayna protested.

"You hesitated," I said. "If there's a possibility, you shouldn't be in here. Bobby can do this."

Bobby better *be able to do this, dammit.* I gave us both lead gloves and throat shields, made Zayna leave the room, then had Bobby help me hold Zuzu straight, on her back. Bobby held her back legs extended, and I gently held her front, holding the IV bag in my teeth.

After a lateral view, we got her back on the treatment table. "I've got to develop these in the darkroom. It'll take about ten minutes. You keep her still." I checked her gums. "She's already pinking up. That's good. Watch her color. Watch her breathing. Come get me if you need to."

In the darkroom, I turned off the lights, opened the cassette, placed the film in the automatic processor, then stood still. I breathed in, I breathed out—relishing my first second to collect myself since they'd arrived with the puppy.

I really didn't *have* to wait in here. I could go start prepping for surgery, but I heard their voices, arguing again. So . . . apparently there was trouble in paradise. You know what? The puppy was stable. I'd stay right here in the peaceful dark, thank you very much.

Please, *please*, don't let these films show any further trauma. Don't let this dog die on my watch. Damn it, why had Bobby put me in this position? Why was I suddenly responsible for saving the life of my ex-husband's dog?

How long had I sat looking at flights? If I'd walked out that door ten minutes earlier, even five, I wouldn't be here, I wouldn't be in this position. I'd be on my way to New York.

But . . . had I left five minutes earlier, Zuzu would surely have bled to death.

When the processor buzzed, I collected the films. Zayna and Bobby fell silent the minute I opened the door. I put the films in a view box and scanned them for broken bones, pulmonary contusions, fluid in the abdomen. I exhaled. Fortunately, the leg was our only issue. In the lateral view, I pointed for Bobby and Zayna. "Fractured radius and ulna."

"Can you fix it?" Bobby asked.

"Yes, but not today."

They looked confused. "That surgery might take an hour and a half. Zuzu's been through a lot already. We have to be sure she's going to—" I stopped myself from saying *live* and revised my words before speaking. "I *will* do surgery today, but just to clean the wound and close her up. I'll splint her leg for now, then we'll get her stronger before we do a more extensive orthopedic surgery in a day or two."

Zuzu was already coming around, wriggling and whining.

I carried her to the surgery room, Zayna holding the IV bag beside us. I gave Zuzu an injection for pain and a dose of ketamine and valium in her IV to induce her for surgery. Bobby, who'd been standing near the table, moved away again—wiping the sweat from his face—when he saw the needle.

Zayna shot me a look and rolled her eyes, I suppose attempting solidarity.

Zuzu stopped trying to sit up. Her head flopped. She was now out of it enough to intubate.

"Remember how I taught you how to assist with an endotracheal tube?" I asked.

Zayna looked at me, her face blank.

"You have to assist me," I said to her.

"Dr. Anderson, I don't think . . . I don't feel comfortable. Not under—"

"You *have* to."

She stammered and shook her head. "Maybe Bobby could—"

I shook my head. "He's worthless."

Her hurt expression exasperated me. "Oh, for God's sake," I said. "I don't give a shit about any of that *right now*. But *look* at him!" Bobby sat on the floor, head on his knees. *Poor Binky.* My voice softened. "Zayna. He *can't do this*. If you want Zuzu to live, you have to help me."

For God's sake, this is why I'd finally taken pity on Bobby and stopped inviting him on rescues!

She nodded. I talked her through it, and she was competent. She held Zuzu's head, keeping the dog's upper jaw open. I pulled Zuzu's tongue to the side and guided the tube into the trachea. When Zuzu coughed, the gentle breeze of her breath traveling up the tube, I said, "We're in."

I did all the things my technician usually did for me while I'd be scrubbing in—tying the tube in place, blowing up the cuff with three cc's of air from a syringe. I hooked the tube up to the anesthesia machine and turned on the gas.

Once I'd clipped a pulse oximeter onto Zuzu's tongue, I turned on the monitor. Her heartbeat beeped into the surgery room, the green bag rising and falling with her respirations.

I tucked my hair under a surgical cap and hooked my mask over my ears, then scrubbed my hands, all the while talking Zayna through cleaning the wound—she'd done that before. I opened a sterile pack and popped open a sterile blade. I unwrapped and shook out my surgical gown. I put my arms through and turned my back to Zayna for her to tie me in.

She had to move the bundle of my cap-covered hair to tie the gown at my neck, then touch my waist to tie the belt snug. An odd intimacy moved through the ritual. Zayna's hands on me, Zayna dressing me. I couldn't help but picture her doing this to Bobby. But she'd probably be *un*dressing him.

I could finally get to work. I checked the bleeder, looking for my ties. All was well. I assessed the damage, then used forceps to clean and debride the wound, picking out hair, dirt, gray tissue too traumatized to recover, and fragments of bone that didn't bode well. Painstaking. Slow. The steady *beep-beep-beep* of Zuzu's heartbeat marked the time.

Every time Bobby asked, "Is she okay?" I wanted to poke him with my forceps.

I had Zayna get sterile water, which I squirted through a syringe to flush the wound.

At last, I was satisfied. I trimmed the edges of Zuzu's skin to "freshen" it and said, "That's good. We can close her."

"Wait," Zayna said, looking confused. "You didn't connect that vein, or artery, or whatever."

I wanted to laugh at her. "I can't," I said. "Those two pieces can't be put back together. I tied them off to stop the bleeding. Now we just hope the collateral circulation kicks in and saves the foot." Blood vessels had the ability to dilate if necessary.

I began suturing the first layer, pulling the muscles together. I didn't want to amputate this puppy's leg. The last time I'd amputated, I realized, was *the day Bobby left me.*

"Save the foot," Zayna repeated. "She might lose her foot?"

"She *might*."

Bobby heaved huge, deep breaths. If he was going to puke, could he please just go to the bathroom?

As if reading my thoughts, he stood and stumbled to the hall.

Zayna looked over her shoulder at the door. When she turned back to me, she said, as if she'd been waiting to say it, "I *told* him we should go to the emergency clinic. I *knew* that."

"Then why didn't you?" My voice was cold.

She looked away. "Bobby said it had to be you. He said you'd save her."

I continued suturing, glad my face was hidden behind my mask.

When I finished that layer, I asked in a calm, quiet voice, "What were you thinking?"

She kept her eyes only on that green bag, but I knew she'd heard me. And I knew she understood what I was talking about—I didn't mean letting her puppy fall out a damn window.

"Did you give any thought at all to what this would do to me?" I asked, suturing the subcutaneous tissue. "To my daughter? To the practice?"

Zayna's face was set as she stared at the bag expand and deflate, expand and deflate.

"I trusted you," I said.

The *beep-beep-beep* was my only answer.

"I trusted you," I repeated. "As an employee. As a friend. I tried to *help* you."

After a long pause, she whispered, "I know. I'm sorry. I am so sorry. I know there will never be a way to make you know that."

———

I couldn't lift my eyes to hers at that moment because I'd begun to close Zuzu's skin, the third and final layer of sutures, but there was something so naked in her voice that I believed her. "You can turn that gas way down now," I said. "But leave her on the oxygen."

When I finished and stood up, Zayna didn't look away but held my gaze.

"Go to the closet and get a meta splint," I said.

While she did, I put gauze over the sutures and rolled the leg in two-inch cast padding.

Zayna brought back three sizes of splints, smart girl, and we selected the right match for Zuzu. The clear plastic splint went from toe to shoulder. As I secured it with stretchy cling tape, Zayna asked, "So you think you'll fix those bones on Monday or Tuesday?"

"*Probably* Tuesday." I made my voice more gentle. "We need to find out how that foot does, so we know exactly what kind of surgery we're heading into."

She nodded. She knew what I meant. There was no point in pinning bones that might be amputated altogether. Just as there was no point in operating on a dead dog.

"I want to ask you one thing," I said.

Zayna's eyes were eager, and I recognized the look from when Bobby'd volunteered to help with barn chores while I was injured. *Give me something—anything—to assuage my guilt.*

"Why did you come to Olive's apartment that morning? Remember, when I was there with Davy and Gabby, the morning of her engagement?"

A shadow crossed Zayna's face, and she looked back at the monitor.

"You can turn that gas completely off now," I said. "But not the oxygen."

"I was scared," she said to the monitor, turning the knob. She looked over her shoulder again, but Bobby hadn't returned. "Bobby was scaring me. It was the morning after he left—" She fumbled with what to call it. "The morning after he moved out of your house. He just came to the apartment and laid on the bed. He wouldn't talk. He just laid there, staring at the wall. I didn't know what to do. It wasn't how I thought it would . . . I thought . . . I thought Olive might be able to help him."

I wrapped Zuzu's leg with a final layer of nasty tasting "No Chew" vet wrap while mulling this information. In some small way it helped to know this, to know that he hadn't run immediately into Zayna's arms, happy to be rid of me. That he'd struggled helped me. If only he'd stayed and we'd struggled to untie our knot together. Even though I was now relieved he was gone, I still felt the gaping wound of being shut out of the decision altogether, of being *left*.

I let Zuzu breathe oxygen for one more minute before disconnecting the endotracheal tube. I waited for the puppy to swallow, then gently pulled the tube from her throat.

"He doesn't love me, Dr. Anderson."

The flatness in Zayna's voice made me stop. She looked into my eyes and said with resignation, "Just so you know. He doesn't love me. I thought maybe I could make him love me. That I could make him happy. But . . ." She shook her head.

I pulled down my mask. "You can't rescue him."

"I know. Now." She looked miserable. Her eyes shone under the glaring surgical light.

I moved the light away from her face. "Nobody can rescue Bobby but Bobby."

We looked at each other, and I saw in her face that she would leave him. Who knew how soon, but she was bailing. Clear as printed words on that young, porcelain face.

Of course she would leave him. How could she be the actress she'd dreamed of being while lugging the heavy anchor of a sad man? Honestly, Bobby couldn't have believed this would end well. To my surprise, though, an ache unfurled in my rib cage, a faint vestige of the broken bones there. Poor Binky. Poor clueless bastard.

Zayna cleaned the blood from Zuzu's chest and other foreleg with gauze and hydrogen peroxide. "I'll be sorry about this the rest of my life," she said. "I'll never do this again. It . . . it sucks to be the other woman. Your daughter *hates* me."

I couldn't deny that. Zayna's honesty, however belated, didn't deserve such a knee-jerk platitude. Besides, Bobby came back, looking a little less cadaver pallored.

He stood looking down at the puppy's neat, intact leg in its hard plastic splint. He looked from the leg to me three times before he said, "You are *amazing*."

Zayna shrank at the heartfelt admiration in his voice.

You clueless, self-absorbed bastard, I thought.

CHAPTER THIRTY-FOUR

I TOOK ZUZU HOME WITH ME, SINCE IT WAS THE WEEKEND. That would save me twenty-minute, one-way drives to check on her. I hooked her IV bag to a wire cage in my kitchen, gave her another pain injection, and sat with her most of the evening. She'd groggily lift her head, snorting a sound of surprise as if to say, "What *happened*?" then fall asleep again.

Gerald sat in my lap as I leaned against the kitchen island with a glass of wine to call Gabby at her tournament. "Dad said you kicked ass, Mom! He said you were absolutely killer. You saved her life."

I stroked Gerald's smooth chest and shoulder—exactly where we'd have to amputate Zuzu's leg if her foot didn't circulate.

I reached into the cage to feel that paw even though I knew it was too soon to tell.

IN THE MORNING, ZUZU'S FOOT FELT WARM—NOT HOT— but was swollen enough for me to know we weren't out of the woods yet.

I was still unsettled by all I'd learned during that emergency yesterday. Shouldn't I be happy to know Zayna and Bobby would fall apart? The knowledge nagged at me, though, rather than bringing any satisfaction.

Although there was nothing really to do for the puppy but wait, I contemplated using Zuzu as an excuse to get out of visiting yet another bakery with Olive. This would be our fifth trip to sample cakes. I didn't know why she was doing this when everyone knew a David's Hot Buns cake was the only way to go.

Fortunately Helen called to offer me a rescue as a legitimate excuse. "Outright abuse," she said, sounding livid. "We need to take your trailer."

I looked out the window. "But it's not raining."

After I'd carried Zuzu outside to use the bathroom, I shut her back in the cage to keep her contained. I called Olive while Helen drove us to the rescue.

"I guess I'll just go by my fucking self," she snapped.

"Why doesn't Nick go with you?"

"He's no help. I swear, we were screaming at each other last night. He says I have to cut at least fifty people from my guest list. There's no way! This is *my* party, dammit."

When I hung up, I said to Helen, "I don't know if I'm gonna survive this wedding."

I didn't need to explain at all. Helen said, "What did Bride Olive do with Sane Olive?"

"And when did I become *slave* of honor?"

By the time we pulled up to a grungy little ramshackle house, raindrops splattered on the truck's windshield.

"Of course," Helen muttered. "You're a jinx."

"How do you know it's *me*?"

We didn't laugh. The circumstances had us too pissed off. "There she is," Helen pointed.

A donkey—a miniature donkey—stood seething in a mud pit of a yard. A huge black band around one leg chained her to a cement chunk that looked like an old post-hole filler. A choke chain behind her jaw, at the top of her throat, tethered her to a tractor tire.

Helen looked at her phone report. "Mr. Pete Early. Lives alone."

"I can see why." Three feral cats lurked around his dilapidated front porch. A Batman sheet hung in the front window. Plastic sheeting rattled in the cold wind where it had come untacked.

We checked the donkey first. Thank God I'd put on my Wellingtons, because the mud went well past my ankles, threatening to steal my boots with every step. Helen stayed on the gravel driveway after the mud sucked off one of her shoes.

"Call the sheriff," I said. "We're taking this girl right now."

Helen nodded and opened her phone.

I'd never worked with donkeys before the Blessing of the Animals. This one seemed a different breed, much smaller than Jenny and Jack in Manhattan, but, oh, this poor girl was sorely in need of a blessing. She was mired mid-shin in the mud. A huge tuft of puffy gray hairs on her forehead gave her a Neanderthal-ish ridge that shaded her eyes, and enormous ears rose toward me, looking like creatures of their own. She watched me approach with lined-black Cleopatra eyes. When I reached out to her, she cringed her face away, eyes shut.

"No, sweetie, I won't hurt you," I said, my throat closing. "I won't ever."

The neighbor woman across the road had called the Humane Society. The donkey had escaped from Mr. Early's yard—smart girl—and hid in the woman's garage. When the neighbor called Mr. Early, he'd arrived with a baseball bat and hit the donkey repeatedly on the back, neck, and even her face. The neighbor woman said she wished she'd never called him.

"C'mere, darling," I said, offering the donkey an apple. She wouldn't take it. I pushed back her hair to get a look at her swollen and crusted right eye. I gingerly felt around her face, finding several spots that made her flinch but nothing that appeared to be broken.

I felt down her neck and withers. She was thin but not starving, like Moonshot had been. Her shape, though, was odd—as though all her muscle and fat had succumbed to gravity and melted off her sides into a big, round belly. When I felt her belly, she turned her neck and nipped at me, swishing her thin tail with its tuft of black.

"Sorry, sweetie. Are you sore?" I offered her the apple again. She turned her head away with a "hmmph" but then swiftly turned back and took it from me.

"See if anyone's home," I called to Helen. She went to the porch and knocked, sending the skinny, wormy cats scattering. Nothing.

Just then a buzzing came from the woods behind the house, growing louder and louder, sounding like power tools. The donkey made one single bray, clearly of disgust, and laid her ears flat on her fuzzy neck. Three men on four-wheelers came into view. They drove into the yard, right up to me, showering me and the donkey with mud. All three men laughed as they cut their engines.

I wiped mud from my face. "Are you Mr. Pete Early?" I asked the skinny one, not giving them the satisfaction of getting a rise out of me with the mud.

"What's it to you?"

"We're here from the Humane Society, investigating a report of abuse."

"What the hell?" another man—heavily tattooed—asked.

Pete Early's grin vanished. "What I do with my animals is nobody's damn business."

"Oh, so you have more animals than this donkey, sir?"

I saw him notice Helen in the driveway. He began to dig at the skin of his neck.

"So what if I did?" Pete Early said.

"We'd like to see those animals, too, sir."

"What if I don't want to show you? You can't come on my property without permission."

"You're absolutely right, sir," Helen said, both of us so utterly polite it cracked me up. "We could get a warrant, though, and return with the police."

"Jesus H. Christ," he muttered.

The tattooed man whispered something to him.

I interrupted them. "Can you please show me where this donkey eats and drinks?" I asked. "There appears to be no water within reach of her ... *restraints* here. And there's no shelter."

Speaking of no shelter, the rain, of course, had moved from droplets to a trickle.

"It's a *donkey*," he said, the way one might say, "It's a *rock*." "I don't even *want* it. I took it as a favor to a friend, and now it's coming back on me. I never hurt this damn donkey."

"Did someone suggest you had?"

He looked confused, then angry. "You know what? You care about this donkey so much, she's yours, okay? Take her. She's a pain in my ass anyway."

I smiled sweetly. "Thank you, sir. We'd be happy to take her off your hands."

"We just need you to sign here," Helen said, "and one of your friends, too, so it's officially witnessed that we took the animal with your permission."

"Jesus Christ on a crutch!" Pete Early slogged over to Helen, as I reached through the mud to unlatch the band tying the donkey to the concrete block.

The third man laughed, a hyena-like sound. "Good luck getting her on that trailer."

I ignored him. In my peripheral vision, I saw Pete Early sign Helen's form. He turned to his friends, "One of you fucknuts get over here and sign this."

"I ain't putting my name on nothing," Hyena Man said.

They began to argue. I worked on the choke chain—a dog's choke chain!—and managed to get it over her ears and down her nose. I let it drop in the mud, where it disappeared.

"You wanna leave this place, old girl?" I whispered. I gave her another apple slice and tugged on her halter. Those ears flipped up, something Muppet-like that made me smile, even in these circumstances. I stepped away and held out another piece of apple.

"What did I tell you?" Hyena Man said.

"The only way to get her to do anything is to smack her," Tattoo said. He got off his four-wheeler and walked to the fencerow, presumably to get a stick from a fallen tree.

The donkey watched him, saw his intent, and began trudging through the mire. I never had to touch her halter again, so willing was she to follow me.

"Well, I'll be damned," Tattoo said. He held a wicked-looking stick as wide as my forearm.

The donkey walked right into the trailer. I'd forgotten to put in fresh hay, but she couldn't care less. She knew an exit when she saw one.

As I put up the trailer door, the sheriff's car pulled in, followed by another cruiser.

Sheriff Stan Metz got out and called, "Everything all right, ladies?"

"Oh, yes," Helen said, so sugary it was hard to keep a straight face. "Mr. Early has signed over possession of the donkey quite willingly."

I wiped my hands on my mud-spattered jeans and said, "We just need a sweep of the property to see the conditions of the other animals."

"Whoa. Hey," Mr. Early said, going pale. "I told you, I don't have any other animals."

"Actually, sir, that's not what you told me. You said, 'So what if I did?' "

He looked like he'd like to take a baseball bat to *me*.

The sheriff said, "Let's take a quick look around. We'll be out of your way in no time. Gentlemen, come with me." He and another officer walked toward the back of the house.

"I don't even live here," Hyena Man said. "I've got to go."

Another officer blocked Hyena Man's exit. Tattoo looked like he might run into the woods.

When a third cruiser parked on the road, I knew this was no routine animal removal.

An officer told us to go ahead and get into my truck. "What's going on?" I asked Helen.

"When I gave Stan the address, he said he'd been waiting for a reason to get on this property."

"What do you think? Drugs?"

Apparently. After about ten minutes, the sheriff leaned into my truck window. "You did that donkey *and* me a huge favor today. Go on and get out of here before the news trucks arrive." He winked and slapped my truck door.

WHEN THE DONKEY WALKED OFF THE TRAILER AT MY FARM, she raised those hand-puppet ears and heaved a sigh that sounded like relief.

Both Biscuit and Moonshot came to their paddock fences to whinny at this newcomer. The donkey brayed—a sound like brakes squealing before an inevitable crash.

Biscuit, although he was five times the donkey's size, trembled.

Moonshot stood, eyes wide, ears forward, every inch of him asking, *What the hell was that?*

Muriel poked her head around a corner of the barn.

The donkey brayed again, and they all bolted.

We gave the donkey some grass hay. She stood eating as Helen and I sat on upside-down buckets on either side of her (she was so short!). We gently curried the mud from her coarse, uneven coat, uncovering the black stripes of fur that intersected at her withers, draping a cross down her shoulders and along her spine. She had several swollen places but nothing I thought warranted an X-ray. I looked in her eyes and in those miraculous ears—fluffy white inside, lined and tipped with black. Her thick brow tapered into a muzzle that eventually went white, with a perfect heart of black velvet tipping her nostrils and extending its point to her top lip.

I washed the cut over the donkey's right eye—a cut that could've used some stitches—then fetched a stethoscope and listened to her heart. Sound and fit.

I felt the donkey's belly. What was up with those skinny ribs but this big tummy? I couldn't imagine that Pete Early would have been very diligent about worming, but it didn't look like a worm belly.

I filled Helen in on the Zuzu trauma the day before.

Helen's eyes were bright. As she listened, she pushed her tongue into that gap between her teeth. "So you think Zayna's leaving him?"

"Yep." I moved my stethoscope to listen to the donkey's belly.

"Are you going to tell him?" Helen asked.

"Not my place. Not my problem."

Healthy gut sounds, all good . . . and something odd—a sensation that pushed my stethoscope away. The donkey lost patience with me and stepped sideways, pushing me off my bucket. I laughed and got up, brushing straw off my butt.

"I thought I'd feel gleeful." I situated the donkey again. "I wanted her to break his heart. But honestly? It feels sort of pitiful."

I leaned over, laying hands on the donkey's belly. There . . . no . . . there it was. A nudge against my open palm. I gasped. "It kicked me!"

Helen looked confused. "The donkey kicked you? When?"

"No," I said. "Her baby did."

Helen's mouth made a pleased, surprised O. "She's pregnant?"

There it was again, as unmistakable as Gabby's own kicks inside my belly once upon a time. "She is."

The donkey folded her knees and lay down with a soft grunt. Even with us standing there, she stretched out on her side. Helen crooned, "No wonder you're tired. Poor thing."

We both sat down in the straw and watched her. "A baby miniature donkey," I said. "I've never handled one of those before!"

Helen cocked her head at me. "I imagine there's not much you can't handle, my friend."

I liked that thought, but then Moonshot whinnied outside. The month was about up. Ms. Porn Star would be coming for him soon.

CHAPTER THIRTY-FIVE

ON MONDAY MORNING, AURORA EXAMINED ZUZU'S SPLINT
and the X-rays. "You did great, Cami." She shook her head, her
nose diamond twinkling. "Damn. I can't imagine pulling that
off by myself. Or rather, I can't imagine pulling that off with my
ex's lover assisting me!"

We laughed. I'd filled her in on all the bizarre details—
including my prediction that Zayna would leave Bobby.

Zuzu wriggled on the exam table, eyes bright, playful. The
little squirt could grow on you.

Gabby had camped out on the kitchen floor with Zuzu last
night, even though it hadn't really been necessary. When the
donkey brayed in the barn, Zuzu had howled. Gabby had sat up,
eyes wide, clutching a hand to her throat. "What is *that*?"

When I told her, she'd rolled her eyes. "Great. A *donkey*? We
have a donkey now, Mom?"

"We are *fostering* a donkey," I said.

"Whatever."

Here in the clinic, Aurora confirmed, "The foot is good.
Excellent job. The pad is warm, skin is pink, no swelling. The
bones, though . . ." She examined the X-ray.

"It'll need a pin," I said.

"Definitely. But all those fragments . . . maybe a plate? I'd recommend they go to an orthopedic specialist. Like Dr. Trick in Cincinnati. Want *me* to call Bobby and give them that recommendation?"

"I'd love you forever."

"Hey! I thought you already did."

"I'd love you *more* forever."

But after I'd neutered two cats—assisted by my brilliant, capable, fabulous technician Bridget, whom I would never ever take for granted again after Saturday's experience—Aurora came to the surgery door. "He wants you to do it," she said. "You saved her life. He trusts you."

I wanted to put my head down on the stainless steel table. An assistant brought in my third neuter, a smoky-gray cat. The assistant and Bridget anesthetized him. "I don't get it. Is he trying to feel less guilty? He thinks *this* will make me feel better? This is *not* a favor!"

"You can refuse," Aurora said.

I mulled this idea. Refusing felt like chickening out. Bridget laid the now-floppy cat on his back, tying his legs spread-eagle, exposing his white belly.

"You know," I said to her, "we *can* do that surgery."

Aurora smiled.

"Dr. Trick might do it faster," I said, "*maybe* better, but we *can* do it."

Aurora laughed and said, "We *are* doing it. I can see it in your eyes."

"We won't do Zuzu any harm," I said.

"Puppies are resilient," Aurora agreed.

"The more I think about it, the more I think it needs cross-pinning."

Aurora's eyes brightened. "We've never done that."

"I know. But don't you *want* to?"

"Ready, Dr. Anderson," Bridget said.

"And you know who we should invite to observe tomorrow, if not to help?"

Aurora cocked her head. "Tyler?"

"Wouldn't that be an impressive essay for a vet program if ever there was one?"

She grinned. But it was nothing compared to Tyler's grin when we told him.

WE KICKED ASS ON ZUZU'S SURGERY.

I'd reviewed my orthopedics notes from school, Aurora had called a former mentor. We were ready. We let Tyler assist, and he was as great as any vet tech I'd ever had.

One hour and seven minutes, no surprises, no setbacks. Beautiful prognosis.

As I sutured Zuzu's leg closed yet again—Aurora said I was neater—Aurora asked, "So, when Zayna leaves Bobby, who keeps the dog?"

I snorted. Should we talk about Bobby in front of Tyler? Why not—I felt a strange bonding after the successful surgery. "Bobby seems pretty smitten," I said. "But he's no good with neediness."

"He's not good with strength, either, if he left you," Tyler said, turning down the gas.

I smiled behind my mask. "Well, thanks."

I held up my tapered needle for more catgut. Tyler picked up the correct cassette without me having to say a word. I'd make this the neatest, tidiest row of sutures ever seen.

"What a dumb ass," Aurora said of Bobby, with surprising kindness.

"I know. When she leaves, I wonder what he'll do? I'd like to hope he learns something."

"I'm not holding my breath." Aurora gave Zuzu an injection of penicillin while I sutured.

Tyler turned off the anesthesia machine.

"Even though this was all his idea, he seems so *lost*, which is weird because even though this was something done to me, I feel like I'm . . ." I searched for the right word as I knotted the final suture.

Aurora's eyes flashed as she pulled down her mask.

"Found?" she and Tyler asked in unison.

"Yeah," I said. "That's it."

I felt strong. Strong as the bones in Zuzu's leg in her postsurgery X-rays. "Those bones are *together*," Aurora said.

She and Tyler high-fived.

RIDING HIGH ON THE SURGERY, I CALLED DUBEY AFTER Bobby (*and* Zayna, I noted) had picked up Zuzu to take her home. Bobby had seemed disturbed by the fact that the pins showed, poking out through the skin. Poor man probably wouldn't be able to look at his dog for six weeks.

To my delight, Dubey had just finished work himself and was free for dinner.

We met at the Pine Club near UD, where we indulged in gin-and-tonics and divine filets.

Once again, our conversation unfolded like a dance we knew well—we fell into rhythm easily, no stumbles, smooth transitions.

He was riveted by the story of Zuzu and toasted to her recovery.

I toasted to Thanksgiving—the day after next.

"I'm thankful for my freedom," he said.

I was tipsy enough that when Dubey asked me what had been the craziness I'd alluded to in my message, I blurted the whole story of Vijay as if we'd drunk truth serum.

As my mouth babbled on and on, my brain screamed, *Shut up! Shut up! Why are you telling him this?* But to my surprise, when I stumbled to a halt, Dubey raised his glass again and said, "I'm honored to know somebody with the strength, heart, and honesty you have. You are a kick-ass, independent woman."

I think I mottled down to my *toes*.

Dubey got it.

"Here's to never walking back into that trap," he said.

"It wouldn't be a *trap* with Vijay. It's just—"

"Never again." He downed his drink.

Well . . . Dubey *sort of* got it.

Close enough to feel like thanksgiving indeed.

Well, that is, until I drove home and saw I'd missed a call from Ginger Avalon. She would pick up Moonshot the Saturday after Thanksgiving.

CHAPTER THIRTY-SIX

IF GETTING GINGER AVALON'S MESSAGE DIDN'T MAKE ME sick enough, the e-mail Vijay finally sent me did.

> I'm sorry I've been quiet so long. Please understand it's hard to talk to you right now. I need to recover, which I know I will, but be patient with me, Cam. I think I'm going to take some time off, all the vacation time I've never taken, and really do some thinking.

My eyes stung at the word "recover." I'd hurt him, which I'd never, ever wanted to do. But, maybe . . . maybe he would figure out what he really wanted in life.

I would love to be able to talk to him about Zuzu, about all that Zayna had said, about losing Moonshot, to have his voice treat all my anxiety and sorrow. I missed him so much. I still held out hope.

That hope made me wretched with confusion over the lovely evening I'd just had with Dubey.

I'D ORIGINALLY WORRIED THAT THE FIRST HOLIDAYS WITH-out Bobby would be difficult, but as it turned out, he wasn't even a blip on my radar.

The Binardis usually had a huge gathering on the Saturday after Thanksgiving in Columbus, so the actual holiday was a small, cozy affair at my mom and dad's. In years past, I'd harass my mother, "What time are we actually eating?" knowing I could only expect Bobby to stay a certain amount of time. This year, Gabby and I went early, and we were surprised to find the Davids already there. "We always come this early," Davy said. "We stay all day."

Ava was there, too—they alternated years with Carol's family—and she was happily icing cookies. (Big David had come up with an ingenious idea: Ava was happiest when busy doing something with her hands. Since she'd always been a baker, he had her roll sugar-cookie dough and cut shapes, then ice them. They delivered copious quantities of their cookies to food pantries around the city.)

Ava iced pumpkins, snowflakes, and Easter eggs. ("Easter eggs?" I asked. Big David shrugged. "It's what she picked.") I iced, too—it was addicting, like filling in coloring books.

When we sat down to dinner, Davy announced, "We were picked by another mother." He said it as exuberantly as he had the first time. I loved that he still had that belief, that hope within him. "After what happened before, we feel a little weird. Don't feel obligated to make a big fuss again."

"Obligated?" my mother asked. "That's hardly the word I'd choose. We're thrilled."

Mom hounded them for details. They told us about Jessie—twenty-four, graduating from a premed program at Northwestern.

"Jess is really smart and together," Big David said, "but not ready to be a mom. She wants her baby to have two parents."

"And she wants those two parents to be us," Davy said, grinning. He handed the bowl of mashed potatoes to David.

See? I thought. *You lose some, you gain some. Concentrate on the gain.*

"The baby is a boy this time," Big David said.

"Have you thought about names?" Gabby asked.

"Jack," Davy said at the exact same moment Big David said, "Michael."

WHEN THE DAVIDS AND AVA HEADED HOME, TAKING GABBY with them, I stayed with my parents to go to the annual Aperjeet Thanksgiving Open House. I'd attended this Open House for as long as I could remember—a fabulous Indian banquet, including my favorite, *gajar ka halva*.

The last time I'd been in their kitchen, I'd kissed Vijay in the pantry. I turned to Mom—we both brushed our hair in the mirror. "Do you know about . . . me and Vijay?"

She nodded, her face suddenly older. "Shivani told me. We were . . . disappointed—not at you! Or Vijay. Just sad it didn't turn out the way we wished."

"He hasn't called me since it happened," I said, my nose burning. "I never wanted to hurt him."

My mother stopped pinning her hair in mid–French twist to put her hands on my arms. Her thick hair fell to her shoulders. We looked at each other in the mirror. "Of course you didn't."

"I . . . I think I would have hurt him worse if we had gotten married."

"Only you know that. And if that's so, you did the right thing."

"Does Shivani hate me?"

"No!" She turned to me instead of my reflection. "Not at all." She hugged me, and with her lips close to my ear she said, "And even if she did, that's no reason to marry the wrong man."

I released the hug and looked in her face, wanting her to understand. "He's not *wrong*. He's so right in so many ways . . . but he's not . . . mine."

She touched my cheek, then returned to pinning up her hair.

"Will he . . . will he be there, do you know?"

She turned sharply, her eyebrows raised. "Don't you know? He's in India."

India? *India?* That threw me. I hated that my mother knew something about Vijay that I didn't. He'd gone to India without telling me? We told each other *everything*.

India. By himself. For *four weeks*. To "recover" and "think."

I missed Vijay with a violence that felt like an injury.

I went home instead of accompanying my parents to the Aperjeets' Open House, going straight to Moonshot's paddock, where I scratched his tail. He shivered in the cold, raw air. "Why don't you finally try your stall, bud?" I urged him. "For your last two nights? Aren't you cold out here?"

He fluttered his nostrils and chose to stay where he was. I tortured myself, replaying that proposal conversation. I didn't understand how, if Vijay really wanted to spend his life with me, my words had made him disappear.

As my fingers ran through Moonshot's now silky tail, I remembered how Vijay and I had found each other at our senior prom—outside with the smokers—commiserating on the lousy time we were having. "We should've come to this together," he'd said.

Would it have been different if we had? Would we be together now? Would he have chosen a different path, one that allowed room for me?

Stop it. There are no what-ifs in life.

I might not have Gabriella in my life if I'd gone to the prom with Vijay.

To imagine this even fleetingly felt like an amputation.

Life unfolded as it should.

You made decisions that led to more.

I leaned against this horse's haunch, here in the church of my barn lot, and prayed for Ginger Avalon to change her mind. Or, if she didn't, for her to be the best thing that ever happened to this horse.

I closed my eyes and breathed in the warmth of Moonshot's earthy coat. *Let the right thing happen.*

ON SATURDAY MORNING, I AWOKE TO *TINK-TINK-TINK*-ING on the glass. The sky was still dark, but the moon shone in the mirror of ice that encased the yard. I couldn't help but smile. Outside, I entered a wonderland. Every twig, every tiny pine needle, every thing imaginable was covered in its own glass sheath. The trees groaned.

St. Francis, encased in his new sugar coating of ice, looked intact.

I slipped and flailed down the treacherous brick path, until I gave up and minced my way on the crunchy grass, where at least there was texture to give me some traction. No sound but the freezing rain rattling down around me, *tink-tink-tink*-ing on the bricks, the barn, the trees, and the aluminum gate. I walked on my own planet, in my own movie, all alone.

Moonshot had pearls of ice beaded in his whiskers and a coat of crunchy ice steaming on his back. His stall door stood open, but he hadn't opted to go in even from this.

"You look like an Appaloosa," I teased him, "with all that white on your back."

He snorted, taking a tentative step toward me, but skidded on the sheet of glass his paddock had become. As he bumped into me, I wrapped my arms around his neck. We slid together in slow motion to the fence, as if dancing a pas de deux in a skating rink. My laughter echoed in the silence the ice had created.

He turned his neck to snuff me where I clutched his shoulder.

"You're not going anywhere," I whispered into his ears tickling my chin. "At least not today." I lifted my face to the sky and let the pellets of ice sting my skin. "Nobody is."

I DECIDED TO BE PRESENT AND APPRECIATE THIS GIFT OF one more day. But the ice *kept* falling, shutting down our area for nearly three days. Branches tore off trees, cracking as loud as gunshots. The power went out, came back on, went out again. The Binardis had to postpone their gathering. I-75 shut down. The airport closed. School was cancelled on Monday.

The animals had trouble walking in the ice—all but Muriel. Surefooted and nimble, she capered about the farm on her built-in cleats as if she walked on gravel.

Each day, Ginger Avalon called, saying, "Well. We'll try again tomorrow," but on Monday evening she called and said,

"I'm afraid I have to be back in Florida on Wednesday. May I leave him with you a few more weeks?"

I wanted to dance for joy.

Muriel did it for me. I hung up the phone and watched her deliberately run, then slide, down the driveway, like a child in socks on a wooden floor.

It's temporary, I reminded myself. What did "a few more weeks" mean, anyway? Three? Six? I hadn't asked on purpose. Whatever the amount of time, I wanted to savor it.

I WENT TO DINNER WITH DUBEY AGAIN, AND HE GAVE ME A salsa CD he'd compiled for me.

When I got home, I put on the music and danced. The cats watched, their faces expressionless. Max wagged his tail, wanting to join this game. Gabriella caught me. She shook her head but smiled.

Moonshot, Biscuit, and the donkey grew their winter coats. Elegant Moonshot looked absurd with thick legs, as if he wore legwarmers. Long hairs grew from his ears and under his jaw.

The donkey sashayed across her paddock twitching her black-tufted tail. When she brayed, Moonshot yanked his head away and went rigid. "I remember when you were a tough guy," I teased him. "It's just a little donkey, you silly thing."

The donkey, we decided, needed a name. A full moon made the barn glow as Gabby and I mulled possibilities, so when Gabby suggested Luna, we agreed it was perfect. Luna lived in the stall next to Moonshot's (which he still never used), and one morning I observed her stealing hay from his pile from under the paddock fence. He laid his ears back but otherwise did not protest.

Each morning, the ice melted a bit more, and the grass crunched under my feet on the way to the barn, until one day I awoke to snow. Muriel gamboled around in the fat, wet flakes— I swear she tried to catch one on her tongue. I watched her cavort around the scrunched-neck St. Francis and laughed.

The Binardis rescheduled their Thanksgiving. Nick and Olive came to pick up Gabby.

When she returned, late that night, bearing Tupperware containers of lasagna, baked ziti, tiramisu, and pignoli cookies, I got out a fork, sat on the kitchen island, and sampled it all. "Oh. My. God," I said. "Damn, I miss this food! That man can *cook*."

Gabby cocked her head at me, an odd look on her face. "That's the only thing you've ever said you miss about Dad."

I set down the lasagna. "Oh, babe, I miss more than that."

She climbed up on the kitchen island and sat cross-legged next to me. She didn't seem angry with me tonight, or judgmental. Just curious. "Like what else?"

I held the lasagna out so that she could reach it, too, but she put a hand over her stomach and said, "I ate *so* much. I can't."

I savored a couple more bites before I said, "I loved your dad so much. I still do, because he made it possible for me to have you."

Gabby smiled but rolled her eyes. "That's such a cliché, Mom."

"Maybe. But it's true. He's a talented, complicated man. Once upon a time we really inspired and challenged each other. I don't think I'd ever have gone for my own practice if I hadn't watched him work for his own restaurant."

I put down the lasagna and peeled open the lid on the tiramisu. I took a bite. Pure heaven. "How does she *do* that?" I asked of Mimi. "How can the ladyfingers not be soggy?" Each bite was the perfect combination of custardy zabaglione and slightly crunchy, espresso-soaked ladyfingers. "How's Mimi? How's everybody?"

"Mimi's Mimi," Gabby said, with a look. "She and Olive argued about the wedding, then Olive and Mr. Henrici argued all the way home."

"If he's going to be your uncle, you can call him Nick."

She made a face. "Maybe after I graduate."

Gabby held her hand out for my fork, even though she'd said she was too full. She took a bite of the tiramisu, then handed the fork back to me.

"Did Olive ask about your wedding speech?" I asked. I took another bite. I loved the slight grittiness of the cocoa-espresso dusting on top.

She slumped her shoulders and glared at me, but not in earnest. "Yes," she moaned. "I was hoping she'd forget all about it. What am *I* supposed to know about marriage?"

"Nobody expects you to know about marriage. Maybe you could write something about love. You know a little something about love, right?"

She rolled her eyes and took the fork. Her face brightened. "Zuzu was there! She's doing great, Mom. She doesn't even *limp*!"

I smiled. "That's a puppy for you. They heal fast."

"Dad told everyone that story. He made you sound like some Superwoman, talking about how amazing you were, how you saved her life, how you did surgery without any help."

"Well, that probably wasn't very fun for Zayna to listen to."

Gabby smiled a big, gleeful smile. "Zayna wasn't there. They broke up."

I kept my face still. "Oh." Poor Binky. What a buffoon. "Wow. Do you know why?"

"Please," Gabby said, keeping the fork for two turns in a row. "Dad and I never talk about stuff like that."

"Stuff like what?"

"Anything real. I guess she left a week ago, but it was the first he'd said anything about it. And it only came up because Aunt Olive asked."

That made me so sad, I couldn't take another bite, even though it was my turn. I loved moments like this with Gabby, talking about "real" things. Bobby never had these with her? He was missing so much of his daughter's life. But that was *his* decision.

"Wait. So *he's* keeping Zuzu?"

"Yep."

"Hey, give me that fork. It's my turn!" We were down to a few bites left. "Wow. Your dad with a *puppy*."

"Maybe we should volunteer to keep her here?" Gabby asked, her face all innocence.

"No. No way."

"But Mom——"

"You can't give me all that crap about 'another animal' and then ask me to take your father's dog!"

She smiled. "I know. But she's so *cute*."

"So are you. So cute and so manipulative."

"But you're keeping *me*, right?"

I ate the last bite of the tiramisu. "Forever and ever," I said. I didn't want to miss any of it, either.

CHAPTER THIRTY-SEVEN

WHEN A NEW CLIENT SAID SHE WAS A DANCE INSTRUCTOR, I perked up. "What kind of dance?"

"Mostly Latin," she said, in a surprisingly deep, melodic voice that didn't match her willowy body. Her pale skin and ice-blue eyes made you expect something other than her warmth.

The geriatric Siamese cat she'd brought in hissed at me, baring its plaque-coated teeth. It was the woman's mother's cat. Her mother had suffered a stroke, and this woman, Colleen Jewell, had moved home from New York City to care for her.

"I used to work in a studio in the city. I danced competitively, but I also taught."

"Are you— Do you think you might have time to do any classes here?"

"I would *love* to," she said. "I actually have a studio in my mother's basement, from when I lived here. Dance floor, mirrors. It would do my heart good to use it."

When I called Dubey to tell him I'd found us another dance class, he said, "Excellent! I'm in."

I gathered other couples for our private class. Colleen undercharged us for the course; she seemed grateful to get to do it. We brought all the makings for a bar and served cocktails before we started. Helen and Hank were in. Olive and Nick. Aurora and her friend Mike. The Davids—how wonderful that they could dance *together*.

"Dubey's cute," Olive whispered to me.

"He smells good," Helen said.

"He can *dance*," Aurora said.

Hank was a good dancer, a natural, but Dubey had finesse and style. Dubey never seemed to get out of breath, the way Hank did.

Everyone seemed to like Dubey, but that overly polite quality remained until Colleen switched all of us around, leaving Big David and Dubey as partners. That traditional tension caused by a lifetime of defending my baby brother from assholes suddenly clenched my neck. Dubey, however, was unfazed. "You wanna lead or follow?" he asked.

Big David said, "I always follow."

Dubey said, "Cool, 'cause I don't know how." They took the dancer stance, Colleen started the music, and I loved that man.

As I danced with Nick, I realized Binky would never have danced with a man. I didn't think Vijay would've, either.

After that dance, the feeling in the room shifted. Everyone got a bit louder, a bit sillier. The profanity flew a little less sheepishly. I knew Dubey was *in*.

The holidays were looking brighter all the time.

GABBY AND I HAD AFFECTIONATELY CALLED BOBBY Scrooge, but really, until I had this distance, I hadn't been aware of the toll his generally pissy attitude about Christmas had taken on me.

For years, when he'd insistently repeat, "God, I hate Christmas," I'd wanted to snap, *You do? Gee, I didn't pick that up from the first seven hundred times you said it.*

I'd begun to dread the holidays, too, because it meant Bobby would brood and drink too much at my family's gatherings. I'd watch him and try to gauge, *Has he had enough? Does he want to leave?* All my energy went into monitoring his moods.

I knew that the root of this holiday misery came from his dysfunctional childhood. Olive had confirmed this. Holidays had typically been horrific, with their father either drunk or absent, but what had made Bobby's reaction to it so different from Olive's? Olive seemed to rejoice as an adult in the season that had been tainted for her as a child. She took control over it.

That's the path I chose to take myself.

GABRIELLA AND I DECIDED TO MAKE A PHOTO CHRISTMAS card with all the animals. What possessed us I'll never know, but we knotted red velvet ribbons in Biscuit's and Moonshot's forelocks and tied both horses with red cotton lead ropes to the heaviest fence near the St. Francis flower bed. We fixed red bows on one of Muriel's horns and on Max's collar.

Luna, once we'd braided red ribbon into her coarse mane, had refused to participate, planting her hooves like fence posts, not even willing to be bribed with carrots.

Helen and Hank came to photograph us, and I laughed so hard I was certain I would pee my pants. Biscuit pulled away and tried to eat grass. Moonshot tried to bite Biscuit. Muriel climbed onto Gabriella, leaving a big manure streak from her hoof on Gabby's new sweater. Gerald growled and Gingersnap answered, their demonic noises growing louder and more insistent.

Hank danced around like an idiot, trying to get the motley crew to look at the camera. He waved a towel. He threw his hat. He did jumping jacks until he panted. He rattled corn in a can—but that made Muriel break free from our group and rush over to him, standing up with her front hooves on his chest just like a begging dog. Max barked at what he knew was Muriel's break from formation. The cats escalated to spitting. I laughed so hard I could barely sit upright.

"Hey! Hey! Over here! Look at me!" Hank called, prancing, jigging, wheezing. He looked so ridiculous that Helen turned to take a picture of *him*.

Moonshot lunged at Biscuit, grabbing his leather halter. Biscuit squealed and reared, striking the fence and knocking off a board, which made Gabby and me leap up. The cats fled. Max chased them, barking, and Muriel happily ate the corn that Hank had dropped.

"Okay, enough!" I said through my giggles. I opened Moonshot's gate and shooed him in, his red ribbon falling into the frozen mud on the way.

We huddled, shivering and laughing, looking through the series of digital photos. When we got to the photo of Hank we howled.

"Delete that this second," he ordered, grinning.

Helen's photo had captured him with his right arm in the air, towel flying, his left hip and arm thrust out, looking for all the world like John Travolta in *Saturday Night Fever*.

Helen tipped her head back and shouted, "I love this man!"

Hank looked at the photo and shook his head. "The things I do for you."

There was one photo that, for a group animal shot, was as good as it gets—everyone's mouth was closed, no teeth or fangs bared. But Gabby and I both kept returning to a more chaotic shot: Gabby holds up Gingersnap, who has her back claws attached to Gabby's jeans. The goat stands on Gabby's thigh, with some of Gabby's hair in her mouth. Max's long muzzle points skyward as he howls at the mayhem. Gerald snarls like a vampire. Moonshot, teeth bared, reaches toward Biscuit. Biscuit cranes his neck away—*doh doh dee doh*—stretching for the grass. Luna's butt is visible in the background as she stands in her paddock. St. Francis's head is turned to the right, although his body faces front. Gabby and I both laugh eyes-squinted-mouths-wide-open laughs.

We printed it as our Christmas card with the words on the front, " . . . and wild and sweet . . ." and continued inside, " . . . the words repeat, of Peace on Earth, Good Will to Men (and women and children and animals)."

I meant it, too. I wished good will to Vijay, wherever he was.

I even wished it to Binky.

I overflowed with good will for Ginger Avalon when a Christmas card arrived from her. It contained a generous board check far exceeding the price we'd agreed upon, an apology, and the words, "It looks like it'll be after the holidays before I can come collect the Ohio horses."

"He's never leaving, is he?" Gabby asked.

"I'm afraid he is," I said. "Just not yet. Ginger gave me a Christmas present."

✿

GABBY AND I DECIDED TO GET A LIVE CHRISTMAS TREE, something I hadn't enjoyed in sixteen years.

We'd always had live Christmas trees in my childhood home. Just like they did all things, Mom and Dad were slow and meticulous with tree selections, so Davy and I would grow bored and run through the display, playing hide-and-seek. Davy would often find some scrawny, lopsided tree and feel sorry for it, growing anxious about how it would "feel" being left behind there, never chosen by anyone. He could get so pale and fretful about it that on three occasions I recall my parents buying two trees—a runty misfit tree for the entrance foyer and a majestic one for the sitting room.

My parents bought Davy and me an ornament each year so that when we moved away to homes of our own, we could take our ornaments with us. They picked things to commemorate some event or accomplishment from that year of our lives. I had a little red bicycle from the year I learned to ride a bike, an Eiffel Tower for the year Vijay and I went on the French club trip to Paris, a stethoscope for the year I became a vet. Davy had a scarecrow for the year he played that role in our high school's performance of *The Wizard of Oz*, an apple for the year he became a teacher, a tiny two-groom cake topper my mother had found the year they had their ceremony.

Bobby had sighed about a Christmas tree. He'd sighed about the fallen needles I was rather nonchalant about vacuuming. He got impatient and profane putting on the lights, so I'd taken over. He just wasn't into it. That's okay, I thought. No big deal.

Our second married Christmas, I heard of a place with great, inexpensive live trees. When we arrived, the lovely snow had turned to rain, and the little dirt road that led to the tree farm had turned into a puddinglike mess. Once we'd selected our tree—a gorgeous one, incredibly cheap for how large it was—our truck got stuck in the mud. We had to be pulled out, and during the process Bobby got sprayed with mud from the spinning wheels.

On the way home, we were hit from behind by a person with no insurance.

Once we finally made it home, the tree turned out to be too big. I had to saw it down.

Then our cat climbed it, tipping it over, narrowly missing Gabby in her baby seat. I had to wire the tree to the ceiling to keep ballistic Bobby from hauling it to the trash.

We woke up one morning to loud "pop!" and "pow!" sounds—the tree was shooting pine nuts all over the room. When I cleaned up the pine nuts (and broke our vacuum sweeper in the process), I didn't realize that the nuts had also spurted out sticky sap that left our new white carpet damp. I set our packages—all wrapped in blue paper—around the base of the tree. After we opened them on Christmas morning, we discovered blue stains on the carpet—stains that proved impossible to remove.

The next year, when I suggested getting a tree, Bobby shot me a look. And that was that.

GABBY AND I SELECTED A MODEST BUT AROMATIC TREE ONE evening on the way home from the clinic. As we put on the lights and made popcorn garlands, I asked, "What are your plans with your dad for Christmas?"

"I'm not sure yet," she said. I hated the worry lines that appeared on her forehead. "But we'll do Christmas Eve like usual, right?"

"Sure." We'd always celebrated Christmas Eve at my parents' with the Davids and then had Christmas Day with the Binardis in Columbus. This saved us from having to do two family gatherings in one day, which invariably got exhausting, especially back in nap-time days.

Gabriella paused, her threaded needle poised in her hand. "If I'm with Dad on Christmas Day, what will you do?" Her sweet eyes darkened with concern.

"I'll be fine." It was a lie. The thought of Christmas Day spent alone felt bleak, but no way would I give my daughter any more baggage to carry. "I might go to Helen and Hank's."

This seemed to please her.

I'd asked Dubey what he was doing, and although he'd seemed happy to be asked, he wasn't sure yet and couldn't commit.

I thought of Vijay, who always came home for Christmas. I could spend the day with him. We could go to a movie, or rent one and watch it here with the fire— If he would speak to me, that is.

As we unpacked the ornaments, most of which Gabby had never seen, I told her how I'd started to keep my parents' tradition. "We bought this one the year you first saw the beach," I said, holding up a little dolphin, "and this one when we took you to Italy"—I showed her a delicate golden blown-glass ball. "You get to take these with you when you have your own place."

"What a cool idea!" Gabriella said. "I need to start getting *you* an ornament each year, too."

I couldn't wait to see what she'd pick for me.

GABBY PRESENTED HER GIFT ON OUR SECOND SNOW DAY OF the year, a morning I'd scheduled off because I had my annual mammogram and gyno appointment (fun, fun—but both ended up being canceled because of the snow). Flakes so small and multiple you could hardly distinguish them in the milky air accumulated in high cake slices on the tree limbs, fence tops, and cars.

I made pancakes after we did the morning feed, then Gabriella gave me my ornaments.

The first was a tiny cat stitched of brown felt with an embroidered face and whiskers.

She'd cut off its left front leg.

"They didn't have one the right color," she explained, "but you'll always remember the year you found Gerald was the year we all lost . . . stuff."

"Lost stuff," I repeated, my eyes burning. "I love it."

"Jeez, Mom, don't cry. Here's another one."

I unfolded the tissue paper to discover a little goat with wings and a halo. I laughed aloud, "An angel *goat*?"

"I know! Isn't it perfect? And look at *this*."

"*Another* one?" I opened a white palm-sized church with a steeple, only three-sided, with the entire back a golden stained glass.

"Hold it up to the light," she instructed.

I did. My breath caught. Inside this church, silhouetted against the golden glass, was a horse. Tail raised, neck arched, about to commit mischief.

I found a perfect spot for them in the tree, with the church in front of a light so that the horse was illuminated against the amber glow. There they were: my guides. My priests. My ministers.

We spent the rest of the morning covered in quilts, a dog, and two cats, watching Christmas specials—crying, "Zuzu's petals!" along with Jimmy Stewart.

DUBEY AND I WENT FOR DRINKS ONE NIGHT AFTER SALSA class. When I asked again about his plans for Christmas Day, he seemed to stiffen. "I'll tell you when I know." Then he softened and said, "Like I said before, if I'm free, I'd love to do something with you."

Later, I asked Gabriella again about Bobby's plans for Christmas and *she* still didn't know. This time, she answered as if I'd asked her a hundred times already, which set off alarm bells.

As the last day of school approached and Gabby's winter break loomed before us, I asked a third time. She said, "He's going away, actually."

I fought not to look pissed. I kept my voice neutral. "Really? Where?"

Her eyes looked sad, but her voice was defiant. "Vegas."

I couldn't speak. He'd always wanted to leave for Christmas and I'd never agreed. I had a sudden, irrational thought: if I'd agreed to go somewhere for Christmas, some ridiculous place he'd suggested to entice me, like Hawaii, Jamaica, or Belize, would we still be married? Is *this* why he'd left? I shook my head. It would never be that simple, the reason. All these months later and I still tortured myself with that game?

"Don't be so judgmental!" Gabby said.

I opened my arms. "I didn't say anything!"

"I can see you thinking," she said. "Standing there hating him."

"That . . . that wasn't what I was thinking at all."

I wanted to ask if he'd invited her to go with him, but she gave me the answer when she said, "He asked if we'd babysit Zuzu. I said we would."

"VEGAS?" I RANTED AT THE NEXT GNO. "HE'D RATHER GO to some cheap-ass, tacky hellhole than be with his daughter? Does he not think about her at all? Does he simply not give a shit?"

"He made Ma cry," Olive said. "How hard can it be? What is so goddamn hard about spending a day with people who fuck- ing love you? The son of a bitch. He says he doesn't want to 'do Christmas' this year. At all."

"And now I'm taking care of his goddamn dog!"

Olive still wanted Gabriella to come over that day, and she and Nick were willing to come get her, if she wanted to come.

"Call and invite her," I pleaded. "Please. I have to stay out of it. I can tell she's crushed, but if I say one word, she attacks me for judging Bobby."

"You can always come play with me and Hank," Helen said.

I loved my friends. We toasted to Christmas, to friends, to the clinic's success, to Olive and Nick's recovery from their latest fight over the wedding guest list (they were up to three hundred!), and to the amazing chicken tikka masala we were eating.

"Have you heard from Vijay?" Aurora asked.

My mouth immediately crumpled. I'd received a postcard

from India that had arrived weeks after its postmark date. It'd said, "I'm trying to reflect and think about the life I want to live. I always want you to be a part of it." I'd analyzed those meager sentences obsessively. Flickers of hope tried to ignite.

I blew my nose and said, "I miss him so much. It's awful."

"But what about that Dubey guy?" Olive asked. "You're seeing him, right?"

I smiled. "I guess so. Kind of. Things are progressing . . . slowly."

"Good," Olive said. "You should be in a relationship."

"Hello." I gestured to the women at my table. "I have lots of relationships."

Olive made her smoke-ring mouth. "You know what I mean."

"I know you're worried about Gabby," Helen said, "but do *you* have plans for Christmas?"

"Maybe. I might be doing something with Dubey. He's not sure he can yet."

Helen studied me. "What? You just gonna sit around and wait?"

I realized that was *exactly* what I'd been going to do.

"No," I said. "I'm coming to your house. For sure. I just might be bringing a date."

Helen nodded. "That's better," she said.

CHAPTER THIRTY-EIGHT

THE COZY CHRISTMAS EVE AT MY PARENTS' HOME TURNED out to be far more fun without Bobby, something even Gabriella admitted.

Had I held my breath my entire marriage, waiting to spring into motion at the first signs of Bobby's unhappiness? There now seemed to be so much room and space for joy.

The Davids brought Jess, the mother of their child, with them. Much to my delight, I thoroughly enjoyed her. Down to earth, smart, with a wicked sense of humor, she fit right in and seemed at ease with everyone. I smiled at the way I caught her often rubbing her belly.

Everyone fawned over Zuzu, who cowered from my parents' miniscule fox terrier and spent most of the evening in my lap. At nine months and forty pounds, she was a bit big for a lap dog.

I already liked Jess, but when Davy explained to her who Zuzu was, Jess looked at me, green eyes flashing, and said, totally deadpan, of Bobby, "That takes some damn *nerve*."

How could I not love her?

Big David helped my mother braid cinnamon-roll dough into a candy cane cake, and Jess and Gabby iced it white and red. I secretly toasted with my glass of wine that if I ever was in a couple again, I wanted a man who loved my family, who'd embrace them like Big David did.

We heaped the Davids with baby gifts again, replacing all the gifts they'd given to Kim and baby Grace. I wondered how Grace's first Christmas was. How often did the Davids think of her? Every waking moment? The guys told us they'd sent Christmas gifts to her. I loved them for their forgiving generosity, but I loved the new mom, Jess, even more when she presented them with a scrapbook of childhood photos of herself and all her family tree, plus an empty photo album to fill with pictures of their baby.

I watched my mother swing her hips to the side so that my father could take a spatula from a drawer, without either of them saying a word. Dad brushed confectioner's sugar off her nose. I ached, watching that familiarity, that language without words.

I looked out a window at the dark Aperjeet house across the street. Mom told me the family had gone to New York for Christmas at Vijay's this year.

I still hadn't heard from Dubey, so I was grateful Helen had made me make plans.

When Gabby and I returned home, it was nearly midnight. "Wanna go to the barn with me?" I asked. "In case the animals have anything to say?"

She yawned. "Nah, Aunt Olive is picking me up *really* early." As she opened the back door, Max, Gerald, and Gingersnap all rushed out to follow me, bowling Zuzu over into the snow.

I felt the childlike belief of *maybe*. Why else would they all want out on a bitterly cold night?

I WAS SEVEN WHEN MY FATHER FIRST TOLD ME THAT AT midnight on Christmas Eve, the animals could speak. We'd just come home from church and I'd fallen asleep in the car, so it was already dreamy and surreal. My mother carried Davy, and my father held my red-mittened hand.

"Shhh," he said. "We have to sneak up." We tried, but the snow squeaked. We got close to the barn and listened at all the stall doors. "Hear any words?" he asked, his breath hanging in clouds.

I shook my head, not sure I could hear anything over my pounding heart.

We crept into the barn aisle and huddled on the floor.

"Why will they talk tonight?" I whispered as our barn cats blinked at us from the hayloft.

"They get to talk for one hour each Christmas because they were so helpful when Jesus was born. The donkey carried Mary, the cow gave up his manger for a crib—"

"What's a manger?" Davy interrupted.

"Like a feedbox," I whispered. "Be *quiet*."

"—the sheep gave him wool to keep warm, and the doves cooed him to sleep."

"What do you think they'll say?" I asked.

Dad rubbed his chin. "Usually they'll tell if they've been mistreated."

"Will God take Myra Engle's pony away from her?" Myra Engle had hit her pony in the face with her crop one day at a horse show. My parents had been mortified, but perhaps even more so by the fact that I'd hit Myra—in the face—with *my* crop.

"We don't know." Mom pursed her lips, no doubt remembering that day.

Myra called her pony names and left him tied to the fence in the hot sun without water at horse shows. If her pony could talk, he'd have a lot to complain about.

My dad squeezed me and asked, "What would *your* pony have to say?"

I wasn't worried about Roscoe. I wanted to know what Stormwatch would say. Would he tell on me? Would he reveal that twice now I'd stood in his feedbox and slipped onto his back?

I felt closer than ever to Stormwatch that year because he hadn't told our secret. My dad had opened the top of his Dutch door. The horse had put his head into the aisle and whinnied toward me. My heart had lodged thick in my throat. But then he'd snorted, sounding only like a horse.

Dad had let me give Stormwatch a shiny red Christmas apple and a candy cane.

None of the animals spoke to us that Christmas Eve or on any others afterward. "Not everyone can hear them," my mother had said, by way of consolation.

I'd had no doubt that *I* could. If they were to speak, *I*'d hear them. They just weren't talking.

HERE IN MY OWN BARN, THERE WAS NO HOPE OF "SNEAKing" up with the entourage that followed me. Moonshot was still out in his paddock, in spite of the cold. I wondered if I should hammer boards up to make him a little shelter until Ginger took him away? Or at least get him a blanket?

I'd led him into his stall a few times, but he always promptly marched back out. If I shut him in, he fretted and paced. I couldn't stand to do that to him, not after all the progress we'd made.

The temperatures had dropped to a point, though, that I needed to close his back door to keep the rest of the barn warm. It hurt me each time I closed the door, shutting him outside.

In the barn, Biscuit snored, lying down asleep. He didn't seem likely to burst into conversation any time soon. Neither did Luna, on her side, her enormous belly rising and falling with her breaths. I hugged myself in my parka, then checked my watch. I had three minutes before the hour. I waded into Moonshot's clean, knee-deep straw and opened his back door. Max snuggled close to me when I sat in one corner. Zuzu clambered onto his back and promptly fell asleep. Muriel snuggled into my other side, occasionally nibbling my thigh through my jeans. Gerald hopped into my lap, which prompted Gingersnap to sulk in the stall door.

"You two can get along for a few minutes," I said. "It's Christmas!" She opted to lie alongside Max. I closed my eyes and tipped back my head. I cringed to remember that last Christmas I'd had sex with Bobby even though I hadn't really wanted to. He'd so rarely initiated it by that point that I'd known not to turn it down. I'd always had this bizarre belief that the coming-together would save us somehow. But I'd turned my head at one point and noticed the clock saying 12:07—*why did I remember that?*—and had thought, "If the animals talk, I'll miss it." I'd felt so guilty at that thought that I threw myself into the sex, giving an Oscar-worthy performance.

An exhalation of breath sounded so like one of Bobby's deep sighs that I opened my eyes. Moonshot stood in the doorway, his neck craned toward us.

"Come on in. Join the party," I whispered.

He stepped into the deep straw, snuffling around. He lowered his velvety muzzle to my nose. "Anything you'd like to say?" I asked. "Now's your chance."

To my amazement, he dropped his haunches to the straw. With a mighty groan he bent his knees, too, and lay down, his legs tucked in like a cat's. He groaned again, a sound much like approval. Then he flopped onto his side, his neck and head in the fluffy straw.

Gerald stood in my lap and reached his one front paw to touch the tear on my cold cheek.

When I crept away—I'd closed his door partway, leaving a crack he could easily nudge open if he felt the need to leave—I carried Zuzu up to Gabriella's bed.

Gabriella murmured, "Did they talk to you?"

My throat tightened. "Yes," I whispered. "They did."

WHEN GABBY LEFT IN THE MORNING, THE DAY STRETCHED before me without a single commitment until I went to Helen and Hank's in the afternoon. I'd expected to feel sad, but instead I felt peaceful.

I found Moonshot still in his stall, as content as if he'd stayed there from day one. I took a chance and put his breakfast in his feedbox rather than outside. He ate it. Progress.

Maybe I simply had to *ask* for what I wanted. I resolved to do just that.

I broke down and called Vijay. I got his voice mail, as usual. I closed my eyes, savoring that deep, rich voice. "Hey you," I said. "Good to hear your voice. This is the first Christmas since we were kids that I won't see you. It doesn't feel right. I . . . I really miss you." I paused. What did I end with? "I—" I wanted to say *I love you*, but the pause grew too long, so I closed my phone.

I knew I'd done the right thing, but damn, did it have to hurt so much?

When my phone rang, my heart leaped. It wasn't Vijay but Dubey. "You know what we should do?" he said. "Go sledding."

We had a blast, careening down my back hill on Gabby's old runner sled and a disk sled. Max, Zuzu, and Booker chased us, barking until they were hoarse. Muriel followed us, too.

We tumbled together in the snow at one point and ended up face to face, me on top of him. I was giddy, and it was on my lips to say, "May I kiss you?" when Muriel climbed on my back, rolling us apart.

Back in the house, I built a fire and opened some wine. I felt terrified at what I'd almost done, but also reckless, looking for another opportunity. I knew I was just switching the Dubey fantasy for the Vijay fantasy. It didn't mean that either man was right for me.

"Where's Gabriella?" he asked. "With her dad?"

I told him the story. "Olive and Nick took her to Columbus today."

"They're engaged, right?" he asked.

"Yep. The wedding's in May."

He sighed. "Ah, well. Everyone makes mistakes."

I'd been raising my glass to my lips but stopped. "You think your marriage was a mistake?"

"Hell, yes. Wasn't yours?"

"No." That surprised me. "It ended badly, but I'll never say I wished it hadn't happened."

I thought about that later, after Dubey and I had gone to Helen and Hank's and eaten ourselves sick on rack of lamb. After we'd laughed and laughed and eaten *good* fruitcake. ("Yes, there really is such a thing," Hank had said.). After Dubey hadn't kissed me *again* at my door.

Before Gabriella came home I thought again, *I will never say I wish I'd never married Bobby.* Our marriage had been reckless, perhaps. Not well thought out. Certainly not maintained. But not a mistake. His leaving me had been the catalyst for the greatest life change I'd ever known.

He'd given me a gift the day he walked out. Okay, so he'd *delivered* the gift wrapped in a poopy diaper, but once I'd picked through all that shit, I'd found *diamonds*. I felt more love for him right at that moment than perhaps I'd ever felt.

Maybe someday I'd even be able to thank him.

That someday seemed very far away when we got the word that Bobby was remarried.

To a woman we'd never heard of.

In Vegas.

CHAPTER THIRTY-NINE

THE CALL CAME ON DECEMBER TWENTY-EIGHTH, AFTER A hellacious day at the clinic. A routine spay had uncovered a poor collie's abdomen full of tumors. A husky was not responding to treatment for lymphoma. A spayed cat had ripped out her stitches. I struggled to remain present with the client in the room rather than all those sullen, waiting faces in the lobby each time I opened the door.

Aurora and I stayed two hours past closing. I was alone and exhausted when Olive called. She got right to the point. "Bobby got married."

Sometimes news is so foreign you have no idea how to wrap your brain around it. In my head I said, *I know that. You were there, you ditz. Eighteen years ago.*

It took a full thirty seconds for my brain to absorb her statement.

Oh. Bobby got married *again*.

"That goddamn son of a bitch," Olive said. "He married some whore in Vegas."

With Olive, I couldn't tell if that *whore* was literal or just an opinion. Had Bobby been *drunk*?

She told me what she knew: the woman's name was Lydia.

She was a real-estate agent from Dayton, divorced also. They married on Christmas Day.

"He called my mom first," Olive said. "She is freaking out."

"Oh, Gabby," left my lips. Hadn't she had enough upheaval for one year?

Olive stopped ranting. I heard the anger now for the pain it truly was. "I'd take a bullet for her. You know that. I told Bobby I'd put the bullet in his head if he kept hurting my niece."

I moaned. "How do I tell her this?"

"Maybe he'll grow a sack and tell her himself."

BELIEVE IT OR NOT, HE DID. THE DAVIDS HAD BROUGHT her back from a movie and we were sitting in my kitchen eating dinner when she got the call. Her face lit up with unmistakable joy at recognizing his ring tone, although she tried to mask it.

"Take it," I said, breaking my own rule that we didn't answer calls at the table.

When she left the room, I told the Davids. It's hard to describe the expression that crossed their faces in unison.

Gabriella returned, looking small and shaken. I hugged her. "I found out today, too."

She sat at the table, her face bewildered.

"Do we even know this woman?" Davy asked.

Big David asked, "Does *he*?"

"He knew her for two days," Gabriella said.

"Two days," Big David repeated.

"And they're married," Davy said. "Legitimate. Official. Married."

The somber mood was broken when Zuzu snatched a biscuit from the table and ran away.

New Year's Eve can be a miserable, fraught holiday for a single person. New Year's Eve is more of a couples' holiday than even Valentine's Day. That level of anxiety only increases when you learn your ex has remarried within a year of leaving you.

Gabriella would be spending the night at Amy's. The Davids went to a midnight 5K race downtown—Davy to run, Big David to help feed the runners afterward. I turned down invites for New Year's Eve parties from Aurora, Hank and Helen, and Olive and Nick.

I'd asked Dubey about his New Year's plans one day when we took the dogs for a hike, but when he replied with that same evasive defensiveness he'd had about Christmas, I dropped the subject.

Vijay called at long last. I stared at his name and didn't answer. So much had changed I didn't think I knew how to talk to him. "Hey, Cam," his voice mail said. God, that voice vibrated into my *fingertips*. "I miss you, too. Sorry to have dropped out of sight for so long. I'd love to talk to you, see you, if you feel like it—I'm in Dayton—although I would understand if you're not talking to me. It was good to hear your voice, even if it's on the machine." I replayed the message four times, just to get high on that voice. I'd see him, and soon, but not tonight.

I went to the clinic, which was open only for half a day today. Bobby came to pick up the now pinless Zuzu while I was gone, which I thought best.

Dubey left a message, "I know it's the height of cheekiness to expect a beautiful woman doesn't have New Year's Eve plans already, but I thought it was worth a try. Call me." For a split second I almost did, but I decided that this New Year's Eve was mine entirely.

On the way home, I picked up my favorite Indian takeout, a good bottle of wine, and some Graeter's ice cream—coconut chocolate chip.

I took a nap, with Max's head on my chest, Gerald in the opposite armpit, and Gingersnap across my feet. I savored the sensation of warm, living bodies cuddled up beside me. Survivors, all of us. Eventually I built a fire and ate my chicken tikka saag. I took a bubble bath, sipping a glass of wine.

I made sure I was at my church when midnight rolled around. I stood with Moonshot in his stall and looked out his open back door at the sliver of moon that matched his own. When the year turned, gunshots and firecrackers echoed through the winter air. My phone trilled in my pocket.

"Happy New Year, Mom," Gabriella said. "Are you at a party?"

"Just a small one." Moonshot turned his mighty haunches to me. "With some close friends."

"SEE? MARRIAGE RUINS EVERYTHING," HELEN SAID WHEN I told her about my strange New Year's Day lunch with Vijay. "The proposal alone was enough to derail a beautiful friendship."

I felt that broken-rib ache as soon as I saw him. I knew his whole history—his first crush, how he couldn't swim until he was in middle school, how he was in a car accident in high school that his parents to this day didn't know about. I knew the sounds he made when sleeping. The smell in the crook of his neck. Those silky black hairs.

And there he sat, a total stranger.

All our former ease was gone. We pushed our food around on our plates. I asked about India and got a lame "It was great. I did a lot of thinking."

At one point I blurted, "Hey. Remember how we said we wouldn't ruin our friendship? We *promised*. We *swore*."

He nodded, looking down at his plate. When he looked up, he said, "I know. But . . . but I wasn't prepared for how I would feel. For what it would feel like when . . ." An unbearable amount of time passed before he continued, " . . . when I realized you didn't want me."

The words punched me in the gut. "I never said I didn't want you, Vijay. You're not allowed to believe that. It's not true."

"But you said—"

"I said 'not yet,' and I told you why I was scared. I told you I worried that I'd never see you, and your answer was to *disappear* for, what? Almost three months?"

He studied me, peering at my face as if something were written there. Eventually he whispered, "What do you want from me, Cam?"

"I want you," I said with no hesitation. "But you're never here. And I don't mean here in Dayton, I mean with me."

"I don't know how to convince you."

"Try something. Try anything."

"It feels like a test."

"It sort of is. But *I*'m not testing you. Marriage is. Marriage is a hard, hard test. Harder than any exam we ever took. We have to decide that we won't fail again."

"Are you dating that guy? The one you danced with?" He looked only at his plate.

"No, Vijay, I'm not. I've gone to dinner with him, on hikes, whatever, but I'm not 'seeing' him. I want *you*, Vijay. I want things to work with *you*."

He looked up and said, "I went on a couple dates."

The old ache in my ribs flared to life. "You *did*?"

"What?" The question was a challenge.

"Nothing. I'm just . . . surprised, I guess. And a little . . ." *Heartbroken? Devastated? Flattened?* I made a face.

"I want to be married, Cam. I can't just wait, you know, forever, for this indefinite test."

Everything I said to him was wrong. "I tried to be honest," I whispered. "If we can't *talk* about being married, then how can we possibly expect a marriage to work?"

"I love you, Cami." His voice trembled as he said it.

"I love you, Vijay." I took his hand. "So much it hurts me."

"And that's not enough." It was a statement, not a question.

I paused too long, forming a response. I felt it happen— those seconds felt like years, that silence became an affirmation. He pulled his hand away.

CHAPTER FORTY

FEBRUARY BEGAN—A GRIM MONTH IN OHIO. ALONG WITH the bleak sky, endless rain, and Valentine's Day decorations that taunted me came Ginger Avalon, with a six-horse trailer. My reprieve was over.

All the false alarms had made me hopeful. I'd fallen into the trap of thinking Moonshot wasn't ever really leaving. My limbs filled with ice water when that trailer pulled into the drive.

Ginger had already picked up the two fillies from my parents and another of the foster horses. She was alone.

"You're not driving all the way to Florida with a full trailer by yourself, are you?" I asked.

She laughed. "No. No way. I'll have two staff members with me."

"What are you going to do with him?" I asked. "He's too old to race, right?"

She nodded as if the fact pained her. "My sister mismanaged his racing career in a big way, and now he's gelded, to boot." I saw in her expression what she thought of her sister's stupidity. "But he's so athletic. I expect he'll have success on the show-jumping circuit."

I tried to keep my face neutral. I didn't tell Ginger my father called the riders on the jump circuit "cowboys," and that he practically spat when he said it.

When Ginger clapped her hands on her jeans-clad thighs and said, "Well," I realized I'd just been standing there, as if by freezing I could keep this moment from happening. I led her to the barn. My hands shook.

She did everything right—she didn't hurry, she let him snuff her over, she fed him treats. I tried not to feel betrayed when he took them.

"You've brought him a long, long way," she said to me, "and I thank you."

"He's brought *me* a long, long way," I said, mortified at my tight, small voice.

"Would you ever sell him?" I blurted.

She cocked her head at me. "He's expensive."

"I know."

She paused. "I know you're attached to him. I don't blame you a bit, but . . . he's not for sale."

I swallowed. "If you ever, ever change your mind, please remember me."

"Of course." She wrapped Moonshot's legs for the journey, and as she led him from his paddock, he high-stepped and stretched at the unfamiliar sensation of the leg-wraps. Ginger laughed at him, but my laughter stuck in my throat.

I followed her on wooden legs as she led him to her huge, fancy trailer, where the other horses waited, munching their hay. She opened up the door for his stall—a step-up, not a ramp. I held back, standing by my broken St. Francis statue. His head had fallen off again. I picked it up and propped it back on his neck.

I stood up in time to see Moonshot balk. As Ginger tried to guide him into the trailer, he planted all four feet square. When she tapped his shoulder to urge him forward, he backed up. When she tugged on his lead rope, he reared.

Uh-oh.

I *hated* watching the struggle. He'd decided he was having nothing to do with it. She was horse-savvy and handled him with calm firmness, but he regressed before my eyes into the wild beast he'd been when he first arrived. He reared, he bucked, he about jerked Ginger's arms from the sockets, he thrashed his head, he dragged her backward.

A childish part of me thought, *She won't be able to load him and she'll say "never mind" and let me keep him*. But I knew that was an impossible outcome. The battle was painful to watch.

He got as nasty as I'd ever seen him, and through it all Ginger never raised her voice or got mean. I had to admire her grace in the face of this tantrum. His fight went on for about ten hideous minutes before I watched Ginger use the tactic I'd seen my parents use on countless occasions and that *always* worked: when he pulled backward, she urged him to *keep* going backward. She tapped his chest and guided him backward all over my yard, all the way around the house. The idea was that if the horse insisted on pulling away, you *made* him move away from you until he was weary of it, until he was *more* than happy to take a step *forward*.

She backed him up, still speaking in a soothing, patient voice, far longer than I would've had the energy to keep it up.

When she backed him up to the trailer, then turned him toward his door, I could hardly believe that he *still* reared up and yanked her off balance rather than loading.

_____

She paused a moment, panting. Then she backed him up some more. She walked him backward all the way down to the road and up the driveway.

When she brought him again to his trailer door, he wheeled around and kicked the side of the trailer, leaving hoofprints in the side. A horse inside whinnied.

She managed to keep hold of him, but I feared for a moment he'd drag her.

I *hated* this. I couldn't stand a minute more of it.

"Ginger," I said.

She hadn't asked me to help her. Two people with a lead rope around his butt could probably get him on that trailer, but I admired that this wasn't her style. I also knew that she was a smart woman—she knew I didn't want him to leave, so she was probably not asking me to help out of respect for me. Unlike Binky asking me to carry his damn computer.

She turned to me, out of breath. Both she and the horse trembled with exhaustion. Foamy sweat flecked Moonshot's neck and chest.

"Bring him back to his paddock," I said. "I'll help you after you both take a breather."

She didn't speak, but she did as I asked.

I brought her a bottle of water and draped a cooling sheet over Moonshot so he wouldn't get chilled in the wintry air. "I want to show you something," I said. I pulled his tail to the side and began running my fingers through the thick hair. "This relaxes him. He loves this."

Ginger's eyes widened and her lips parted. "My . . . my father did that. He always did that with his horses."

I invited her to take my place. She did, and Moonshot visibly softened his body language as she stroked his tail.

When she went to check on the other horses in the trailer, I leaned my forehead against Moonshot's. "All right, my friend. Enough of this silliness. This is really happening, and we have to stop pretending."

He ground his teeth, amplified through our touching skulls.

When Ginger returned, she said with forced cheer, "Okay. Round two."

"I'll lead him if you like."

Her smile faltered. "But I need to be able to handle him without you around."

"I think," I said, "I think once he's away from here, he'll be different."

She paused, then nodded. Moonshot did his absurd high-stepping again as I led him to the yard. When we got to the trailer, he followed me on. Just like that. I felt like Judas.

Ginger closed the door behind us. I took his lead rope and tied it to the ring in the wall. A giant pile of clover hay lay before him.

He turned his head and before I could blink, he took my forearm in his mouth. He didn't bite, he didn't exert any pressure—he just held my arm in his teeth. I stroked his forehead with my other hand, leaning forward to kiss that crescent moon. "I know," I whispered. "We're not the same as we were that day, are we?"

He released my arm and clipped me on the chin with his muzzle. "Ow!" I rubbed my chin.

I leaned my forehead against his again. "Go and be brilliant, my friend. Promise?"

———

He began to munch his hay.

After Ginger had hauled that horse trailer away, I sat down on the cold, damp gravel. I waited for them to *come back*. That couldn't really have just happened, right? He couldn't be gone. That would be like my *lungs* being gone. Or my *blood*.

Gerald hopped over to me, butted his head against my thigh, then leaped onto St. Francis's head, which wobbled but stayed in place. He posed there like a tripod, his tail curling over the statue's face, giving the saint an outrageous mustache.

Moonshot was gone. I made myself say it aloud. After I did, my arm ached with phantom pain from that old wound all day.

It ached for days, as if it had just happened.

GABRIELLA GAVE ME A CARD WITH THE DR. SEUSS QUOTE "Don't cry because it's over. Smile because it happened."

I called Dubey and left a message about what had happened. He showed up about two hours later—as I was clearing the straw out of Moonshot's stall—to take me to dinner. "We're going on a picnic," he said.

I looked at the gray sky, at the clouds of our breath.

He watched me and smiled. "You'll see. Come on."

He drove us to the University of Dayton campus, where he unfolded a blanket in an enclosed, beautiful Gothic cloister. Once again, he unpacked wine, good cheese, fresh bread, grapes. The cloister was secluded, hushed, warm. Someone practiced piano—well—nearby, and the sound seemed to tiptoe to our alcove. We sat shoulder to shoulder, leaning against a stone wall, and whispered. As I told Dubey about the morning with Ginger and Moonshot, he took my hand.

Flutters. *And* comfort. A combination most welcome.

When I turned my head to look at him, he kissed me.

At long last, he kissed me.

It was well worth the wait.

"I was wondering when you were going to do that," I whispered, teasing.

He smiled. "I like to take my time."

AFTER A LINGERING PICNIC, PUNCTUATED BY BOUTS OF kissing, we went back to the farm and walked the pastures, holding hands. Max limped along beside us. I told Dubey about Bobby's new wife.

Dubey actually stopped walking, looking at me in disbelief. "Does this guy never learn?"

"I know! I feel so disappointed watching him make the same mistake again. Especially after telling me he didn't think he'd ever be with *anyone* again. I don't think he's spent a total of a *week* alone since he left me."

Dubey shook his head, and we resumed walking.

"I feel like my time alone has given me a lot," I said. "The distance helped me look at myself, look at my marriage. There's a lot my marriage taught me."

"My marriage taught me never again, that's for sure."

He didn't get it. I let the topic drop. Back at the house I thanked him for cheering a very bleak day. Light snow had begun falling, and I wondered how far Ginger would drive tonight.

"February's just bleak in general," Dubey said, looking up at the snowflakes.

"We should make plans for Valentine's Day," I said. "So the day's not so depressing."

He nodded, still looking at the sky. "We could do that."

"What sounds good?"

"We'll see." He kissed me and left me too flustered to care that he'd evaded me yet again.

ALTHOUGH WE WENT OUT TWO MORE TIMES AND EVEN MADE exquisite, unhurried love in his sister's guest cottage (he did indeed like to take his time, much to my delight), he slipped away from any definite plans for the holiday until it was too late to get reservations anywhere decent.

He delivered flowers to the clinic on Valentine's Day, though—*not* roses—along with a card that said, "Don't let the bastards get you down!" I smiled. I mottled. I felt the flutter.

Maybe, I told myself, maybe he's so commitment-phobic because his divorce was so awful. He'd been damaged, he had baggage. Didn't we all?

"You don't," Aurora said. "You don't seem to be carrying all that much baggage. Not like Bobby. Have you met this new wife yet?"

I hadn't. Gabriella had. After meeting her stepmother for the first time, Gabriella had dubbed poor Lydia "the Christian pudding maker."

"What the hell is Christian pudding?" I asked.

"No, not Christian pudding. She's religious. *And* she makes pudding." Apparently, Lydia was very fond of banana pudding—from a box—with peanuts and vanilla wafers, something I felt fairly certain was an abomination in Bobby's eyes.

"Oh. One more thing," Gabby said, her voice jumping too light, too innocent, sending up red flags along my spine. "She's allergic to dogs."

I let this sink in. "Don't you *dare*," I said.

"Dad asked if we'd take Zuzu."

I closed my eyes.

"I said we would."

And so it was the week I lost a horse, I gained a dog.

OLIVE HATED LYDIA. "SHE'S AGGRESSIVE. SHE FINISHES your sentences. I *hate* that. She bosses him around and he *takes* it. *And* she has a huge ass."

"Oh, stop it. I bet she does not."

"Honest to Christ. No lie. You could serve tea off her ass."

I asked Gabriella about that later, waiting patiently until the topic of Lydia came up without my leading. "Olive said she had a really big—"

"Butt?" Gabriella volunteered. "It's ginormous."

I was intrigued by this big-butted, allergic, aggressive Christian pudding maker. If she hadn't been drunk, then this took a bit of reckless daring I couldn't help but admire. Taking on a wildly brooding man, probably an alcoholic, with an ex-wife, an angry teenage daughter, and a frosty clan of Italian women all crossing their arms over their considerable chests. She'd sense the *whore* Olive called her even if no one so much as breathed it aloud in her presence.

Surely they couldn't really have known each other for only two days.

"No, it was two days. They both live in Dayton, but they didn't *meet* until Vegas," Mimi said as I sat in her kitchen, making plans for Olive's wedding shower. Since it looked as though Olive and Nick were really, truly getting married, in spite of their frequent arguments and shouting matches—and since I no longer had Moonshot to keep me occupied at home—I knew I'd better get down to it and do what a maid of honor was supposed to do.

I knew Mimi would take over, but I'd made peace with that, deciding to embrace it.

I vowed to treat interactions with Mimi like a dance, like when I'd had to dance with Big David in salsa class. He was clunky, bless his generous, good-sported heart, and when he said, "I'm an oaf," I remembered thinking, *That's it. That's the* perfect *word*. But if I stayed open and present and really focused on *following*, we could pull it off. Maybe not graceful, maybe not beautiful, but what anyone could recognize as a dance.

I decided to let Mimi lead and to be the most gracious of followers.

Mimi made me a glass of espresso, and we planned the shower while she made some "gravy." Mimi wanted me to host the shower at the farm. I tried to convince her to have it at *her* house, since most of the female relatives lived in Columbus, an hour's drive away. "Plus, won't that be weird for everyone?" I asked her. "Since Bobby doesn't live there anymore?"

She stopped chopping an onion and pointed the knife at me. "You belong to this family, Camden. Even if you end up marrying that fucking Indian, you belong to this family."

A sincere laugh escaped me, its echo bouncing in the kitchen. Mimi looked startled.

"I'm not," I said. "I'm not marrying that fucking Indian."

"Oh. Well. Whatever you do, you're Gabriella's mother, and you belong to this family."

I took it. *Just follow. Just follow.* "Thank you," I said.

She continued chopping, then asked, almost shyly, "What happened to the Indian?"

I looked out her window at the gray mounds of snow melting in the rain. "It just . . . it just didn't work out. I'm not looking to replace my marriage quite so quickly."

"Don't take too long about it or you'll wind up old and alone like me."

I bit my lip. *Just follow.* "Old and alone sure beats lonely with the wrong guy."

Her expression made it clear that she thought I was nuts. *Fucking* nuts, if she'd said it aloud.

DUBEY CONTACTED COLLEEN JEWELL ABOUT ANOTHER salsa class—he said that was just the thing I needed to distract me from missing Moonshot. He called the Davids, Hank and Helen, Nick and Olive, and Aurora, inviting them back. He asked me to be his partner again. "So, I didn't scare you off?" I joked. "Trying to pin you down for a Valentine's date?"

"I don't think there's much of anything you could do to scare me off," he said.

Again, the flutter.

"So," I said, "am I allowed to say I'm dating you?"

"You're allowed to say whatever you want."

"But are you okay with that?"

"I'm okay with what we're doing. More than okay." That made me happy. But then he said, "I don't think we need to call it anything in particular."

ONE DAY I GOT AN E-MAIL FROM GINGER AVALON. JUST *seeing* it sent me into a frenzy—had she changed her mind? Was she willing to sell him? Oh, *shit*, where would I get that kind of money? But the e-mail was to let me know Moonshot was doing well, to thank me for sharing the secret of his tail, and to include two photos of him jumping *incredible* heights. God, he was gorgeous. I was pleased to see it was Ginger herself on his back, looking like a child atop his magnificent size. She had good form, and Moonshot had his ears forward, clearly enjoying himself.

It took a prayer in my barn lot and a long walk with Muriel to truly accept that Moonshot was gone, that he wasn't coming back.

IT NEVER OCCURRED TO ME, UNTIL THE SHOWER, THAT Bobby's Whore—as the Binardi women called her—would *be* at the shower. Thank God Olive called me the night before. "Look, Mom and I thought, as a peace offering within the family, we should invite her. We never thought she'd say yes! Why the hell would she say yes?"

"*Of course* she'd say yes!" I snapped. "Why wouldn't she want to be part of the family?"

"I'm so, so, sorry," Olive said. "I owe you big-time."

I looked out the window at Luna and Biscuit grazing side by

side. "Stop worrying," I said. "This is *your* day. None of this is your problem, and it's going to be fine." Sometimes you have to say what the other person needs to hear even if every word of it is untrue.

This woman. This Lydia. She was now a part of my daughter's life. And I would do anything to make life easier for my daughter. That's what I told myself. This wasn't about Mimi, or even Olive, anymore. This was about Gabriella.

THE MARCH MORNING OF THE SHOWER WAS CHILLY BUT blindingly sunny. When Mimi first widened her eyes at the kitchen, it took me a moment to recognize that it was new to her. I had trouble remembering it before my new colors, including the turquoise Gabby had coined "hope blue."

I'd missed the aunts and cousins, which surprised me.

Max was calm in a crowd, but Zuzu was underfoot and excitable. I cringed when she left a glob of drool on mean Aunt Jen's leg but couldn't help but smile when Jen didn't notice. Gabby caught my eye and said, "I'll watch Zuzu, Mom."

As I got everyone situated with drinks, they all were warm and welcoming to me.

Then Lydia arrived.

The shift was subtle, but it was there. I felt outside myself, looking on, as the family threw their love and attention her way and I became the hired help.

This is for Gabriella. Just follow. Just follow.

Lydia, by the way, was not what I'd expected. What *had* I expected? A young bombshell, like Zayna, but with a giant butt? Lydia was older and shorter than me. The only feature I envied was her curly hair. The red curls were streaked through with white, though, and the effect brought to mind a strawberry roan horse. She was wide in the hips but by no means "ginormous." I almost caught myself saying aloud, *Her ass is not that big.*

She walked in with Olive, and a hush fell over the room before I called out, "The guest of honor!" and prompted everyone to applaud.

I waited until the focus was somewhere else and introduced myself to her. "I'm Camden," I said, holding out a hand.

She shook my hand. "Thank you," she said, and I swallowed the urge to ask, *For what?*

"It's nice to meet you," I said.

She cocked her head and looked at me with narrowed eyes that said, *You do not mean that.*

I laughed, caught. So did she. And there it was, I liked her. A little.

Whenever anyone needed anything, Mimi called, "Camden? Fran needs a drink." "Camden? Louisa needs more ice." "Camden? Are there more lemon bars? The platter is empty."

"Jesus, do you want me to slap her?" Olive asked, getting her aunt Louisa more ice. Olive turned to Lydia and said, "She's in rare form today," referring to her mother.

When Olive left the room, I said to Lydia, "Nothing rare about it," and we laughed.

Helen and Aurora helped me wait on everyone, and we were surprised when Lydia pitched in, too. Lydia shot me a worried look when Mimi told her to sit next to her. Helen and Aurora were at Olive's table. I'd been delegated to a table with deaf Aunt Lucy and mean Aunt Jen.

Before I'd finished my lunch, Mimi snapped her fingers to get my attention ("What are you, a dog?" Aurora huffed later) and held out her empty plate to me. "You should clear plates, doll, and get coffee going." *This is for Gabby. Just follow.* I pictured myself escaping to the barn later, to comb Moonshot's tail. I felt socked in the gut to remember *Moonshot is gone*.

After lunch, as we arranged ourselves for the torturous Opening of the Gifts, Mimi passed out a little blank book and instructed every guest to write some "marriage advice" for Olive.

Olive called me to sit next to her. I had to record who had given her which present. The gifts were endless, the ritual tedious. Gabriella took Zuzu upstairs. Helen and Aurora made up some reason to busy themselves in the kitchen. I envied them.

When the advice book made its way to me, I welcomed the distraction, flipping through the book for entertainment. But the "advice" was so sad. Page after page of "Hide the checkbook," "Keep your own account," "No checkbook, no sex," and bullshit like that. "Don't give in early or you'll give in forever." "Be the boss." "Get your way, but make it seem like it's his idea." I looked at the women's faces before me. Did they *believe* that? *This* was the marriage advice they'd offer their niece, their cousin, their daughter?

I wrote, "Always be honest, kind, and generous with each other. Never take each other for granted. Go to bed with the promise 'More fun tomorrow.' "

I held up the book, "Anyone still need to write advice?"

Aunt Jen smirked. "*You* have marriage advice? Consider the source, Olive."

There was a slight inhalation from the group, but Olive

made that smoke-ring mouth and said, "I'd treasure anything my best friend has to offer me. Consider the source? She made it eighteen years with my piece-of-shit brother, so I think she knows a little something!"

Jen and Olive exchanged profanity. Mimi yelled at them both. Gabby came downstairs to see what was going on. Zuzu barked at the skirmish. Helen stood in the kitchen doorway, her mouth agape as if she were watching the *Jerry Springer Show*. Old Lucy shouted, "What did she say?"

Mimi said, "You've had too much goddamn wine in the middle of the afternoon! I knew we shouldn't have wine. Have some fucking manners, for Christ's sake!"

Lydia stood up and said, in a surprisingly deep, authoritative voice, "Ladies. Come on. Let's remember what this occasion is for. This is Olive's day. Let's end on a nicer note."

Everyone glared at her but stopped shouting. In the silence, the donkey brayed down in the barn. Several women jumped and clutched their hearts. "What the hell is *that*?" Mimi asked.

When Luna brayed again and Zuzu howled in response, a laugh rumbled up from deep in my belly. I couldn't stop. It was that same kind of laughter that possesses you in church or in school—the harder you try to stop, the more helpless you are. I shook with it as the party broke up.

The women formed a procession to kiss Olive's cheeks. Jen left first and waited in her car for the other women she'd driven with. Muriel clambered onto the hood of the car. Jen kept honking to try to get the goat off, but it made everyone inside think she was trying to hurry everyone up. Mimi went outside and shouted at her.

———

In the kitchen, Lydia whispered, "Oh, my God."

I wiped my eyes, took a deep breath, and got my giggling under control enough to say, "Welcome to the Binardi family."

"It's like *The Sopranos* without all the guns."

That did it. Laughter took me again. Gabriella joined me. "You haven't seen the guns?" we asked.

CHAPTER FORTY-ONE

MIMI

A LOT OF DAMN GOOD IT DID HER, ALL HER WORK TO GET Bobby to go back to Cami. She'd told him from day one, "Your sorry ass is not spending one fucking night on my couch. You go back home to the best woman you'll ever have." The problem was he didn't *need* her couch. He already had an apartment with that redheaded tramp. What's with the red hair? His new wife had red hair, too. For the love of Christ, if that's what he was after, Cami could've gotten a dye job.

What a disaster today, this shower. Jen. They never should've invited her. And Lydia! Bobby should've told her not to come. Why the hell did she want to be there? Poor Cami. As if she hadn't been through enough.

Cami. Mimi loved her like a daughter. She *was* her daughter, and she always would be. Mimi had stayed to help her with all the dishes after the shower. She needed to make it up to her, the whole Jen incident. Cami was a strong woman. She was strong enough for Bobby; this Lydia wasn't. What Bobby saw in that pale, frumpy Lydia was beyond her, not that anyone asked.

Bobby should be home. What was this shit about not being happy? He'd told her, "We've drifted apart." Well, Christ, put your oars in the water and row the hell back together. What was he, a moron? Where did everyone get off thinking happiness was going to be handed down to them from on high? You had to *earn* your own goddamn happiness.

Like Olive and Nick writing their own vows. For a while, they'd actually wanted to pledge to honor and cherish each other "for as long as our love shall last" instead of "for as long as we both shall live." Thank God, Mimi had talked them out of that. Why get married at all if you were gonna cut out the minute you weren't feeling loving? What, were all her children half-wits? When you weren't feeling loving, then you rowed harder. Christ, everyone had to put up with a certain amount of shit. It was worth it to belong, to be somebody.

"It's been a long day," Cami said. "You still have to drive home. I can take it from here."

"No, no. I can't leave you with all this, doll. Especially after how it ended."

Cami laughed. She actually laughed. "Don't worry about that. It was entertaining, at least."

Mimi couldn't believe it was over with the Indian. She wanted Cami taken care of. Cami said she didn't feel lonely, but she'd see. You were invisible without a man. Cami thought her life was full, but she'd get tired of going out with couples, riding in the backseat like a child. You weren't somebody in this world unless you were with someone.

Mimi scrubbed the tile island. "Who did she think she was?" she couldn't help but say out loud of Lydia. "Chatting with you? Laughing with you? Like you were long-lost friends!"

Cami stopped washing dishes. "I *liked* her. I'm glad she talked to me."

Mimi kept scrubbing the cracks between the tiles. "And who did she think she was standing up and bossing everyone around? She needs to know her place. Whore."

"All right. *Enough*." Cami's tone stopped her. "You tell me what's so bad about her, Mimi. Name one thing."

Mimi's mouth wrinkled up like a baby's. She felt a decade older. One thing? She sniffed and whispered, "She's not you."

CHAPTER FORTY-TWO

Helen and I met in the outer lobby of the Humane Society office for the monthly meeting.

"I'm not feeling it," I admitted. "Let's ditch this meeting."

Helen was walking out the door before I finished the sentence. "They can carry on without us," she said once we were outside. "You know we'll both end up splitting that box of kittens if we go back in there."

Although the days now hinted at spring, the evenings were still cold and damp. We linked arms for warmth, heading—without discussion—for the river.

"How's Dubey?" Helen asked.

I sighed. "Like a feral animal I've humanely trapped."

"Uh-oh."

"I have to approach very slowly in order not to scare him. I can't make eye contact or move too fast."

"Hmm," Helen said, nothing more. She seemed as moody as I was tonight. I missed Moonshot. Ginger had sent me a brief video of the two of them jumping a training course. Along with his athleticism, he had an elegance over jumps that was truly breathtaking.

I liked watching him move forward and took comfort in

knowing I'd helped him do that. I didn't really want him pining away, kicking walls again.

But I missed him. And I missed Vijay. And I missed Dubey, which troubled me. I shouldn't have to miss *him*, should I? I'd called him after that insane shower day, needing to talk, needing to detox it with someone who hadn't been there, but he had yet to call me back.

"I can't ask too much of him," I said. "If I try to pin him down, he gets all slippery."

"What?" Helen asked.

"Dubey," I said.

"Oh." She wasn't really listening.

It'd been a nice idea to skip the meeting, but still a block from the river, I felt naked, the insistent wind penetrating my clothes and skin with its raw chill. "I'm freezing," I said.

She turned around as answer. Heading back, we faced into the bitter wind.

We walked fast, clutching each other. I held a hand over one ear. "What's Hank doing tonight?" I asked, hoping that maybe we could call him and all go to dinner somewhere warm.

She made a funny sound—sort of a laugh, with something uncomfortable underneath it. "He's cooking."

"Ooh, cooking what?" Even better than going out would be going to their house.

"His mac 'n' cheese, apple pie, meatloaf, you name it."

That seemed odd. I was about to ask if they were planning a party when a warning buzzer vibrated up my spine.

I stopped walking.

Helen didn't question my halt. I saw she hadn't wanted to

go into that meeting for a *reason*. How could I not have seen it in her eyes, felt it in her distraction? "Helen? What's wrong?"

The wind whipped her hair across her eyes and almost stole her words as she said, "Hank has cancer, Cami. We just found out."

I TOOK HER HAND, LED HER TO MY CAR, AND DROVE HER TO a coffee shop that had a fireplace.

Hank had testicular cancer. Before she even told me it had metastasized in his lungs, I thought back to his shortness of breath in salsa class. The man ran marathons, for God's sake. A little dancing shouldn't have made him wheeze. Why hadn't I registered that?

I pictured the cancer making those sunspots all over his lung X-ray. I knew enough about human medicine to know what that meant. It was the same for dogs, after all.

"He has surgery this week, to remove a testicle," Helen said. "Then he'll start chemo."

I'd just advised a family with a beautiful twelve-year-old black lab not to go the chemo route. Dog's lives were so short, the amount of time such misery bought—and it was *misery*, misery the dog couldn't understand—did not seem worth the price. I was overcome with the urge to call them back and say, *Do it. A few months is a few months.*

"He never had any symptoms in the early stages," she said, staring at the fire. "I mean, we thought maybe he had a hernia once, but it just . . . went away." She rubbed her eyes. "His back had been hurting lately, though. A lot. And he was getting out of breath—you saw him."

"You have a good doctor?" I'd show up on Vijay's doorstep if I had to, to get him to find them the finest, most skilled doctor who existed.

But Helen nodded.

"The survival rate is high," I said. "Even with advanced." I left out the word *sometimes*. "Think of Lance Armstrong."

She didn't even flash her gap-toothed smile. "I do," she said, in all seriousness. "Every minute of every day since we found out. I *dream* about Lance Armstrong."

I squeezed her hands in both of mine.

"I love that man," she said. The words seemed so flimsy compared to the sincerity in her eyes. "I'm gonna need you, friend."

"You have me," I vowed. "Anytime of the day or night."

AT THE NEXT SALSA CLASS, WHEN I HUGGED HANK TIGHT, he whispered, "Let's just dance. For now."

So we did. He and Helen didn't change partners between songs.

"You okay?" Dubey whispered at one point. I was pleased he'd sensed my sorrow.

At the end of the class, as we all sat chatting and drinking, Hank cleared his throat and said, "I've got some news to share with you all," and he told us. Helen held his hand the whole time and never took her eyes from his face.

When we got to the car, Dubey pounded his fist on the steering wheel. "Why *them*?"

I knew what he meant. They'd figured it out, they didn't *need* to be tested.

But life tests all of us over and over again.

I went to sleep that night intentionally visualizing Lance Armstrong. I dreamed I galloped on Moonshot, chasing that yellow jersey on the bike, leaping fluidly over cars and corner coffee carts. We stopped, panting, in a deserted cobblestoned square. Even in my dream, I wasn't sure if it was good or bad that Lance had gotten away.

HANK'S SURGERY WAS TEXTBOOK, AND, AT HIS REQUEST, I made him a batch of Hanky-Pankies the next day, when he was over his anesthesia queasiness.

Dear, sweet Vijay spent hours researching Hank's cancer when I told him the news, providing Helen and Hank with several case studies of treatment and good prognoses, helping them translate what doctors told them, talking to doctors himself. Because of Vijay I *believed* Hank's oncologist when he said the outlook was excellent.

Luna showed no signs of giving birth. She cracked me up with her stubborn, willful ways. My father was sweet on her, for reasons he couldn't explain. My heart lifted each time I pulled into my drive and saw my father's old blue pickup truck—he'd taken to dropping in on her.

"She looks like a wine barrel on toothpicks," Dad said of her. He liked to sit on a bucket and feed her handfuls of beet pulp. If beets were, according to old wives' tales, supposed to induce labor in women, he thought perhaps beet pulp would do the same for a donkey. The only effect it seemed to produce, though, was fuchsia foam around her lips and pink-tinted teeth.

"According to Dr. Coatney, she's overdue," I said. "She says donkeys gestate twelve months on average, but some go thirteen or more."

We didn't have the exact date she'd been bred, of course. Mr. Pete Early, now in jail, had responded to the Humane inquiry with, "Fuck you. How the hell should I know?"

"Everything is healthy and on track," Dr. Coatney assured us, but the donkey was not at all serious about getting this show on the road. Sometimes you could see one of the foal's hooves, or a folded knee, pressing against Luna's sides. How amazing that a whole donkey, with four legs, a tail, and a head was folded up in there like origami.

Then I'd look at Gabriella, touch my own stomach, and think the same thing: this amazing human being was once all folded up inside of me.

One night, Gabby and I were at the kitchen island, both of us studying (she, news magazines for current debate statistics; me, a foaling book I'd ordered online).

"Who will be your date to the wedding?" she asked. "Vijay? Or Dubey?"

I closed my foaling book. "Maybe neither."

"You need a date, Mom. Dad will be there with Lydia."

"So? I don't care." She stared at me. "It's not a competition. I *could* be remarried, but I chose not to be. I don't care what any of them think of me."

Gabriella cocked her head. "How do you get there, Mom?"

"You get there by living, I guess. You live and you learn."

"You're a quick study, then," she said.

"What does that mean?" I was pretty sure she was complimenting me, but I wanted to be sure.

"You seem so . . . happy. You're way more fun and cool now than when you and Dad were together. Which is weird, because he's the one who left, but he's the one who seems so sad and . . . stuck. You had this shitty thing happen to you . . . but it's like you used it as a springboard, you know?" She grinned. "You don't need a man."

"I *want* one," I admitted.

"But that's totally different than *needing* one," she said.

Amen. I wanted to *dance* to hear her say those words.

CHAPTER FORTY-THREE

THE WEATHER GREW WARMER, LUNA GREW FATTER, AND Hank grew thinner.

Olive became more frantic about the wedding, but at salsa class, at least, Olive and Nick never argued. Hank and Helen continued to come as Hank began his chemo—and for all but one class Hank even danced. His hair thinned after the second cycle but wasn't entirely gone (although Helen told me it filled the shower drain and came off in her hands). He and Helen held a focus, an intention so bright it sometimes blinded me to look at them. They talked of the future, of Olive and Nick's wedding, of next year's garden, of where they'd dance. Rather than denial, it seemed like determination. When that determination was so sharp it cut me, Dubey would sense it and gently ease the wound. His timing was impeccable.

I began to doubt I truly wanted to have a new partner. Not yet anyway. There were moments I thought, *Good God, what did I just do, turn away the best single man in the world?*

Other times I'd break out in cold chills at the close call.

And at yet other moments I was smitten with Dubey like a schoolgirl.

Aurora said it best one day. I was in her house, with her

two greyhounds lying at my feet and her luscious paella in a bowl before me. "I look around sometimes," she mused, tapping her bowl with her spoon, "and I think, *What would a man add to this picture?* Most of the time, I can't think of any way he wouldn't *detract* from it. When I find the guy who enriches the picture, then fine. In the meantime, though, my life is pretty damn good."

When Gabriella earned the place of valedictorian, her humble response was, "Great. Another speech? It'll be easy after the wedding one."

Bobby and his Vegas bride parted ways after just four months. "Separated," Olive said. "Figuring some things out."

"Dad," Gabriella said, rolling her eyes. "What is he doing?"

Vijay was seeing someone else. I learned this in a grocery store aisle, where I crossed paths with Shivani, who blushed and burst into tears when she saw me.

"Shivani, what is it?" She wiped her eyes with the end of her sari and told me. She and Lalit had met the woman when they'd gone to New York for Easter. Her name was Tara, and she was one of the producers of Vijay's TV show.

I felt trampled, humbled, undone to recognize that Vijay perhaps wasn't interested in marrying *me*, but in simply being married again.

I had to go to my church to recover from that news. I'd wanted to scratch Moonshot's tail but brushed Muriel and Luna instead. *Try anything*, I'd asked. I guess this was my answer.

I'd learned so much about myself in this past year. Were these men learning *anything*?

❧

BOBBY CALLED. "HOW'S HANK DOING?"

I filled him in, wondering why he couldn't find the courage to call Hank himself. Once upon a time our families had vacationed together, for God's sake.

When I tried to picture going through a catastrophic illness with Bobby, I felt claustrophobic.

"Hey," I said. "Gabby told me about you and Lydia . . . separating. I'm sorry."

After a guarded pause, he said, "Thanks."

"Can I ask you what that was *about*? I mean, was it really only two days and you were ready to marry again?"

When he spoke, his voice was honest, naked in some new way. "I hate to be alone, Cam."

It wasn't anger but bewilderment that surged through me. "Then why did you *leave*?"

Without changing his tone of voice, he said, "I felt alone a lot when we were married."

Clarity—immediate, miraculous. "I know what you mean," I said. "I felt that way, too."

We were silent, but it felt easy, amiable.

"I'm trying to learn from all this, you know?" I said. "To work on myself."

"You seem like you're doing great." I could picture us in the living room, feet up, with glasses of wine after a long day. "I, um . . . I'm trying to work on myself, too. I think I might finally sell the restaurant."

A floating sensation lifted me. "Bobby, that's wonderful. Good for you. That's brave."

He laughed a self-deprecating laugh, but I could tell he was pleased. "It might be fucking nuts more than brave. I could end up completely broke just in time for Gabby to be in college."

"I doubt that. We'll figure it out."

It was odd to say *we*, but there'd always be a *we* because of Gabby.

"I just need to get enough money to buy some time," Bobby said. "You know, to figure out what I'm supposed to be doing with my life."

I felt a twinge of sorrow at the fact that he hadn't felt able to do this with me, but the sorrow now seemed as old as the faint ridge of scar where Moonshot's teeth had once crushed my skin.

Bobby cleared his throat and said, "I was hoping to come get Zuzu. If, um . . . if that's okay."

I smiled. "Of course." I sincerely believed Zuzu might help him. He wouldn't be alone, but perhaps he could stay out of another disastrous relationship long enough to reflect and learn something. Learn *anything*. Learn to at least make a *new* mistake. I felt hopeful that maybe his life would open into space and light like mine had, that so much heartbreak and disruption might lead to *two* happier lives.

I DID ERRANDS FOR HANK AND HELEN AS HANK proceeded through chemotherapy. I walked dogs, cleaned gutters, mowed grass, took cars for oil changes, and grocery shopped. His oncologist marveled at Hank's plucky endurance, and I was determined that when Hank felt well, he and Helen could do what they *wanted* to do.

They were nearly always smiling. I often heard them laugh.

"Anything. Anytime," I said to them both whenever I left. "Day or night."

ONE DAY AT THE CLINIC, AS I SAT IN MY OFFICE BETWEEN appointments, Gabby came storming out of the kennel and slammed herself into the bathroom.

I got up from my desk, crossed the hall, and tapped on the bathroom door. "You okay?"

"God, Mom," she said through the door. "Can't a person have some privacy?"

For the rest of that afternoon, she and Tyler were back to their old stiff dance of avoiding eye contact. Although Tyler blushed every time she was near him, the tables seemed turned and it was Gabby who looked knocked down and trampled this time.

Once she and I got in the car to go home, it didn't take long to get the story. Immediately upon closing her car door, Gabby wailed, "Tyler is taking Amy to the prom!"

I studied my daughter for a moment. As gently as I could I asked, "Why shouldn't he, sweetie?"

"Because *I* love him! *We* should be going to prom! Everyone knows it!"

I didn't start the car. Like in triage, I assessed what Gabby needed first: comfort. I hugged her as she cried into my shoulder. "I'm sorry," I said, stroking her hair.

Once her breathing returned to somewhat normal, I could start other treatment. "Babe, how was Tyler supposed to know you love him?"

She sniffled.

"You've spent nearly a year convincing yourself that you didn't love him, and in the process, I think you managed to finally convince Tyler to give up."

"But *nobody* believed me! Everyone knew we'd end up together. That's how it's supposed to be."

"Things don't work like that, babe. Nothing ends up how it's 'supposed to be' unless you *make* them how you want them to be."

She leaned her head back against the passenger seat. "Oh, I messed this up so bad."

"Most mess-ups can be fixed."

"But he already asked her! Amy said yes! I can't believe she'd say yes!"

"Don't hate me for saying this, but why shouldn't she say yes? Tyler's a fun, great guy."

Silence.

"Most mess-ups can be fixed," I repeated.

"*How?* They're already going to prom together and he's too nice to un-ask her."

"Prom's just one night. I'm talking about the bigger mess-up. You might not get your prom, but if you're honest about your feelings, you might get what you really want, which is to have Tyler back in your life, right?"

Eventually I started the car. After stopping for ice cream— which everyone knows can ease heartache—we went home. I kept thinking that perhaps I should take my own advice.

I KNEW THAT BOBBY AND I HAD BEGUN TO UNRAVEL WHEN we'd stopped talking, stopped telling each other the truth. So, on the first really warm spring Saturday in late April—that first day people sit out in the sun, shed long sleeves, wear shorts that bare white winter skin, those days that make you want to *drink* the sunshine—I packed a picnic and drove out to Dubey's guest cottage. He was playing piano as I arrived, which trickled out through the open windows. I waited until he finished to say, "Lovely," through the screen.

He spun around on his piano bench. "Oh. Hey, Cam." He let me in and kissed me, but when his eyes went to the picnic basket, his jaw tightened.

"I thought I could entice you away on a picnic. To celebrate beautiful days."

He paused.

"You should've called." He laughed, but the sound was forced.

I set the basket down and said, "You've just shown up at my place before to whisk me away somewhere. I loved it."

He frowned. "I just . . . I don't think—" He stammered a moment, then said, as if he'd been *wanting* to say it but holding back, "I'm not comfortable with this, Cami."

I sat down. I gestured for him to do the same, but he didn't. "We need to talk. You're not comfortable with *me*? Or you're not comfortable with not being in control of our plans?" To my surprise I wasn't angry. I looked at the gashes hacked out of his piano legs and couldn't be.

He shook his head. "Every time a woman says, 'We need to talk,' the relationship is doomed."

I laughed. "I personally think if two people *don't* talk about their feelings, a relationship is doomed. I'm pretty confused by how things are playing out with us. Confused and a bit irritated, to be honest."

"I've *been* honest, Cami," he said. He still didn't sit down. "I've always said I didn't want another relationship. I've been as clear as I could be that I'm not going down that path again."

"That's true," I said. "You did. But your actions didn't match your words. You'd say 'never again,' but you'd be sweet and romantic and give me great gifts and lots of attention. We've slept together, Dubey."

"I knew that was a mistake."

"Wow. Really?" I tried to be kind, gentle. If only he could see how *afraid* he was. "I didn't think it was a mistake. I thought it was pretty damn nice."

"It *was* nice," he said, suddenly mortified. "I didn't mean it wasn't—I just meant it was a mistake because . . . because you can't leave it at that. Now you show up and act like you own my time, my schedule."

"Asking you to come eat some cheese on a hillside with me is not trying to own your time."

"But that's where it will lead." He paced. "That's how it is with relationships, with marriage."

"Marriage? I'm asking you to go on a *picnic*."

"But I know how it will turn out."

"Based on what? *Your* marriage? That's just one example."

He finally sat—but on the piano bench across the room from me. "I thought you 'got it' when you told me about turning down Vijay's proposal. I thought you wanted to be independent, to live your own life. When you're with somebody, you can't do that, not with real freedom. You're always . . . you've always got . . ." He paused, as if searching for an image. His face brightened. "It's like a horse, right? If you're with someone, it's like someone always has a hand on one rein, keeping you checked."

I wanted to laugh but managed not to. *What the hell?* That didn't even make sense! Who rides holding *one* rein? If you did that you'd just turn in circles.

Oh.

That's exactly what I was doing, wasn't I?

I stood and retrieved my basket. "I'm really glad I met you, Dubey." I wanted to kiss him, perform some farewell gesture, something, but his stiff posture didn't welcome that. "You crossed my path when I needed you most. Thank you for being such a great dance partner."

He seemed confused, wary even, at my kindness. "We can still do stuff like that. We're going to dance at Nick and Olive's wedding this weekend, right?"

I thought about being snide and throwing his own game back at him, saying "We'll see" or "That could be nice" without giving him a definite answer, but instead I said, "No, Dubey. I don't think so."

He looked sad, even though I'd never officially asked him to be my date. Looks like I'd be a free agent at the wedding, which suited me just fine.

Besides, all that riding in circles had made me dizzy. I needed to get my balance.

"Do you have your wedding speech?" I asked Gabriella as we drove to the rehearsal dinner.

"I'm almost done."

My stomach bottomed out at her nonchalance. "It's the *rehearsal*," I said. "They're going to want you to *read* it."

"I think we just hit our marks, right?" she asked. "It's not like they'll actually say the vows tonight. Lighten up. It'll be fine."

I took deep breaths and reminded myself, *This was not my problem.*

"You've got straw in your hair, Mom."

"Great." I looked in the rearview mirror, trying to see it.

"God, Mom, watch the road! I'll get it!" Gabby combed through my hair. I understood why Moonshot loved it. I hoped Ginger indulged him often. "Jeez. Can't take you anywhere."

"I was just trying to look at Luna's udder," I said, "She's so short!"

"You really think she's close?"

I nodded. *Finally.* Just tonight, crouching down in the clean deep straw, I'd seen "waxing"—opaque white liquid—on her teats. My books said waxing occurred "anytime from forty-eight to four hours before birth." I'd called Dr. Coatney, who'd warned that Luna might seem anxious, paw the ground, and get up and down frequently. I figured we had time to spare, since she stood serenely eating all the hay I'd put before her.

"Your grandparents are going to check on her while we're at the rehearsal dinner. They promise to call if she starts. Do I look okay? No other straw? I don't smell like horses, do I?"

She laughed. "You *always* smell like horses."

I frowned. "I *do*?" That's what was on my mind as I went into the rehearsal.

Gabriella was right. All we had to do was hit our marks. No one said vows, gave the sermon, or read poems. She was off the hook. Was I the only one nervous?

I was last up the aisle, before the bride. I was paired with Nick's brother, a very attractive, funny best man. I spent most of my time chatting with him as we waited, to avoid having to talk to Bobby. Although he and I had had an honest phone conversation, it still felt awkward being in a room with him.

Everyone asked me about Hank. "He's doing great," I told them. "He's managing really high doses his oncologist didn't think he could." Helen had originally been in the bridal party but had bowed out, preferring to sit with Hank at the ceremony. Olive was gracious, although Mimi had mumbled about how changing plans on the bride was rude and made the sides of the wedding party uneven.

The dinner seemed endless.

I kept hoping Luna would go into labor so I'd have an excuse to leave.

Alas, she didn't. Once we were home, we found Mom and Dad camped out in the straw, with wine and cheese, on cushions they'd brought from home.

"I don't think it's tonight," Dad said, pushing his reading glasses up to his forehead.

I looked at the donkey, shaking my head. "She doesn't do anything she doesn't want to do, so I guess she's going to wait until she's good and ready."

"Can we sleep down here?" Gabriella asked.

"You need to finish that speech, young lady."

She waved her hand as if to say, *Whatever.*

Please don't let tomorrow be a disaster.

I COULDN'T SLEEP. I'D SET UP BABY MONITORS IN LUNA'S stall and my room, but only heard the donkey's gentle snoring. *Sleep. Otherwise you'll look like shit tomorrow.*

I e-mailed Vijay:

> You are an asshole and here's why: NOT because you're seeing Tara, but because your MOTHER had to tell me you were seeing Tara. If you've found someone you're willing to introduce to your parents (I know how neurotic you are about that! Don't forget, my friend, I know you!), that's a big deal, and I was once the first person you'd call with news like that. We SWORE not to wreck our friendship. Don't tell me this is how the book ends! Love, Cami. P.S. I hope we'll figure out a way to include each other in our next chapters. I miss you.

I checked the baby monitor, certain it didn't work. I turned up the volume all the way but was rewarded with a donkey fart that shook the walls and made Gerald dash under the bed.

I turned the monitor back down. I lay down, but after an hour, knowing I wasn't going to sleep, I dressed and walked down to the barn.

Biscuit paced his paddock on his dinner-plate hooves. He nickered, long and low.

I didn't turn on lights, because I didn't want to disturb Luna. We'd left a light on over the feed box for this very reason. When I got to Luna's stall, she lay on her side, a sac of blue membrane peeking out from below her tail—and visible through it were a tiny muzzle and two little hooves.

CHAPTER FORTY-FOUR

GABRIELLA AND I HELD HANDS AS I LED HER BACK TO THE barn.

We peered through the stall slats. "How you doing there, lady?" I whispered. Luna rolled her eyes toward me and snorted once, her breathing pronounced but not labored.

I thought about calling Dr. Coatney, but I'd been dragged out of bed unnecessarily by clients enough times to have a little restraint. She was near enough to get here fast should we need her.

Luna lay quietly for several minutes and at some natural cue gave a mighty heave. The foal's nose, resting on two front hooves—"diving" position, just what we wanted—came another inch into view.

Gabriella started to undo the latch, but I put my hand on hers and shook my head. I gathered up the cushions Mom and Dad had left, and we stayed in the aisle where we could watch through the slats in the boards. "Let's leave her alone," I whispered. "She's doing great."

Gabby gripped my hand, her face bright, eager. "You know who would *love* to see this?"

Together we said, "Tyler."

"You can call him," I said, "but he better hurry."

She went outside to make the call, then came back in grinning. "He's coming!" We knelt shoulder to shoulder. For nearly ten minutes we were silent, watching Luna's progress.

"Is it scary?" Gabby asked.

"Look at Luna's face. Does she look scared?"

The donkey's face was regal, her white muzzle closed, her velvety black nostrils flaring.

"She looks . . . focused," Gabriella whispered.

I nodded. "That's it. Our bodies take over. You're just along for the ride."

Another heave, and a whole foal's face, almost to the ears, became visible, still wrapped in the silver-blue, shiny membrane, the front legs now extending to mid-shin.

I feared Tyler might not make it in time, but after another ten minutes or so, I heard Max's greeting bark just as Luna gave another push, her legs momentarily extended straight out to the side with her effort. Most of the foal's neck slid into slippery view, its seemingly endless legs in their elegant dive.

Tyler rushed into the barn. He made no noise and knelt beside us, saying only, "Thank you."

"I think you just made it," I whispered. "Once we get to the shoulders, the show's nearly over."

After moments filled only with Luna's deep breaths, Gabriella asked, "Does it . . . hurt?"

"Are you fucking *kidding* me?" flew out of my mouth before I could help it.

She clapped a hand over her mouth to muffle her laugh. Tyler's shoulders shook.

"*Yes*, it hurts," I said. "A lot." I didn't tell her that her arrival had felt like a freight train grinding on my spine. I didn't tell her that part of the awe was the realization we could *take* such pain. Or that pain could come in white-hot waves in levels I'd never imagined. How it wasn't even the pain itself but the *stamina* required that had over and over again stunned me with *there's more*.

I simply said, "But it's worth it."

"I read somewhere," Tyler whispered, "that we can't recall pain. Humans can't re-create pain the way they can other emotions."

I nodded. "It's a handy survival skill. That's the only reason people have second children."

Or ever risk loving a second time.

It made sense that labor hurt so much: it was the only preparation for how much it would hurt to love your child so completely.

Love wasn't even a word that came close.

I looked at Gabriella peering through the slats, her head almost touching Tyler's sleep-rumpled hair.

A groan from Luna turned my eyes back to the slat in time to see the foal's shoulders emerge.

The front hooves pierced the membrane and it peeled back, revealing the foal's face and open eyes. Its little nostrils fluttered in surprise.

Just as the book and Dr. Coatney had said, thank God, the rest of the foal slid out of Luna's body with a wet whoosh, and there it lay, perfect, whole, and in the world.

We all gasped aloud. "Good girl," I said. "Good job, Luna."

Luna tucked her front legs under her and curled her neck around to meet this miniature version of herself. The foal's rabbit ears unfolded toward its mother, and we laughed. I was crying, with happiness, relief, emotion. Just plain old emotion—any of them, all of them, you name it—coursing through me. Gabby held my hand. I saw that Tyler held her other.

As I quietly predicted each action for Tyler, Luna did all the right things: she tore off the rest of the membrane and licked the foal dry, so that its wet black coat turned gray, like her own. She climbed to her feet, her own sides slick with sweat, her back legs shiny with blood, and nudged the foal to stand. The foal pinned back its ears, closed its Cleopatra eyes, and turned its head away in a comical impersonation of the mother it had just met.

"Wow," Gabby said. "It's its own little creature already."

You have no idea. I only nodded, my professional side taking over, watching the foal breathe, watching for the afterbirth, watching Luna's bleeding. Check, check, check. Textbook.

Luna nudged her nose under the foal's belly and prodded it to unfold those impossibly long legs. It looked, for all the world, like some giant, fuzzy spider—bent black legs all around it.

It rose to standing. We cheered.

It toppled over in a nosedive.

It stood again. Wobbled. Sat down.

Luna let it rest a few moments, then helped it as it rose again. This time it stood long enough for me to say, "We have a baby girl."

She began to nurse. For a moment the only sound was strong, greedy suckling, then my phone vibrated in my pocket. I read the text from the Davids: "Jess in labor! Here we go!"

I thought, *There's more. Love so sharp and clear it hurts.*

"Something must be in the air this morning," I joked as I told the kids the news.

Biscuit whinnied from his stall, and Luna brayed in answer.

The foal pulled away from the teats, white milk dribbling from her gums as she raised a high-pitched, ridiculous bray of her own. Like someone hiccuping on helium.

CHAPTER FORTY-FIVE

THE REALIZATION THAT IT WAS NINE-THIRTY IN THE MORN-ing made us finally stop fawning over Luna and the filly. We were due at the salon with Olive in less than an hour.

We drove to the salon after having called Mom and Dad, who agreed to be there for Dr. Coatney's postpartum checkup. Tyler had offered to stay, but Gabriella had said, "Is it too late to ask you to be my date to the wedding?"

"I would *love* to be your date to the wedding."

"Then you better go home and shower."

There's more.

"YOU'RE *LATE*," MIMI GREETED US. SHE WAS ON EDGE, crazed energy coming off her in waves. I braced myself for the day. Olive waved from under a dryer. Aurora was being sham-pooed. Cousin Chrissie's hair was being blown dry.

"Luna had her baby!" Gabriella announced. "We couldn't miss it."

"And the Davids' baby is on the way!" I said.

As I sat there, relishing the stylist playing with my hair, I was hyperaware of the ring burning in my bra, pressed up against the soft white flesh of my left breast.

It wasn't Olive's ring for Nick.

No, this was *my* wedding ring—I'd discovered it this morning as I frantically dug through my drawer for the strapless bra I needed to go under my bridesmaid dress. When I saw it—I'd honestly forgotten it was there—I knew immediately what I should do with it.

My phone buzzed in my bag. "Sorry," I said to the stylist, "But I have to take this, in case it's the vet." I looked at the number. *Helen.* I'd seen Hank yesterday morning and he was fine. Well . . . fine for a person getting his ass kicked by chemotherapy, that is. For a split second, I considered not answering. I'm so glad I did.

"I need you, Cami."

A chill tiptoed across my shoulders. "Hank?"

"He's . . . okay right now. But we need you. It's important."

"But . . . you said Hank's . . . what's up?"

Helen paused, and I felt a flicker of irritation. If everything was okay couldn't it *wait?*

But then she pulled the trump card. "You said anytime. Day or night."

I took a breath. There was only one right answer. "Where and when?"

I saw Mimi pretending not to listen.

"Right now. Miami Valley Hospital."

"The *hospital?* You said everything was fine."

"It is for now. Are you already dolled up?"

"My hair's done. Almost," I said, wondering why the hell she cared. "I haven't had my manicure."

"Skip it. Get here now." She told me the floor and room, then hung up.

I looked in the mirror at the stylist behind me. "I have to go," I whispered.

He looked scared, and I knew he feared Mimi. "Two secs," he begged.

But Mimi was on her feet. "You're *leaving?*"

Everyone's head swiveled toward me.

Gabriella ducked from under her stylist's hands. "Is it Luna?"

"You can't leave," Mimi declared.

I pulled a trump card of my own. "Hank's in the hospital." I didn't explain to anybody that Hank was fine . . . because I wasn't at all sure it was true. Helen had sounded so . . . panicked.

When Olive opened her mouth I had no idea what would come out. "Go," she said. "If you can't make it back, I understand."

I would've hugged her if my frantic stylist hadn't still had tools enmeshed in my hair.

"If she can't make it back?" Mimi bellowed. "She's your maid of honor!"

"And the husband of one of our best friends could be dying," Olive said. "So shut up. We'll deal."

Dying? No. No. Why had she said *that?*

Mimi opened her mouth to retort, but Olive held up her hand. "Honest to God, Ma. Shut. Up. Helen needs Cami, so that's where she should be. I wouldn't want it any other way." She turned to me. "If you make it back, it's icing on the cake. But . . . if you don't—I get it." She looked at the stylist. "Now, hurry up and finish her goddamn hair."

"Done!" he said, stepping back, holding up his hands.

I planted a huge kiss on Olive's cheek. Then on Gabby's. Then the stylist's. I moved to Mimi but she turned her back.

"Tell them I love them!" Olive called as I ran out the door.

I SQUEALED INTO THE HOSPITAL PARKING LOT JUST AS the first raindrops hit my windshield. Too bad this wasn't a rescue—the weather was right on cue. Once I found a spot in the garage, I ran for the elevator, then drew concerned looks as I rushed down halls to the right room.

"Hey," I said breathlessly. "I'm here."

Hank sat upright in a hospital bed, fully dressed, holding a milk shake, laughing and chatting with Holly and an older man I didn't recognize.

"Excellent," Helen said, rising from beside Hank on the bed. "That was record time." She wore a peach dress embroidered with flowers and strappy sandals with heels.

"What's going on?" I asked. "What happened?"

Holly and Hank grinned.

The older man stood and extended his hand. "Hi, I'm Adam. I'm Hank's brother."

"He just flew in from Chicago," Hank explained.

"Nice to meet you," I said to Adam, then turned to Hank and Helen. "What. Is. Going. On?"

"Do you have your dress for the wedding with you? Or any-thing else to wear?" She eyed my outfit—a pair of khaki pants and a T-shirt from the Kentucky Horse Park.

"It doesn't matter, Helen," Hank said.

"Am I speaking Swahili or something?" I snapped. "*Why* are you in the hospital?"

Helen flashed that gap-toothed grin. "Oh, calm the hell down. I can't believe you haven't guessed. We're getting married, okay? I want you to be there."

I knew my mouth hung open, but I felt incapable of closing it. *There's more.*

"Let's be fair," Hank said. "We're a little silly on relief, but we need to bring Cami up to speed." He took my hand to pull me down on the bed beside him. Helen sat on the other side, one hand on Hank's bald head.

"We had a big scare yesterday," Helen began.

They filled me in. Yesterday, after I'd left, Hank felt a strange weakness on the right side of his body. When he stumbled going up the stairs, he at first attributed his clumsiness to chemo fatigue, but then late last night, he couldn't lift his right leg at all or hold silverware or a toothbrush with his right hand. They'd gone to the ER, where a CT scan revealed a mass in his brain somehow missed— probably microscopic—at the time of his initial cancer workup. Swelling from this mass caused the neurological symptoms.

I covered my mouth at the words *mass in his brain* but looked at Hank, who was holding his milk shake with his right hand. "But—" I said, gesturing. "Steroids?"

He nodding, smiling. The beauty of steroids was their immediate effect.

"Everything's okay for now, but—" He looked at Helen. She kissed his head. "But I'm a candidate for surgery to remove it. It's a single lesion. The docs feel I've done well enough to warrant this surgery." He chuckled. "They used the phrase 'the possibility of long-term survival.' I could have complete remission."

"But brain surgery?" I whispered.

They nodded.

"We talked to Vijay," Helen said.

An involuntary zip raced through my pulse.

"He was incredibly helpful," Helen said. "He wants us to tell him when the surgery is and he's going to try to be here."

Because I felt raw and vulnerable—about Hank, about Vijay—I went snarky as a defense. "Did he say anything about his new girlfriend?" I asked, too flip, too glib.

Helen and Hank looked at each other. "No, he did not," Helen said. "As a matter of fact, he asked about you."

I didn't know what to say. I cursed the mottles I felt blooming.

"So," Helen said, looking at her watch. "We're not trying to be assholes messing up Olive's big day, but the surgery might be as early as this week. We could get the chaplain for sure *today*, so we felt we should just do it."

"You know how we feel," Hank said as Helen stroked his head. "This is 'just in case.' "

They looked at each other and smiled, already accepting what that 'just in case' contained.

"We love you, and we want you to be here," Hank said.

There's more. There's more.

"Come on," Helen said, taking my arm. "We need to go. We have another wedding to get to, after this, you know."

ADAM AND I WERE WITNESSES, HOLLY THE ONLY GUEST. A chaplain met us in a soothing, cavelike chapel at the hospital where the rain tapped on the skylight above us. "I discovered this place when Hank had his first surgery," Helen said. "I love this room."

I changed in the restroom in less than five minutes and decided a few wrinkles in my red halter-style bridesmaid dress wouldn't matter.

· The ceremony was simple, quick, and pure. I stood beside my friend as she and her companion of nineteen years vowed to honor, love, and cherish each other in sickness and in health, in good times and hard times, for better and worse, for long as they both should live.

I wished with all my might that that would be for a very long time.

WHEN I MADE IT BACK TO HOLY TRINITY, THE PRE-pictures had started and it rained in earnest. Since I didn't have a raincoat or an umbrella, I took the floor mat from my truck and used it as a shield to protect my spectacular updo.

"Nice of you to be here," Mimi huffed, not even asking about Hank.

Olive, Gabby, and Aurora asked, though, and I assured them he'd had a scare but was fine. I'd wait until after the ceremony to tell them about the surgery. I'd let Olive have her spotlight.

The photographer began to coax us into formation. As I posed for four wedding party shots, Bobby entered the church and sat in a back pew, watching. As soon as I wasn't in a photo, I walked back to him. His suit was spattered with raindrops.

"You ready for this?" I joked.

He smiled. "I'm ready for my mother to calm the hell down, that's for sure."

We gazed at the rest of the wedding party for a moment. Bobby said, "Gabriella is so *beautiful*."

She stood near the altar, looking down at what I *hoped* was her speech. The rainy day's feeble light came through the stained-glass window to the left of us, bathing her in a muted rainbow. She was the most exquisite thing I'd ever seen, the feeling even more intense than the day she was placed in my exhausted, waiting arms.

I don't know if it was my lack of sleep, my hope for the Davids' baby, the strange mix of emotions from witnessing Luna's labor, or the weight of Hank's prognosis, but I felt raw and vulnerable, and I *had* to tell someone. I couldn't carry this secret all day. "Hank has a lesion on his brain," I whispered.

When Bobby reached out to take my hand, I let him. He looked at me with such tenderness that for a moment I could remember how we once cherished each other. I had a flash of his face full of hope on our wedding day, a flash of his face beside mine as I labored to deliver Gabriella, a flash of his dark eyes alight to see me enter a room.

"We need to clear the chapel!" Mimi called. "People are arriving, and we need to get the bride sequestered."

Sequestered? Bobby and I looked at each other and cracked up.

Mimi's footsteps clicked down the aisle toward us. "Bobby? Thank God you're here——" She stopped. I turned my head and saw her open mouth. I realized Bobby still held my hand. I saw the *hope* in her eyes. Hope, happiness, and *relief*.

"For the love of Christ," she muttered. "This day is going to be the fucking death of me!" She clattered back away, tossing over her shoulder, "You kids clear out of here soon."

"Oh," I said, pulling my hand from Bobby's. "She thinks—"

"She hopes," Bobby said. "She wishes. She tells me every damn day."

I didn't know what to say, or what to do with my hands.

"So," Bobby said. "There's been something I've been wanting to tell you."

"Wait! There's something I want to give you." I dug into my bra and retrieved the warm ring. I held it out to him.

His lips parted for a moment before he said, "I . . . I thought you sold—"

I shook my head. "I had it appraised," I said. When I told him the worth, his eyes widened.

"That should buy you the time you need to find some clarity."

He stared at me as if he hadn't understood what I said.

"You know," I said. "To figure out what you want to do after the restaurant."

"You'd do that?" he whispered.

I held the ring out on my palm, but Bobby closed my hand over it. His mouth trembled. "I regret what I did," he said in a rush. "I regret it nearly every moment of every day. I want you to know that."

The ring cut into my palm, the way he pressed my hand closed. After a moment, I pulled my hand away and put the ring into one of his. "Thank you for telling me that. Truly. That . . . that's a generous gift."

Olive called from the side door. "Cam! C'mon!"

I heard Mimi hiss, "Leave them be!"

"Listen, I know you need to go." He sidestepped out of his pew. He held out the ring. "Keep this. Please."

"It's yours," I said. "I should've given it to you when we were working out the divorce."

He turned the ring in his fingers, and I knew he was reading the Italian inscription. "Thank you," he said.

Thunder rumbled in the sky.

"What is *this*?" Mimi yelled. "Who left this here? We're about to start a goddamn wedding, for Christ's sake!" She held up my truck's floor mat.

"That's mine! Sorry!"

As I took it from her, a huge crack of lightning and thunder made us both jump. "What next?" she asked, but her eyes twinkled as she looked at me.

I NEARLY FLOATED THROUGH THE DAY. BECAUSE OF THE rain, the wedding party couldn't go to the building next door as planned, so we squeezed into a side foyer of the church to wait. The pile of guests' umbrellas grew to look like some kind of prehistoric jungle flower garden.

Helen and Hank arrived. I watched him lean on Helen's arm as he slowly tackled each step, then I dashed into the rain, ducking under their umbrella to take his other arm.

"What do you know about llamas?" Helen asked me.

"Uh . . . not much. Why?"

"I just got a call about an abuse case." We paused a moment to let Hank catch his breath. "Maybe we could check it out after the reception? After a stop to see your new nephew, of course."

Hank nodded, and we proceeded up the next step.

"Helen! It's your wedding day!" I said. "We're not going on a rescue *today*."

But Hank laughed and said, "Hey, we swore getting married wouldn't change a *thing* about our relationship."

I kissed them both and let Bobby usher them to their seats.

My parents arrived.

"How's my baby?" I asked my mother, the wind fluttering our dresses as we stood near the open doors.

"Healthy as can be. Mama, too."

"And opinionated as all get out," my father said. "Already."

"Anything new from Uncle Davy?" Gabby asked them.

They beamed. "All progressing well. We'll head there after the ceremony."

I floated on their love. I floated down the aisle with Nick's brother and stood beside my former sister-in-law as the priest told us why we were gathered there this day.

From my vantage point I saw Helen and Hank hold hands, their faces emitting enough joy to light the stormy, gray sky outside.

I saw my mother whisper something into my father's ear. He smiled and put his arm around her shoulders, pulling her close.

I saw Tyler gaze at Gabriella with such naked love I had to look away.

A cold wind blew all the way into the church, ruffling people's hair in the pews.

I recognized how easy it would be to respond to that look of hope in Mimi's eyes. To marry just to please someone else. Because it would be *easy*. Convenient even. But there was no going back with Bobby. The marriage I once treasured with him was over, and rightly so.

We sat down, and Gabriella did her reading. I would love to say she had amazing insights that made us all gasp, that she left us changed. But she didn't. She was winging it. She was, as I'd heard her say of certain debate rounds, "pulling it out of her ass." I silently wished for her valedictorian speech to be much better prepared. I saw that the others were too impressed by her poise and vocabulary to recognize how naïve and shallow her thoughts were. I saw it had been ridiculous to ask an eighteen-year-old to have any real thoughts on marriage. On love, perhaps, but marriage? Marriage took some *time*. Marriage took some living that Gabby hadn't done yet. You couldn't ask someone who'd never been married to comment on it. You couldn't *know*. No one knew unless you were one of two people wrapped up in a marriage's arms.

While Cousin Chrissie sang "Ave Maria," my mind wandered to Dubey. And to Vijay. To Vijay being here for Hank's surgery. Then I thought about llamas and what creature I might meet later today. What would *it* teach me?

We rose again, and I stood beside my friend as she vowed to love one man forever. I handed her the ring that symbolized their union.

What a risk love was. But the riskier the venture and greater the chance of failure, the higher the reward.

My dad had once tried to teach my ten-year-old self this fact about horse-racing: why a two-dollar bet to win made more money than a ten-dollar bet to show. "It's worth more because you risk more," he'd said. "You're betting you'll be absolutely right, no 'maybe' or 'close' about it."

A whip crack of lightning and a crash of thunder made everyone jump, then laugh in nervous relief.

Mimi, in the front row, next to Bobby, crossed herself, her muttered "Oh *merda*" audible to the wedding party. We all chuckled.

The lights flickered.

The priest picked up his pace.

"What do you give them?" Aurora had asked me once.

I shamefully remembered I'd quipped, "Three years. Tops."

Thunder boomed, and the rain stopped abruptly. Every head turned up to the stained-glass windows just as the city's tornado sirens rose in mournful warning.

A collective groan ran through the church.

I caught my mother's eye. Her mouth twitched in a smile, and I knew exactly what she was thinking.

The priest presented to us the now married couple, then immediately announced, over the distracted applause, that the assembled should move downstairs to the basement classrooms.

I remembered reaching out for that moving wall of air. Trying to do the impossible. *Believing* I could do it. Believing it wouldn't hurt me.

Olive and Nick kissed each other. They were attempting to do the impossible, too.

So were the Davids and bold, generous Jess.

I looked out at Gabriella and her father, at Tyler, my parents, Helen and Hank, Aurora.

All of us so brave.

We were all—every one of us—rushing out into the hail.

Dancing out into the hail every single day.

ACKNOWLEDGMENTS

If you write nonfiction, you have to fight to prove every fact, but if you write fiction, everyone assumes it's all true. Because I got divorced during the writing of this book, there will be several people who assume this book is about my own life. Anyone who even remotely knows me or my ex will recognize that this book is entirely a work of fiction. The only characters taken "from life" are some of the animals, so let me begin by thanking Booker T., George, Humphrey, Jenny, Max, Peggy Eileen, and, most of all, Degas—the equine love of my life.

Huge love and thanks to my agent and friend, Lisa Bankoff, who not only demonstrated great patience and belief but generosity in the form of a New England autumn retreat in her beautiful Connecticut home, where I at long last finished the novel. Here's to Scrabble, bears in the yard, and heated mattress pads!

Thanks to the amazing Elizabeth Perrella and Tina Wexler at ICM for their cheerful assistance and expertise.

I am so grateful for my publishing home at HarperCollins and the many talented people there who bring my books to life and get them in readers' hands—Amy Baker, Erica Barmash, Jonathan Burnham, Kevin Callahan, Mary Beth Constant,

Mareike Grover, Samantha Hagerbaumer, Jennifer Hart, Gregory Hart, Emily Krump, Julia Novitch, Jennifer Pooley, and Stephanie Selah. A special class of gratitude goes to the brilliant Carrie Kania and to Claire Wachtel—even if she wasn't my editor, there's no one I'd rather talk politics or go coat-shopping with. Thank you for saving me from my worst writing mistakes. You are "awesome" (couldn't resist).

Thanks to all the independent booksellers out there (with special love to Jill Miner of Saturn Books), to Heather Martin and Susan Strong for sharing honest insights about open adoption, to Marie Dzuris for speech and debate details, to Judy Keefner for animal rescue stories and her description of broken-rib pain, and to Michelle Tedford for Web site assistance and unbelievably scrumptious meals (thank you, Kevin, too!).

Bryan Lakatos, Dan Florio, and Michael Cetrangol answered odd questions about all things Italian at any hour of the day or night.

Dr. Rajeev Venkayya generously offered medical guidance—both real and fictional—from at least four different time zones.

Portions of this novel were written while I had the good fortune to be in the Spalding University's MFA in Writing Program. To Sena Jeter Nasland, Kathleen Driskoll, Gayle Hanratty, Karen Mann, and Katy Yocom my deep thanks for that experience. I was privileged to have Roy Hoffman, Rachel Harper, and Jody Lisberger as my mentors, and Crystal Wilkinson, Robin Lippincott, Mary Yukari Waters, Joyce McDonald, and Charles Gaines as my workshop leaders. I learned from and was inspired by all my fellow writers there but must single out Brad Riddell, Tanya Robie, Grace Farag, and Sam Zalutsky in honor of gin-and-gingers in the lobby of The Brown.

There aren't really words for the gratitude I feel toward my mom and dad, my talented sister, Monica, and Rick, Amy, and Nathan for their inspiration, encouragement, and support.

Love and "I owe you" to Rachel Moulton, Anne Griffith, Katy Yocom, Sharon Short, Kathy Joseph, and my parents for close, careful reading and feedback.

Big love and gratitude to every book club who has ever chosen one of my novels, and to all the wonderful readers who have written to me. Special thanks to Jayne Patton of the Cincinnati "Wine, Women and Words" book club for permission to use her "inexpensive" Christmas tree story!

In addition to Ted and David, to whom I dedicate this book, a shortlist of other couples keeps me believing in miracles. A few who've made it in the long haul and epitomize true, inspiring partnerships are Ed and Anne Griffith, Beth Common and Marv Thordsen, Mike and Lauren Reed, and the Beckies (my Queens of Carpe Diem).

Rachel Moulton writes circles around me and can talk me through any meltdown. She is, hands down, the most fiercely loyal, honest, fellow zombie-loving, and fun friend I've been lucky enough to find in my life. She read this entire novel at least four times in as many years and helped make it better each time.

Dr. Kathy Joseph not only answered countless veterinary questions and allowed me to shadow her at her clinic, but she is a strong, kick-ass woman, brave enough to trek out solo for what's authentic. Here's to goats in the house, to long talks over biryani and chai, and to "not interfering." Thank you for my stay in your magical cottage, for my big, silly boy-cat, and, most of all, for your inspiration, affirmation, and friendship.

About the author

About the book

Insights,
Interviews
& More ...

Read on

My Year as a Gypsy

I WAS RECENTLY HOMELESS for a year. Not "on the street" homeless but quite by choice without a home of my own. I called the experiment my "Year as a Gypsy." It was one of the best things that's ever happened to me . . . but it grew out of one of the worst things that's ever happened to me.

My divorce was not my choice and a total blind side. I was unraveled for a blurry couple of years, unsure of what I wanted to do, where or how I wanted to live.

Self-pity is dangerous, shark-infested water to swim in, and very boring to boot, so I eventually took stock: this had happened. There was no changing it. So, how could I turn my divorce into an opportunity instead of a loss? What could this sudden single status and freedom allow me to do that I wouldn't have done if I'd remained married?

And so it was that I left my salaried teaching position with good benefits (just as the economy was tanking, mind you) to take a stab at writing full-time. I gave up my apartment, put my most beloved possessions into storage—selling or giving away the rest—and kept only what I'd need for my year as a nomad.

Lauren Reed

The goal was to "experience the new"—which opens us to inspiration: to pare down and travel light, so that I could see more clearly; to give myself a year to explore what would be my next step in life.

I kept a journal along the way, recorded on my blog at www.katrinakittle.com.

May 19, 2008: After the garage sale, I'm down to one chair in my apartment. It belongs to my sister now, but she's letting me keep it until I'm out of the apartment and on my adventure. I carry it upstairs when I use my desktop computer (now set up on my one remaining file cabinet). I carry it downstairs when I eat at the table. I'm realizing what I need and what I don't. I can get by with so much less than I have been. Feels liberating.

I've always been a fan of the expression "Leap and the net will appear." I've truly leaped. I better get busy weaving that net!

June 13, 2008: Last day of school. The movers came today. I turned in my apartment keys. I have done it. I have begun my journey. I'm officially homeless. I am in my first temporary home (house-sitting for friends on vacation). I've had this magnet on my fridge for years that says, "Go confidently in the direction of your dreams. Live the life you've imagined." I have. I am. I can't stop grinning.

At first I still kept too much stuff. I arrived at my first house-sitting gig in a car so loaded down I looked like a Beverly Hillbilly. With each move (and early that summer, I was moving nearly every ten days or so) I streamlined more.

I think the possessions we think we "need" are very characterizing of us. Along with the obvious writer tools—my laptop, my printer, my ten-pound thesaurus—I also carried a French press, a coffee- ▶

> ❝ I can get by with so much less than I have been. Feels liberating. ❞

My Year as a Gypsy *(continued)*

bean grinder, a spring-form cake pan, and a small Godzilla figurine to eighteen different "homes" over the course of the next three hundred sixty-five days.

I set up my writing space next to a pool, in a lush garden full of hummingbirds, in a kitchen with a giant Frisch's Big Boy looking down on me, on a deck overlooking a Dayton MetroPark, and in a magical cottage where a goat sometimes danced down my sidewalk. I kept my former school schedule as my writing schedule that first summer.

In September, I drove to Connecticut—in a car less packed than it had been in June—where I lived for three months in a spacious home in the woods, the second-to-last house on a dead-end country road in a teeny-tiny town in the Litchfield Hills. Secluded. Coyotes serenading at night. A bear in the yard on occasion. Horses down the road. A bloodhound puppy who'd mysteriously emerge from the woods and join me on my runs (well, sometimes he ran with me, and sometimes he'd just hurl himself into my knees, but he'd always manage to leave a glob of drool hanging on my body). Autumn foliage that more than once made me slam the brakes to stop and stare. The Ten Mile River Metro-North station just a twenty-minute drive away, where I could get on a train and be in Grand Central Station in under two hours (and did so frequently).

Next, I shipped just three boxes ahead (one contained my printer) and took two suitcases on a plane to spend three months in a fabulous sun-drenched Park Slope loft in Brooklyn while a friend was on

66 I set up my writing space next to a pool, in a lush garden full of hummingbirds, in a kitchen with a giant Frisch's Big Boy looking down on me . . . 99

4

sabbatical. My companion there was an older, nearly blind, epileptic dog named Stella who ferociously barked at the neighbor dogs through the door but wagged her tail in greeting if she met them in the hall or on the street. Deep snowfalls all through January. Running in Prospect Park. Volunteering at Housing Works Bookstore. Taking a tango class. Overdosing on live theater options. Walking the Brooklyn Bridge. City-hiking once from Park Slope all the way to Times Square. Visiting Angel of the Waters, the Bethesda Fountain in Central Park. Eating at the divine Angelo's in Little Italy. The first spring flowers peeking up through the dirt at the Brooklyn Botanic Garden.

When you're removed from everything you know, from all your comfort zones, from all your own "stuff," you can't help but confront the perceptions and conceptions you've held about yourself—or that others have put forth and you've accepted. I made daily discoveries about who I really am at this juncture of my life. I overcame some fears and learned new strengths. The "shoulds" fell away, as did the need to prove anything to anyone else, and I began to hear what I wanted, what I missed, what would truly make me happy.

February 14, 2009, Valentine's Day in Brooklyn: While being single can at times be tough, it sure beats being in a bad or even mediocre relationship that asks you to give up any part of yourself. If there's anything I've learned on this Year as a Gypsy, it's that few of us devote the kind of energy, attention, ▶

> " The 'shoulds' fell away, as did the need to prove anything to anyone else, and I began to hear what I wanted. "

and romance to ourselves as we do to others. Why do so many (women especially) change themselves or deny themselves just to be in the company of an other? We'll go out of our way, clear our schedules, hugely inconvenience ourselves to woo a love interest . . . but do we ever romance ourselves? How often do we pay attention to the things that truly make *us* happy (as opposed to the things that make the ones we love happy?)

Traveling alone can at times be . . . well, lonely. (It can also be exhilarating, stimulating, and inspiring.) There's time for reflection and self-discovery. I have rediscovered the joys of romance even while on my own. Why wait for someone else to buy me flowers? Why wait to have a date to hit a restaurant I've been eyeing? Why not *always* use the best sheets, the good china, the sexy lingerie? Trust me—life is lots richer when you behave as if you're *always* in the midst of a love affair.

True romance means listening to *yourself* as attentively as you'd listen to a lover. I've learned to listen to what truly makes me happy instead of doing what I think might impress other people. Sure it might be hip to be the kind of person who lived in New York, especially the kind of *writer* who lived in New York . . . but that's not the authentic me. The authentic me likes to go barefoot all summer, likes the fresh baked cornbread scent of crop fields on a

" Why wait for someone else to buy me flowers? "

6

hot summer night, likes seeing deer wander through my neighborhood munching all the hostas.

> *At the center of your being*
> *you have the answer;*
> *you know who you are*
> *and you know what you want.*
>
> Lao-tzu

Some of what I wanted surprised me. I longed for roots. My own home. When I daydreamed, I was nearly always designing gardens. I wanted *space*. I wanted to plunge my hands in dirt. I wanted to make things grow. I found myself following people on horseback in Prospect Park, feeling the deficiency from the lack of equine presence in my life.

I'd been happily rolling along, having fun, and then one day I wasn't. I was about to head overseas to stay with friends in Portugal (their invitation was what had planted the seed of this adventure in the first place). I'd already changed the ticket twice when I realized Portugal would *not* be the next step.

April 2, 2009: Big changes to report here. I'm not going to Portugal next on my Year as a Gypsy. I am being "called" to land somewhere and have a home again. I'm so glad I gave myself space and time for adventure and to let my life shake itself out. It was time to listen to what truly made my heart sing. And I heard it—the clarity I'd asked for. ▶

66 When I daydreamed, I was nearly always designing gardens. **99**

When I leave Brooklyn on April 15, I'll be heading home to Dayton to look for a house. I've been feeling downright gleeful since deciding.

And if life is like the draft of a novel, I'm not deleting the chapter "Living in Portugal." I'm just moving it to a later slot in the manuscript, because something more powerful came bubbling forth in the story, with more energy.

I've learned I can label these chapters . . . but I can't write their endings in advance.

I love asking for clarity, then getting it. More than that, I love listening to it!

And listen I did. Now, when I wake up in my lovely little dream house, with my silly boy-cat snuggled next to me, and I pad into my sanctuary of a writing office—three walls of windows overlooking my privacy-fenced garden (I tilled flower beds before I unpacked a single box)—I have no regrets and no doubts. I know for sure this is where I want to be right now.

It feels like such a privilege, such a gift, to be doing what I've dreamed of doing for so long. My alarm goes off early in the morning and I smile and do a little dance (like a kid on Christmas morning), eager to get to the page.

My year was incredible. Life altering, just like the divorce had been.

Change is inevitable. Growth is an option. I'm growing much more than flowers out in my garden. ∽

> ❝ I have no regrets and no doubts. I know for sure this is where I want to be right now. ❞

8

My Own Defense of Marriage Act

"Marriage, as an institution in Western culture, is obsolete. Marriage is no longer necessary."

THE SEED FOR THIS NOVEL came with these words. Delivered by a guest on NPR with a clipped British accent, they caused a knee-jerk reaction in me: of *course* marriage is necessary! But as I drove along in the rain, I thought to myself, *Why?* As the woman on the radio listed the many historical reasons for the creation of marriage—and argued that these reasons no longer exist—I caught myself scrambling to defend marriage. Just like the students in my English classes, I was trying to figure out how would I support my argument. What defense would I use? It troubled me that I couldn't come up with much ammunition.

Actually, it more than troubled me. It deeply disturbed me. As my windshield wipers squeaked across my vision, I felt I should be able to grab something unequivocal, something concrete: Marriage is necessary because of X. X should be obvious. But why couldn't I think of it?

The woman wasn't attacking marriage. She was simply pointing out that women no longer *need* marriage to have status, to own property, even to have children and raise healthy families. The windshield wipers kept time as she explained that fewer people were marrying at all these days, that those who did were waiting ▶

9

until much later in life, and that more than half of those marriages ended in divorce.

Bleak. Nothing new or earth-shattering, but bleak as the gray, rainy Ohio February day.

The radio segment tugged at me in some odd way. I didn't recognize it as a story idea just yet—I didn't recognize it until the report that followed it: a report about President Bush's Defense of Marriage Act, which sought to alter the U.S. Constitution to ban same-sex marriage.

And it struck me as interesting: here was a group of citizens fighting relentlessly for the right to enter into this "obsolete" institution, while the group of citizens who already enjoyed that right were treating it rather cavalierly.

The beginnings of a story started simmering in my brain. I caught myself thinking about marriage a lot, asking people questions at dinner parties and gatherings—"Why did you get married?" and "Why shouldn't gays be allowed to marry?"—even running a contest on my Web site at one point, inviting readers to write a brief essay defending their answer to the question "Is marriage necessary?"

Every one of my books has begun with a social issue I care deeply about, so this seemed part of my process. But when readers asked, "So what's the social issue in your next book?" they'd chuckle when I said, "Marriage."

The chuckling intrigued me. Okay, so marriage was certainly not as "edgy" as AIDS, alcoholism, and child sexual abuse—issues I've taken on in the past. But marriage *is* a social issue, and one that

66 Marriage was certainly not as 'edgy' as AIDS, alcoholism, and child sexual abuse—issues I've taken on in the past. But marriage *is* a social issue. 99

touches many, many more people than my previous topics.

The chuckling affirmed something my initial research had led me to believe: most people don't spend much time thinking seriously about marriage. Even if they *are* married.

Oh, they spend a lot of time and energy thinking about *weddings*, but not about marriage.

Most married people I talked to couldn't answer the question "Why did you get married?" beyond a "We love each other." Most eventually admitted that they married because "that's what people do." So, why, then, in an era where we have the luxury of marrying solely for love, do so many of those unions end in divorce?

I'd been working on the novel for two years—already with my protagonist going through a divorce—when I got divorced myself.

My divorce caused some pretty serious rewriting. At first, I was such a mess that I couldn't read or write. The novel sat for nearly ten months. When I returned to it, I was a totally different person and had to start over. I did—for a time—fall into that self-indulgent, boring literary trap of forcing my fiction into the straitjacket of my own life story. I will love my editor forever for her response to that draft. After having read one hundred pages of it, she said, "This ex-husband is not at all an interesting or satisfying character." Instead of insisting, "But that's really how it happened," I laughed out loud, grateful that her honesty freed me from that trap. I rewrote again. ▶

" I did—for a time—fall into that self-indulgent, boring literary trap of forcing my fiction into the straitjacket of my own life story. "

My Own Defense of Marriage Act *(continued)*

To this day, I could not come up with a clear defense for marriage's existence, and neither could I come up with a clear defense of preventing same-sex couples from entering into it if they so chose. I have yet to hear an argument or a reason that convinces me. Some argue that the legalization of same-sex marriage will lead to people wanting to marry their children, multiple spouses, or their pets. Really? Is it so difficult to define marriage as between any two consenting adult human beings? Some argue that the majority of Americans is still against it. Well, the majority of Americans was in support of slavery when it was abolished; the majority of Americans was against women's right to vote when it was granted (same with biracial marriages). To allow two consenting adults to publicly declare a monogamous commitment to each other—explain to me how that threatens marriage. The gay and lesbian couples I know in no way contributed to my divorce. They didn't cause my marriage to crumble. In fact, the couple to whom this novel is dedicated has served as a model to me—while I was married and now that I'm not—of the kind of true partnership I want to have. Ted and Dave in every way epitomize the marriage vows they're not allowed to take.

No, what wrecked my marriage was lack of stamina. We were in no way trained for the long haul; we were not conditioned for the marathon of two individual people creating one life together—a life that must naturally change and evolve. When it didn't evolve *easily*, the instinct was to simply get rid of it. I think our cultural instinct when

> ❝ The couple to whom this novel is dedicated has served as a model to me—while I was married and now that I'm not—of the kind of true partnership I want to have. ❞

12

something isn't working is to throw it out and get a new one. That's where the connection to the tattered saddle and the rescue animals came together for me in the story: I don't believe marriage is *necessary*. But I *do* think every adult should have the *right* to marry if they so choose. And if they do, there's a richness that only comes from the repairs. Until you've *truly* committed to something— the damaged saddle, the horse that's become a dangerous nuisance, the relationship you feel you've outgrown— you never get to experience that sweet satisfaction, that deeper layer of love that comes only from the arduous work of salvaging it. As Cami's dad describes the stitched-up saddle in the novel, the scars ". . . add to the beauty of the saddle, to the value. They announce it was worth saving."

66 Until you've *truly* committed to something . . . you never get to experience that sweet satisfaction, that deeper layer of love that comes only from the arduous work of salvaging it. 99

Excerpt: *The Kindness of Strangers*

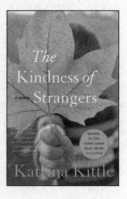

A YOUNG WIDOW RAISING TWO BOYS, Sarah Laden is struggling to keep her family together. But when a shocking revelation rips apart the family of her closest friend, Sarah finds herself welcoming yet another troubled young boy into her already tumultuous life.

Jordan, a quiet, reclusive elementary school classmate of Sarah's son Danny, has survived a terrible ordeal. By agreeing to become Jordan's foster mother, Sarah will be forced to question the things she has long believed. And as the delicate threads that bind their family begin to unravel, all the Ladens will have to face difficult truths about themselves and one another—and discover the power of love necessary to forgive and to heal.

"Katrina Kittle's compulsively readable *The Kindness of Strangers* is a powerful public-service narrative about child abuse and its effects on a family."

—*Chicago Tribune*

Excerpt

Danny wondered if people looked at his family and knew. Did it show?

Sitting there, in his childhood home, hours before the wedding, he was astounded they'd all come so far. He looked back and remembered a time he'd never dreamed there'd be a scene like this. He wondered if anyone else looked at them and still thought, *My God, it's amazing.*

He knew that his family still thought it.

And that's what he loved about them. On days like this one, or on their graduations or holidays, they sometimes caught one another's eyes and it was there. That sparkle of "we did it, didn't we?" This light of how lucky they were.

Danny loved the days when they remembered that.

Because they didn't always. They couldn't. He knew that it went against human nature to truly savor every moment and continually remain aware of all they had to be grateful for. They couldn't *live* like that. They'd never get anything done. There wasn't always time to savor every damn little thing, like electricity, or your car starting, or the shipment of specialty cheeses arriving on time. He thought about how much effort and energy it would consume to perpetually relish everything. It wasn't practical.

But he thought his family did it more than most.

And with good reason.

His favorite days were when he knew they were all doing it at the same time.

The bustle here in his mother's kitchen gave him a rush. Mom looked great, but he was careful not to tell her too many times. He'd finally convinced her to color her gray hairs, and he didn't want to make too big a deal out of being so obviously right; he just grinned every time someone else told her, "You look fabulous, Sarah."

Danny had already taken off his tux jacket and tucked a cloth napkin into his shirt as an apron. He envied how Mom could stir up the brown-sugar frosting and never get a drop or a splatter on her ivory dress. It was so like her to make the cake herself. Danny had told her he would do ▶

66 They sometimes caught one another's eyes and it was there. . . . This light of how lucky they were. 99

it—she had a ton of other things to worry about today—but, as usual, she tried to do everything. At least she was letting them all help, even though that added to the chaos. She'd embraced the frantic quality of the day and turned it into a party instead of a hassle. She caught his eye and laughed, then dipped her finger into the melted butter and brown sugar she stirred. She closed her eyes to express her approval.

Danny's brothers stood nearby, looking like movie stars in their tuxes, eating the scraps of the buttermilk chocolate cake Danny had trimmed off. They laughed at something, and Danny tilted his head and studied them; his brothers looked as different as two members of a family could look.

Most of the time Danny forgot to remember. But today that was impossible. Odd things brought it all back to him. Sometimes the triggers were obvious, but occasionally they surprised him— the scent of a swimming pool, the sight of a flowering dogwood, a glimpse of a black-and-white cat, the sound of his laser printer, police in uniform, or a blond woman wearing pink.

Today it was everyone taking pictures. The flashes and the video cameras reminded him. They always had, since the discovery on that rainy, cold day twelve years ago.

Twelve years. Damn. Sometimes the memory seemed so recent it could still make the panic thicken in Danny's chest. Other times it was difficult for the man he was now to recognize the boy he had been

> 66 She'd embraced the frantic quality of the day and turned it into a party instead of a hassle. 99

then. But Danny couldn't pose for a picture, or have someone film him, without remembering it all.

"That summer," his family called it. Even though it started in the spring, in April. Or "that year." If they just said "that summer" or "that year," they all knew what it meant. Anything else would be specific: "the summer that Nate left for med school," or "that summer I was sous-chef at Arriba Arriba in Manhattan." But if someone just said "that summer," the rest of them knew what was meant.

Danny didn't believe that everything happened for a reason. He refused to believe it. He hated that image of a God, of a world. Too many things were just petty and mean if he looked at them that way. But in college he'd studied a bit about reincarnation in a comparative-religions class. Some people who believed in reincarnation thought that there was a place somewhere, a place they couldn't ever recognize in this world, from which they chose the path of their lives on earth.

Danny pondered that when he encountered certain people or contemplated his family's history. If it were true, what made some people choose a remedial, cush life and others choose an advanced placement course? What would have made his family *choose* the shock, the betrayal, the heartache? He wished he understood it.

On days like this, he felt he got a little closer. Knowing everything he knew now, seeing how it had turned out so far, from this better place, he thought ▶

66 Danny didn't believe that everything happened for a reason. . . . He hated that image of a God, of a world. 99

he'd choose this life again. He really thought he would.

"Ready with the raspberry?" Mom asked.

Danny opened the raspberry preserves he'd canned himself. Certain items held a family history. A jar of raspberry preserves was bound to set off a family story.

Danny knew he loved the family stories more than anyone else did. Everyone else would complain and cry out, "Not again!" but Danny adored them, longed for them, and secretly devised ways to get them started.

He spread the raspberry preserves between the three layers of dense chocolate cake. When served with homemade vanilla ice cream, this cake was, as Mom called it, "just about as close to culinary ecstasy as is possible." This cake had been his father's favorite, and so it touched Danny that it had been requested for today. Thinking about his dad reminded Danny of a family story. An old one. One that used to be told at all the weddings, the Thanksgivings, the bar mitzvahs, and the birthdays. Always on Danny's birthday. At Danny's expense. Before, back before Dad had died, Danny was embarrassed when the story was told. But now he sometimes asked his mom to tell it.

He'd been very small. Four, maybe five. And he'd been playing by himself in the backyard of this very house. Mom and Dad loved to tell how Danny came running into the house and shouted, "Did you know that when you jump, both your feet come off the ground?"

66 Danny knew he loved the family stories more than anyone else did. Everyone else would complain and cry out, 'Not again!' but Danny adored them. 99

Everyone thought it was so cute and dumb, but really, to Danny, it had been a scary moment and an amazing realization. He had seen his shadow against the garage. He had jumped into the air and had seen this space between his body and the grass. Against the white wall of the garage, he saw himself floating, not connected to anything.

What kept you from floating away?

Dad had told him about gravity, but it was Mom who listened to Danny explain his fear and who hugged him and said, "I'll keep you from floating away. There's a connection between us, even though you can't see it. You'll always be connected to us."

When Danny used to think about his father dead, he sometimes thought of a shadow floating. Dad was like Danny's own shadow. Danny couldn't really touch it, and it was sometimes really hard to see, but it was always there. Danny knew it. He couldn't lose it.

And that was family. That was the feeling of safety.

And so even though he used to be embarrassed when they told that story, now he liked it. That story was a connection, too. It connected everyone who told it to each other.

But that story was from Before.

There were new stories. The stories of After.

And the story of how Before became After.

The story of how they became who they were now.

> " He saw himself floating, not connected to anything. What kept you from floating away? "

Have You Read?
More by Katrina Kittle

TRAVELING LIGHT

"Travel light and you can sing in the robber's face" was the best advice Summer Zwolenick ever received from her father, though she didn't recognize it at the time. Three years after the accident that ended her career as a ballerina, she is back in the familiar suburbs of Dayton, Ohio, teaching at a local high school. But it wasn't nostalgia that called Summer home. It was her need to spend quality time with her brother Todd and his devoted partner, Jacob. Todd, the golden athlete whose strength and spirit encouraged Summer to nurture her own unique talents and follow her dream, is in the final stages of a terminal illness. In a few short months, he will be dead—leaving Summer only a handful of precious days to learn all the lessons her brother still has to teach her . . . from how to love and how to live to letting go.

Traveling Light is the deeply moving debut novel from Katrina Kittle, the acclaimed author of *The Kindness of Strangers*—an unforgettable story of love, bonds, and promises that endure longer than life itself.

"Wonderfully moving . . . hard to put down and harder still to forget."
—*Booklist* (starred review)

TWO TRUTHS AND A LIE

Dair Canard has long been a master at weaving stories out of thin air. A natural actress, she leads a life that's a minefield of untruths she can never admit to anyone— especially not to Peyton, her husband of eight years. But the bizarre death of her best friend and fellow actor—initially thought a suicide, then believed to be murder—is forcing Dair to confront the big lie that led Peyton to fall in love with her in the first place. Haunted by the terrible events that are suddenly ripping her life wide open, Dair is struggling to find answers—taking steps that could well lead to the destruction of her marriage, her career . . . even her freedom.

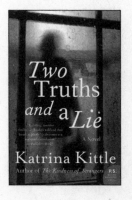

But everyone around her has secrets and something to hide. Dair's determination to unravel the decade-old web of her own tightly woven deceptions is awakening inner demons she has fought hard to control . . . and revealing that she's closer to a killer than she ever imagined.

Have You Read? *(continued)*

"A chilling, sensitive thriller. . . . Readers will hold their breath as her tale comes to a suspenseful conclusion."
—*Publishers Weekly*

"A tale of suspense, lies, and redemption."
—*Tacoma News Tribune* (Washington)

"Always surprising. . . . Ms. Kittle follows up *Traveling Light* with equal aplomb."
—*Cincinnati Enquirer*

"Fiction as it ought to be. . . . A superbly tense and witty novel that offers a fresh angle on the human soul. It will leave you craving more from this deliciously talented writer."   —Chris Gilson, author of *Crazy for Cornelia*

Don't miss the next book by your favorite author. Sign up now for AuthorTracker by visiting www.AuthorTracker.com.